Poul Anderson
THE AVATAR
AN SF MASTER'S GREATEST WORK!

JUMP.
Light, everywhere light. And at the center of it a sweetly curved ellipsoid. A webwork extended from it...

Here are the Others! blazed in Joelle. *No beings but the Others could have wrought this! They are coming, and I am she who will converse with them. I, alone among humans, who have gone beyond the human...*

"THIS NOVEL HAS EVERYTHING: MARVELOUS ALIEN SIGHTS AND BEINGS, COLORFUL AND SYMPATHETIC CHARACTERS... AND AN INVOLVING AND TRAGIC PLOT. A MAJOR WORK BY ONE OF SF'S MATURE TALENTS..."
—*Publishers Weekly*

THE AVATAR

POUL ANDERSON

A BERKLEY BOOK
published by
BERKLEY PUBLISHING CORPORATION

This Berkley book contains the complete
text of the original hardcover edition.
It has been completely reset in a type face
designed for easy reading, and was printed
from new film.

THE AVATAR

A Berkley Book / published by arrangment with
the author

PRINTING HISTORY
Berkley-Putnam edition published October 1978
Berkley edition / October 1979
Second Printing

ISBN: 0-425-04213-8

A BERKLEY BOOK ® TM 757,375
PRINTED IN THE UNITED STATES OF AMERICA

ACKNOWLEDGMENTS

The T machine is not entirely a figment of my imagination. Its basic principle was described by F. J. Tipler in *Physical Review*, vol. D-9, no. 8 (15 April 1974), pp. 2203-1; *Physical Review Letters*, vol. 37, no. 14 (4 October 1976), pp. 879-82; and his thesis *Causality Violation in General Relativity* (University of Maryland, 1976). He is in no way responsible for my use of his idea, especially since I have departed considerably from his mathematical model.

Likewise, the concept of life on a pulsar is from an interview with Frank Drake in *Astronomy* magazine, December 1973, pp. 5-8, as well as a lecture he gave at the 1974 meeting of the American Association for the Advancement of Science. He too is a reputable scientist; he does not advance the notion as anything but highly speculative, at best; moreover, I may have committed grievous technical errors for which he has no responsibility.

My thanks to both these gentlemen for permission to borrow their thoughts. I can but hope that these are herewith returned in not too badly battered a condition.

Parts of Chapters II and XXIII appeared, in slightly different form, in the Fall 1977 issue of *Isaac Asimov's Science Fiction Magazine*, in a story entitled "Joelle," copyright © 1977 by Davis Publications, Inc.

The quotation in Chapter IV is from the poem "Sussex," by Rudyard Kipling, in *Rudyard Kipling's Verse, Definitive Edition*, published by Doubleday & Co., and is used by agreement.

For suggestions, information, and general helpfulness I am especially indebted to Karen Anderson, Mildred Downey Broxon, Victor Fernández-Dávila, Robert L. Forward, Larry J. Friesen, and David G. Hartwell. Several good things in the book are due to them. The bad things are all my own invention.

POUL ANDERSON

To Bubbles
Go raibh maith agat, mo chroí

THE AVATAR

I

I WAS A BIRCH TREE, white slenderness in the middle of a meadow, but had no name for what I was. My leaves drank of the sunlight that streamed through them and set their green aglow, my leaves danced in the wind, which made a harp of my branches, but I did not see or hear. Waning days turned me brittle golden, frost stripped me bare, snow blew about me during my long drowse, then Orion hunted his quarry beyond this heaven and the sun swung north to blaze me awake, but none of this did I sense.

And yet I marked it all, for I lived. Each cell within me felt in a secret way how the sky first shone aloud and afterward grew quiet, air gusted or whooped or lay dreaming, rain flung chill and laughter, water and worms did their work for my reaching roots, nestlings piped where I sheltered them and soughed, grass and dandelions enfolded me in richness, the earth stirred as the Earth turned among stars. Each year that departed left a ring in me for remembrance. Though I was not aware, I was still in Creation and of it; though I did not understand, I knew. I was Tree.

II

WHEN *Emissary* passed through the gate and Phoebus again shone upon her, half of the dozen crewfolk who survived were gathered in her common room, together with the passenger from Beta. After their long time away, they wanted to witness this return on the biggest viewscreens they had and share a ceremony, raising goblets of the last wine aboard to the hope of a good homecoming. Those on duty added voices over the intercom. *"Salud. Proost. Skål. Banzai. Saúde. Zdoroviye. Prosit. Mazel tov. Santé. Viva. Aloha"* each spoke of a very special place.

From her post at the linkage computer, Joelle Ky whispered, on behalf of those who had stayed behind forever, *"Zivio"* for Alexander Vlantis, *"Kan bei"* for Yuan Chichao, "Cheers" for Christine Burns. She added nothing of her own, thought what a sentimental old fool she was, and trusted that nobody had heard. Her gaze drifted to a small screen supposed to provide her with visual data should any be needed. Amidst the meters, controls, input and output equipment which crowded the cabin, it seemed like a window on the world.

"World," though, meant "universe." Amplification was set at one, revealing simply what the naked eye would have seen. Yet stars shone so many and bright, unwinking diamond, sapphire, topaz, ruby, that the blackness around and beyond was but a chalice for them. Even in the Solar System, Joelle could have picked no constellations out of such a throng. However, the shape of the Milky Way was little changed from nights above North America. With that chill brilliance for a guide, she found an elvenglow which was M31; and it had looked the same at Beta, too, for it is sister to our whole galaxy.

Nonetheless she suddenly wanted a more familiar sight. The need for the comfort it would give surprised her—she, the holothete, to whom everything visible was merely a veil that reality wore. The past eight Earth-years must have drunk deeper of her than she knew. Unwilling to wait the hours, maybe days until she could see Sol again, she ran fingers across the keyboard before her, directing the scanner to bring in Phoebus. At least she had glimpsed it when outbound, and countless pictures of it throughout her life.

The helmet was already on her head, the linkage to computer, memory bank, and ship's instruments already complete. The instant after she desired that particular celestial location, she had calculated it. To her the operation felt everyday: felt like knowing where to move her hand to pick up a tool or knowing which way a sound was coming from. There was nothing numinous about it.

The scene switched to a different sector. A disc appeared, slightly larger than Sol observed from Earth or Luna, a trifle yellower, type G5. Photospheric luminance, ten percent above what Earth got, had been automatically stopped down to avoid blinding her. Lesser splendors remained undimmed. Thus she made out spots on the surface, flares along the limb, nacre of corona, slim wings of zodiacal light. *Yes,* she thought, *Phoebus has the same kind of beauty as my sun. Centrum does not, and only now do I feel how lonely was that lack.*

Her touch ranged onward, calling for a sight of Demeter. This problem her unaided brain could have solved. Having newly made transit, *Emissary* floated near the gate; and it held a Lagrange 4 position with respect to the planet, in the same orbit though sixty degrees ahead. The scanner must merely course along the ecliptic to find what she wished.

At a distance of 0.81 astronomical units, unmagnified, Demeter resembled the stars about it, stronger than most and bluer than any. *Are you still yonder, Dan Brodersen?* Joelle wondered; and then: *Oh, yes, you must be. I've been gone for eight years, but a bare few of your months have passed.*

How many exactly? I don't know. Fidelio isn't quite sure.

Captain Langendijk's general announcement interrupted her reverie. "Attention, please. We've registered two vessels on our radars. One is obviously the official watchcraft, and is signalling for tight-beam communication. I'll put that over the intercom, but kindly do not interrupt the talk, or make any unnecessary noise. Best they don't know you are listening."

For a moment Joelle was puzzled. Why should he take

precautions, as if *Emissary*'s return might not be the occasion for mankind-wide rejoicing? What put the note of strain into his tone? The answer struck inward. She had been indifferent to partisan matters, they scarcely existed for her, but once recruited into this crew, she couldn't help hearing talk of strife and intrigue. Brodersen had rather grimly explained the facts to her, and they had often been a subject of conversation at Beta. A considerable coalition within humanity had never wanted the expedition and would not be happy at its success.

Two vessels, both presumably in orbit around the T machine. The second must be Dan's.

"Thomas Archer, commanding World Union watchship *Faraday,* speaking," said a man's voice. His Spanish was accented like hers. "Identify yourself."

"Willem Langendijk, commanding exploratory ship *Emissary* [Spanish *Emisario*]," replied her captain. "We're passing through on our way back to the Solar System. May we commence maneuvers?"

"What—but—" Archer obviously struggled with amazement. "Well, you do seem like—But everybody expected you'd be gone for years!"

"We were."

"No. I witnessed your transit. That was, uh, five months ago, no more."

"Ah-ha. Give me the present date and time, please."

"But—you—"

"If you please." Joelle could well imagine how Langendijk's lean face tautened to match his sternness.

Archer blurted the figures off a chronometer. She summoned from the memory bank the exact clock reading when she and her fellows had finished tracing out the guidepath here and twisted through space-time to their unknown goal. Subtraction yielded an interval of twenty weeks and three days. She could as readily have told how many seconds, or miroseconds, had passed out of Archer's lifespan, but he had only given information to the nearest minute.

"Thank you," Langendijk said. "For us, approximately eight Terrestrial years have passed. It turns out that the T machine is indeed a time machine of sorts, as well as a space transporter. The Betans—the beings whom we followed—calculated our course to bring us out near the date when we left."

Silence hummed. Joelle noticed she was aware of her

environment with more than usual intensity. Free falling, the ship kept her weightless in a loosened safety harness. The sensation was pleasant, recalling flying dreams of long ago when she was young. (Afterward her dreams had changed with her mind and soul, as she grew into being a holothete.) Air from a ventilator murmured and stroked her cheeks. It bore a slight greenwood odor of recycling chemicals and, at its present stage of the variability necessary for health, coolness and a subliminal pungency of ions. Her heart knocked loud in her ears. And, yes, twinges in her left wrist had turned into a steady ache, she was overdue for an arthritis booster, time went, time went. Probably the Others themselves could not change that....

"Well," Archer said in English. "Well, I'll be God damned. Uh, welcome back. How are you?"

Langendijk switched to the same language, in which he felt a touch more at ease and which was in fact used aboard *Emissary* about as often as Spanish. "We lost three people. But otherwise, Captain, believe me, the news we bear is all wonderful. Besides being anxious to get home—you will understand that—we can hardly wait to spread our story through the Union."

"Did you—" Archer paused, as if half afraid to utter the rest. Quite possibly he was. Joelle heard him draw breath before he plunged: "Did you find the Others?"

"No. What we did find was an advanced civilization, nonhuman but friendly, in contact with scores of inhabited worlds. They're eager to establish close relations with us, too; they offer what my crew and I think are some fantastically good deals. No, they know nothing more about the Others than we do, except for the additional gates they've learned how to use. But we, the next several generations of man will have as much as we can do to assimilate what the Betans will give.

"Now I'm sorry, Captain, I realize you'd love to hear everything, but that would take days, and anyhow, we have orders not to linger. The Council of the World Union commissioned us and requires we report first to it. That is reasonable, no? Accordingly, we request clearance to proceed straight on to the Solar System."

Again Archer was mute a while. Was something more than surprise at work in him? On impulse, Joelle called on the ship's exoinstrumental circuits. An immediate inrush of data lured her. It wasn't a full perception, but still, as far as possible, how easy and how blessed to comprehend yonder cosmos as a whole and become one with it! Resisting, she concentrated solely on radar and navigational information. In a split pulsebeat, she calculated how to bring *Faraday* onto her viewscreen.

There was no particular reason for that. She knew what the watchcraft looked like: a tapered gray cylinder so as to be capable of planetfall, missile launcher and ray projector recessed into the sleekness—wholly foreign to the huge, equipment-bristling, fragile sphere which was *Emissary*. When the picture changed, she didn't magnify and amplify to make the vessel visible across a thousand kilometers. Instead, the sight of two dully glowing globes, red and green, coming into the scanner field, against the stars, snatched at her. Those were markers around the T machine. The Others had placed them. Her augmented senses told her that a third likewise happened to be visible on the receiver; it was colored ultraviolet.

Vaguely she heard Archer: "—quarantine?" and Langendijk: "Well, if they insist, but we walked on Beta, again and again for eight years, and we have a Betan native with us, and nobody's caught any diseases. Pinski and de Carvalho, our biologists, studied the subject and tell me cross-infection is impossible. Biochemistries are too unlike."

Caught up in the beacons, she quite stopped listening. Oh, surely someday she, holothete, could speak mind to mind with their makers, if ever she found them.

Though what would they make of *her*, perhaps in more than one meaning of the phrase? Even physical appearance might conceivably not be altogether irrelevant to them. It was an odd thing to do in these circumstances, but for the first time in almost a decade Joelle Ky briefly considered her body as flesh, not machinery.

At fifty-eight Earth-years of age, her hundred and seventy-five centimeters remained slim, verging on gaunt, her skin clear and pale and only lightly lined. In that and the high cheekbones her genes kept a bit of the history which her name also remembered; she had been born in North America, in what was left of the old United States before it federated with Canada. Her features were delicate, her eyes large and dark. Hair once sable, bobbed immediately below the ears, was the hue of iron. Clad now in the working uniform of the ship, a coverall with abundant pockets and snaploops, she seldom wore anything very much more stylish at home.

A smile flickered. *How silly can I get? If one thing is certain*

about the Others, it is that none of them will come courting me!
Could it be the thought of Dan, yonder on Demeter? Additional
nonsense. Why, at Beta I became eight years his senior.

Somehow that raised Eric Stranathan for her, the first and
last man with whom she fell wholly in love. Across a quarter
century—plus the time she had been gone on this mission—he
came back, seated opposite her in a canoe on Lake Louise,
among mountains, in piney air, under a night sky nearly as vast
as what lay around *Emissary*; and staring upward, she
whispered, "How do the Others see that? What is it to them?"

"What are they?" he answered. "Animals evolved beyond us;
machines that think; angels dwelling by the throne of God;
beings, or a being, of a kind we've never imagined and never can;
or what? Humans have been wondering for more than a hundred
years now."

She mustered pride. "We'll come to know."

"Through holothetics?" he asked.

"Maybe. Else through—who can tell? But I do believe we
will. I have to believe that."

"We might not want to. I've got an idea we'd never be the
same again, and that price might be too high."

She shivered. "You mean we'd forsake all we have here?"

"And all we are. Yes, it's possible." His dear lanky form
stirred, rocking the boat. "And I wouldn't, myself. I'm so happy
where I am, this moment."

That was the night they became lovers.

—Joelle shook herself. *Stop. Be sensible. I'm obsessive about*
the Others, I know. Seeing their handiwork again serving not
aliens but humans must have uncapped a wellspring in me. But
Willem's right. The Betans should be enough for many
generations of my race. Do the Others know that? Did they
foresee it?

She was faintly shocked to note that her attention had drifted
from the intercom for minutes. She wasn't given to introspection
or daydreaming. Maybe it had happened because she was
computer-linked. At such times, an operator became a greater
mathematician and logician, by orders of magnitude, than had
ever lived on Earth before the conjunction was developed. But
the operator remained a mortal, full of mortal foolishness, *I*
suppose my habit of close concentration while I'm in this state
took over in me. Since I'm not used to dealing with emotions, the
habit got out of hand.

She knew peripherally that an argument had been going on. Hearkening, she heard Archer state:

"Very well, Captain Langendijk, nobody foresaw you'd return this early—if ever, to be frank—and therefore I don't have specific orders regarding you. But my superiors did brief me and issue a general directive."

"Ah?" replied the skipper of *Emissary*. "And what does that say?"

"Well, uh, well, certain highly placed people worry about more than your bringing a strange bug to Earth. The idea is, they don't know what you might bring back. Look, I'm not saying a monster has taken over your ship and is pretending to be you, anything paranoid like that."

"I should hope not! As a matter of fact, sir, the Betans—the name we gave them, of course—the Betans are not just friendly, they are anxious to know us well. That is why they will trade with us on terms that would else be unbelievably favorable. They stand to gain even more."

Wariness responded: "What?"

"It would take long to explain. There is something vital they hope to learn from us."

It twisted in Joelle: *Something that I have never yet really learned myself, nor ever likely will.*

Archer's voice jarred the thought out of her. "Well, maybe. Though I think that reinforces the point, that nobody can tell what the effect might be . . . on us. And the World Union is none too stable, you know. You plan to report straight to the Council—"

"Yes." Langendijk said. "We'll proceed to the neighborhood of Earth, call Lima, and request instructions. What's wrong with that?"

"Too public!" Archer exclaimed. After a few seconds: "Look, I'm not at liberty to say much. But . . . the officials I mentioned want to, uh, debrief you in strict privacy, examine your materials, that sort of thing, before they issue any news release. Do you see?"

"M-m-m, I had my suspicions," Langendijk rumbled. "Go on."

"Well, under the circumstances, et cetera, I'm going to interpret my orders as follows. We'll accompany you through the gate, to the Solar System. Radio interlock of our autopilots, of course, to make sure the ships come out at the other end simultaneously. You'll have no communication with anybody but us, on a tight beam—we'll handle everything outside—until you hear differently. Is that clear?"

"Rather too clear."

"Please, Captain, no offense intended, nothing like that. You must understand what a tremendous business this is. People who, uh, who're responsible for billions of human lives, they're bound to be cautious. Including, for a start, me."

"Yes, I agree you are doing your duty as you see it, Captain Archer. Besides, you have the power." *Emissary* bore a couple of guns, but almost as an afterthought; her fire control officers doubled as pilots of her launch. Though she could build up huge velocities if given time, her top acceleration with payload and reaction mass on hand was under two gravities; and her gyros or lateral jets could turn her about only ponderously. No one had imagined her as a warcraft, a lone vessel setting off into what might be a whole galaxy. *Faraday* was designed for battle. (The occasion had never arisen, but who knew what might someday emerge from a gate? Besides, her high maneuverability fitted her for rescue work and for conveying exploratory teams.)

"I'm trying to do our best for our government, sir."

"I wish you would tell me who in the government."

"I'm sorry, but I'm only an astronautical officer. It wouldn't be proper for me to discuss politics. Uh, you do see, don't you, you've nothing to worry about? This is an extra precaution, no more."

"Yes, yes," Langendijk sighed. "Let us get on with it." Talk went into technicalities.

Signoff followed. Langendijk addressed his crew: "You heard, of course. Questions? Comments?"

A burst of indignation and dismay responded; loudest came Frieda von Moltke's *"Höllenfeuer und Teufelscheiss!"* First Engineer Dairoku Mitsukuri was milder: "This is perhaps high-handed, but we ought not to be detained long. The fact of our arrival will generate enormous public pressure for our release."

Carlos Francisco Rueda Suárez, the mate, added in his haughtiest tone, "Furthermore, my family will have a good deal to say about the matter."

A dread she had hoped was ridiculous lifted in Joelle, chilled her flesh and harshened her contralto. "You're supposing they will know," she said.

"Good Lord, you can't mean that," Second Engineer Torsten Sverdrup protested. "The Ruedas kept in ignorance—that's impossible."

"I fear it not," Joelle answered. "We're completely at the mercy of yonder watchship, you realize. And her captain isn't acting like a man who only wants to play safe. Is he? I don't pretend to be very sensitive where people are concerned, but I have had some exposure to cliques and cabals on high political levels. Also, the last time we talked on Earth, Dan Brodersen warned me we might return not simply to hostility from some factions, but to trouble."

"Brodersen?" asked Sam Kalahele, von Moltke's fellow gunner.

"The owner of Chehalis Enterprises on Demeter," said Marie Feuillet, chemist. "You must allow for him exaggerating. He is a free-swinging capitalist, therefore overly suspicious of the government, perhaps of the Union itself."

"We have to commence acceleration soon," Langendijk declared. "All hands to flight posts."

"Please!" Joelle cried. "Skipper, listen a minute! I'm not going to debate, I admit I'm hopelessly naive about many things, but Dan—Captain Brodersen did tell me he'd keep a robot near the gate, programmed to look out for us, just in case of trouble. He foresaw the possibility—the likelihood, he called it—that we'd return on a date soon after departure. Well, what else can that second craft be, orbiting far off—we have a radar pickup of it, you remember—what else can it be but his observer?"

Rueda's voice rang: "Holy Virgin, Joelle, in all these years, why did you never mention it?"

"Oh, he felt we shouldn't be worried about something that might never happen. He told me because, well, we're friends, knowing I'd shunt the information off in my own mind. I put it on my summary tape, for the rest of you to play back if I should die."

"But in that case, there is no problem," Rueda said happily. "We cannot be held incommunicado, if that's what you fear. Once the robot reports to him, he'll tell the world. I might have expected this of him. You may have heard he's my kinsman by his first marriage."

Joelle shook her head. The cables into the bowl-shaped helmet were flexible and allowed that, though the added mass forced a noticeable effort and, in weightlessness, caused her torso to countertwist slightly.

"No," she answered. "Notice how distant it is. No optical system man has yet built has the resolution to tell *Emissary* apart from—seven, is it?—similar ships, at such a remove. She's simply a modified *Reina*-class transport, after all."

"Then what's the use of parking an observer out here?" snapped Quartermaster Bruno Benedetti.

"Isn't it obvious what's happened?" retorted planetologist Olga Razumovski. "But tell us, Joelle."

The holothete drew breath. "Here's what Brodersen planned to do," she said. "He'd dispatch the robot ostensibly to study the T machine over a period of years in hopes of gaining a few clues as to how it works. The watchships don't really carry on a very satisfactory program, so the project could hardly be forbidden. Besides, he wouldn't do it in his own name. He'd get the Demetrian Research Foundation to front for him. He's been generous enough with donations there. Anyway, the craft would be carrying out bona fide observations.

"Then why is so valuable an instrumentality forced to stay more than a million kilometers from the thing it's supposed to be investigating? I daresay the authorities made some excuse about safety, possible collision if a ship came through with the wrong vectors. I make the probability of that happening to be on the order of one in ten to the tenth. But they could enforce the regulation if they were determined to.

"So the fact they would have done it, doesn't that show their true motive? They don't want to lose control over news about the gate—another Betan ship appearing, maybe, or us returning, or anything marvelous. They want to exercise censorship.

"Will they censor *us*? There is a powerful antistellar element on Earth, in more than one national government. They could have gotten hold of the right levers in the Union hierarchy. They could have plans that they've not consulted their colleagues about."

Curses, growls, a couple of objections grated from the intercom. Lonely among them went Fidelio's fluting sound of bewilderment. What is the trouble? the Betan sang. Why are you no longer glad?

Langendijk silenced the noise. "As captain of a watchcraft, Archer has authority over me," he said. "Prepare to obey his instructions."

"Willem, listen," Joelle pleaded. "I can pinpoint a beam to the robot so they'll not detect a whisper aboard *Faraday*, and give Brodersen the truth—"

Langendijk cut her off: "We will follow our orders. That's a direct command of my own, which I'll enter in the log." His tone gentled. "Let's not quarrel, after we've come such a long, hard way together. Calm down. Think how large the chances are that some of you are overwrought, building a haunted house on a grain of sand. Archer communicates secretly, with the secret connivance of the watchship captain in the Solar System— communicates secretly with his secret masters, who tell him to take us to a secret place? Isn't that a little melodramatic?" Earnestly: "Think, too—the law of space is above politics. It has to be. Without it, man doesn't go to the stars, he dies. Every one of us has given a solemn oath to uphold it." After a pause, during which only the ventilator wind had utterance: "Take your flight stations. We will accelerate in ten minutes."

Joelle slumped. Hopelessness overwhelmed her. She could in fact have sent the uninterceptible message she spoke of, if her computer linkage were extended to the outercom system; but the switches for that were not in this chamber.

And Willem does have a point about the law. He could well be right, likewise, about this whole idea of a plot against us being a sick fantasy. Who am I to judge? I've been too remote from common humanity for too many years to have much feel for how it works.

Ultimate reality is easier to understand, yes, to be a part of, than we are, we flickers across the Noumenon.

"Are you ready, Joelle?" Langendijk asked mildly, well-nigh contritely.

"Oh!" She started. "Oh, yes. Any time."

"I've signalled *Faraday* our intent to start blasting at one gee at fifteen thirty-five hours, and they concur. They'll pace us; they are maneuvering for that right now. Interlock of autopilots will be made at one hundred kilometers from Beacon Charlie. Do you have assembled the information you need? . . . *Ach*, you're bound to, I'm a forgetful idiot to ask."

Herself wishful of reconciliation, Joelle smiled a smile he couldn't see and answered, "It's easy for you to forget, Willem. I'm holding down Christine's job"—Christine Burns, regular computerman, who died in Joelle's arms a bare few months before *Emissary* started home.

"Navigation is yours, then," Langendijk said formally. "Proceed upon signal."

"Aye."

Joelle got busy. Information flooded her, location vectors, velocity vectors, momenta, thrusts, gravitational field strengths, the time and space derivatives of these, continuously changing, smooth and mighty. It came out of instruments, transformed into digital numbers; and meanwhile the memory bank supplied her not only what specific past facts and natural constants she required, but the entire magnificent analytical structure of celestial mechanics and stress tensors. She had at her instant beck the physical knowledge of centuries and of this unique point in space-time where she was.

The data passed from their sources through a unit that translated them, in nanoseconds, into the proper signals. Thence they went to her brain. The connection was not through wires stuck in her skull or any such crudity; electromagnetic induction sufficed. She, in turn, called on the powerful computer to which she was also linked, as problems arose moment by moment.

The rapport was total. She had added to her nervous system the immense input, storage capacity, and retrieval speed of the electronic assembly, together with the immense mathematico-logical capacity for volume and speed of operations which belonged to its other half. For her part, she contributed a human ability to perceive the unexpected, to think creatively, to change her mind. She was the software for the whole system; a program which continuously rewrote itself; conductor of a huge mute orchestra which might have to start playing jazz with no warning, or compose an entire new symphony.

The numbers and manipulations did not stream before her as individual things. (Nor did she plan out the countless kinesthetic decisions her body made whenever it walked.) She felt them, but as a deep obbligato, a sense of ongoing rightness, *function*. Her awareness went over and beyond mechanical symbol-shuffling; it shaped the ongoing general pattern, as a sculptor shapes clay with hands that know of themselves what to do.

Artist, scientist, athlete, at the brief pinnacle of achievement... thus had linkage felt to Christine Burns.

It did not to Joelle. Christine had been an ordinary linker. Joelle was a holothete who had transcended that experience. Perhaps the difference resembled that between a devout Catholic layman at prayer and St. John of the Cross.

Besides, this present work was routine. Joelle had merely to direct, by her thoughts, equipment which sent the ship along a standard set of curves through a known set of configurations.

The unaided computer could have done as well, had it been worth the trouble of readjusting several circuits. Brodersen's robot performed the same kind of task.

Christine, the linker, had been signed on because *Emissary* was heading into the totally unknown, where survival might turn on a flash decision that could never have been foreseen and programmed for. She herself, had she lived, would have found this maneuvering easy.

Joelle found it soothing. She leaned back in her chair, conscious of regained weight, and enjoyed her oneness with the vessel. She could not hear and feel, but she could sense how the drive whispered. Migma cells were generating gigawatts of fusion power, to split water, ionize its atoms, hurl the plasma out through the jet focuser at a speed close to that of light itself. But the efficiency was superb, a triumph as great as the cathedral at Chartres; nothing appeared but the dimmest glow streaming aft for a few kilometers, and the onward motion of the hull.

Motion—it would last for several hours, at ever-changing orientations and configurations, as *Emissary* wove her way through the star gate between Phoebus and Sol. However, at present there was only a straightforward boost toward the first of the beacons. Joelle stirred and scowled. With less than half her attention engaged, she could not for long dismiss her fear of imprisonment ahead.

But then the viewscreen happened to catch the T machine itself, and she was lifted off into a miracle which never dulled.

At its distance, the cylinder was a tiny streak among hosts and clouds of stars. She magnified and the shape grew clear, though the dimensions remained an abstraction: length about a thousand kilometers, diameter slightly more than two. It spun around its long axis so fast that a point on the rim traveled at three-fourths the speed of light. Nothing on its silvery-brilliant surface told that to the unaided eye, yet somehow an endless, barely perceptible shimmer of changeable colors conveyed a maelstrom sense of the energy locked within. Humans believed that that gleam came from force-fields which held together matter compressed to ultimate densities. There were moons which had less mass than yonder engine for opening star gates.

In the background glowed two more of the beacons which surrounded it, a purple and a gold; and through the instruments, Joelle spied a third, whose color was radio.

This thing the Others had forged and set circling around

Phoebus, as they had set one at Sol and one at Centrum and one at ... who dared guess how many stars, across how many light-years and years? What number of sentient races had found them in space, gotten the same impersonal leave to use them, and hungered ever afterward to know who the builders truly were?

Out of those, what portion have crippled themselves the way we're doing? Joelle questioned in an upsurge of bitterness. *O Dan, Dan, it's gone for nothing, your trying to get the word that could set us free—*

And then, like a sunburst, she saw what must have come to him early on. He was bound to have thought of it; she remembered him drawling, "Every fox has two holes for his burrow." Hope kindled within her. She didn't stop to see how feeble it was, how easily blown out again. For now, the spark was enough.

III

DANIEL BRODERSEN WAS BORN in what was still called the state of Washington and had, indeed, not broken from the USA during the civil wars, as several regions attempted and the Holy Western Republic succeeded in doing. However, for three generations before him, the family chief had borne the title Captain General of the Olympic Domain and exercised a leadership over that peninsula, including the city of Tacoma, which was real while the claims of the federal government were words.

Those barons had not considered themselves nobility. Mike was a fisherman with a Quinault Indian wife, who had invested his money in several boats. When the Troubles reached America, he and his men became the nucleus of a group which restored order in the neighborhood, mainly to protect their households. As things worsened, he got appeals to help an ever-growing circle of farms and small towns, until rather to his surprise he was lord of many mountains, forests, vales, and strands, with all the folk therein. Any of them could always bend his ear; he put on no airs.

He fell in battle against bandits. His eldest son Bob avenged him in terrifying fashion, annexed the lawless territory to prevent a repetition, and set himself to giving defense and rough justice to his land, so that people could get on with their work. Bob felt loyal to the United States and twice raised volunteer regiments to fight for its integrity. He lost two boys of his own that way, and died while defending Seattle against a fleet which the Holies had sent north.

During his lifetime, similar developments went on in British Columbia. American and Canadian nationalism meant much less than the need for local cooperation. Bob married John, his remaining son, to Barbara, daughter of the Captain General of the Fraser Valley. That alliance ripened into close friendship between the families. After Bob's death, a special election overwhelmingly gave his office to John. "We've done okay with the Brodersens, haven't we?" went the word from wharfs and docks, huts and houses, orchards, fields, timber camps, workshops, taverns, from Cape Flattery to Puget Sound and from Tatoosh to Hoquiam.

John's early years in charge were turbulent, but this was due to events outside the Olympic Peninsula and gradually those too lost their violence. With peace came prosperity and a reheightening of civilization. The barons had always been fairly well educated, but men of raw action. John endowed schools, imported scholars, listened to them, and read books in what spare time he could find.

Thus he came to understand, better even than native shrewdness allowed, that the feudal period was waning. First the federal military command brought the entire USA under control, as General McDonough had done in Canada. Then piece by piece it established a new civil administration, reached agreement of sorts with the Holy Western Republic and the Méxican Empire, and opened negotiations for amalgamation with its northern neighbor. Meanwhile the World Union created by the Covenant of Lima was spreading. The North American Federation joined within three years of being proclaimed, according to a promise made beforehand. This example brought in the last holdout nations, and limited government over the entire human race was a reality—for a time, at least.

At the start of these events, John decided that his call was to preserve for his people enough home rule that they could continue to live more or less according to their traditions and desires. Over the years he gave way to centralization, step by step, bargaining for every point, and did achieve his wish. In the end he was nominally a squire, holding considerable property, entitled to various honors and perquisites, but a common citizen. In practice he was among the magnates, drawing strength from the respect and affection of the entire Pacific Northwest.

Daniel was his third son, who would inherit little wealth and no rank. This suited Daniel quite well. He enjoyed his boyhood—woods, uplands, wild rivers, the sea, horses, cars, watercraft, aircraft, firearms, friends, ceremonies of the guard, rude splendor of the manor until it became a mansion, visits to his mother's relatives and to cities nearer by where both pleasure and culture grew steadily more complicated—but restlessness was in him, the legacy of a fighting house, and in his teens he often got into brawls, when he wasn't carousing with low-life buddies or tumbling servant girls. Finally he enlisted in the Emergency Corps of the World Union Peace Command. That was very soon after its formation. The Union itself was still an infant that many wanted to strangle. A Corpsman hopped from place to place around the globe—later, off it as well—and most of them were full of weapons seeing brisk use. For Brodersen, here began a series of careers which eventually landed him on Demeter.

His latter-day acquaintances assumed that that youth was far behind him in space and perhaps, at fifty Earth-years of age, farther yet in time. He himself seldom thought about it. He kept too busy.

Settling his bulk into a chair, he drew forth pipe and tobacco pouch. "Damn the torpedoes," he rumbled. "Full speed ahead."

The Governor General of Demeter blinked at him across her desk. "What?"

"A saying of my dad's," Brodersen told her. "Means you asked me to come to your office in person, because you didn't want us gabbing about whatever 'tis over the phone; and now you're tiptoeing around the subject as if 'twere a cowbarn that hadn't been cleaned lately." He grinned to show he meant no harm. Actually, he suspected he did. "Let's not keep me here, mixing up my figures of speech, longer'n we must. Lis expects me home for dinner, and she's unforgiving if I cause the roast to be overdone."

Aurelia Hancock frowned. She was a sizeable woman, rather overweight, with blunt features and short gray hair. A cigarette smoldered between yellow-stained fingers; smoking had hoarsened her voice, and rumor was that she took an uncommon lot of cancer booster shots. As usual, she wore clothes which were Earth-modish but conservative, a green tunic with a silver-trimmed open collar above bell-bottomed slacks and gilt sandals. "I was trying to be pleasant," she said.

Brodersen's thumb tamped the bowl of his briar. "Thanks," he replied, "but I'm afraid that nohow can this be a nice subject."

She bridled. "How do you know what I want to talk about?"

"Aw, come down off that ungainly platform, Aurie. What else'd it be but *Emissary*?"

Hancock dragged on her cigarette, lowered, and said: "All right! Dan, you have got to stop spreading those tales about the ship returning. They simply are not true. My staff and I have our hands full as is, without adding unfounded suspicions that the Council itself is lying to the people."

Brodersen raised his shaggy brows. "Who says I've been telling stories out of school? I haven't made an appearance on any broadcast, or mounted a box and orated in Goddard Park, have I? Four or five weeks ago, I asked if you'd heard about *Emissary,* and I've asked you a couple of times since, and you've answered no. That's all."

"It isn't. You've been talking—"

"To friends, sure. Since when have your cops been monitoring conversations?"

"Cops? I suppose you mean police detectives. No, Dan, certainly not. What do you take me for? Why would I want to, even, with only half a million people in Eopolis and the way they gossip? Word gets to me automatically."

Brodersen regarded her with fresh respect. She was a political appointee—prominent in the Action Party of the North American Federation, helper and protégée of Ira Quick—but by and large, she hadn't been doing a bad job on Demeter, mediating between the Union Council and a diverse lot of increasingly disaffected colonists. (A tinge of pity: Her husband had been a high-powered lawyer on Earth, but there was little demand for his services here, and in spite of his putting on a good show, everybody knew he was far gone into alcoholism, without wanting to be cured of it. If anything, though, that made Aurelia Hancock the more formidable.) He'd better play close to his vest.

"I did speak to you first," he said.

"Yes, and I told you I'd surely have heard if—"

"You never convinced me my evidence was faulty."

"I tried to. You wouldn't listen. But think. At its distance, how could your robot possibly tell whether that was *Emissary* passing through?" Hancock frowned again. "Your deception of the Astronautical Control Board about the true purpose of that vessel could affect the continuance of your licenses, you know."

Brodersen had awaited that line of attack. "Aurie," he sighed elaborately, "let me just rehearse for you exactly what happened."

He struck fire to his pipe and got it under weigh. His glance roved. The room and furniture were to his taste, little of synth about them, mostly handmade of what materials were handy some seventy years ago, when the settlement on Demeter was about a generation old. *(That'd be half an Earth century,* flitted across his mind. *I really have soaked this planet up into me, haven't I?)* Creamy, whorl-grained daphne wainscoting set off a vase of sunbloom on the desk and, on a shelf behind, a stunning hologram of Mount Lorn with both moons full above its snows. On his right, two windows stood open on a garden. There Terrestrial rosebuds and grass reached to a wrought iron fence; but a huge old thunder oak remained from the vanished forest, its bluish-green leaves breathing forth a slight gingery odor, and slingplant grew jubilantly over the metal. Ordinary traffic moved along the street, pedestrians, cyclists, bubble of a car and snake of a freighter whirring on their air cushions. Across the way, a modern house lifted its pastel trapezoid. Yet overhead the sky arched deeper blue than anywhere on Earth, and Phoebus in afternoon had a mellowness akin to Sol at evening. For a half second he recalled that barometric pressure was lower and so was gravity (eighty percent), but his body was too habituated to feel either any longer.

He drew on the pipe, savored a bite across tongue and nostrils, and continued: "I never kept my opinion secret. Theory says a T machine can scoot you to anywhere in space-time within its range ... which means space *and* time. *Emissary* was on the track of an alien ship that'd been observed using a gate in this system, obviously to pass between a couple of points we knew nothing about. I figured the crew and owners 'ud be friendly. Why shouldn't they be? At a minimum, they'd help *Emissary* return after her mission was completed. And in that case, why not send them home close to the same date as they left?"

"I've heard your argument," Hancock said, "but only after you began agitating. If you felt it was that plausible, that important, why didn't you file a report beforehand with the appropriate bureau?"

Brodersen shrugged. "Why should I? The idea wasn't absolutely unique to me. Besides, I'm a private citizen."

She gave him a narrow look. "The wealthiest man on Demeter is not altogether a private citizen."

"I'm small potatoes next to the rich on Earth," he replied blandly.

"Like the Rueda clan in Perú—with whom you have a business as well as family relationship. No, you are not entirely a private citizen."

Still she stared at him. He sat back, cradling the warmth of his pipe bowl, and let her. Not that he had illusions about his handsomeness. He was a big man, a hundred and eighty-eight centimeters tall and thickboned, muscular, broad in the shoulders, deep in the chest; but of late years he had added girth till he appeared stocky. His head was likewise massive, mesocephalic, square-faced, with heavy jaw and mouth, jutting Roman nose, eyes gray, wideset, downward-slanted, crow's-footed, skin weathered and furrowed. Like most men on Demeter, he went clean-shaven and cropped his hair above the ears; it was straight, coarse, black with some white streaks, a last inheritance from his great-grandmother. For this meeting, as for most occasions, he wore casual colonial male garb: bolero of orosaur leather above a loose blouse, baggy pants tucked into soft half boots, wide belt holding assorted small tools and instruments in its loops plus a sheath knife.

"Regardless," he said, keeping his amicable tone, "I don't know of any laws I've broken, nor bent unrepairably far out of shape."

"Don't be too cocksure about that," she warned.

"Hm? Maybe we'd better run through the story from the beginning, and see if you can point out where I went illegal. Otherwise, relax and enjoy."

Brodersen took a breath before he continued: "I thought, and mentioned to miscellaneous people, that *Emissary* might come back early. Few paid me much heed. Yes, as you've guessed, I did sponsor that robot observer the Foundation sent to study the T Machine—but it was mainly doing legitimate scientific work, and I've yet to get a satisfactory explanation of why it was required to take up such a distant orbit.

"Hold, if you will. Let me rant for a minute longer." Though his eyelids crinkled, belying the imperious note, his voice tramped on. "Space regs don't demand that research plans be explained in detail. And what harm in keeping a lens cocked for

Emissary, anyway? You accuse me of deception? Blazes, Aurie, 'twas the other way around!

"Just the same, after a few months the observer did return, and beamed a message to the station it was supposed to, under certain circumstances. I called you and asked—sort of tactfully, I think—if you knew anything about the matter. You said no. I checked with Earth, and everybody I contacted there said no too. Now I'd hate to call them all liars. Especially you, Aurie. Nevertheless, today you invited me down for a confidential discussion, which seems to be about gagging me."

She straightened in her chair, gripped her desktop, and defied him: "You were jumping to conclusions from the start. Absurd conclusions."

"Must I run barefoot through the cowbarn for you?" His note of patience was not spontaneous; he had planned his tactics en route to this house. "Directly or indirectly, you've got to have heard my reasoning before. But okay, here 'tis again."

She pulled smoke into her lungs and waited. He thought fleetingly how much human discourse was like this, barren repetition if not mere tom-tom beat, and wondered if the Others were free of the necessity, if they could speak straight to a meaningful point.

"The robot spotted a *Reina*-class transport popping out of a gate," he said. "Sure, it was too far off to identify the ship, but we humans have built nothing bigger and the shape was right. Either that was a *Reina* or it was a nonhuman vessel of the same general kind. The robot then tracked *Faraday* closing in on the newcomer, and then tracked them both as they followed the Phoebus-to-Sol guidepath. That was enough for its program to decide it should come home and report.

"Still, Aurie, I didn't swan-dive whooping off the deep end. I began by having my agents on Earth learn exactly where every other *Reina* was at that time. It turned out none of them could've been what my observer saw; we were accounted for, in the Solar System or this one.

"Meanwhile *Faraday* returned to Phoebus and resumed her duties. I had a Foundation director beam Captain Archer a polite inquiry as to what had happened. He answered that there had been nothing unusual, a freighter had developed some trouble in transit from Sol and he escorted her back as a precaution, and no, she was not a *Reina* but a *Princesa* and if our robot claimed otherwise, we'd better have its instruments overhauled.

"Now look, Aurie, I know that observer is in perfect shape. So what the devil do you want me to think? Either that was a nonhuman ship, or she was *Emissary,* which I imagine you'll agree is more likely by a whisker or three. Whichever, 'tis the biggest story since...take your choice...and nobody in authority has a bloody damn thing to say about it!"

Brodersen leaned forward. His pipestem jabbed the air. "I give you, probably most of those I've queried, or my agents have, are honest," he said. "They really had no information. In a couple of cases they took the trouble to send off inquiries of their own, and got back a negative. It's understandable that they didn't then dig further. They consider their time valuable, and I've got the reputation of being a troublemaker. Why should they assume my data were valid? Doubtless several of them decided I was lying for some obscure purpose.

"Well, you've been on Demeter long enough to know me better than that, no? And for my part, when I first contacted you about this and you said you'd heard nothing, I believed. When I asked again later and you said you were investigating, I believed also. Since then, however—frankly, I've grown more and more skeptical.

"So why have you summoned me today?"

Hancock tossed the stub of her cigarette down an ashtaker, took another from a box, and struck it alight in a savage motion. "You mentioned my wanting to gag you," she said. "Call it what you please. It's what I mean to do."

Not quite a surprise. Brodersen willed his belly muscles to untighten, his response to be soft: "For what reason and by what right?"

She met his gaze square on. "I've received an answer to my communications about this affair. From an extremely high quarter. The public interest demands that for an indefinite time there be no release of news. That includes the allegations you've been making."

"Public interest, eh?"

"Yes. I wish—" The hand that brought the cigarette to Hancock's lips was less than steady. "Dan," she said almost sadly, "we've been at loggerheads before. I realize how much you oppose certain policies of the Union and how you're becoming a spokesman for that attitude among Demetrians. Nevertheless, I've esteemed you and dared hope you believed I also wanted the best for this planet. We've worked together, even, haven't we? Like when I talked the Council into making the extra appropriation for the University you wanted, or you lobbied your stiff-necked colonial parliament into approving the Ecological Authority that I'd persuaded you had become a necessity. May I ask today for a bit more of your trust?"

"Sure," he said, "if you'll tell me the reasons."

She shook her head. "I can't. You see, I haven't been given the details myself. It's that crucial. But those who've requested my help, I must trust them."

"Notably Ira Quick." Brodersen couldn't neutralize the acid in his reply.

She stiffened. "As you like. He *is* the Minister of Research and Development."

"And a drive wheel in the Action Party, which leads all those factions on Earth that'd rather not see us go out into the galaxy." Brodersen curbed his temper. "Let's not argue politics. What are you free to tell me? I presume you can give me some argument, some reason to dog my hatch."

Hancock streamed smoke while she stared at the glowing butt she held on the desktop. "They suggested a hypothetical case to me. Imagine you're right, that *Emissary* has in fact returned, but she was bearing something terrible."

"A plague? A swarm of vampires? For Pete's sake, Aurie! And Paul's, Matt's, Mark's, Luke's, and Jack's."

"It could simply be bad news. We've taken a lot of things for granted. For instance, that every civilization technologically advanced beyond us must be peaceful, else they couldn't have lasted. Which is a logical *non sequitur,* actually. Suppose *Emissary* discovered a conquering race of interstellar Huns."

"If nothing else, I doubt the Others would sit still for that. However, supposing it, why, I'd want to alert my species so we could ready our defenses."

Hancock gave Brodersen a pale smile. "That was my own offhand example. I admit it's not very plausible."

"Then feed me one that is."

She winced. "All right. Since you mentioned the Others— suppose there are none."

"Huh? *Somebody* built the T machines and lets us use them."

"Robots. When the first explorers reached the machine in the

Solar System, the thing that spoke to them did not hide that it was only a robot. We've built up our whole concept of the Others from nothing more than what it said. Which is awfully little, Dan, if you stop to think. Suppose *Emissary* has brought back proof that we're wrong. That the Others are extinct. Or never existed. Or are basically evil. Or whatever you can imagine. You're a born heretic. You don't find any of this unthinkable, do you?"

"N-no. I do find it extremely unlikely. But supposing it for the sake of argument, what then?"

"You could keep your sanity. But you're an exceptional sort. Could humankind as a whole?"

"What're you getting at?"

Once more Hancock raised her tormented head to confront him. "You like to read history," she said, "and as an entrepreneur, you're a kind of practical politician. Must I spell out for you what it would mean, the shattering of our image of the Others?"

Brodersen's pipe had died. He resurrected it. "Maybe you must."

"Well, look, man." (He was oddly moved by the American- ism. They shared that background, though she came from the Midwest. *And Joelle was born in Pennsylvania,* he remembered. *Where are you now, Joelle?*) "When they found out what the strange object was, an actual T machine, and heard what the robot had to tell them, it may have been the greatest shock the human race has ever undergone—the whole human race. You had to take Jesus or Buddha on faith, and the faith spread slowly. But here, overnight, was direct proof that beings exist superior to us. Not merely in science and technology—no, what the Voice said indicated they were beyond us in their own selves. Angels, gods, whatever name you care to give. And seemingly benign but indifferent. We were told how to get from Sol to Phoebus and back; we were free to settle Demeter if we chose; the rest was left to us, including how to go onward from here."

"Yeah, sure," he encouraged her.

"Probably that was a large part of the shock: the indifference. Suddenly humans realized for a fact that they aren't anything special in the universe. But at the same time, there is something to aspire to. No wonder a million cults, theories, self-assertions, outright lunacies sprang up. No wonder that after a while, Earth exploded."

"M-m-m, I wouldn't blame the Troubles entirely on the revelation," Brodersen said. "The balance that'd been reached earlier was almighty precarious. If anything, I think the idea of the Others helped keep everybody from running amuck—helped keep the real planet-killer weapons from seeing over-much use—so Earth is still habitable."

"As you like," Hancock replied. "The point is, that idea has made a tremendous difference, maybe more than any traditional religion ever did."

She braced herself to go on: "Okay. Suppose the *Emissary* expedition learned it's a false idea. As I suggested, maybe the Others are dead, or moved elsewhere, or less than we think, or worse than we think. Let that news out with no forewarning, let hysterical commentators knock the foundations loose from under hundreds of millions of people, and what happens? The Union isn't firmly enough grounded that it can survive worldwide mania. And next time around, the planet-killers might well get unleashed.

"Dan," she begged, "do you see why we have to keep silence for a while?"

He puffed his pipe. "I'm afraid I'll need the details," he answered.

"But—"

"You admitted this was hypothetical, didn't you? Well, I don't buy the hypothesis. If the Others were monsters, we wouldn't be sitting here; we'd be wiped out, or we'd be domestic animals of theirs, or whatever. If they're extinct—hunh, tell me how a species capable of building T machines is going to let itself become extinct. Nor do I imagine they're not better than us; with that kind of technology, wouldn't you improve your own race, supposing evolution had not already done it for you? And as for them collectively going off to live in some kind of parallel universe—why should they, when this one we've got is loaded with more fun than anybody can use up before the last star burns out?"

"I didn't claim any of those was the case," Hancock said. "I was only giving you some examples."

"Uh-huh. Ever heard of Occam's razor? I've shaved with it from time to time."

"Choose the simplest explanation for the facts."

"Right. And in this case, what is the simplest? I propose that *Emissary* did return; that the story she brought was of how we might go beyond these two planetary systems we have; that certain politicians on Earth don't like that possibility and want to suppress it; and that you, Aurie, have now gotten your marching orders. I imagine you agree in principle anyway. You belong to the Action Party."

Brodersen barked it forth. He might as well, his back to the wall of a decision already made; and perhaps he could provoke a little truth out of her who had become his enemy.

Yet he was jarred when she said in her coldest manner: "I consider that an insult, Captain Brodersen. But never mind. If you won't cooperate freely, we'll have to apply duress. You are not going to continue talking as you have been."

Chill rammed through him. He had come expecting that she would lay heavy pressure on him, but not a grabclaw. "Ever read the Covenant?" he asked low. "I mean the free speech clause."

"Have you read the provision for emergencies and the laws enacted under it?" she retorted, though he could see her hurting.

"Yeah. So?"

"I declare an emergency. Come back in five years and take the matter to court." Hancock reached for a fresh cigarette. "Dan," she stated unhappily, "I've got the cops, as you call them. Until we can agree about this business, you're under arrest."

She meant he would be confined to his home, his mail and phone monitored. Maybe she was sincere in her promise that her surveillance men would only activate their electronic eavesdroppers when he had visitors. He could conduct his business as usual from the house—these days, it mostly ran itself anyway—and could give whatever reason he chose, such as a prolonged attack of the galloping collywobbles, for not leaving the place. If he said it was on her orders, though, she'd tell the news media that he was being held while his company was investigated on suspicion of fraud.

She thought she could probably let him go in a month or two. That would depend on what she heard from Earth.

He didn't waste energy roaring. "You're being a government, Aurie," he remarked. When she gave him an inquiring glance, he explained: "The single definition of government I've ever seen that makes sense is that it's the organization which claims the right to kill people who won't do what it wants."

He could have gone on to admit that he was oversimplifying,

since she was obviously acting on behalf of a group whose own behavior might well be unlawful; but he didn't think it was worth his while.

IV

TWO COURTEOUS PLAINCLOTHES policemen escorted Brodersen from the governor's house and rode home with him in his car. By then, Demeter was completing another day, ten percent shorter than Earth's. The sun was hidden behind Anvil Hill, which loomed blue-gray at the end of Pioneer Avenue with the dome of the Capitol shining gold on its brow. Right and left the city reached, an uncluttered view of intermingled dwellings, small factories, stores, service enterprises, most buildings surrounded by lawns and flowers. At his back, the Europa River gleamed broad on its way to Apollo Bay and thence the Hephaestian Sea. The opposite shore was farmland, fields of wheat and corn vividly green at this season against a few remaining bluish stands of mariflora and raincatch. A moon stood high at half phase, wan and mottled amidst cloudless azure. Wings cruised up there, frailies and bucearos seeking their nests, starlarks rising to hunt through the dusk. The air blew cool and bore wild scents from the hinterland eastward.

How beautiful this is, passed through him as he came outdoors, together with a few lines from his favorite poet, penned more than two centuries ago:

> *God gave all men all earth to love,*
> *But, since our hearts are small,*
> *Ordained for each one spot should prove*
> *Belovéd over all;*

—and at the same time: *No, damnation, it* isn't *enough! We have a whole universe to live in, if we can break past the powermongers.*

Sharply to him came the memories—Earth seen from space, tiny, gorgeously beswirled, infinitely precious; Lunar craters beneath a blaze of stars; a Martial dawn, red, red, red over sands

29

and boulders and colors; the mighty sight of many-banded
Jupiter; his first glimpse of Phoebus athwart new constellations.
What else had Joelle witnessed? What else could he?

"Nice weather," said one of the officers. "Looks like we won't
get the summer storms till Hektos or Hebdomos this year."

"Yeah," Brodersen responded like a machine. A part of him
noted that the young men beside him had been born here. They
used the Demetrian calendar automatically. Few were the atoms
in them that had come from Earth. What did they individually
think about the prospect of humankind getting the freedom of
the cosmos? Doubtless they'd say that was a great idea . . . until
some neo-collectivist gave them an estimate of the social cost.
What then? He forbore to ask.

Instead he steered for the Église de St. Michel suburb.
(Traffic was not so thick in Eopolis that autopilots were
mandatory.) Hidden Mountain Road lay gold at evening,
houses and gardens widely separated, native meadows and
woodlands in between. His own dwelling was designed for the
climate, a Hawaiian-style bungalow in half a hectare of lodix
lawn and Terrestrial flowers. "How do you fellows plan to get
back?" he asked as he pulled into the carport.

"We'll be around here till we're relieved, sir," was the answer.

"M-m-m . . . hm. Want to stop in for a cup of coffee?"

"We'd better not, sir. Thanks anyway."

Brodersen grinned at his passengers' embarrassment, which
very slightly eased the anger in him, and got out. They moved off
the property and vanished behind a tall davisia hedge, doubtless
to take stations watchful of both his front and rear entrances.

After patting his German shepherd hello, he went on into the
house. The living room was long and high, paneled like the office
where he had been, a stone fireplace that he had built himself
standing archaic opposite a broad window showing the patio. It
was full of fragrances from the blooms his wife had brought in.
She had music going, some of her cherished Sibelius, but softly,
while she sat in a lounger, the cat on her lap, and studied an
engineering report. (After he hired her, he soon found she rated
rapid promotion; after they were married, he made her his full
partner. These days Elisabet Leino occupied much of her time
with matters outside of Chehalis Enterprises—civic, theatrical,
horticultural, not to mention two lively youngsters—but the
company still could not have managed well without her.)

"Hi," she said, laid the papers down and rose, expecting to

kiss him. She was a rangy woman, ivory-skinned, brown-haired, husky-voiced, today clad in a dress whose shortness did justice to her legs. Sharp, almost Classical features lost their look of gladness. "You've got a faceful of riptides. It went badly, didn't it?"

"I want beer," he growled, and hauled a bottle from a cooler cabinet behind a small bar. His manners came back to him. "Uh, you too?"

She walked across to embrace him lightly. "I'll wait for cocktail hour. What happened, darling?"

"Plenty, and all ungood." He poured into a silver mug from a set he'd brought back from his last trip to Earth, baggage charges be damned, for their ninth wedding anniversary this Demetrian year. The feel of it in his fist and the chill pungency in his mouth were comforting.

She studied him. "You've made up your mind what to do," she said.

"I'm working on it. You're involved, of course, starting as chief consultant."

"Then tell me." She took his hand and led him toward the couch.

He let her sit down while he paced and talked, gulping between harsh passages. At the end, he summarized: "Seems obvious to me. A bunch of antistellar types have formed a cabal. They must have members in several national governments, plus doubtless the Union Council, the bureaucracy, and the space corps. Quite likely they took more seriously than they let on, the notion that *Emissary* might return earlier than expected, and kept sort of on the ready. So she's being held incommunicado while they decide how to handle her. Meanwhile I've been getting too noisy. So Hancock got word to muzzle me. I doubt she was ever in on any conspiracy, but she is loyal to the Action Party in general and her political sponsors in particular. If they tell her it's her duty to enforce silence, she'll accept that without asking inconvenient questions." He shrugged. "I suppose I should give thanks she isn't the type to take stronger measures than she has."

Lis let silence fall for a moment, together with twilight, before she murmured, "I don't suppose there is any possibility that they may be right?"

"What do you think?"

"Oh, we've been over this territory often enough, and you

know I agree with you. I simply wondered. One does hate to imagine corruption in high levels of the Union—the Union!—doesn't one?... What do you plan to do?"

He stopped, stared down at her, and said, "What can I, except be a good boy? And you be a good girl. Hancock understood I'd tell you how things are, but warned me you'd be in Dutch too if you talked. We'll let out that I'm—um-m, 'indisposed' for weeks isn't believable.... I've turned hermit in order to work on a new idea for the business, which has to stay secret till it's ready. You take over in the office for me."

"What?" She was astounded. "You, Dan, that tamely?"

He shook his head and laid a finger across his lips. "What choice have we got? I could be worse off than taking an enforced vacation. Might read some of those books you're always urging me to. Now look, sweetheart, I'm tired and grumped and won't appreciate your dinner unless I can relax first. Okay?"

Her gaze upon him grew knowing. "Okay," she said.

Accordingly, for the next while, they went through their family routine. After a second beer he took the children to the rec room for the half-hour-plus with Daddy which was theirs by right. Mike, going on three (two, Earth calendar), was content to stump around laughing, get jounced on an ankle, and join wordlessly in some songs. He came closer to carrying the tunes than his father did, though that wasn't saying much. Barbara, at seven, demanded as well that he draw a picture and tell her the latest installment of his saga of Slewfoot the orosaur. (In his childhood, Captain General John had told him about Slewfoot the bear, but that was on Earth.) He ended the current adventure rather abruptly, with a safe return to Queets Castle.

She sensed his haste. "Are you goin' away again?" she asked.

"I'm not sure, darling," he said. It twisted within him. "I may have to." How warm she sat between his hands.

"For long?"

"I certainly hope not. You know how I've got to make trips sometimes to find money. If I must go, well, I'll come home as soon as may be, with a load of presents and a lot of new stories." Hugging her: "You'll help Mother same as before, right? That's my lassie." She cast her arms about his neck.

He supposed that eavesdroppers, who might be using pickups in spite of Hancock's promise, wouldn't attach any importance to such an exchange. Nevertheless, after the kids were back in the nursery and he had settled down for a drink with Lis, he took the precaution of remarking, "About my confinement to quarters, I do wonder if I can't get leave to visit *Chinook*. There are several things that need my personal attention. Even Barbara could feel I'm anxious to take care of 'em. They can send a couple of their damn guards along to make sure I don't blurt."

"Well, you can try," she answered.

"In a few days I might, when tempers have cooled."

As aware of his mood as their daughter, she changed the subject. They always had plenty to talk about. The business itself was endlessly varied. Chehalis held most spacecraft in the Phoebean System and conducted most undertakings off Demeter, on its own or under contract—transport, prospecting, mining, manufacturing, exploration, pure research. This inevitably involved it in widespread aspects of the colony's economy and politics, and increasingly with Earth. Beyond that, without having ambitions for public office, they both took a close interest in public affairs; they went sailing or on wilderness trips together, skied, figure skated, played tennis and slapdash chess and Machiavellian poker, worked on their house and grounds; they often strolled out to watch the stars and wonder what dwelt yonder. This evening they got onto some recent discoveries, about an odd relationship between the dominant hypersauroids and the primitive theroids along the Ionian Gulf littoral, and almost forgot their troubles. Afterward the children made dinner enjoyable.

But when man and wife alone were awake, Brodersen said, "I feel restless. Think I'll tinker with that monofilm recorder. Why don't you come along and help?"

Such projects were not among Lis' hobbies, but she caught his meaning and replied, "Sure."

They sought his workshop. In half an hour he had cobbled together the apparatus he wanted from an ample supply of spare parts and activated it. A whine filled the equipment-crowded chamber. He clicked his tongue. "Dear me. Inefficient."

"Is that to cover our voices?" she inquired.

She had realized what worried him. People spoke Finnish on her parents' farm in the Trollberg region, and he had acquired a few extra languages in the years when he knocked about Earth. But all he and she had in common were English—their everyday tongue—and Spanish, both of which would be known to any detective.

"No," he explained. "Sonics wouldn't work, at least not without a lot of fancy heterodyning gear. This is no more'n a high-powered wide-band radio noise generator, which ought to jam electronic communications within a couple hundred meters, and seem accidental. I'm assuming the opposition has planted bugs along our walls, to pick up speech inside and buck it on to a receiver. Easy to do. Those things are small. You could lob 'em into the shrubbery with a slingshot."

Dread touched her. "Do you really believe Aurie Hancock would order that, or the police would obey? Demeter's supposed to be a free society."

"Supposed to be. It's actually a set of societies, you know, and a lot of mother countries aren't exactly libertarian. If I were governor, I'd keep a few men on the force whose background doesn't include scruples about privacy. Might need 'em someday to deal with criminals who were finding this planet a happy hunting ground." Brodersen hitched himself onto the workbench and sat swinging his legs. "Anyway, Lis, I don't *believe* we're bugged, I'm *assuming* it. This matter's too big for optimism. Tomorrow you have Mamoru Saigo come around with a detector and check for spy gadgets. If he finds any, hm, I'd suggest you destroy them, but first speak a sharp message that if this happens again, you'll go to court and the news media both."

She was mute among the tools while her gaze searched him. The window behind her was closed and blinded, but from it breathed a slight chill, like a sense of the darkness beyond.

"You won't be here, then," she foreknew.

He fumbled after pipe and tobacco. "'Fraid not, honey. We can't let the bastards ream us out, can we? Judas priest, the whole future of human spacefaring! Besides—have you forgotten?—the mate aboard *Emissary* is Carlos Rueda Suárez, my friend, Toni's cousin. I don't write family off."

"Also Joelle Ky, if she's alive," Lis said quietly.

He winced from the pain he saw on her. "Yeah, well, an old friend too."

"More than a friend." Lis raised a palm. "No, don't bother pretending. I've never objected to your little flings, have I? I'd like to meet Joelle myself. She must be rather special, to mean this much to you. You've never mentioned her to me as casually as you imagined you did."

"You win," he said, fiery-faced. "Not that we got romantic, understand. She's too...strange for that. But—Anyway, the main point is, I don't see how the cabal can ever let *Emissary* go. The publicity would wreck their whole aim, and their personal careers to boot. At the same time, it's dangerous maintaining prisoners. They may decide on a massacre."

"If they are that villainous. If there is a cabal."

He nodded. "The chance I take, that I'm mistaken."

"As well as chances with your life, Dan."

"Not too bad. Honest. I value my hide. It's the only one I've got."

"What do you want to do, essentially?"

"Go to Earth. Investigate. Act. Mainly, I suppose, alert the Rueda clan. At most, they'll've heard vague rumors. I haven't written to them directly, as you know, because I wasn't that sure of my facts; and then when I was, I trustingly asked Aurie to push her queries harder, and then today she dumped this crockful over me. Our mail is bound to be intercepted, stopped if it says anything inconvenient. Nobody that I know on Demeter whom I might somehow pass the word to, nobody knows his way around Earth or has the connections I do there. No, I must get to Lima in person and talk to the Señor."

"How?"

He paused in stuffing his pipe to give her a lopsided grin. "Lis, that plain and practical a question alone, right in this hour, would make me love you."

He had not seen her blush and drop her glance in a long time. She squeezed his thigh. "We're partners, remember?" she whispered.

"I'm not about to forget." He set his smoking apparatus down to lay a hand over hers. "Okay, we haven't a truckload of time, we'd better conspire onward.

"I don't yet have an exact plan. Mainly, I figure it's needful I bust free, out of reach. And immediately. If nothing is seen or heard of me for the next two-three days, I think Aurie'll take for granted I'm sulking in my tent. After that, however, it'd seem funny if I didn't at least make an occasional phone call. So I'll skite off tonight."

She didn't require details. None but the two of them knew about their tunnel. A few years past, he'd rented a burrower to add a wine cellar to their storm shelter. While he was at it, he excavated a crawlway to the middle of the woods north of their land, reinforcing with spraycrete. That was during the bitter dispute, on and around Earth, regarding jurisdiction and property rights among the asteroids, when for a while it looked as if the Iliadic League would secede. If that federation of orbital and Lunar colonies left the Union—and the Union probably resorted to arms to bring it back—God knew what would happen, also on Demeter. The crisis faded away in grumbling compromise, but Brodersen still jawed himself for not having provided a secret exit from the house before then. He'd seen enough disasters, most of them due to governments, that he should have taken out that insurance at the start.

From the woods he could hike five kilometers to a lonely airbus stop, fly to a distant town, and rent a car. He had established a couple of fake identities, complete with excellent credit ratings, to protect privacy when he and his traveled. In the pond that was Demeter, population less than three million, he'd become a bigger frog than he liked.

"What next?" Lis asked.

"Let's think," he said, kindling tobacco and drinking smoke. "Obviously I'll need transportation to Sol, transportation that'll do me some good after I get there. *Chinook*—what else?—the crew she can carry, the supplies aboard, the auxiliary boat. Besides, *Williwaw* is practically designed for jobs like snatching me unbeknownst from wherever I am on this planet."

"How do you hope you'll get *Chinook* through the gate, past the watchship?"

He chuckled. The prospect of operating, instead of being operated on, cheered him immensely. Not that he welcomed the present mess. Yet in recent years his days had gotten too predictable for his taste. "We'll figure that out. If you can't handle the negotiations, dear, we'd better both report to the gero clinic. Off hand ... hm ... well, Aventureros"—the parent company of Chehalis—"certainly could use another big freighter within the Solar System; and with no prospect now of *Chinook* going starward, why, we might as well put her on charter there." He snapped his fingers. "Hey, yes, that'd give her the perfect official reason to contact the Ruedas." Leaning forward, going earnest: "Yes, let's count on that. Tomorrow you buzz the crewfolk. Speak about a possible trip to Sol on short notice, and invite them here for a conference about it. La Hancock did tell me quite frankly we'd be bugged whenever we had visitors, and jamming at that time would look too suspicious. But you can prepare written summaries to hand out, and all the real talk can be in writing, while harmless things are spoken that you can also have written out beforehand. They're bright people I picked, quick studies. They'll put on a convincing show."

Lis frowned. "Will they necessarily go along with such a risky venture?"

"Well, some may be too law-abiding or something. However, I feel sure that if any refuse, they'll still be loyal enough that they won't run off and blab. I didn't choose them to be my crew on a possible voyage to new planets without getting to know each one of them pretty well."

"Even so, Aurelia is no fool. If she learns that *Chinook* is about to leave, she may slap on a hold, on whatever pretext she can think of, just to play safe."

"Need she know? The Governor General's office doesn't usually keep track of spaceship comings and goings. I've little doubt you can hit on an arrangement."

Brodersen hesitated before adding: "Uh, in due course she will grow certain I've vamoosed, and quite likely speculate that I was smuggled aboard. You'll be in for considerable static, I'm afraid."

"I can give as good as I get," she assured him.

He smiled. "Yeah. How well I know. I don't see how she can make really serious trouble for you without tipping her hand, which she mustn't. What can she legally prove, except maybe that you helped your husband break out of a dubiously legal custody? And if that came to trial, wow!"

"She might trump up something worse," Lis said. "Not that I think she'd want to. She's not basically a commissar. But she might be ordered to."

"Our lawyers can drag out any court case for months," he reminded her. "By that time, I should've gotten the whole stinking business busted to flinders." He frowned. "Of course, if I fail—"

"Don't worry about me," she interrupted. "You know I'll manage."

Again she grew quiet, standing beside him. "I'll be afraid on your account," she said at last.

"Don't be." He shifted his pipe and laid an arm around her shoulders.

"Well, since you are bound to go, let's plan things carefully. For openers, how do we keep in touch?"

"Through Abner Croft," he proposed. That was among his fictitious personalities. Abner Croft owned a cabin on Lake

Artemis, a hundred kilometers hence. His phone possessed more than a scrambler. It had a military gadget Brodersen had learned about on Earth and re-created for himself, as an extra precaution during the Iliadic crisis. A tap on the line would register a banal pre-recorded conversation. He and Lis had had fun creating several such, using disguises and voder-altered voices. He could get in circuit from any third instrument by requesting a conference call; the switching machinery didn't care.

"M-hm," she said. "Where do you expect you'll actually be?"

"In the uplands. Logical area, no?"

She paused. "With Caitlín?"

Taken aback because she spoke so gravely, he floundered, "Well, um, that's where she is this time of year. Everybody local'll know how to find her, and think it quite natural that an outside visitor would want to hear a few songs of hers. And who else could better keep me concealed, or tell what's a safe rendezvous in those parts, or ... or whatever?"

He puffed hard. Lis touched him anew, and now she did not let go. "Forgive me that I asked," she said low. "I'm not protesting. You're right, she's a fine bet to help us. But you see—no, I'm not jealous, but I might never see you again after tonight, and she means a great deal more to you than Joelle, doesn't she?"

"Aw, sweetheart." He laid his pipe aside, to slide from the bench and stand holding her.

Head on his breast, fingers tight against his back, she let the words tumble forth, though she kept them soft. "Dan, dearest, understand. I know you love me. And I, after that wretched marriage of mine broke up, when I met you—Everything you've been says you love me. But you, your first wife, you were never happier than when you had Antonia, were you?"

"No," he confessed around a thickness. "Except you've given me—"

"Hush. I've made it clear to you I don't mind—enough to matter—if you wander a bit once in a while. You meet a lot of assorted people, and I don't usually go along on your business trips to Earth, and you're a mighty attractive bull, did I ever tell you? No, shut up, darling, let me finish. I don't worry about Joelle. From what little you've said, there's a kind of witchcraft about her—a holothete and—But you didn't ever invent excuses to go back to her. Caitlín, though—"

"Her either—" he tried.

"You haven't told me she was anything but a friend and occasional playmate. Well, you haven't told me that, openly, about anyone. You're a private person in your way, Dan. But I've come to know you regardless. I've watched you two when she came visiting. Caitlín is quite a bit like Toni, isn't she?"

He could only grip her to him for reply.

"You said I didn't have to be a monogamist myself," Lis blurted. "And maybe I won't always." She gulped a giggle. "What a pair of anachronisms we are, knowing what 'monogamy' means!...But since we got married, Dan, nobody's been worth the trouble. And nobody will be while you're away this trip and I don't know if you'll get back."

"I will," he vowed, "I will, to you."

"You'll do your damnedest, sure. Which is one blazing hell of a damnedest." She raised her face to his. He saw tears, and felt and tasted them. "I'm sorry," she got forth. "I shouldn't have mentioned Caitlín. Except...give her my love, please."

"I, I said earlier, your practical question reminded me what kind of people you are," he stammered. "Then, uh, this—You're flat-out unbelievably *good*."

Lis disengaged, stepped back, flowed her hands from his ribs to his hips, and said far down in her throat: "Thanks, chum. Now look, this'll be a short night—you'll want to catch your bus when the passengers are sleepy—and we've a lot of plotting to do yet. First, however...m-m-m-m?"

Warmth rose in him. "M-m-m-m," he returned.

V

THREE HUNDRED KILOMETERS east of the Hephaestian Sea,
two thousand north of Eopolis, the Uplands rose. There a
number of immigrants from northern Europe had settled during
the past century's inflow. Like most colonists, once it became
possible to survive beyond the original town and its technological support, they tended to clump together with their own kind.
Farmers, herders, lumberjacks, hunters, they lived in primitive
fashion for lack of machinery; freight costs from Earth were
enormous. Later, when Demetrian industry began to grow, they
acquired some modern equipment—but not much, because in
the meantime they had developed ways well suited to coping
with their particular country. Moreover, most of them didn't
care to become dependent on outsiders. They or their ancestors
had moved here to be free of governments, corporations,
unions, and other monopolies. That spirit endured.

The folk who bore it had evolved a whole ethos. In their
homes, many of them continued to speak the original languages;
but given that variety, English was the common tongue, in a new
dialect. Traditions blended together, mutated, or sprang
spontaneously into being. For instance, at winter solstice—cold,
murk, snow, in this part of the continent which humans called
Ionia—they celebrated Yule (not Christmas, which still went by
the Terrestrial calendar) with feasting, mirth, decorations, gifts,
and reunions. Halfway around the Demetrian year they found a
different occasion for gatherings, more frankly bacchanalian.
Then bonfire signalled to bonfire across rugged distances, while
around them went dancing—drinking, eating, singing, japing,
gaming, sporting, lovemaking—from sundown to sunrise.

For the past three years, Caitlín Margaret Mulryan had given
music at that season to those who met on Trollberg, when she
wasn't busy with associated pleasures. She was again on her

way, afoot along a dirt road, since the journey was part of the fun. As she went, she practiced the latest song she had made for the festival, skipping to its waltz time while her clear soprano lifted.

> *In silver-blue, the dew lies bright.*
> *The midsummer night*
> *Is abrim with light.*
> *Come take each other by the hand,*
> *For music has wakened*
> *All over the land.*

Fingers bounced across the control board of the sonador she held in the crook of her left arm. Programmed to imitate a flute, though louder, the mahogany-colored box piped beneath her chorus.

> *Go gladly up and gladly down.*
> *The dancing flies outward like laughter*
> *From blossomfield to mountain crown.*
> *Rejoice in the joy that comes after!*

Dust puffed from under her shoes. Around her, the heights dreamed beneath the amber glow of a Phoebus declining westward, close to its northernmost point in a sky where a few clouds drifted white. The road followed the Astrid River, which rippled and gurgled, green with glacial flour, on her right, downward bound to Aguabranca where it would enter the mighty Europa. Beyond the stream lay untouched native ground, steeply falling into a dale already full of dusk, clothed in bluish-green growth wherever boulders did not thrust forth—lodix like a kind of trilobate grass or clover, gemmed with petals of arrowhead and sunbloom, between coppices of tall redlance and supple daphne. Insectoids swarmed, gorgeously hued flamewings, leaping hopshrubs, multitudinous humbugs. A bright-plumed frailie cruised among them, a minstrel warbled from a bough, a couple of bucearos swooped overhead, and a draque hovered lean, far above—not birds, these, but hypersauroids, like every well-developed vertebrate which Demeter had brought forth. Pungencies that roused memories of resin and cinnamon drifted on a south breeze which was rapidly cooling off the afternoon.

On Caitlín's left ran a rail fence. Somewhat level, till it met a
scarp three or four kilometers off, the soil thus demarked had
been converted to pasture for Terrestrial livestock and, further
on, barley fields for humans. To the invaders from space,
Demetrian meat and vegetation were often edible, occasionally
delicious; she had been plucking moonberries, pearl apples, and
dulcifruct ever since she got off the bus at Freidorp. But they
lacked the whole complement of vitamins and amino acids,
while containing several that were useless. The imported plants
were intensely verdant, the cattle that grazed them fantastically
red.

Behind her, the road twisted out of sight around a hill.
Ahead, it climbed like a snake. Beyond the next ridge she could
see Trollberg, wooded and meadowed to its top. Ghost-faint at
its back floated the Phaeacian snowpeaks, Mount Lorn their
lord.

> *The music sparkles fleet and sweet.*
> *She sways there before him*
> *On eager feet,*
> *So lithe and blithe, and garlanded*
> *With roses and starshine*
> *Around her dear head.*
> *Go gladly up and gladly down.*
> *The dancing flies outward like laughter—*

Caitlín halted. From a wilderness thicket had appeared a
garm. Gray-furred, round-snouted, bob-tailed, tiger-sized, it
flowed along in a gracefulness that brought a gasp of admiration
from her. Neither need fear. Demetrian carnivores didn't like the
scent of Terrestrial animals and never attacked them. For their
part, human hunters tried to preserve the balance of a nature
which provided them skins for the market, and the Upland
Folkmeet had declared garms a protected species.

The beast stopped too, and stared back at her. It saw a young
woman. (Her exact age was thirty-four, though being Earthborn she thought of it as twenty-five.) Of medium height, full-
bosomed, withy-slender, long in the legs, she bore aloft a curly,
bronze-brown mane which fell to her shoulders. Her face was
wide in the brow, high in the cheekbones, tapering to the chin;
but her mouth was broad and full. Beneath arching dark brows
were emerald eyes and a short, tilted nose. Weather had turned a

fair skin tawny and added a dusting of freckles. Her tunic and trousers had seen rough use. A crios belt, gaudy rainbow sash, encircled them. A backpack carried changes of clothing, sleeping bag, a little dried food, the poems of Yeats, and other travel gear.

"Glory be to Creation," she breathed, "you're beautiful, me bucko!"

The garm vanished back onto its domain. Caitlín sighed and continued along her route.

> He spurns the turf that once he paced.
>   His arm throws a glowing
>   Around her waist,
> And whirled across the world, she sees
>   Him light as the wind and
>   More tall than the trees.
> Go gladly up—

She broke off. A man had stepped into sight, rounding a huge rock behind the fence ahead of her. Equally surprised, after an instant he raised a hand and cried a greeting. Caitlín jogged toward him. He was young, too, she saw, stocky, blond. Clad in coveralls, he bore a horn made from a tordener's tusk wherewith to call his cows home.

"Good day, my girl," he said in his lilting accent when she reached him. Hereabouts that was courteous. "How goes it for you?"

"Very well. I thank you, sir, and wish the top of the day to you," she replied in the soft English of her homeland, which long since had taken unto itself the speech of its conquerors and made that its own.

"Can I ask where you fare?"

"To Trollberg for Midsummer."

His eyes widened. "Ah. That I guessed. You are Cathleen, true? I'd call you 'Miz' like a gentleman ought, but ken not your last name. Nobody seems to use it."

She tolerated his pronunciation. Few Sassenachs or squareheads knew any better. "Aye, for I'm only here at the turning of the sun, when all the province is one great shebeen. It's a fine country you have, and dear people, but there's too much else of the planet to be traveling in. Who might you be, now?"

"Elias Daukantas. Of Vilnyus Farm." He jerked a thumb backward. Above a windbreak of poplars rose what must be chimney smoke. Shyly: "I've heard much about you, and wish Trollberg was in my neighborhood. Or, leastwise, that I'd had hap to see you come by afore. Uh...walk you always?"

She nodded. "What for would I be driving, and never knowing through what I passed?"

"But where stay you the nights over? I've heard nil talk of your visiting our scant inns, though more than two landlords tell how they'd pay you well for an evening's entertainment."

She smiled to show she took no offense as she replied, "Bards sing not for gain, Freeholder Daukantas, and a bard I reckon myself to be, if scarcely any Brian Merriman. We may receive gifts, but we sing for love or hospitality. I stay where they give me welcome, else spread my sack on the lodix."

In his awkwardness he exclaimed, "But what live you on?" and then burned in the cheeks at his gaucherie.

"Are you embarrassed, now?" she said cheerfully, with a pat for his hand where it clenched the rail. "Why, they all ask me that." She shifted on purpose into flat Eopolitan. "I'm medically trained, though no physician. Winters, I work in the city and its hinterland, out of St. Enoch Hospital. The doctor shortage pretty well lets me set whatever terms I want. Of course, were I a decent person, I'd work full time. But when my lifespan won't reach to exploring Demeter—" She tautened. "And when I have to see people hurting—" She broke off, shivered the tension out, and laughed. "Mercy alive, but I've talked about myself, right enough! Shall we be speaking of you?"

"There's naught to tell, my lady. This is my father's stead, and I his third son."

She cocked her head. "You're a bachelor, then?"

He nodded. "*Tja,* you know our custom in the uplands. When I am married, we can stay in the big house as partners, or we can get help to clear land and raise a dwelling for ourselves. I, I think I'll pick that. The new start."

"And you've no girl to tell you her wishes in the matter?"

"No. Someday—But this is a scoopful about me, uh, uh, Cathleen," he said in a rush. "Will you spend the night with us? I promise the whole gang will be delighted."

She glanced west. Though shadows were getting long and the mountains turning purple, Phoebus had an hour or better before the horizon captured it. "I thank you and I thank your kin," she answered. "But I should be at Trollberg inside three days, and my plan was for keeping on past sunset, since Persephone will be rising full, big and bright as Luna over Earth." Erion, half that apparent size, was already up, its curve ivory upon indigo.

"I'll drive you tomorrow, as far as you like," he offered. Her expression betokened reluctance. He grew clever. "Yes, you want to be near the land. Well, here's a family in it you've nay met. Our home, our manners, they should interest you, they're unusual, I swear; we're no Swedes or British or—Please! You'd make us hurrah. We'd never forget."

"We-ell. . . ." She eased, smiled, moved closer, fluttered her lashes the least bit. "It's too kind you are, Elias Daukantas, and sure I'd be of a good evening, stayed I there. So if you are certain that himself will not object—"

A whirr loudened. Turning, they saw a small car approach. Its air cushion threw dust right and left like the foam at the bow of a speeding boat. It reached them and braked in a roar. Tripods slammed down. The bubble top dilated. A big man tumbled out. "Caitlín!" he bawled.

She dropped her sonador. "Dan, oh, Dan!" She sped to him.

They grabbed each other. After a while his mouth left hers and sought her ear. "Listen, macushla," he whispered. "I'm on the run. Hunted. My name is Dan Smith. Okay?"

"Okay," she breathed back. He felt the elastic slimness of her, smelled sunlight odors of hair and warmer odors of flesh. "What is your wish, my heart?"

"Get the devil out of here, to some safe hiding place. Then we'll talk." Brodersen had all he could do to stay wary, rather than cast her down and him above.

The same effort shuddered in her, stronger than his. She pulled free, wrenched herself around, and said waveringly to the gaping farmer: "Elias, dear, it's a grand surprise I've had. Here is my own fiancé, Daniel Smith. We'd looked not to meet before the festival; he's been upon the road. But since the gods are so kind—Can you pardon me at all, at all? I'll be back, the Powers willing, and then I'll sing for you."

He and he shook hands and uttered clumsy politeness. Caitlín snatched up her instrument and tugged on Brodersen's sleeve. He and she scrambled into the car. It leaped onward. Daukantas stood for a long while staring the way it had gone, before he raised his horn and summoned the cattle.

●　　●　　●

A moon and a half shining. Phoebus not far out of sight, the sky was violet more than black and showed few stars. Of the constellations, only Medea and Ariadne appeared complete. Aphrodite and Zeus, sister planets, stood candle-bright. Three small clouds glowed. Silver washed across treetops and splashed on the ground beneath, which lay in a translucent dusk. Through a break in the forest shimmered Mount Lorn. Torchflies flitted about like tiny lanterns. Choristers trilled in their tens of thousands, calling from among stalks and leaves for their mates; a starlark chanted; near the cave, a spring flowed forth in crystalline clinking.

Caitlín had guided Brodersen here, down a game trail after he parked the car. He had brought outdoor kit of his own, including a fuel-cell heater which gave the shelter a welcome warmth. Sleeping bags on mollite pads made the floor comfortable. But they two did not sleep. After a while, amidst tender jesting, they cooked and ate dinner. When that was done, they did not sleep either.

Toward dawn, she raised herself on an elbow, the better to regard him. The cave faced west, and Persephone's beams were now streaming straight in, so eerily bright that against the whiteness of her he thought he could see how rosy were her nipples. He reached up to cup a heavy softness; it pressed itself around his hand as she leaned down to kiss him, a kiss which lingered.

"My love, my darling, my life," she nearly sang, "had I words to tell the wonder of you, humans would remember me when Sappho and Catullus lie forgotten. But not Brigit herself commands that magic."

"Oh, Christ, how I love you," he said, hoarse from the power of it. "How long for us? Three years?"

"A snippet more. I count months as well, from when first I knew what you were doing to my soul, till the chance came for me to be seizing you."

"And I thought it was only another romp. How fast you proved me wrong! You, not just a delicious body and hell on wheels in bed, but everything that's *you.*"

"Were it not trouble that brought you on my trail, I would be in isotopically pure bliss, Dan, my Dan. And as is, I praise your enemies for that much while scheming how to cut the guts out of them. I'd no idea I'd see you before fall."

"If you stayed in Eopolis—"

The lustrous locks moved, shadowing her features, as she

shook her head. "No." She became altogether serious. "Haven't we worn this question bare yet? It would not be fair to Lis. Or you. You love her too, as well you should. I do myself, and would never cause her more sorrow than I must, and hope the friendship she gives me is not from duty alone—for sure it is she knows what's between us, though she's never spoken aloud of it to me."

Caitlín sat straight, hugging her knees, looking over him to the argent wilderness. "Also, because I lack her gift for figures and organization, I couldn't share in the adventure of your enterprises," she said. "I'll not be a parasite. And a steady, safe job in a single place would soon have me daft. A bird of passage have I been since the hour I was born."

Mirth crowed from her: "Och, I'm moonstruck! How would a bird get born?"

He hoisted himself to sit cross-legged beside her. "The same way an idea gets hatched," he suggested.

"Aye," she responded quickly, "see, Einstein brooded long over his—they had to bring him his food and tobacco where he sat—until one fine day the egg went *crack* and a little principle of special relativity peeped forth, all wet and naked, and then the poor man must scurry to and fro fetching long wiggly equations to stuff down its beak, but at last it was grown to be a grand big cock of a general relativity theory and the quantum mechanics came to build a proper perch for it."

"Ye-es." He laid an arm around her. "As for launching a project, I see it lying on the greased ways, and you come and break a bottle of champagne across the director—he's the figurehead, of course—"

Their foolishness went on. Her merriment was an indivisible part of what he held dear about her.

"Hey," he remarked eventually, "you haven't told me how you found this cave. Not that I wasted time asking. But since we're taking a rest, how did you?"

She grinned. "How do you think?"

"Uh—"

"The handsomest hunter last year...Do you know, my treasure, I could almost wish—almost—you'd set out a single day later? I was developing designs on that lad when you came by. Ah, well, no doubt he can bide for a bit."

He tried not to stiffen. She felt it, embraced him, and said, "I'm sorry. Have I hurt you? I mourn."

"Well, naturally, I can't expect you to stay celibate months on end," he made himself reply. "You've got too much life in you."

"You are him I love, Daniel. True, there've been past loves, and they flamed too, but none like this. Your strength, your knowledge, the skill in your darling hands, och, you are wholly a *man,* and yet you are kind and generous and caring. You I will love till they close my eyes. The rest . . . some few turn out bad, most are good, none have been dull, but frolic is all they really ever are. Or, at most, a making of closer comradeship."

"Yeah, sure," he said. "I'm not exactly a monogamist either."

She tried to get past the barrier in him: "I've told you, my heart, I'm no she-cat. An impulse now and again, aye, but mainly I must think well of him first, and after that reckon I would not be the harm of anybody else, before I will give more than a kiss. It's no vast number of lovers I've had. A score, maybe, since I turned sixteen on Earth?"

"And me, I've not always been choosy," Brodersen admitted.

He caught her to him and held her there a minute. "Forgive me," he said thereafter, shakenly. "I didn't mean to react like that to a little teasing. But—"

"But?" she urged, seconds later.

"I think what did it was your kidding me that I might've left home today instead of yesterday. Suddenly I remembered that I did leave home, and why."

"And you stepped back into jealousy because the real thought pained you too much. O beloved." She knelt before him, stroked his face, regarded him through tears.

"Could be," he said. "I'm not in any habit of probing my psyche." He pulled his lips upward. "As long as the damn thing runs, not rattling a lot, I'll simply give it an occasional change of oil. Okay, let's drop this subject with a dull, sickening thud."

She remained grave. "No, Dan. You are in danger, and everything you care about is, Lis and the children foremost. How could I deserve being your mistress if you must shelter me from your griefs? Tell me."

"I did while we drove here."

"You laid out a skeleton for me. Breathe on it now, that it may rise alive."

"I, uh, I don't know what to say, Pegeen." That was a name for her which they had private between them.

"Let me lead you, then." She settled beside him fresh; they touched, arm to arm and flank to flank, while they gazed outward at torchflies, trees and fugitive stars. Save for the springwater, the night was growing still as it grew old. "Why are you in rebellion?" she asked. "Sure, and I hunger to explore yonder suns myself. But you have *Chinook,* that you got remodeled and crewed for the same purpose."

"Yeah, after the alien ship passed through the Phoebean gate. Have you forgotten, though? Only a watchship was around, to see what precise guidepath she followed—which, actually, only a couple of specialist officers did. Damn them, they didn't release the information except to their high command, and the Union government promptly declared it super top secret. Don Pedro himself—the Señor, the head of the Rueda clan and combine—he's never managed to pry the data loose. If the rest of the crew hadn't babbled, maybe you and I would still not know that an outworld vessel ever did come by.

"Oh, yes," Brodersen went on, out of the acridness in his gullet, "I could see the reasoning. Why, I could agree, sort of, would you believe? We'd no idea what kind of beings were at the far end of that gate. We couldn't let any random team charge through, to raise any possible kind of havoc. That had to include me and my company. When I commissioned *Chinook,* I did it on sheer hope, that the official expedition would come back bearing good news, so the government could freely let responsible private parties go. Or else, if the expedition did not come back, the Union Council would some year let me make a second attempt. At that, I kept her fully stocked, so I could take off too fast for a politician or bureaucrat to get my clearance cancelled.

"And God damn it, *Emissary* did return! And they're suppressing the fact! They want to kill our chance for going, ever—"

He slumped. "Hell and damnation," he said, "you've heard me drone on, over and over, about what's common knowledge. Last time we met, you heard me talk about my earliest suspicions. Today you heard me rant about what's happened since. Why do you put up with my repeating like this?"

She laid her head against his shoulder. "Because you have the need, my dear, my dear," she answered. After a moment: "But tell me next, what was the need in you to charge forward like O'Shaughnessy's bull? You steer yourself well. Why could you not be patient and cunning, till at last you held the truth gathered between your fingers for a noose to do hangman's justice?"

More than the words, her tone calmed him. "Well," he said,

"I'd already compromised myself to a degree. Then I trusted Aurelia Hancock too much, and look what happened."

"You could have outwaited that. How many years, or millions of years, blew by while the Others were growing into the galaxy and we abiding blind on our single globe? Would a few more matter?"

"They will to the *Emissary* crew," he grated. "You know that the mate, if he's alive, is family to me. And another is a, a good friend of mine. Not to mention the rest. They have their rights too."

"Aye. Yet against this you surely set the welfare of Lis and Barbara and Mike, to say naught of hundreds who get their livelihood from Chehalis." Caitlin gripped his nearest hand. "Dan, dearest, something beyond is driving you. What might that be? Yes, many a time you've told me how marvelous it will be for humans to have the freedom of the stars, more than fire or writing or the end of disease. And have I differed with you? But why this terrible haste, at whatever cost? We'll die, darling, old and wicked if I have my desire, before we've known all there is to know here on Demeter by herself."

He knotted his fists while his mind groped for clarity. "Pegeen, on Earth I saw too much of what big, passionate convictions do to people, especially when governments have them. Then I started reading history, and found what horrors they've brought in the past. That made me swear I'd stay objective. If nothing else, I figured I could keep from orating at everybody in sight.

"Except . . . I guess when we get right down to bedrock, I can no more set my strongest beliefs on a shelf to wait for a convenient moment than anyone else can."

Briefly, a part of him wondered if she noticed the mixed metaphor. Probably. But she kissed him and requested, "Tell me them. How I wish you had earlier."

He heard how strained his voice was but couldn't amend that: "This is what I'm afraid of. If the human race doesn't take off soon for the stars, it dies.

"The Union is in bad trouble. I thought, when I quit the Peace Command as a young fellow, that we'd pretty well worked ourselves out of a job. Earth looked orderly and sane. Well, I was wrong. Too many two-legged animals are jammed onto the planet. More and more lunacies keep boiling up. Religions like Transdeism. Heresies like New Islam. Political faiths like Asianism. Nations where mobs, or cabinet ministers, scream for secession if they can't get what they want when they want, no matter if it's feasible. And the worst is, a lot of those grudges against the Union are legitimate. More and more, the world government is trying to run everything—everything—from the center. As if an Oceanian mariculturist, a Himalayan knight, a businessman in Nairobi, and a spaceman working out of an Iliadic base didn't know best what their special problems are and what to do about them. Judas priest, are you aware that dead-serious talk is going on in the Council about resurrecting Keynesian fiscal policies?

"I suppose you've been spared the knowledge of what those were.

"The point is, whenever I visit Earth, I see it more sick. A lot of sociologists claim that the revelation about the Others, a completely superior race of beings, had considerable to do with bringing on the nuttiness that led to the Troubles. I dunno. Maybe. But if that's correct, then the Covenant didn't buy us anything except a breathing spell. We haven't yet come to terms with the fact of the Others. We never will, either, unless we can get out there. No, I'm sure that the way things are going, Earth will explode pretty soon. The best result of that would be a kind of Caesar; and the Caesars weren't really very durable. The worst that can happen—the worst doesn't bear thinking about, Caitlín.

"And don't suppose we can safely sit out the disaster here. My personal experience, these past several weeks, says different. Demeter may be two hundred and twenty light-years from Earth—the latest estimate I've seen from the astronomers—but that's just a skip through the gate for a ship armed with fusion missiles.

"Oh, yes," he ended, "maybe I am being too apocalyptic. I said I try to steer clear of fanaticism. Maybe they'll muddle through somehow. But I know for certain, if I know nothing else, that Earth won't get any new ideas except from the stars, and meanwhile the old ideas are killing people. Same as they killed my first wife."

He stopped, exhausted.

"Dan, you bleed," she half wept, and cradled him as best she was able.

At last: "You've never really told me what happened with Antonia. You loved her, and married her, and she died a bad death. Would you tell me the whole story this night?"

He stared before him. "Why saddle you with it?"

"So I can understand, my most dear. Understand you and what is in you; for sure it has become to me that this is your great wound and the reason why you could not stay quiet about *Emissary*."

"Perhaps," he mumbled. "You see, it was a political assassination, and the politics wouldn't have existed if we weren't stuck in these two miserable planetary systems."

"Speak, Dan. About your Antonia. I'd make a song in honor of her memory, if you would like that."

"I would. I would."

"Then first I must know."

He was merely average articulate, and full of grief; he groped and croaked:

"Okay, to start, how we met. After my discharge from the Peace Command, I wanted to go into spatial engineering, and had the luck to be accepted for the academy that the Andean Confederacy runs. When I'd graduated, I went to work for Aventureros Planetarios—*the* big corporation, you know, that the Rueda clan dominates. I did pretty well, got invited to some parties they threw, and there was Toni.

"She herself said she'd be damned if we sucked the timocracy's tit. She was into astrography, and good at it, too. We wangled locations for us both at Nueva Cíbola. That's an Iliadic satellite, you may recall, but an office of Aventureros is there, and so is Arp Observatory.

"Six Earth years . . . I traveled a lot, necessarily, as far afield as Jupiter; but you know, Pegeen, though women were usually along on our jobs, through that whole time I really was a monogamist. Not that Toni'd have disowned me; but she was, and that settled the matter."

He fell mute, while Caitlín held him.

"At last we decided to start a family," he resumed. "She loved children. And animals and . . . everything alive. She wanted to have the baby at home, in the Rueda mansion, for the sake of her grandparents. They were too frail to leave Earth, but it'd mean a cosmos to them to see the next generation arrive.

"Why not? I had an assignment ahead of me on Luna, which'd keep me away for several weeks. She might as well return to the clan at once and enjoy them. They're grand folk. I expected I'd finish before birthtime, take leave of absence, and join her.

"Well—Quite soon after she landed, the *residencia* got

bombed. By terrorists. They issued an anonymous announcement that they were protesting the Ruedas' hogging the benefits of space development from the masses. It was an incident in a wave of revolutionary violence going through South America.

"That's faded out. Temporarily. It's rising again. The Ruedas are still targets. Yes, of course they're rich, because their ancestors had the wit to invite private space enterprise to Perú. But hogging the wealth? Why, suppose that money was divided equally among the *oprimidos*. What sum would each person get? And where'd the capital come from for the next investment? Pegeen, Pegeen, when will these world savior types learn some elementary economics?

"Anyway . . . this bomb didn't do much. Destroyed a wing of the house, and three servants who'd been around for most of their lives—and, aye, aye, Toni and her baby.

"She didn't die immediately. They rushed her to a hospital. She asked if she could see the Moon in the sky—the last thing she asked—but the phase wasn't right. And I was off on Farside in a lunatrac, and a solar flare lousing up communications—

"Well. That's the story. I went on the bum for a year, but the Ruedas bore with me, and helped me straighten out, and staked me when I decided to go to Demeter and start a business like theirs. You see why I worry about Carlos aboard *Emissary*?"

Brodersen and Caitlín sat silent together. The night waned. Finally he said, "Toni was a lot like you."

Being a bard, she knew when not to speak. She only gave him whatever was hers to give. At first he was passive, then he tried to respond and she let him understand that that was not needful, then slowly he realized with his whole being that the past was gone but she was here.

Later they did sleep a while.

She woke before he did. Rousing, he saw her seated in the cave mouth, limned against the mysterious blueness that on Earthlike planets comes just before sunrise: She had programmed her sonador for unaccompanied guitar, making the instrument ring. Most quietly, she gave forth the last of the many stanzas in her festival song:

> *The peaks grow gold, the east grows white,*
> *A breeze pipes the end*
> *Of the summer night,*
> *And wide across a widespread land*

The dancers turn homeward with
　Hand laid in hand.
Go gladly up and gladly down.
　The dancing flies outward like laughter
From blossomfields to mountain crown.
　Rejoice in the joy that comes after!

VI

I WAS A CATERPILLAR that crawled, a pupa that slumbered, a moth that flew in search of the Moon. The changes were so deep that my body could not remember what it had formerly been; I was as if reborn to wings. Nor had I the means to wonder at this. I simply was. Yet how bright was my being!

Even my infant self, a hairy length of hunger, lived among riches: juice and crisp sweetness in a leaf, sunlight warm or dew cool or breezes astir over his pelt, endless odors with each its subtle message. Then at last dwindling days spoke to his inwardness. He found a sheltered branch and spun silk out of his guts to make himself a place alone, and curled within its darkness, he died the little death. For a season his flesh labored at its own transformation, until that which opened the cocoon and crept forth belonged to an altogether new world. Soon my outer skin sloughed off me, my freed wings grew dry and strong, and I launched myself upon heaven.

Mine was the night. In my eyes it glowed and sparkled, full of vague shapes that I knew best by their fragrances. My food was the nectar of flowers, taken as I hovered on fluttery wingbeats, though sometimes the fermented sap of a tree set me and a thousand like me dizzily spiraling about. Wilder was it to strive as high as might be after the full Moon, more lost in its radiance than in a rainstorm. And when the smell of a female ready to mate floated around me, I became flying Desire.

Another blind urge set our flock on a journey across distance. Night by night we passed over hills, valleys, waters, woods, fields, the lights of men like bewildering stars beneath us; day by day we rested on some tree, decking it with our numbers. While I was thus breasting strange winds, One gathered me up, taking me back into Oneness, and presently We knew what my whole life had been since I lay in the egg. Its marvels were many. I was Insect.

VII

COLD AND EMPTY, *Emissary* orbited Sol a hundred kilometers behind the San Geronimo Wheel. Dwarfed by remoteness, the sun gave her only a wan light, and she seemed lost among the stars. The Wheel was more impressive, two kilometers across, majestically rotating to provide Terrestrial weight for the workshops and living quarters around its rim. The hub, at the middle of the spokes which were passageways, could readily have accommodated the ship in its dock. Its radiation sheilding aluminum-plated, the whole structure shone as if burnished.

Yet it was a failure. Men had constructed it a century ago, to serve as a base for operations among the asteroids. Thinly scattered though those remnants of a stillborn world are, they could profitably be worked by robots, as could the Jovian moons at times around inferior conjunction. Soon improved spacecraft made that whole idea obsolete. It grew cheaper, as well as more productive, for men to go in person, boosting continuously at a gee or better, directly between these regions and the industrial satellites of Earth. The Wheel became a derelict. There was talk of scrapping it for the metal, but incentive was insufficient. Already then, the price of every metal was tumbling. Eventually title went to the Union government, which had it refurbished and declared it a historical monument. It got few visitors.

When Ira Quick, Council Minister of Research and Development, authorized its occupancy, nobody paid much attention. He declared that it was well suited for studies of interplanetary gas. This would be the merest detail work, with nothing fundamental to be learned, but presumably worthwhile; besides, a private institution was underwriting the project. The measurements being delicate, the Wheel and its vicinity must be

56

barred to outsiders for some weeks or months. This would scarcely inconvenience anyone, least of all the custodial staff, who would enjoy a salaried leave of absence. The item rated a line or two in various astronautical journals, and about thirty seconds on perhaps a dozen newscasts.

A port in Joelle Ky's apartment showed her the heavens, the view rendered vertical by a set of prisms. They did not stream by too fast to watch, for a turn took almost three hours, and the sight was glorious. But she soon wearied of it and would have spent most of her time in the holothetic state, had the equipment been on hand. Thus far her prisonkeepers had declined to remove it from the ship or take her there.

They were apologetic, explaining that they dared not act without orders. The twenty men who guarded *Emissary*'s crew and passenger were decent enough in their fashion, North American secret service agents on special detail. They sincerely believed that what they did was right and necessary. But then, they were hand-picked, raised in the cult of discipline and obedience which had prevailed in the former military régime. Their chief, who presided over interrogation and exhortation of the captives, was less *simpático*. He was no brute, though, and when he told Joelle that Quick himself was coming to see them, he promised to request permission to fetch the apparatus over for her.

"Of course, Dr. Ky," he added, "if you'd cooperate better, if you'd appreciate what your duty is, why, you should go free altogether." She felt too weary to respond.

She had withdrawn into books, recorded visual art, and music. The director had not refused to have the vessel's enormous bank of references, recreational material, and data transferred—especially since the major part of his task was to find out what the explorers had done and learned in their eight years agone. Except for meals, Joelle virtually abandoned social life.

Her former companions remained more outgoing. While Captain Langendijk was icily correct toward the agents, Rueda Suárez calculatedly condescending, and Benedetti sometimes abusive, the rest fraternized in varying degrees. Frieda von Moltke even found a long-desired sexual newness among them. The other women disdained that, keeping their favors for their friends, but were not above a game of cards or handball.

Lonelier still, not in quite the same way that a human among nonhumans would have been, Fidelio first sought Joelle's kind of solace, then increasingly sought her. He asked for elucidations of things that bewildered him. He had studied Spanish before embarking, but not the thousand cultures of a foreign species. She could best help, because she had been most engaged in learning his two languages, originally using holothetics to assist Alexander Vlantis, then taking over leadership of the research after a tidal bore drowned the linguist.

She was screening Swinburne on a particular daywatch when the Betan called. Much fiction and poetry left her unmoved, or else puzzled; she had too limited an experience of ordinary emotional relationships, too wide an experience of that which underlay the universe. However, the romantic sensualists appealed to her viscera, as the precisionists did to her cerebrum. She believed she understood—

> —*Time and the Gods are at strife: ye dwell in the midst thereof,*
> *Draining a little life from the barren breasts of love.*
> *I say to you, cease, take rest; yea, I say to you all, be at peace,*
> *Till the bitter milk of her breast and the barren bosom shall cease.*

Her thoughts drifted from the text, as they had been doing since she began to read. The impulse behind both was the same; she had shown these words to Dan Brodersen, the last time they were together. In this her present isolation, his image often arose, ever more vividly until she could smell his pipe and almost count the crow's-feet around his eyes. She wondered if that was because he was alive (oh, he must be alive!) while Christine was dead, or because his maleness was somehow safer than the memory of her, or—*Forgive me, Chris,* passed through her as she surrendered to what had been.

"Well," he said, "It's pretty. No, more than that. He was tackling something real." He paused. "Excuse me, though, isn't it kind of longwinded? Kipling would've gotten the same across in one page at the most."

"Perhaps that is why I have never managed to appreciate Kipling," she answered.

He cocked a brow at her. "Not even the poems about machinery? And yet you, the holothete, whose soul is supposed to be a computer program, you enjoy Swinburne?" With a shrug: "Well, people are paradox generators."

Suddenly, irrationally hurt, she blurted, "I don't quite understand you, for sure. But I assumed you normal types sometimes resonate with each other. Do you mean you can't either?"

For an instant she imagined she did comprehend an ancient myth. It felt indeed as if the daimon of this place possessed her. They were spending the few days they could arrange to be together on an island in the Tuamotu Archipelago which he knew of old (yes, with another woman, he admitted unabashed). From the verandah where they stood, her gaze went past a red-and-green riot of hibiscus, down a path to the beach, which curved around a lagoon. Ranked palms nodded and whispered in answer to a blowing mildness. The water was lapis lazuli strewn with stars, save out on the reef where it creamed and thundered. The only clouds stood opposite the sun, a wall with a rainbow for portal. She had no names for the sweetnesses and pungencies the air cast at her. This morning she and Brodersen had wandered hand in hand along the shore, stripped (save for sneakers against the beautiful sharp coral) to go swimming, afterward lounged about—the light soaked through her skin to the marrow—until he warned against burns and they dressed. On the way back they encountered a brown man who smiled, chatted in broken Spanish, invited them to his nearby home for a bite to eat, and later fetched out a guitar and swapped a few songs with Brodersen. The rain which came along about then was like sky and Earth making love.

Now he who had come to her from Demeter implied that he too dwelt forever within walls. The daimon knew horror. The pain mounted.

"Oh, well, I dunno, never worried about it to speak of—" He broke off. "Hoy, what's the matter? All at once, you look sandbagged."

She shook her head, eyes squeezed shut. "It's nothing," her tongue formed.

He trod forward, took her by both arms that trembled just a little, and growled, "The hell it's nothing. Anything that can shake *you*, Joelle—"

"I don't know, I don't know," she answered before she could stop herself. Control returned. "I . . . have my . . . irrational moments too." Observing his shock: "Didn't you realize that?"

He gulped, which astonished her. Surely he'd experienced enough women and their vagaries. After a while he said slowly, "Well, yes, you must enjoy my company—aside from bed, I mean—which doesn't make a lot of sense."

She saw that, beneath the easy manner he'd acquired with her over the years, he was still wonder-smitten by her intellect.

"But if you also have a real weakness—" He lost his words as she cast herself against him.

"Hold me close, Dan," she begged and commanded, for she did not want to be reminded of the contemptible psyche beneath her aware mind. "Let's go inside." *Let's appease the animal part.*

—But this time she couldn't make it work. He was as kind and strong as always, and there was some relief in it, and afterward more in reassuring him that she was merely out of sorts and everything would soon be fine again: which was doubtless true.

Still—*None of us escape the fact that it's often difficult, too often impossible for us,* thought Joelle in the Wheel. *Worse for the Betans, of course. What can it be like, having to pin your hopes for love on an alien and barely half-civilized race? Is that part of the reason, quite aside from our shared holothesis, why I feel so close to Fidelio?*

The door chimed. "Come in," she said, and was more than pleased when it proved to be him. Not only had she been thinking of him. Against the bleakly functional room, which pastel paint did nothing to make cheerful, he stood like a solid avowal that there was more to reality.

"Buenos días," he greeted in the harsh, guttural voice of his breed upon land. Whistling overtones made the words hard to follow.

"Bienvenido," she replied, and suggested he employ his native speech, the one intended for air. She would stay with Spanish. Without computerized voder equipment, she could not render Betan vocables, and she didn't feel like taking him down to the lab and talking under the eyes of the guard posted in the hall, who would come along. If the conversation required phrases of his, she could write them. To be sure, lacking her holothetic

assembly, she had but limited knowledge. The languages held more nuances strange to her than an unaided brain could master. (The underwater "tongue" was worse, from the standpoint of pronunciation and comprehension both.) However, if things didn't get complicated today, she could manage.

"Are you engaged, female of intellect?" he asked politely. "I would not interrupt a dream-logic." That was her rendition of a certain concept, not very satisfactory but doubtless better than "meditation" or "philosophical thought" or "purposeful day-dreaming."

"No, I'm idle and wish I weren't," she assured him. "How are you? I haven't seen you since—I don't know. Time is meaningless in this damned place."

"I was in the pool," he said. Early on, *Emissary*'s biologists had warned that Fidelio would sicken and die if he couldn't spend several hours per week in water like that of his native sea. The composition was not identical with that of Earth's oceans, but not exotic either; any chemical laboratory could supply the ingredients. They had been fetched from the ship to the Wheel and a bath constructed. The trade in salt between coastal and inland communities had conditioned a great deal of Betan history.

"Good for you," Joelle said, and thought how inadequate that was. What a tragedy it would be to lose him: for both species, and perhaps many more. Besides, he was brilliant and gentle, worth a million Ira Quicks.

We will *lose him, if his food runs out,* she remembered. He couldn't get nourishment from Earthborn tissues; most were poisonous to him. The returning expedition had carried a year's rations for Fidelio, chiefly in freeze-dried form. They took for granted that well before then, the Union would have opened regular traffic with Beta.

She was not given to rage, but abruptly she tasted it. Seeking calm, she regarded him as he sat on feet and tail before her lounger. She always found something, a matter of shape or motion or less easily identifiable subtlety, which she had not noticed before.

Well, we two are the products of four billion years of separate evolution, from the primordial stuffs that went into our two very unlike planets. Names are necessary, but they mislead, they give us the impression that we have an insight when we actually don't.

Their arbitrariness made them twice deceiving. The explorers dubbed the sun to which the star gate transported them "Centrum" for lack of a more imaginative proposal, and its attendants "Alpha," "Beta," "Gamma"...in outward order. "Fidelio" was bestowed by Torsten Sverdrup, who adored Beethoven, and stuck. At home the being was called, approximately, "K'thrr'u" on land, "Gaoung Ro Mm" in the water; but no Terrestrial alphabet rendered either appellation right.

He was as typical of his species as she was of hers, which ranged from Chinese to Papuan, Celt to Pygmy, Negro to Eskimo, and onward. Specifically, he came from the eastern seaboard of the principal continent in the northern hemisphere, at a middle latitude, and belonged to that society which had taken the lead in an industrial revolution a millennium ago. Civilizations didn't seem to rise and fall on Beta as they had on Earth. Nevertheless, today his whole world, and its colonies around other stars, faced a peculiar crisis—

Fidelio was a six-limbed biped. His body was the size of a large man's, exclusive of a powerful tail, ending in horizontal flukes, which added half again the length. Because of his forward-leaning posture, he stood about a hundred and fifty centimeters tall, and blubber hid the formidable muscles. His legs, which reminded her of Tyrannosaurus Rex, ended in broad, webbed feet, the upper arms in long claws with webs between, the smaller lower arms in hands with three fingers and a thumb, not especially human-looking. The skeletal anatomy made limbs and digits, plus the torso, tail, and slender neck, so flexible as to seem almost boneless. His head was narrow, bulging backward to hold the brain. A short, sharp muzzle surrounded by stiff whiskers bore a single closable nostril and a mouth whose omnivore's variety of teeth included a pair of alarming fangs. The two ears were small. The two eyes were large and of a uniform blue; nictitating membranes could change their optical properties for underwater seeing. Sleek dark-brown fur covered his entire skin, lighter on the belly. A tangy, iodine-like odor came from him. For clothing he wore a kind of bandolier with pockets. His reproductive organs being retractible, and not much like a man's anyway, he wasn't obviously male...except at home, where just for a starter he had two-thirds the bulk of the average female....

His distance vision in air was not equal to the human, though he saw far better when submerged or in the dark, and at least as well at close range. His hearing was superior, and he possessed chemosensitivities which Joelle had decided not to label "taste" or "smell." For his part, he was constantly amazed at the discriminations she could make with her fingertips.

Here he is, she thought, *the good-faith goodwill ambassador of his people, slammed into jail; and I don't even know how he feels about it. He's tried to tell me, but he can't make himself clear unless I go holothetic, and maybe then he can't quite.*

"What can I do for you, Fidelio?" she asked softly.

"I seek to bring into my dream-currents [to know with his entire being?] how your kind first came to the transport engines and to information about the Others."

"Why, you've heard," she said, surprised. "We simply found the machine in the Solar System, the same as your interplanetary explorers earlier found the one that orbits Centrum."

Earlier? she wondered. *What does that mean? Simultaneity is not a concept that applies across interstellar distances. Moreover, it turns out that the "T" in "T machine" stands not only for "Tipler" and "Transport," but also for "Time." The Betans themselves aren't sure whether, in a passage through a different system, they visit their future or their past. For that matter, we don't know what our temporal relationship is to our colony on Demeter. All that astronomers can determine is that the three gates open on the same general era of this galaxy.*

And, for whatever it's worth, which may be nothing, we have the fact that the Betans have behind them centuries more of being scientific-civilized than we do on Earth—if we are civilized yet.

"That is a truth cast onto a reef and bleached dry," Fidelio said. "I am in search of the living coral. [Of course, Beta had no coral, but it did have a genus which behaved similarly.] You have told me, Joelle [indescribable pronunciation], you did not predict this detention. I begin to doubt that what has happened is the result of deviation [Villainy? Misguidedness? Disagreement? The word contained the possibility that Quick and his minions were right.] The impact of that original disclosure was tremendous upon Beta. It must have been comparable on Earth. Still, the wave it raised bore a shape peculiar to your kind, in whatever condition contemporary humanity was. And the ripples cannot have died out.... I have been reading histories, Joelle, but they are gorged with references to events and personalities that mean nothing to me."

"I see," she answered slowly. (*"Comprendo"* = "I grasp." English and Spanish idioms are not equivalent. As for his, at sea he would have said, "My teeth close on it," ashore he would have said, "I sense it in my vibrissae.")

"Well," she went on, "I hardly think I can give you a complete answer, when I myself am rather lost. But let's make an attempt." She stroked her chin, pondering. "Yes, I remember a documentary on the whole subject, intended for schools, which contains much original material. I'll try to retrieve it."

Like every apartment in the Wheel, hers had a computer terminal, with display and printout. The piece she had in mind was such a classic, and went back such a number of years—back to when folk expected a permanent population here, including children—that she supposed it was in the data bank. She activated the keyboard and tapped out her request.

It was.

VIII

(VIEW OF THE MACHINE seen from afar, a thousand-kilometer length like a needle afloat in space, dwarfed by the Milky Way.)

NARRATOR

—unmanned probes reported indications of something curious, orbiting the sun on the same track as Earth but a hundred and eighty degrees off, so that it was always on the opposite side. A flyby confirmed that it was strange indeed. No asteroid could have a perfectly cylindrical shape. Most certainly, none could be so massive, nor spin so fast....

(An astrophysicist, famous at the time, speaks from his desk, occasionally screening an animated diagram for illustration.)

IONESCU

—should not be possible. That thing is as dense as a collapser, barely short of the black hole condition. Its atoms must have been compressed down to where they are no longer true atoms but nearly continuous nuclear matter, the stuff we call neutronium. Only the gravitational field of a larger star than Sol, falling in on itself after its fires are extinct, can bring them to that condition. The cylinder cannot. Gigantic though it is, its mass is far too small—in fact, not enough to perturb the planets identifiably. Besides, a natural body would form a spheroid.

Yet there the thing is. Forces of a kind we know nothing about shaped it, gave it its unbelievable rotational energy, and hold it together. I have no doubt whatsoever that here is the product of a technology farther advanced from ours than ours is from the Stone Age....

(Scenes of excitement, speeches, crowds, demonstrations,

65

sermons, prayer meetings everywhere on Earth and in the satellites. Excerpt from a press conference held by Manuel Fernández-Dávila, Donald Napier, and Saburo Tonari, the three men who are to go, the most nearly international team that chaos throughout much of the world has left it possible to assemble. Liftoff of the shuttle, blast vivid against an austere cordillera. Rendezvous with *Discoverer,* the ship, and transfer to her.

(Scenes during the flight, which at that time took weeks, mostly in free fall. Shots through the ports: the cylinder waxing in view until its enormousness begins to be apparent and the glowing attendants are visible. Spacesuited men go outside, at the ends of tethers, to take pictures and instrumental readings. They speak at Earth via a relay which has been orbited especially for them. The words are usually dry, but shaken by awe.)

FERNÁNDEZ-DÁVILA

—they are not satellites. They don't go around the cylinder, they stay in place relative to the sun and each other. God knows how that is done, but we guess they're held by some of the power that keeps the main body in one piece. We've counted ten. They appear featureless except for the different wavelengths they emit. They're spaced around the spin axis of the cylinder— which is exactly normal to the ecliptic—at various distances and orientations, the farthest about a million kilometers out, the closest about a thousand. When we watch the whole system through our main telescope, it's a pretty sight. Well, anything astronomical is....

(At a later date, when the goal is looming.)

TONARI

—glowing attendants are definitely spheres, diameter estimated at ten kilometers. They don't seem to be material. More like balls of energy, nexuses in a force-field. We have confirmed that they are not absolutely stationary. The configuration changes, extremely slowly but continuously, according to a plan we cannot decipher....

(Outside view taken by Tonari in EVA: a glimpse of the ship, a straight look at the cylinder, whose length now fills the screen, and a pair of its moons which are not moons, and behind and around everything, the stars.)

NAPIER
(meanwhile, aboard)

—satisfactory approach curve. We'll swing around it at a distance of ninety-five hundred kilometers, recede to one hundred thousand, establish ourselves in a circular orbit, and—*Name of God! What's that?*

VOICE

(melodious, androgynous, speaking Spanish like an educated denizen of Lima)

Your attention, please. Your attention, please. This is a message to you from the builders of the device you are seeking. You are welcome here. But you must change your course. Your present path is dangerous to you. Prepare for acceleration and stand by for instructions. Please record. You will need the information you are about to receive. Please record. In five minutes, these words will repeat for that purpose, followed by the necessary data. They are words of welcome, of joy that you have finally reached this far. Thank you.

(Interior scene. Fernández-Dávila has started the movie cameras for the sake of the history books.)

NAPIER

How in Christ's name—?

FERNÁNDEZ-DÁVILA

Probably sonic vibrations set up in the hull. No trick at all for *them*—Saburo! Saburo, get your ass back in the airlock!

(No repeat of the greeting; this documentary has used the replay that was promised, since the original was captured only at the end of a radio beam two hundred and ten million kilometers long, after which it was passed an equal distance to Earth, losing quality along the whole way.)

VOICE

—understand that the truth will not be easy to make clear.
Now, while you calm yourselves, you should retreat to
approximately five hundred thousand kilometers and take
orbit. Otherwise you will not likely see your homes again. Here
are the timing and the vectors for you—

(Miscellaneous shots, exterior and interior, taken during the
days that follow: the titanic artifact, star, Milky Way,
Magellanic Clouds, the sister galaxy in Andromeda, the men,
who somehow continue their routines, actually joking or
playing games, in between grave discussions of what they have
learned each time a message comes.)

VOICE
(excerpts)

You hear a kind of computer-effector system, a robot, if you
will. No living being could or should abide out here, awaiting
your arrival....
The universe is a cornucopia of life....
The builders have existed through age after age. They wish
the cosmos well, but for that very reason do not seek to be
overlords, let alone gods. Best that each race make its own
destiny, tragic though that may prove. Only thus can it grow, in
strength, mind, and spirit. Too, the builders have lives of their
own to live, dreams of their own to pursue. Thus you will hear
little more than this about them, ever. To you, to countless
beings more among the suns, they must remain the unknown
Others....
Yet they are interested in you. They love you. Plain to see,
they have observed you at length and in depth. Having made
your way here, you are free to use their engine for interstellar
travel. You will be guided to a system wherein is a planet akin to
your mother world, save that it has borne no sentience to claim
it—yours for the taking, if you choose....

NARRATOR

When *Discoverer*'s transmissions reached Earth, few indeed
were the persons who kept a measure of calm.

(The office of the astrophysicist)

IONESCU

—speculations that began to be heard when the flyby observations came in, seem now to be confirmed. As far as we can tell, that thing is a Tipler machine.

I call it that in honor of the theoretician who, extending the work of Kerr and others, published in 1974 a paper on this exact subject, which afterward he pursued farther with imagination as well as mathematical rigor. True, he was forced to make certain simplifying assumptions. However, he did use strict, well-established principles of physics to show that transport across space-time was conceptually sound though apparently requiring conditions impossible to achieve in the real universe. (Smiling) I'm afraid the proof is rather esoteric. What it amounts to, in everyday terms, is this. A cylinder of ultra-dense matter, spinning at a speed in excess of one-half light's, will generate a field. Not a force-field, in the proper sense. Call it, instead, a region in which some quantities vary according to your position. A body passing through that field can be transported directly from event to event. In more popular language, depending on what path it takes, it can go from any point in space-time to any other in range of the machine.

As I said, this effect seemed to demand impossible conditions. For instance, it called for matter densities many orders of magnitude greater than that of nucleons themselves, such as might conceivably exist within a black hole but nowhere else. I therefore suspect that the density we have measured for yonder cylinder, high though it be, is only a mean; that it increases within, to the point where black hole-type phenomena occur; that at the very center is an actual singularity. How the Others have achieved this, we can only guess—we can speculate that the weak energy condition may, after all, in the right circumstances be violated—and most likely our guesses are dead wrong. With a little more confidence, we think that the finite length of this real-world object limits the range of its effect: though obviously that range is interstellar and perhaps it is interepochal.

We are also beginning to get an inkling of how the cylinder stays in position with respect to Earth. That position is not stable. Planetary perturbations should cause a body there to drift away from it in a fairly short time. Yet presumably the device has been where it is for centuries at least. What gives it its station-keeping capability? Analyzing available data, we think

probably there is a continuous interaction with the interplanetary and the galactic magnetic fields, though this too must take
place throughout awesome distances.

I hope to live long enough to see us gain a little more
knowledge about the creation the Others have added to
Creation. We may even, at last, find a way to make our findings
comprehensible to the layman—or to ourselves.

(The professorial contenance glows) But no matter now.
What matters above everything else today is that we have been
given the chance for a fresh beginning!

NARRATOR

Before *Discoverer* returned home, the Voice offered to
conduct her through the star gate and back. As Fernández-
Dávila said afterward, "How could we not have accepted?"

(Views of a vessel which later traced the route, photographed
from a companion ship. They are interspersed with simulations
and animations, as well as pictures taken during the maiden
venture. This and the narration make clear what happens. The
spacecraft moves from sphere to sphere in a precise order.)

VOICE

The globes are simply markers, navigational aids. With their
help, you can follow the exact path through the transport field
which will bring you to the place prepared for you.

Have care! Any different path will take you to quite a
different destination. It may well be that no machine exists
there. You would perish somewhere out in those light-years.
When the builders wish to establish a new foothold, they must
send all needful materials and equipment through an existing
engine and make a new one at the new site, before they can
return.

Even if you emerged at a machine, you would never find your
way back. Consider. Ten globes, taken in their various orders,
define 3,628,800 paths. In truth the combinations are many
more, since not every path requires passing by every beacon; if
you ignore the markers altogether, the number becomes
virtually infinite. You would blunder blind until you died, or
more probably until you emerged someplace where no machine
was.

You must have noted that the configuration of the spheres is not constant, but gradually changes. Doubtless you have guessed that that is to compensate for the changing positions of the stars. Do not worry about it. Simply follow the same order of close passage by each, as you have been instructed. Likewise, the correct order at the far end of this trip of yours will always bring you back from there to here. You will note that it is entirely unlike the course which took you from here to there.

Beware, repeat, beware of deviating from either of those patterns. Send unmanned probes on random paths if you like, but never a live crew, for it could never return.

(The study of a famous philosopher)

SAMUELSON

—I don't believe any human is equipped to understand the Others. They must have what is infinitely more important than a science and technology superior to ours by perhaps millions of years. I feel convinced that they have superior minds . . . and, yes, I suppose, superior, nobler souls. I cannot believe they'd exist for such reaches of time, with such powers as are theirs, and not *evolve*.

Nevertheless, in the case of the T machines, I'll risk a guess about their motives. Why hasn't their Voice described any paths to us except the ones between Sol and this single distant star? Why hasn't it even hinted at what the mathematical relation is between a given path and two given points in space-time, so we can work out how to get from A where we're at to a B which we'd like to visit? Why, indeed, has the Voice been silent since that first advent of humans?

I think this is part and parcel of their doctrine of non-interference.

Think. They put the Solar System machine opposite Earth, and we didn't dream it existed till we had developed a substantial capability in space. But the machine in the other system orbits much more handily, in a stable path, sixty degrees ahead of the planet we'll probably be colonizing, clearly visible to any astronomers there. However, apparently no astronomers, no truly thinking creatures, are native to it: nobody that might be lured by the sight into feverish, unbalanced efforts or a deadly struggle for control.

The Voice said the Others love us. They must; they have given

us a whole new world. But they must love all sentient races. I
suspect a breed like ours, with its history of war, oppression,
rapine, and exploitation, would bring disaster if it burst
overnight into the galaxy. I suspect also that we are not
unusually bad or short-sighted, that many a species would
become an equal menace if it got the chance.

At the same time, the Others seemingly refuse to take us, or
anybody, under tutelage. I am sure that, from their viewpoint,
they have far better things to do. And from the viewpoint of our
well-being, they may feel it would be wrong to domesticate us.

So they leave us our free will, they permit us to use their star
gates, but they make no further gifts. We must endure the
frustration of seeing Alpha Centauri and Sirius shining still
unattainable in our skies, until we have groped our own way out
into the cosmos. I hope that they hope the long, cooperative
effort that this requires will mature us a little....

(View of a spacecraft completing her path. Suddenly she
vanishes. View of the T machine in the Phoebean System.
Suddenly the spacecraft appears, about half a million kilometers
from the cylinder.

(Shots taken on the original faring. Fernández-Dávila,
Tonari, and Napier stare from their cramped cabin. They
babble. Two of them offer prayers. Presently they master
themselves and look outward with trained eyes. A groundling
cannot see constellations in space; the visible stars are too many.
An astronaut can. Here, none are familiar. After a while, the
men think they can puzzle out a few, changed though the shapes
are; and extragalactic objects do not appear different. They
reckon roughly that they have gone more than one hundred and
less than five hundred light-years northwest of Sol.)

VOICE

—The planet that will interest you most is in the sky hard by
the Crab Nebula....

(The view settles on a point of sapphire, infinitely lovely.)

NARRATOR

The world we have since named Demeter—

(Stopped-down view of Phoebus. View of *Discoverer*'s cabin and three men stunned with glory.)

VOICE

Your ship has not the reserves to go there. You had best return to the Solar System at once. Surely more vessels, outfitted to explore, will come after. You yourselves may be aboard....

(Scenes of the path back through the gate being traced out, not the least like the earlier pattern. Scenes of emergence at the other end, of jubilation, of solemnity, of the long haul home. Scenes of tumult, parades, ceremonies, parties, extravagant predictions, and in between an occasional word of foreboding.)

NARRATOR

—we are at last ready to send our first colonists. Beforehand, we had to spend years of research, learning the most elementary things about Demeter. The Others promised it would be worth our trouble, but not that it would be Eden....

(The home of a famous spaceman)

FERNÁNDEZ-DÁVILA

—The price is high per person we send, and we cannot tell what they might send back that would repay it. On this account, we hear protests, we hear demands that the whole program be dropped. Well, I maintain that the stimulus to space technology it has given, the order-of-magnitude improvement in ships and instruments, has already recouped the entire cost plus a high profit. Then there's the scientific revolution, especially in biology, that we've gotten out of Demeter. An entire independent set of life forms! We need decades, maybe centuries, to examine them further, with their implications for medicine, genetics, agriculture, mariculture, and who can foresee what else? That requires a permanent settlement.

Beyond this, in the crassest economic terms, I claim that within a generation, humans on Demeter will be returning

Earth's investment to Earth a thousand times over. Remember what America meant to Europe. Remember what Luna and the satellites mean to us today.

Far beyond *this,* think of the imponderables and unpredictables: challenge, opportunity, enlightenment, freedom....

The beginning of our growth toward the Others....

Joelle found that a sequel had been added. She thought it was equally honest, but the honesty was that of a later generation.

It went into Demetrian history. No more than a few thousand individuals per year could be boosted to the gate and landed on the planet. Conveyance capacity did expand as the colony started to yield dividends—but slowly, because of conflicting claims on that wealth. Emigrants went under national auspices, according to an elaborate quota setup. However, through bribery or lawful agreement, many traveled under flags different from their own.

The reasons for going were as various as the people who went. Ambition, adventure, utopian visions were among them. But certain governments subsidized the departure of dissident citizens, and pressured them to accept; certain ones aimed to found outposts of power for themselves; certain more had crazier motives, as did assorted unofficial organizations and individuals.

Initially, everybody must live in or near Eopolis, and close cooperation was a requirement of survival. A notion that the Others might be somewhere around, watching, reinforced solidarity. This faded with time, and meanwhile population and the economy grew. Likewise did knowledge. People learned how to live independently of the city. The countryside became a patchwork of ethnic clusters and social contracts.

At last a Demetrian legislature was a perceived necessity. It remained subordinate to the Union, represented by the governor general, and its authority was further limited by the fact that most communities ran most of their affairs without reference to it.

Elsewhere, time had also been riding. What precarious order had prevailed on Earth had broken down, and the Troubles begun. No few rhetoricians claimed that the fact of the Others brought this on; it was too disturbing, too provocative of heresy; there were things man was never meant to know. In Joelle's opinion—derived in large part from conversations with Dan

Brodersen, who was thoroughly opinionated—that was non-sense. If anything, the miracle was that the equilibrium had lasted, seesawing, until then; and the fact of the Others gave enough pause for reflection that lunacy did not lay waste the entire globe. Be this as it may, indisputable was that, though millions died and whole nations went under, the world survived. Civilization survived, in more areas than not. Space endeavors survived; no important hiatus occurred beyond Earth, whether in industry, exploration, or the settlement of Demeter.

One ongoing effort was reckoned more important than even the dispatching of unmanned probes toward neighbor stars. It was the sending of such craft through the gates, along arbitrary paths, programmed to return from wherever they went by taking equally arbitrary paths. None did.

Slowly, mankind appeared to settle down. In Lima they signed the Covenant.

(The office of a famous astrophysicist, still alive.)

ROSSET

—the theory we've been developing says that a T machine has a finite range. We estimate it as five hundred light-years in space, perhaps more, perhaps less. The point is that if you want to go across a greater span than that, you must go through an intermediate machine, which acts as a relay.

Now we've had no luck thus far with our probes. But let us keep it up long enough, and sheer statistics guarantees that eventually one will find its way back to us, with a record of the routes that it took. Let this happen a number of times, and we'll at least have the information we need to reach that many stars. We may also begin to get a glimmering of the basic principles, of how to plot a course for ourselves.

This will be especially true if we encounter another race that is likewise probing. We can compare notes. . . .

The presentation ended at that point, twenty-odd years in the past. Joelle wondered how the tape had gotten here. Maybe a fussy curator decreed that, if the San Geronimo Wheel was to be a monument, historical references in its data bank should be kept current.

For a minute she imagined another update, starting four

years back in the time of Sol or Phoebus, twelve years back in her own life.

(View from the watchship at the Phoebean machine, of an unknown craft suddenly arriving. Long, blunt-nosed, serrated, surrounded by a blue haze, she is obviously not human-built. She makes no response to signals, but at high accelerations traces out a path among the markers which officers aboard the watchship closely note, until she disappears.

(Scenes of public furor and of secret debate after the news has broken. Officialdom has come to despair of the cost effectiveness of robot probes and sent none for quite some time. The decision is reached not to send any now, but, instead, a manned vessel, along that path. Volunteers for the crew will not be lacking.

(*Emissary* goes through the unknown gate and vanishes.

(Astoundingly soon, *Emissary* returns.

(Interview with a famous holothete, who explains what she has learned from the Betans. They have been using this transport engine, which they discovered by sheer cut-and-try, for the past three centuries—but infrequently, as a relay to or from a part of the galaxy which they seldom have occasion to visit. No planet in the system attracts them as a colony site, and as for scientific research, they already have more going than they can handle. Hastily homebound, accustomed to employing neutrinos rather than radio or lasers for communication in space, the crew of this particular craft did not notice that newcomers were present.

(This sequence differs from previous ones in that the famous holothete is not addressing the whole human world, but those few men who hold her captive.)

"Well," Joelle asked, "do you understand better?"

"No," Fidelio confessed.

"Nor I," Joelle said.

IX

THE WORDS Lis spoke made Brodersen glance around him. The sole public phone in Novy Mir was on a wall of its tavern. However, nobody appeared interested. Sunlight entered through the windows and an open door, along with odors of soil and growth, to set an ikon aglow and brighten the whole dim little room. A pair of oldsters sipped tea and played chess. A younger man sat near the samovar, though he drank vodka, and talked idly with the landlord. Their eyes did keep drifting elsewhere—but toward Caitlín, who occupied a table by herself and scowled at a glass of what these Russians imagined to be beer. *Anyhow, few people hereabouts know English,* Brodersen recalled. *Maybe none.*

"Okay." He turned back to the screen. "How's that again, sweetheart?"

For an instant, seeing the image of her face and the signs of sleeplessness on it, he felt how sundered they were. The physical distance was trivial. But he dared not come to her, nor she to him, that they might touch. They could not even call other directly. From here his voice went to the cabin on Lake Artemis, where it was scrambled and passed on to their house, where Lis' instrument strained out the pre-recorded conversation between "Abner Croft" and her husband—which ought to help convince Hancock's linetappers that he was home—and reconstructed his message. Her answer must retrace the same long route.

"I said, only five of the crew agreed to go." Lis named them. "The rest promised to keep silence, and I believe they will, but, well, the way Ram Das Gupta put it was, he has a family to think about, and this venture isn't just desperate, it could become lawless."

"Damn and double damn!" Brodersen snarled. "They were all ready enough to go through the gate, to wherever *Emissary* did, if we could get clearance and the guidepath data—with God knows what at the far side, and He not telling."

"That's not the same. I, I can't help sympathizing. The Union does mean so much. Defying it is a kind of blasphemy."

"The cabal are who're defying it, subverting it."

"You may be wrong, darling. You may be. And whether or not you are, if you try this thing and fail—" She strove to hold pain out of her speech and features. "I'll always be proud, you know that, but maybe I won't be able to convince Barbara and Mike that their dad did not die a criminal."

Brodersen's fist slammed the wall. Those in the room gave him a startled glance. He took a deep breath and felt his throat loosen a bit.

"We went through this before, the other night," he said. "I tell you again, I do not aim to get reckless." He constructed a grin. "Would I have lasted to date if I were a bold type?"

"I'm sorry, I'm sorry." She blinked hard. "I can't help being afraid for you. If I could come along, oh, for that I'd give whatever years of my life I may have to live without you."

Overwhelmed, he could mumble nothing but, "Aw, shucks, honey."

Showing merely her head, the screen nonetheless told him how she straightened. "If I back you up from here, that is my way of going along," she said. "Do your job, Elisabet Leino, and do it right!"

"Say, look, I never meant—"

"Let's stick to business." She spoke briskly. "Can you get by with those five crewmen?"

He wrestled himself down into her kind of calm. "As far as conning *Chinook* or *Williwaw,* sure, no problem. Besides, remember, the first thing I figure to do is contact the Señor. He may well be able to take over completely from there. Everything may turn out downright disappointingly safe and easy."

"In which case, after you come back, we'll raise some private hell."

"Sure." The smile flew between them, and away. "All right, we've got a skeleton crew standing by. What about leave to go?"

"I'm working on that."

Brodersen frowned. "Um-m-m. How long d'you reckon it'll take? Hancock's pretty soon bound to suspect I've furloughed myself."

"I'm doing nothing to remind her of us. Instead, I've gotten hold of Barry Two Eagles." As the Astronautical Control

Board's commissioner for the Phoebean System, he held authority over space traffic. "Confidential-like, you understand. We had dinner yesterday evening, *tête-à-tête*, at the Apollo House. He's got hot pants for me, you know.... You didn't?" Lis laughed. "You're nowhere near as depraved as you claim to be, Dan, dearest."

"Um, yeah, he's a good fellow," Brodersen said with a reluctance that surprised him.

"True. I like him, and do not like using him, because he'll get no satisfaction, though he doesn't know that yet. Anyhow, he'll do nothing illegal, of course, but he'll be within his rights to clear *Chinook* for Sol without telling the governor. Especially since he doesn't know you're supposed to be under arrest. I explained you're busy, but you've heard how Aventureros badly wants to charter your ship and asked me to handle the matter. To him it looks like a typical Brodersen-Leino snap decision.

"I explained furthermore that Aurie Hancock would veto it if she knew beforehand, because she and her husband have stock in a rival corporation—oh, you'd have enjoyed the yarn I spun. He was shocked, denied she'd be that venal, but I prattled him into agreeing to keep silence, and then offered him a bribe. He's thinking it over."

"Huh? Barry don't bribe."

"Not exactly. But when I remarked that if this deal went through, we'd be in a position to make a substantial donation to research on brain tissue cloning—" She saw the man wince, and did herself. Two Eagles had ordered a doctor to switch off the machine that maintained what was left of his son after a skull-shattering accident. "Dan, we *will*. Regardless."

"For certain. I wish you hadn't had to, though."

"Me too. But I did have to."

After a moment, Brodersen said: "Well. Expect he'll agree?"

"I've little doubt. He ought to call me this afternoon."

"What about picking me up?"

"That's in the package. I told him several of *Chinook*'s crew had last-minute business groundside, and because of the need for discretion couldn't engage a shuttle to the ship. They'll meet at a spot where *Williwaw* can fetch them, if he issues a permit." Lis paused. "Where should it be?"

Brodersen had already considered that. "East shore of Spearhorn Lake. Well off in the backwoods, you recall, though there's a road of sorts—easy landing site—okay?"

"Okay." She glanced at her watch. "Hold on." He realized

she was punching a keyboard. "There. Our tape was running out. I patched in the extra section."

"Good girl." He stood helpless to kiss her. "Oh, good girl."

"I'm not sure we have much else to talk about," she said forlornly. "If the boat doesn't come tonight, I suppose you'd better find a phone and check with me tomorrow morning."

"Naturalmente, querida."

"The kids are fine, except for missing you. Barbara's having her nap. I could wake her."

"Don't."

"She said to tell you hello from her and Slewfoot both."

"Tell her hello right back, and—and—"

They stumbled along for a minute or two till Brodersen exploded: "Hell! This isn't getting us anywhere, is it?"

"No. And you'd better move. That lake's a ways from Novy Mir."

"Yeah. Right. I love you, Lis."

"Goodbye, darling." She operated controls to segue in a canned farewell. "I mean, 'So long. *Hasta la vista.*' But don't worry if it takes you a while. I'll always be here."

The screen blanked. Not quite steadily, Brodersen sought Caitlín's table. The chair creaked when his weight thumped down.

She reached to clasp his hand. "Is all well, my heart?" she asked low.

"Seems like it," he muttered, staring down at the scarred surface.

"And underneath, all is ill. That poor brave lady. It's fine judgment you showed in choosing her, Dan, so it is."

He met her green gaze and essayed a smile. "I'm a good judge of women. Drink up and let's clear out of here."

"Gladly will I go with you anywhere, my own, but—" she made a wry mouth—"must I drink up?"

"No, never mind. Leave it for the poor."

"What, and be starting a revolution?"

Somewhat cheered, he bade the landlord, *"Adiós"* and accompanied her forth. Phoebus was approaching noon, most settlers were out in the communal cropland, houses dreamed side by side along a single dusty street. Their timber smelled tarry in the warmth, though bright images adorned the gables. A cat strolled by. A *babushka* sat on her stoop, knitting, while she kept watch on a couple of small children at play, whose shouts were almost the only sound. Beyond, the valley reached green to the mountains whose sheerness enclosed it. The scene might have come out of a book of nursery tales, Brodersen thought.

But fusion-powered spacecraft had brought its creators here; agrochemists guided the conversion of the soil until Terrestrial plants, duly modified by geneticists, could flourish; ecological technology, working mostly on the microbial level, held at bay the native life which else would return and reconquer; at night, the constellations bore names like Aeneas and Gryphus, and only a powerful telescope could find the star which was Sol.

"Where are we bound?" Caitlín inquired as he opened the car bubble.

"To meet with the boat that'll take me off," Brodersen said. "Will you return this runabout to the rental agency for me, please?"

"What, has it not an autopilot you can be setting for that?"

"Yes, but you'll be to hellangone from anywhere."

"What do you mean I will?"

"Hey, wait, you don't think—"

"Get in," she said. "Drive while we fight, so we can be done with that when we arrive and ready for more interesting pastimes."

"Pegeen," he sighed, casting off guilt, for Lis would not begrudge him what comfort he could seize, "you've got a one-track mind."

"True," she agreed. "Isn't it a *nice* track?"

Chinook swung about Demeter like a near moon. Later she would be a comet.

Modeled on *Emissary,* since hers was to have been the same purpose if the gods were kind to Brodersen, she was a sphere, two hundred meters in diameter, mirror-burnished. (Her powerplant could easily keep her warm; getting rid of heat was the occasional problem.) Aft, the focuser for her jet traced out, with its framework, a graceful tulip shape. Amidships were the auxiliaries, swivel-mounted chemical rocket motors. Around the forward hemisphere, locks, turrets, housing, and electronic dishes broke her smoothness. At the pole opposite the main drive, two cranes flanked a great circular door.

Her crew were aboard. That had gone more easily than Leino intimated to Two Eagles. They had taken the regular ferry to

Persephone, unnoticed among the other passengers. At the port they engaged a private boat, whose owner-pilot cleared for Erion and then took them to their ship instead. Intersatellite traffic was only loosely monitored, and most spacemen were willing to break a regulation or two if it would help a lodge mate.

Fetching the captain unbeknownst presented more of a problem.

Word came. The door swung aside. A conveyor thrust *Williwaw* halfway out. The cranes laid hold on the boat, hauled her forth, swung her around so her blast wouldn't touch the mother vessel. In shape her seventy-five-meter length suggested a torpedo, fins at the rear, wings recessed near the waist, lanceolate boom projecting from the nose.

Vapor gushed from her, too hot to be visible. The cranes let go and she accelerated. A portion of the water condensed kilometers behind, making a cloud that roiled spectral white before dissipating. It was an inefficient system compared to a plasma drive, but it could endure rough passage through an atmosphere. For all her size and the unimaginable energies that her engine released and channeled, *Chinook* was too fragile for that, or for ever landing anywhere.

Obedient to an officially approved flight plan, *Williwaw* spent a couple of hours curving toward the planet before she reached the fringes of its stratosphere. Much velocity remained to be shed: slowly, lest she burn. Stubby wings extended. The rockets fell silent; valves closed them off. For a time the pilot and his computer nursed the boat through a long glide. Eventually she was at a level where the jet motors on the wings had a sufficient intake. He kicked in power to them. A rising whine filled the cockpit. Still furiously decelarating, *Williwaw* was now an aircraft. Solid-state optical transmitters revealed to the pilot a sea of sunlit clouds, far and far below. He had half the globe to round before he landed.

The moons of Demeter orbit faster than does the Moon of Earth. On this night, Erion was down and Persephone would not rise till after dawn. Thus a larger number of stars showed than before, soft in a violet-blue dusk. The hour was past for torchflies and choristers; quietness dwelt here. Walled by shadow masses of forest, the lake sheened sable. Across the middle of it, Zeus cast a perfect glade. Because the vale which cupped it lay much less high than the cave, warmth lingered, to raise a ghost of smoky fragrance from the sunbloom growing amidst lodix on the open ground where Brodersen and Caitlin sat.

He stirred upon springy turf. It was becoming damp. "Damnation, Pegeen," he said, "you cannot go, and that's that." At the back of his mind he felt how his vehemence profaned the peace around them.

She curled calf beneath knee, leaned against him, rumpled his hair, nibbled his ear. "I love you when you're firm," she murmured. "You may take that in any sense you please."

"This is ridiculous! How often must I repeat? You've no training—"

"Yourself have promised you'd give me the same, and the learning is easy and there's nothing to equal free-fall screwing."

"Be serious, will you? I meant a short pleasure trip, no further than to Aphrodite or Ares."

She dropped her hand to rest her weight on it. Forearm, hip, and thigh continued pressing gently on him. He felt her breath on his cheek as her tone dropped mirth. "Well, then it's serious I will be, dear wurra-wurra-wart. You've confessed you'll have no quartermaster and, what's worse, no medical officer. Can I not be both? Should I let you fare off into danger without me when I might help? Think also of your crew, Captain Brodersen. Would you be denying them what might save a life, to be free of fear on my account?"

"But the trip *won't* be dangerous."

"In that case, why refuse me the experience? You know what flying barracks the emigrant ships are. I've more sense of a universe around me here—or, aye, watching a newscast from space—than ever I got aboard *Isabella*."

"Well, uh, well, no telling what'll happen. We're steering mighty close to the wind, and—uh—"

"And your mistress must not be at your side? Daniel, Daniel, it's angry I'd be at you were I not so disappointed."

"Oh, hell, Pegeen!" He reached around to draw her closer yet.

"Of course," she said slyly, "if you fear scandal, I could keep decorous with you. Sure some boy aboard would console me."

"Stop that, you witch." He had known this was the last skirmish in a fight she'd won, by her special weapons, soon after they reached this place. "I give up. You're on." The surrender gladdened him. She sealed her victory by waiting for him to kiss her—thirty seconds?—though immediately after, nobody knew quite who was in charge.

They halted there, since the boat might appear at any minute, and sat for a while letting serenity well up within them. Presently Caitlín rose. "I will make my farewells," she said. He saw her clear through the twilight, but changed by it to a sight not altogether real, the hue of the Milky Way, moving around the meadow. She dipped a hand into the lake and drank, she plucked a sunbloom petal and crushed it lovingly between lips and teeth, she cast arms around a man-tall koost and hugged the bush to her, burying her face in its leaves. . . . At last she came back to him.

"You really try to be part of all this, don't you?" he half whispered.

"No, I am." Her hand swept an arc from stars to water and across the woods. "And you are, Dan. Everything is. Why cannot people feel it?"

"We can't be you, I suppose. You said something once about maybe having faerie blood. I thought it was just your figure of speech. Tonight I wonder."

She stared before her. "I wonder my own self."

"You mean that? I could pretty near believe it, old agnostic me."

"Oh, no, I'd not give you any mystical blarney. Not even from Yeats will I buy his metaphysics." She looked upward. "Yet sure, and this is a strange cosmos, more strange than we can guess, is that not so, my joy?"

He nodded. "The size of it alone. I've tried and tried to imagine a light-year, a single light-year, but of course I can't. Then I've tried to imagine the smallness of an atom, and can't. Wave mechanics. Background radiation left over from the Beginning. Expansion forever—into what? Black holes. Quasars. T machines. The Others. Yes." After a silence, touching her: "I think, though, you were getting at a particular mystery."

"Well, it was a queer story my mother told me, and she a good Catholic."

"Want to tell me?"

"That I do, but och, I don't know how. For it is not really a story, anything that truly happened or else was a lie. No, it is in the way and the time of telling, and herself who told it. Would you indeed like to hear?"

He tightened his arm about her. "Why do you ask me that?"

Caitlín responded. "Thank you, dear bear that you are.

"You must first understand, Mother was from Lahinch in County Clare. That's among the parts of Eire which grew poor during the Troubles, until none were left but smallholders, and many of them unlettered. There again they believe in the Sídhe, if ever they stopped believing, though I suppose Lady Gregory would not recognize their tales. And knowing about the Others, why under the winter stars should they not believe?"

Out in the lake, the great black bulk of a wassergeist surfaced, uttered its eldritch whistle, and sank.

"Well, as I've told you before, Mother came to Dublin on a scholarship to study music, after a professor on a fishing trip had heard her sing," Caitlín went on. "But she was only a little in the opera, for she married Padraig Mulryan and soon bore him two children. Then she fell homesick. He, a physician, could not take free, but he sent her back on holiday to the cottage of her parents, and glad she was to roam about the countryside she loved."

Caitlín sat straight, twining her fingers hard together, searching her thoughts. Brodersen waited. Her profile against the light night was dear to him.

"This she related long afterward, and I the first to hear except her priest. My father, that good dry man, fifteen years older than she, would have called it a mere dream, as likely it was. But Mother was seeking to reach me, when she saw me breaking from faith and family both. She wanted me to know that she too had felt what I did, so that she could warn me to beware.

"And yet she could say no more than this. She had been on a week's tramp, where she would sleep at whatever house the sunset found her near, and they always happy to meet a new person. But this moonlit night beneath Slieve Bernagh was so fair that she spread her bedroll on the moss, and late she lay while her vision lost itself upwards.

"Then there came a music out of the moonlight like flame, and one whose beauty was such that she wept to see, and he asked her would she go into the mountain with him. No woman born could have refused, or would have been a saint if she could, my mother told me. She left the sod like a bird, and he nested her in his arms and bore her away. But as for what followed, she could only speak of rainbows and suns, purple and gold, wind and wild seas and everything a glory. If that was how he made love to her, then that was how he made love to her. She awoke where she had lain down, and a sunbeam tickled her nose till she sneezed.... I've given you in English, Dan, a song I made about it in Gaelic, for Mother lacked the words; I do myself, but I saw her eyes and heard her voice."

Nor had he aught he could say.

"Nine months later, I was born, and grew to be the image of her," Caitlín continued after a spell during which a meteor streaked overhead. "Aye, well do I know what you are thinking. My father, the dear, never did. To him, she had carried me a little time long or a little time short, no matter which it was. And how he spoiled me, for I was his single daughter and the last child they had. Dan, he was right. You'll grant me, won't you, I read people well? She has known no other man than him, ever."

"Oh, I didn't mean that," Brodersen protested clumsily. "Not that I'd give a damn, but—No, I just guess at maybe a fantasy she was nursing—you'll agree she might, huh?—maybe without quite realizing she did—And she got a little high."

"She was never one for the poteen or the pot." When he tried to apologize, Caitlín laid a palm across his lips. "Aye, you mean she got drunk on moonlight."

"It happens," he replied when she let go. "Why, I remember an old juniper behind the house that'd talk to me. I forget what it said, but I remember it talking as well as I remember learning to ride a horse at the same age, four or five or whenever that was. Dreams hang on in the oddest ways. And ... if you're like her, Pegeen, then she's like you, and you're a dreamer—

"—except sometimes when you're so practical you scare me."

She didn't ease and laugh as he'd hoped, though she did smile. "I'm simply a woman, Dan. You men are the romantic sex."

"All right, what do you suppose happened? If you think she really went into Elhoy—what we call it where I come from—if you think that, I won't scoff. In the same world as the Others, no trouble to accept Underearth."

"Or devils?" He felt her shiver. "That's what Mother feared it was, hell tempting her and she falling. The priest said not to believe that; likeliest she'd had but a gust in the brain. Yet in her soul she bears the fear to this day. My father has told me how she was light-hearted in her youth, but from about that time grew very devout."

The pressure toward that would certainly be there, Brodersen reflected. *Where the fact of the Others hadn't destroyed religions, it's inspired new ones, or repowered the old. Was any of that their intention?* "What is your guess?"

"Mine? I have none. I know what scientific evidence consists of, and here is naught."

"But you must have speculated. It obviously matters a lot to you."

"Naturally. Norah is my mother. Far though I've drifted, I love her and my father and brothers, and hope to see them again on our journey."

Caitlín took his hand in a close grip. "You recall what started this talk was when you asked about the sense of belonging in the whole universe," she said. "I think she had it that night, stronger than ever myself have. Were she a Buddhist, she would have been speaking of Nirvana or enlightenment or some such wonderful thing. Being an Irish peasant girl, for all she was wedded to a Dublin doctor and had sung in the opera, she recoiled in horror, and dreadful is the pity of that. But as for what brought on her experience and gave it such form, I will not guess."

"May I?" he responded. "She was as adventurous by nature as you are, as hungry for life, except she never fought her way to freedom the way you did. So—"

Br-r-roo-oom-m said the sky. They sprang to their feet. Metal high aloft caught light from the hidden sun and glimmered, then dived into eclipse. Nonetheless they could track it as it neared them. The rumble became a roar, leaves trembled, air buffeted. The spaceboat rotated wings, descended vertically, lowered wheels, touched ground, cut motors, and rested. Silence thundered back.

Brodersen and Caitlín grabbed up their gear and ran toward her.

X

THE AUDITORIUM in the San Geronimo Wheel included an offstage room where speakers or entertainers could wait, preparing themselves if they needed to. Ira Quick didn't, but he spent a few seconds before a mirror, checking out his appearance. It showed him a trim, fine-boned Caucasoid man of forty-four with a high forehead above thin regular features, brown eyes, black Vandyke beard and wavy black hair, barely frosted, which had gotten sparse on top but fell abundant behind the ears and halfway down the neck. That was the mode, as were the quiet iridescence of his tunic and the flare of his dark slacks, noticeably less than last year's: the mode, not the ultra-fashion. "Be not the first by whom the new are tried."

My, quite the actor, readying for an entrance that will capture the hostile audience, aren't we? he thought, appreciating his ability to jest at himself. Underneath, he felt how he was aware of the deadly seriousness behind his errand here, yes, the tragedy. Tragedy did not consist of a clash between pure good and pure evil; that was mere melodrama. Tragedy occurred when the conflict was ineluctable between persons of equal morality, equal (well, almost equal) intelligence and sensitivity.

Henry Troxell, director of the guards, stirred. "Are you, uh, about set, sir?" he inquired.

"Yes," Quick said. "No fancy introduction, please."

"I couldn't handle that anyway, sir. Okay."

Troxell went forth. His bull tones reverberated back through the open door: *"Damas y caballeros.* I have the pleasure—I've explained plenty of times to you that my men and I have just been doing our duty, as assigned us by our government and yours. You've demanded a meeting with somebody who is in charge. Now he's arrived. I have the honor to present Ira Quick, member for the Midwest in the Assembly of the North American

Federation, Minister of Research and Development on the Council of the World-Union. Sr. Quick." He backed off stage as the newcomer entered, leading the applause until he noticed that he alone was clapping.

Quick went to the lectern, which he felt was a psychologically valuable prop, and smiled outward. Intended for hundreds, the chamber reached huge and hollow. Twelve prisoners sat in the front row and glowered—the alien not among them, he saw, unsure whether to be annoyed or relieved. Guards, seated or standing, added a similar number; the rest were on station, minuscule though the chance of an emergency was. Everybody wore spaceman's coveralls. The secret service agents bore holstered handguns, mostly sonic stunners, a few pistols.

Through the silence, he heard ventilation whirr. The air smelled properly fresh; surely a slight mustiness was all in his imagination. Given its near emptiness, the auditorium had bad acoustics, a hint of echoes. *Well,* he thought, *I've spoken in worse.* Briefly through him flashed memories, a small-town schoolhouse crammed with well-manured field hands, a rainy evening in a Masonic hall partly bombed out in the last civil war and not yet repaired, a cruel winter dawn outside the gate of a factory whose workers knew they'd be laid off when automation was restored, the kind of thing to which a bright young attorney who had become a bright young politician must grow accustomed. *Desirable in its fashion. Helped me understand the common man.*

"Do you mind if I speak English?" he began. "It's my native language, and you used it as much as Spanish aboard your ship, didn't you?" The sullenness before him was unchanged. "Thank you." Having sounded a note of informality, he leaned his fingertips on the lectern and gave full play to his famous baritone.

"Good day, ladies and gentlemen. And a good day I hope this will prove, for you and for mankind. More than any language can say, I regret, I grieve at what has happened to you. There you were, back from your expedition, an expedition whose significance dwarfed that of Columbus'. You had toiled, you had suffered, you had lost three comrades who were dear to you, and meanwhile you had endured. But at last you were bringing back the prize which you sincerely believed would open a new and brighter era. You had every right to expect a triumph, honor for the rest of your lives, immortality in history. Instead—"

"*Ach*, drop that shit," called a large blond woman. "Don't throw it at us. We haff had plenty already."

She must be Frieda von Moltke, gunner and boat pilot like the brown man, Sam Kalahele, who sat beside her. Captain Willem Langendijk turned around in the ultra-correct way that Quick remembered, to shush her. Mate Carlos Francisco Rueda Suárez gave his brows the least aristocratic lift in order to cast a look of scorn . . . stageward. Expressions on the rest varied from grins to embarrassment—save for the lean gray-haired woman, Joelle Ky, who stayed impassive.

Quick lifted a hand. "No offense," he said. "Believe me, I sympathize. I've come the whole way from Earth in order that we can have a meaningful dialogue and reach a *modus vivendi* that will satisfy you too. I thought I'd give a short talk, and then we would hold a free discussion. Is that agreeable?"

"Hear him out," Langendijk ordered.

Quartermaster Bruno Benedetti folded his arms, leaned back, and gave an artificial yawn. "We may as well," he said. "We have nothing else to do."

"Please." Esther Pinski, medical officer and assistant biologist, spoke timidly (though she had gone through the gate to an unknown destination like the rest, there to study life forms which for all she knew would prove lethal). "Let us be polite."

"Yes," added engineer Dairoku Mitsukuri. "How else shall we win release?"

The crew settled down. Quick reassumed his speaker's posture.

"Thank you," he said. "You are most generous." *You are mortally dangerous,* he thought, and at once: *No, it isn't their fault. They don't know any better. I must try to educate them. Education is the key to the future.* He felt tolerance stand tall within him.

"Colonel Troxell, and no doubt his men, have done their best to make clear to you why you have been held this weary while," he began. "However, with due respect, perhaps they aren't the most articulate people alive. Talking isn't their business. It is mine—or it better be, if I hope to stay in office." Nobody gave him back his chuckle. Planetologist Olga Razumovski briefly pinched her nostrils. "I intended to speak with the, ah, Betan too," he proceeded. "May I ask why he isn't present?"

Glances sought Joelle Ky. She crossed her legs and stated flatly: "I advised him otherwise. We'll play back this scene later and try to interpret it for him, point by point."

Quick stepped from the lectern and reduced his smile. Nothing lost an audience faster than a fixed stance or an unresponsive countenance. Besides, holothetes gave him the crawlies. They weren't *human*. . . . He must never admit to his prejudice. He was big enough to recognize that it was a prejudice.

Marie Feuillet, chemist, softened Ky's reply when she said, "Fidelio is so puzzled already, and I think so hurt."

"Well, his shipmates know him best," Quick conceded. "Fidelio, please accept my very good wishes and my government's welcome to the Solar System."

Focusing on the crew: "A hell of a welcome, I agree. I've come to apologize, and at the same time lay out for you why the government has had no choice. The custodians can only have outlined the reasons. I intend to fill in those outlines. Ask me the toughest questions you're able, and I'll give you the straightest answers I'm able. First, though, I think we'll be wise if I describe the situation to you from the start, the way my colleagues and I see it. Please don't tell yourself, 'I've heard this before.' Please listen. Maybe you have not heard every bit of it before.

"You realized when you signed on that probably you'd be quarantined for an unspecified period on your return, no matter what your researches seemed to prove. Even in the case of Demeter, which the Voice of the Others had assured was free of any disease our race could catch, even in that case, ten years went by before any scientist who went there set foot again on any body of the Solar System. You would not have to wait that long in orbit, of course. But the time might well have been longer than you have spent thus far here in the Wheel."

Floriano de Carvalho, chief biologist, flushed. "A different kind of time, Quick!" he shouted in anger.

The speaker retreated slightly upon the stage, as a matador of old might retreat. "Yes, certainly, certainly. You would be in audiovisual contact with your loved ones and the whole world, you would receive gifts, you would—well, enjoy better food and drink than I'm afraid you've been getting—oh, yes. Above all—am I right?—you would be conveying your message. The message that mankind now had the freedom of the galaxy."

"Well, not quite that yet," said a lanky fellow. "In a thousand years, the Betans have puzzled out the paths that take them to about a hundred stars and home again. It's a beginning, though."

For an instant, Quick didn't recognize him. A mental block.

He'd personally met each crewman and backup, and studied each dossier, after he failed to prevent any expedition. But he'd expected years would follow; if luck was really decent, *Emissary* never would return. Then came the catastrophic word, and he almost wished he had a God to thank that Tom Archer was commanding the watchship at that moment. There'd been no chance to persuade many such officers to cooperate. The contingency had seemed remote anyhow—that a T machine could as easily flick you through time as through space— theoretical, yes, as e=mc² was once theoretical—

The message from Archer: *Faraday* had escorted *Emissary* through the gate to the Solar System, after cleverly misleading his opposite number there, and was mounting guard on her; what should he do? Quick later took pride in the speed with which he had crystallized arrangements about the Wheel and, incidentally, about *Faraday*. (Send her back to her post in the Phoebean System. Before that tour expired, assign her to a hastily authorized mapping survey of distant Hades, with the usual fat bonuses for her crew. That bought a number of weeks in which to devise something more permanent.) Still, it had been a nightmare scramble to accomplish the task while keeping the secret. No single man could have done it. A bond of more than brotherhood would always exist between those people, in high places and low, from a dozen different countries, who had laid their careers on the line as they strove behind the scenes to forestall disaster.

And subsequently— Radio messages between Wheel and Earth could not well go in code, when nobody was supposed to be out here but a few harmless scientists. Courier boats took days, and in any event could not make frequent runs. That would excite comment also. (Besides, the available discretionary funds wouldn't stretch. Oh, damn those pinchpenny reactionaries who forever were hobbling persons of vision!) Thus Quick arrived here with the sketchiest notion of what Troxell's team had learned.

Fortunately, I'm a quick study. His standard joke broke the spell. It had lasted no more than a second, while he stood overcome by the magnitude of what he was doing for humanity. He knew the name of the latest troublemaker, *Emissary*'s second engineer, as well as he knew his wife's.

"I was being metaphorical, Mr. Sverdrup," he said. "As I understand your account, though, the Betans can guide us to planets we might colonize after we've filled Demeter. More important—am I right?—they can introduce us to about twenty sentient races, from each of which we should be able to learn incalculably much: science, art, philosophy, who can predict what?"

"Starting with the Betans themselves," Rueda snapped. "Technologically, they're the farthest advanced. Compared to their engineers, ours play with jackstraws in a sandbox. For a bare start, they can show us how to make spacecraft with capabilities that are science fiction to us, as cheaply and easily as we do automobiles. And they are willing to. They offer us trade terms so generous that I am still dazed. We told them that on Earth the person of an ambassador is sacred. Sir, where is theirs at this hour? What are your intentions toward him?"

The matador swayed aside from the charge. "Please, Sr. Rueda, that's what we'll discuss today. Surely you don't consider me antiscientific. I *am* the Minister of Research and Development."

Rueda replied with his eyebrows. *Curse him, he's passed his adult life as a spaceman,* Quick thought, *but he remains a member of his blasted timocratic clan, and they must have talked politics in his presence. He knows I didn't aim for R & D in the Cabinet because I wanted to give those blind forces free rein. No, I have a mission to tame them. They are good servants but bad masters.... Ah-ha, Ira, quoting your usual speech to yourself, are you?*

"Let me hark back to the twentieth century," he said, "and the moratorium on research into recombinant DNA techniques that responsible scientists imposed until they had worked out rigorous safety regulations. The result was that no new plague swept the world, but instead man reaped the countless benefits of new, basic knowledge in the field of genetics.

"Ladies and gentlemen, you today are in the position of those pioneers. I salute your heroism, I sympathize with your plight, and I appreciate the vast potential for good to come out of your accomplishments. Yet I feel sure you would never wish to release a horrible disease upon humanity. What I call for is not an end to exploration but a moratorium. My prayer is that you will agree.

"'What disease?' you ask. My friends, the same question was asked in those genetic laboratories. 'What disease?' Nobody knew. If they had known there would have been no problem. However, they did have the wisdom to admit the limitations of their knowledge.

"Your government takes its stewardship seriously. When

that Betan ship was observed passing through the gate at Phoebus, an expedition to follow it was authorized only after long debate, both public and official." *After one hell of a political battle, which my side lost, though we did extract a few concessions and afterward some of us got together to plan how we might win the next battle.* "To a large extent, the decision to go ahead turned on the assumption that you'd be away for years. If nothing else, it seemed clear that you would need much time to establish communication with a totally foreign species. Meanwhile, we at home could imagine contingencies and prepare for them." *And jostle for those who would have the final say.* "But instead, having spent those years, you returned within months!"

Quick switched from excitement to solemnity. "Fidelio, dear friend from the stars, forgive me what I must say. I am morally certain that you and yours are benign. Yet moral certainty is not enough, when a government must watch over billions of lives. And in fact, what do you know about us? Do you have proof positive of our honesty and peacefulness? I think our duty to both our posterities is that we both exercise the greatest caution."

A couple of his listeners were snickering. The von Moltke bitch laughed aloud and called, "He only knows Spanish, Mr. Eloquent Statesman. Do you want I should translate?"

Quick suppressed a surge of fury, considered repeating himself in the second language, decided that would only underline the contretemps, and replied with his sharpest smile, "If you like, at your leisure, *madam.*" The riposte seemed wasted on her, though.

He aimed at the crew again: "Quite aside from possible aggressive intent, which I agree isn't likely—quite aside from that, think of the impact on society. The Others gave us Demeter; they also gave us the Troubles. The Union remains frighteningly vulnerable. The Peace Command is daily more overstrained. You are idealists. You suppose that a flash flood of revolutionary information, technology, ideas, philosophies, faiths—you suppose this can only be desirable, can only stimulate a renaissance.

"My friends, I remind you that the original European Renaissance was indeed brilliant in art and science, but it was likewise an era when civilization exploded, the era not just of Leonardo and Michelangelo but of the Borgias and the Cenci.

And the strongest thing they had to kill with was gunpowder. We have fusion warheads.

"I apologize for repeating arguments which were heard over and over before you departed. But you have, after all, spent eight years of your lifetimes away, in an exotic setting. The enthusiasm of discovery and achievement has dimmed these cautions in your memories. And evidently Colonel Troxell and his staff haven't succeeded in impressing their gravity upon you.

"Let me repeat, we who look after the common weal counted on years in which to prepare for your return. Foreseeing the danger, we intended both to strengthen institutions of law and order and to educate the public. Frankly, by coming back this early, you yourselves have precipitated the emergency."

Rueda flipped an arm upward. "Don't you know why we did?" he called.

Taken aback, the minister heard his own voice: "What? Well... well, no. I guess not. It's doubtless in the reports— Colonel Troxell tells me you've been pretty frank—but that's a huge amount of material and I didn't want to keep you waiting longer—" He rallied. "Very well, Sr. Rueda. I took for granted that that was how the gate works."

"Wrong, Mr. Quick," the mate said. "The Betans have had a thousand years to study the T machines. They developed cheap probes that they could send out by the billions, where we've sent a few thousand. So they got some back. Given that much information, they could begin to see traces of a pattern, begin to get inklings of a theory. They are far from a complete understanding, true. But they have found how slight variations in a guidepath, not enough to take you to a different destination in space, will take you to different moments in time. The range isn't great, a matter of a decade or two either way. Beyond that, their information is still too incomplete. But they told us they could calculate a guidepath around the machine at Centrum which would bring us out before or after the hour we left Phoebus, by anywhere—anywhen—within several years.

"We elected to return to a few days after our departure. That it was months, instead, is because we can't conn *Emissary* as precisely as they control their ships.

"It was our decision. Ours."

Langendijk frowned. Rueda shook his head at the captain.

Appalled—he felt his lips go numb—Quick breathed, "Why?" though already he guessed the response.

"We did not forget the debates beforehand," Rueda said. "No, we spent eight years thinking. We saw the risk that your faction, sir, would prevail, because it knows exactly what it wants, while our kind of people promise nothing except hope. We decided we had better arrive home early."

Above his dismay (because, Jesus Christ, time travel on top of everything else!), Quick was pleased to note how ready was his counterattack. "Thank you, Sr. Rueda," he purred. "I wish you'd tell me what my faction, as you call it, does want. I'd be interested to know. I thought the Action Party and like-minded organizations simply aim at the well-being of mankind."

Rueda shrugged. "What is the well-being of mankind? Who determines? Let me cite a little history too. Several centuries back, the shoguns of Japan excluded foreigners—anything new, anything fresh. Mr. Mitsukuri has told me how they then tried to regulate the whole of life, down to the price you might pay for a doll to give your child."

"*Festung Menschenheim,*" von Moltke added nastily. "But this hermit kingdom could last. Keep missiles at either T machine and blow to bits whatever strange may show itself. Oh, yes."

Not altogether a bad idea. Quick raised his hand. "What sort of monster do you take me for?" he cried. "How do you expect me to reply to that kind of charge? Have I stopped beating my wife? Ladies and gentlemen, I don't want to believe those years at Beta made paranoids of you. I beg you, stop talking that way!"

Captain Langendijk intervened. "If you please, everyone, if you please. Let us stay civilized." He got up and addressed the stage. "Sir, we did not advance our return date because of a persecution complex. It merely seemed sensible. Besides, you can imagine personal reasons. In eight years, a number of those we care for would have died, the rest aged. We hoped to escape that."

Quick attempted a reply. Langendijk's polder-level voice went on: "As Carlos said, we remembered the big arguments before we left. Over and over, we discussed them—including the danger of reviving the Troubles. We found the danger is negligible.

"You speak of a flood of newness. Well, this cannot happen. In a hundred years, we have barely begun to know Demeter, and it has no intelligent native race. As for Beta—the Betans, who are experienced at meeting different species, they estimate fifty years before they and we can move beyond the exchange of cultural and scientific missions. We will need that long to get acquainted. Earth will have ample time to adapt.

"Please. Let me finish. Technology will enter faster than that, yes. But what of it? Or what *not* of it? The technology most immediately significant will be astronautical. Routes through the gates; cheap, plentiful, truly serviceable spacecraft; uninhabited Earthlike planets—the safety valve, can you not see? Freedom to get away and start fresh, not a few thousand per year crammed in a transport, but unlimited. Freedom. This is what we bring back with us."

He sat down, red-faced, unused to orating, and waited. The whole room waited.

Quick let silence grow, to emphasize the words he was assembling, before he took to the lectern again, reassumed his pastoral posture, and told them:

"We're all idealists here. You wouldn't have gone to Beta if you weren't. I wouldn't serve in Toronto and in Lima if I weren't. For that matter, the men who've been taking care of you here wouldn't have accepted their hard, thankless job if they weren't."

I shade the truth a trifle, he thought. *Emotionally speaking, it must be I, Ira Wallace Quick, who forces destiny into shape. There is no ecstasy like that. On the crudest level, hearing a crowd cheer me, seeing them adore me, beats taking a woman to bed.*

How very honest I am with myself. (I am being wry. I often am. I like that trait, in moderation.) Therefore I dare be frank and add that somebody has to assume the stewardship and I, over the years, have come to know the common man and what he needs.

"Captain Langendijk," he said, "I admit you're sincere, but have you really considered the consequences of recklessly introducing that kind of astronautics? You spoke of a safety valve. Let me, instead, speak about the wretched of Earth, whole nations that have not yet climbed back from starveling barbarism, millions of poor and downtrodden within the so-called advanced countries. Have they no call upon us? Surely you don't imagine they could pack up and go. Where would they get the price of the cheapest ticket, of the tools necessary at the far end? Where would they get the education required for survival? Demeter has claimed her hundreds of lives already, from carefully selected emigrants to a carefully researched world. Where, even, would the poor get the incentive to go, the bare energy?

"No, what you propose would divert vitally needed resources and still more vitally needed skilled labor. For the benefit of a privileged few, the many would be cast into suffering deeper and more prolonged. Have you no sense of obligation toward your fellow humans?"

"Mamma mia," Benedetto yelled, "have you no sense of elementary economics? You cannot believe that *sciocchezza!"*

Quick stiffened. "I believe in compassionate government," he declared.

Ky stirred in her chair. "'Compassionate government,'" she said, "is a code phrase meaning, 'There will be absolutely no compassion for the taxpayer.'"

That can't be her jape, thought Quick in anger. *She's too divorced from reality. I'll bet she heard it from Daniel Brodersen, that bastard on Demeter. The detectives told me she and he had a close relationship.*

He mastered himself, relaxed muscle after muscle, leaned across the lectern and urged with all the mellowness at his command:

"Ladies and gentlemen, I realized you'd feel bitter. I did not foresee our meeting would stray this far or get this hostile. Look, I shunted my other responsibilities aside and spent days traveling from Earth in order to work out a plan with you that'll satisfy you in your private lives while fulfilling the duty we share to mankind and civilization. Let's hold a genuine dialogue, shall we?"

Hours later, he sat in the apartment given him, a Scotch and soda in his grip, and fumbled after a decision. Soon he must join Troxell for dinner. No doubt he could fob off undesirable questions and suggestions, pleading weariness. It wouldn't be feigned, either. Under no circumstances could he be candid. And he mustn't stay here long, caged in outer space while events ran wild at home. For him, the Wheel was bad karma. So if he could structure the conversation this evenwatch, he might elicit clues as to how best to proceed. But this involved having at least a tentative scheme of action, which in turn demanded that he stare down some rather horrible facts.

A hot shower had washed the sweat off him, a change of clothes rid him of the stench. The lounger cuddled his body. The tumbler was cool in his hand, moist, each sip reminding him of smoke—bonfire at a political rally, campfire in the Rockies, hearthfire *après-ski* in a Swiss chalet, cigar after a four-star dinner and, across the table, a worshipful young female from the governmental programmer pool.... Haydn lilted. Stars marched magnificently across a port in the wall. He barely noticed any of it.

What to do, what to do?

Tragedy, real tragedy, a light-year past what he went through as a junior attorney in the Judge Advocate's bureau under the old martial government, helping prosecute malefactors who were actually the products of a society in chaos. They who boarded *Emissary* for Beta were in their fashion the finest Earth had to offer, gifted, educated, high-minded. He could not even call them rabid technophiles, any more than they could properly call him a rabid xenophobe. He and they held separate parts of the truth, like the blind men feeling the elephant.

He had to confront the hard questions, though, or stop thinking of himself as a statesman. Which position was more nearly right, or less grossly wrong? What was more essential to the elephant, its tail or its trunk?

I've seen too much misery in the wake of the Troubles, read the statistics on too much more. He would forever be haunted by a little girl he never knew. A border clash had occurred between units of the United States and the Holy Western Republic, a mortar shell went astray, he as an officer of the joint armistice commission had poked around for evidence of culpability and found, instead, her holding a teddy bear against the wound that bled her to death. And at that, she'd gone fast, in the ruins of her home. Famine was worse, pellagra worse yet. *What raison d'être does government have, except to care for people? And who will care for them except government?*

Quick gulped a mouthful, paid attention to it going down his throat, became consciously sardonic. *Now I'm quoting Speech No. 17-B.* That helped calm him, without changing the facts.

The foremost fact was that Homo sapiens had no business among the stars. Eventually, yes, when he was ready, then let him go forth. But first he should put his own house in order. One could actually argue that interplanetary enterprises, from the original Sputnik, had been a mistake. Granted, this was heresy. Quick had never publicly uttered it. The technophiles would have come down on him like an avalanche, with their figures of increases in real wealth due to minerals and manufactures, their citations of advances in scientific knowledge and everything that that meant in every field from earthquake control to medicine; and they would have been truthful. What they never stopped to wonder was what mankind might have done in the way of building a decent, stable world, had mankind stayed quietly at home.

Be that as it may—*Oh, damn the Others! If they aren't already damned. They're enough to make a man believe in Satan.*

Helter-skelter, off to Demeter, at whatever cost in work and material, to give new hope to thousands out of Earth's billions.... Yes, yes, the investment was paying off, Demeter was returning a nice profit, some of which the general public was getting in the form of higher wages and lower prices—but what about the poor who must scrounge along while the investment was being made? That capital would have bought them a lot of welfare.

More important, fundamental, unhealing, was the drain on *attention*. The best of Earth, in ever-increasing numbers, no longer cared much about the government of Earth. They were off into space. Turn them completely loose, let in the Betans, and that would spell the end of Ira Quick's program for a humane and rational civilization.

He stroked his beard. The silkiness was minutely soothing as he continued to review. His was far from the sole interest at stake. No two of his allies had identical motives. Stedman, of the Holy Western Republic, feared the collapse of a faith and a way of life already weakened by secular Terrestrial influences. Makarov, of Great Russia, foresaw his dream of reunification with Byelorussia, Ukrainia, and Siberia coming to naught. Abdallah, of the Meccan Caliphate, suspected that Iran, already committed to high-energy industry, would gain a decisive advantage over his part of Islam. Garcilaso, of the Andean Confederacy, had brought his corporation into a viable relationship with its chief competitor, Aventureros Planetarios, and didn't want that upset, less because he would lose money than because his family would lose standing. Broussard, of Europe, talked practical politics, but basically dreaded the oblivion into which his culture and tradition might sink. The list went on.

Quick halted his reverie and clenched his drink. A realist must accept reality. He couldn't wish away Demeter, the star gates, the Others, or even the Iliadic League. Water does not run uphill. However, you can dig a catch basin to stop it. After that, perhaps, given luck and devotion, you can install a pump to force it back where it belongs.

Today I confirmed my fears. There is no way to make that crew cooperate. I can only be thankful that none of them have the skill to pretend, with the aim of betraying me later.

They are valuable human beings; and no doubt the alien among them has the same claim on my conscience. We can't hold them captive till they die of age, can we? No. Too many chances for the secret to escape.

Well, what is the alternative? Release them? That would not only negate everything we've striven for, it would doom the Action Party and every group that collaborated with me. What then of my hopes?

All right, what are the facts? The Emissary *crew have evidently been quite outspoken under interrogation.*

(a) Though the Betans could enter the Phoebean System whenever they wanted, they had no idea of how to reach the Solar System, from that machine or any other. No matter how close they got to the Betans, the human visitors had honored their pledge to keep that path secret.

(b) The Betans recognized the possibility that contact with mankind might not be good after all, from their viewpoint or ours. They sent an ambassador, who was also an investigator, but would send nobody else to Phoebus. The next step was up to us. If no Terrestrial vessel sought them to initiate regular relationships, they would wait long before they took any initiative. (Quick had difficulty believing in such restraint, till he remembered that he was thinking like a human, not a Betan. Their primary interest in us had a thoroughly nonhuman motivation, and could scarcely be satisfied if they forced their way in.)

(c) When *Emissary* left, nearly everyone took for granted she'd be years gone at the least, and might well never return. Thus time remained to organize Earth and Demeter properly.

(d) They knew aboard *Faraday* that *Emissary* was back. To judge by a recent report from Aurelia Hancock, apparently the noxious Brodersen had suspicions, and thus doubtless associates of his did. Moreover, the San Geronimo Wheel contained twenty-one men who knew still more, if not all. However, such small quantities weren't impossible to handle. Appeal to duty or vanity; persuasion, of several kinds; pressure, since any person has vulnerable points; and, of course, the creation of a climate of opinion, such that nobody in his right mind would heed the accusations of an isolated crank or two. That took time and money, but it worked. Despite tens of thousands of witnesses, the Western intellectual community did not accept the truth about Stalin's empire for decades, and was slower yet to acknowledge it about the Maoists'.

Not that Ira Quick meant to set up concentration camps or anything like that. The example merely showed what a strong propaganda effort could accomplish, for good or ill. Mostly a doctrine was spread by people who didn't even subscribe to it as a whole, but simply took for granted that certain key assertions were true. These got into the textbooks....

(e) The *Emissary* folk themselves. That was what hurt. Let them loose to spread their tale—

—for the tale was not merely that they had been there, it was exactly the revelation that Rueda and Langendijk preached—

—and you might as well forget about social justice. *Plus the career of Ira Quick. Oh, my associates and I would avoid criminal charges. We checked the legal technicalities most carefully.* The Dangerous Instrumentalities Act gave his ministry broad discretion to sequester matériel it judged to be a menace. The Finalist case—members of a nihilist sect, about whom evidence appeared that they had discovered several fission warheads left over from the Troubles—gave precedent for holding persons incommunicado. While the *Emissary* matter would bring on a ruinous scandal, he'd be immune from prosecution ... unless he kept his prisoners too long, say more than three months. *Perhaps I could revive my law practice after the furor died out. With the world turned upside down, I suppose lawyers would have a field day. But what would be the meaning of it all?*

Therefore: what to do?

For the sake of humanity.

Quick gulped hard. Troxell was dutiful; he had been told that the Union Cabinet in executive session had ordered this arrest. That was not exactly the case. Instead, a determined handful within the government had acted.

What next?

Quick doubted that the Union itself, open and aboveboard, could make Troxell agree to a massacre.

Foul word. For a foul idea.

And yet very easy to carry out. For instance, by a merciful gas.

Relieve Troxell's team. Find them individual assignments that will disperse them. Then two or three wholly dedicated men—

On my head be it, and the heads of my colleagues. I could never wash clean these hands.

But that dead little girl. Poverty. Ignorance. The best and the brightest gone off in search of mere adventure, when they could be serving. Is this situation basically different from a war?

He drained his tumbler and banged it down. *I don't know. I must think. Consult. Share guilt. Soon, though, something final must be done about that crew.*

"I do not understand," Fidelio said.

"Nor I," Joelle answered, there in her quarters.

"Nor he. The male called Quick [Kh'eh-yih-kh-h-h]. Has he not seen in summaries and heard related what our dilemma is on our world? Can he not realize how we wish to come to you, if you will receive us?"

"Either he can't, or he doesn't want to," Joelle said. "It may be too subtle for him. Or—I don't know. I'm not sorry to be as remote from these things as I am."

Her gaze went to the port. In the crystalline night of space, the Pleiades had become visible as the Wheel turned. In that general direction, the Betans had calculated, lay Beta. Lay three humans whose corners of a foreign planet were forever Earth. "If Chris were here," Joelle said, scarcely to be heard, "maybe she could explain."

XI

The Memory Bank

THE SUN that humans named Centrum is a K3 dwarf, its luminosity 0.183 that of Sol. Revolving about it at a mean distance of 0.427 astronomical unit, the second planet, Beta, gets about as much total irradiation as Earth does—more infrared, far less ultraviolet. The orbital period is approximately 118 Terrestrial days. Rotation had become locked to two-thirds of this. Hence the time from sunrise to sunset upon that world is one Betan year, and axial tilt operates to keep the southern hemisphere permanently glaciated. (Precession changes that, but over geological epochs, since Beta has no moon.) There is also a large ice cap on the north pole.

The slow spin makes a weak magnetic field. Thus auroras are few and dim, sky glow at night stronger than on Earth or Demeter. Likewise feeble are cyclonic winds. However, violent weather is common along the terminator, where day meets night. In the northern temperate and tropical zones, the characteristic cycle is: early morning thaw; midmorning to noon, rainstorms; afternoon drought; evening rainstorms; later snowstorms; eventual freeze and quiet until dawn, at which time new gales herald the next thaw. Life has evolved to fit these conditions.

It is of the same basic sort as life on Earth or Demeter, proteins in water solution, plants which photosynthesize, animals which eat the vegetation and each other. That is no surprise, on a globe as similar—mean diameter 11,902 kilometers, mean density 5.23 g/cc, liquid water covering sixty-five percent of the surface. Compared to, say, Mercury or Jupiter, the three worlds are practically triplets.

Yet their slight differences condition the nature and fate of everything that is alive upon them.

• • •

Joelle Ky and Christine Burns wandered along an eastern shore. Around them reached wilderness. It lay within fifty kilometers of a megalopolitan complex holding fifteen million souls; but the Betans cherished their countrysides. Indeed, you might never recognize a city from above. You would see a historic core, buildings crowded into a thousand hectares or less, otherwise a parkscape interrupted by an occasional road, garden around an artificial lake, or elegant spire. Most of the city was underground. Even agricultural regions lacked the regimented look of human fields and pastures.

Joelle and Christine had parked their aircar and gone off afoot. The vehicle was one lent them—instantly, upon request—by a local matriarch eager to oblige. Neither seats nor controls suited their bodies, but the autopilot took charge once Joelle had given instructions, and on a short flight like this they could sit any old way.

They walked for a while, silent, before Joelle gathered resolution to say, "You wanted us to find a place where we could talk in private, Chris," and wondered why that should be hard. Could she be flinching from what she might hear?

Emissary's computerman drew breath. "Yes, I did," she replied in her musical Jamaican English. She was tall and lissome, with gentle features and fawn eyes. Her skin was almost ebony, her hair a black aureole. Today she wore a dress whose scarlet defied the landscape. "You needn't have brought us this far. Anywhere beyond earshot of camp would have done." She laughed. Ever since they met, Joelle had envied the ease with which she laughed. "Our hosts would scarcely eavesdrop, what?"

"Oh, a change of scene," the holothete replied. She struggled to express: *You wish to confide in me. My cold self feels the warmth of your need. Do you not deserve a beautiful setting for your confessional?* She failed. "I've visited here before. I like it."

"Me too. Why did you never tell the rest of us about it?"

"Plenty of other areas are equally good. You know I have to go off alone every now and then."

"Well, this is right for you, Joelle."

That awakened an awareness of it, almost leaf by leaf. Habituation dropped away and she felt how the gravity took seven or eight kilos off her Earth weight and altered slightly the

manner of walking, of every motion. She couldn't sense a
reduced air pressure, but she noticed heat relieved by a salt blast
from the sea on her right, and odor after odor, sweet, sulfurous,
rosy, cheesy, spicy, indescribable. Surf boomed; wind skirled; a
flying creature on leathery wings fluted.

The sky was deep purplish blue. Centrum stood low in the
west, well-nigh motionless, three-fourths again the angular size
of Sol viewed from Earth, an orange disc at which she could
safely gaze for a second at a time. Opposite, clouds towered
immense above the eastern horizon, darkling in their depths
save where lightning winked, red and gold on their edges. They
cast that glow 'down onto the ocean, which elsewhere ran
gunmetal color and whitecapped till it crashed on a shingly
beach.

The Terrestrials walked above, through bushes that scraped
at their calves and sprang shut behind them. Inland, canebrakes
rattled together and solitary trees fluttered fronds along thin,
wildly whipping boughs. The level sunbeams brought forth
infinite shades of brown, sorrel, ruby, apricot, ocher, gold, a
somber, Rembrandtesque richness.

Eight years, Joelle thought. *Can I still truly remember a
Kansas cornfield, a Tennessee greenwood?*

The surroundings fled, for Chris had taken her hand.

Joelle's fingers replied, shyly, and the two women paced
onward. At last Christine said, her tone muffled, "I hope you'll
not mind if I . . . unload my trouble on you."

"No. Go ahead." Joelle's pulse stammered. She picked her
words: "You realize, though, I am the last of our crew who
should try giving personal advice. What do I know of
emotions?"

"More than the rest of us. Would you stay a practicing
holothete if you didn't find that a full kind of existence?"

"Hardly a human existence."

"It is, it is. Whatever a human can do is human."

"By definition, if you insist. That doesn't mean a, an ascetic
and a libertine are the same. I've had nowhere else to go but
where I am."

Christine regarded her. "I don't want to pry," she said at
length. "If I start that, slap me down, please. But I think you
know more about people than you realize you do."

"How? I grew up in the project that developed holothetics,
since I was two years old, a war orphan adopted into a military

research reservation. It turns out a holothete must begin almost that early. You were—eighteen, did you tell me?—when you started training to become a linker. My first memory is of being linked. It marks a person." Joelle squeezed the clasp that joined hers. "I'm not complaining. On the whole, I've had a satisfactory life. However, it's not been like yours."

"Not in the least? I ... well, you've shunned intimate relationships on this trip, I've seen you fend off advances that weren't always casual, but—Forgive me, I do *not* want to pry. Still, gossip—no, common knowledge, to speak plainly—you've had your involvements."

Eric Stranathan, Joelle remembered, and for an instant Beta was altogether gone, he and she were at Lake Louise and there was nobody else. Afterward he, a proud man, a son of the Captain General of the Fraser Valley, could not endure the idea of being a mere linker *vis-à-vis* her (for this was when the understanding of what it meant to be a holothete had exploded into bloom) and bade farewell. *You wouldn't have heard of Eric, Chris. You weren't born then. You're thinking of my occasional lovers since, mostly fellow holothetes, bodily pleasure and little else, except, I suppose to a degree, Dan Brodersen.*

"Nothing profound," she said. The hand in hers belied her.

"You've been like a mother to me," the Jamaican said. "That's why I dare turn to you now."

A mother, a mother? No, a mother image. In your mind, Chris, you are an ordinary linker, I am a godlike holothete. The truth is, I've simply been an easy-going superior who gave you some advanced instruction. (You are youth and loveliness. I am agedness that suddenly is reaching—against its own will, reaching.)

Joelle felt the wind stiffen, minute by minute. She had to raise her voice: "Thank you. Ha, let's stop talking about me and attack your problem. Tell me whatever you wish, dear."

Dear.

"I've been nerving myself to this for weeks," said Chris, as if around an obstacle. "Ever since we all agreed we've accomplished enough, we can soon head home. Not that I was scared of you. I was scared of myself, afraid to look straight at the conflicts inside me. Can you help?"

"I can try."

"You, you'll recall it was jolly at first aboard ship. [When six women and nine men applicants won top grades in tests for the crew assignments, the girls had a fine thing going for them, especially after Joelle opted out of that particular sport.] Then Chi and I got serious. When he died—[Yuan Chichao, planetologist, went into a ravine to examine a granitic outcrop, and fell dead. Later analysis showed that plants growing there exuded a lethal gas in the heat of noontide, which an inversion layer trapped and concentrated. The Betans were heartbroken. They had had no idea. That vapor was harmless to them.] Looking back, I suppose I did go a bit wild, grieving, afterward flinging around. [She handled her tasks gallantly well. They were somewhat menial, too, demand for a computerman being small while the expedition endeavored to learn about an entire world.] Torsten stabilized me. He's been incredibly kind, strong, thoughtful. I shudder to think what a mood drug zombie I might be by now if it weren't for him."

I could not have done that for you, could I? twisted within Joelle. Aloud: "You underrate yourself. You're healthy, you'd've recovered on your own." Reluctantly: "Still, it's obvious he gave you a large boost. You feel in his debt." *I have watched you and him day by day, I have watched you hour by hour, Chris.*

"I do that. When we get back to Earth, he wants to marry me."

"Why, how splendid," Joelle said automatically.

Chris gulped. "I'm in love with Dairoku."

Similar appearance to Chi's? I never thought so, but—"How does he feel?"

"I'm his good friend, respected shipmate, and enjoyed bedfellow," said Chris in a rush. "Along with Frieda, Esther, Marie, and Olga. And you'd be too, if you wanted. Since we heard of the time travel capability, he's been talking more and more about a girl he knew in Kyoto. . . . He's courteous to me, considerate, yes, I'd call him affectionate, but that . . . that's where he stops."

"Have you told him how it is with you?"

"No. Not really. The things one says on a mattress—they're discounted afterward, aren't they? Should I?"

"I'll have to think about that," Joelle said. "And then quite probably I'll guess wrong."

They tramped on. The wind loudened, the sea ramped. Clouds in the east lifted their wall higher, startlingly fast. Wrack blew off them, to scud across indigo heaven.

Chris hunched shoulders against a gathering chill. "What of Torsten?" she asked.

"You don't have to marry anybody, you know," Joelle bit off in abrupt irritation.

"Of course not. But—"

"He won't pine away. He'll find someone else after we return. Or a series of someone elses."

"Yes, to be sure. But . . . if I can't have Dai . . . do I want to let Torsten go? I'd like to tell you more about him, little things, and have you advise me what's wise. Not that I'm being totally selfish, I trust. He does love me. . . . But then, you know Dai, you and he have worked together, maintaining the engine and the jet. Maybe you can give me an idea if I might—just maybe I might—" Chris hugged Joelle's hand to her bosom.

Do not respond!

How curious are the ways of love. I doubt they are less powerful in us than in the Betans, and here they have brought history to a turning point. Joelle found strength in a rehearsal of facts.

The ancestors of the Betans were omnivores turned hunters along the coast, specialized neither for land nor water, though they could swim faster than they could run. Perhaps dexterity and intelligence were selected for when shifts in ocean currents, due to shifts in hemispheric glaciation, made for poor "fishing" but abundant game ashore, large beasts such as cold climates often favor. Eventually, fully sapient, the species spread widely, some of its members too far inland ever to visit the sea. They remained bound to the cycle of day and night.

The female was half again as big as the male, her body proportionately stouter but her limbs the same length. Thus she was more powerful, more agile in the water, but comparatively slow and awkward on land. She had four outlets for nourishing infants. You could scarcely call these teats, their structure was so different, nor call their product milk. As a rule, she bore four young in a litter, of which three were male; her equivalent of chromosomes determined the sex of offspring, not her mate's. Ova had been released one at a time over a period of some one hundred hours during breeding season, and had ordinarily been fertilized by separate partners.

This occurred about noon. Parturition came in the late

afternoon of the following day, making the gestation period comparable to man's. The infants arrived, out of a compartmented womb, at intervals roughly corresponding to their conceptions. Due to the mother's size, this went more easily than for humans. She nursed them through the night, during which they grew fast, then started weaning them in the morning. While nursing she was not breedable, and she continued to give suck, diminuendo, long enough that she stayed infertile until the next midday. Hence the normal spacing of births was four Betan years, or seventeen Terrestrial months.

In primitive milieus, the mother was handicapped ashore, yet must remain there to care for the young during the initial night of their lives. Her mates—three, on the average—usually brought in food, while she worked around the rookery or camp and guarded it. (Betan eyes have superb dark adaptation.) As marriage customs developed, they naturally took a polyandrous form.

Perhaps because of infrequent sexual intercourse, as well as the somatic disparity, inherent psychomental differences between male and female became much clearer on Beta than on Earth. The former tended strongly to be aggressive, inventive, handy, abstraction-minded, but not very creative in those arts that appeal directly to the emotions. The latter tended to be staid, persistent, ruthless at need, practical-minded, but artistic, with a feeling for the living world that males could never quite fathom. Nearly all societies were matriarchal, and the Great Mother was *the* religious archetype.

This was the case because of the means of bonding, which kept parents together and thus assured proper care of the slowly maturing young. In man, it was year-round libido. In the Betan, concupiscence was if anything a disruptive force, rousing passions that could prove uncontrollable. Many institutions in many distinct cultures evolved to keep a wife in heat the exclusive partner of her husbands and to protect the virtue of a daughter.

Rather than permanent low-grade rut, nature on Beta used nutrition to weld male to female. Besides nursing their babies, she nursed him.

Garbling a single word (there were thousands) for the fluid she produced, *Emissary's* scientists called it *enin*, and the process of its production they called *enination*. Enin fed sucklings of either sex. It also contained a hormone which promoted their growth—and was essential to the health and vigor of the adult male. He needed only small quantities, and tapping them from her gave him such intense pleasure that soon he was sated; but he must come back several times per planetary rotation. (She enjoyed being tapped, though for her the sensations were mild and diffuse.) In this way the normal female was sure of retaining her spouses.

At breeding time she went dry. The pheromone she then gave off incited her mates to lust. At the end of the period they were famished. When, early in pregnancy, she resumed limited enination, it was an occasion of joy, the highest feast of numerous faiths.

This direct dependence generally gave males a sense of mystery and awe about females. In some areas the sexes even formed two distinct sub-societies, with separate laws, rituals, and languages; the common "tongue" might be a pidgin.

Universally, a basic unit was the husbands of a given wife, together with adolescent sons. They were supposed to form an indissoluble fraternity. Of course, in practice this could fail. Bachelorhood was everywhere rare, requiring outré sorts of prostitution, and homosexuality unheard of. After civilizations grew sophisticated and cosmopolitan, efforts increased to make the sexes—not "equal," which was hardly thinkable—but more closely integrated.

As on Earth, the state eventually appeared, both sedentary (along the fortunate seashores) and nomadic (in the grim continental interiors). As on Earth, it brought forth public works, wars, conquests, enslavements, tyrannies, corruptions, decline and fall. Also as on Earth, it was the agent of considerable material and intellectual progress.

Yet no Betan state was really comparable to any Terrestrial one. The heads were invariably female—a monarch might be proclaimed divine—and kept male combativeness curbed. Family structure preserved their subjects from being mobilized into machine-like armies or atomized into anomie. Furthermore, given access to the sea, any healthy person could live by old-fashioned marine hunting, and so swim away from oppression. Accordingly, most nations were either quietist and tradition-bound, or active but rational. Their imperialistic ventures were usually for well-defined objectives, and ceased when these had been attained.

On the whole, then, Betan history, with its ups and downs,

was less harrowing than Terrestrial. On the other hand, private violence between males was commoner.

At last came a scientific-industrial revolution. It brought its hazards and disasters, but never passed as near the abyss as did Earth's, in large part because it took place quite gradually in these conservative, female-dominated civilizations with their strong environmentalistic ethics. In the long run, though, it changed the character of Betan life more thoroughly than Earth's changed the human condition.

This came about through biological science, which had been favored above physics. Researchers learned how to synthesize the key hormone in enin.

Upheaval did not come overnight. Countervailing forces were custom, habit, religion, law; emotions, including those associated with tapping; recurrent sexuality; desire for progeny. Nonetheless, now males could live apart from females for as long as they chose, and stay hale.

Young individuals started postponing marriage and seeking mates who would be more than pragmatically suitable. For the first time, Beta saw an analogue of romantic love. Meanwhile the mystique surrounding the female in the male mind (and often in her own) began to dissipate.

Some males turned celibate in order to explore—explore Beta and the neighbor planets, science, philosophy, achievement. Monastic orders were founded. Extreme idealism engendered fanaticism, with all that that entailed. A larger number of males simply realized they were free to go as far as they wished into areas like engineering, for which the matriarchs had had sharply limited enthusiasm. A high-energy industry came into being and proliferated.

By no means did the revolution take place in a single convulsion. Thoughtful individuals of both sexes worked to contain it. One result was world government. Another was space travel. Since much of the ancient reverence for life, embodied in the female, remained, it came natural to direct the new technology outward, where it could not harm the mother planet but would, rather, bring in new resources.

Free enterprise, in a human sense, had never existed here. As if to compensate, war and similar follies had always, by human standards, occurred on an incredibly small scale. The world state had ample reserves for a space program.

Soon Betans discovered the T machine orbiting Centrum,

exactly opposite their planet. In the next ten centuries, with vast effort and patience, they found guidepaths through a hundred separate star gates; they colonized half a dozen uninhabited globes; they met a score of other intelligent races, learned from them, and thereby enriched beyond measure their own civilization.

But at the same time, the foundations of that civilization were being eroded away, ever faster. The biological revolution went far more slowly than anything that important would have gone through mankind; still, it went, inexorably. While males, having overcome their physical dependence on females, were generation by generation losing their spiritual dependence as well, chemistry made controllable the reproductive cycle. A female could be in heat or not as she chose, whenever she chose.

The psychological effects of this were at once liberating and devastating. The primordial harmony with sun and stars was no more—or was, at most, a matter of conscious decision. If she entered a hitherto masculine field like spacefaring, she had to settle not just her working relationships, but the question of her identity, who and what she truly was. She never quite succeeded. Confusion and embitterment spread, also to those who stayed home. Too often sexuality became a weapon.

Prophets, philosophers, and common folk alike sought after a viable, satisfying new ideal. The example of alien sentiences, the knowledge that the Others existed, made their quests doubly intense, their disappointments doubly agonizing.

When *Emissary* arrived, the psychosexual dilemma had brought Beta to a crisis. Restlessness, eccentricity, mental illness, crime, tumult were steeply on the rise. No matter how busy, prosperous, interested in what they were doing, few of the more fortunate were altogether happy, and in many the sadness underlay their whole beings.

Some actually urged using time travel to abort the entire development of science; but if nothing else, this was impossible because no path was known which would fetch a ship out at Centrum very far in the past, nor did it seem likely that any could be found. Proposals heard much more often, that the race go "back to nature" by an act of will, were equally quixotic. Without modern technology, nearly the whole population, belike the whole species, must die; and that technology could only be run by the sexually emancipated. There was nowhere to go but forward . . . in what direction, though?

Then *Emissary* arrived.

As communication improved, year by year, excitement waxed among the more discerning Betans. What had been an intriguing academic project took on a gigantic significance. These bipeds were not simply a new type of sophonts. They were by birthright what the Betans were struggling to become.

Their sexual pattern occurred in several breeds elsewhere, but there too many differences existed as well, too profound, affecting too much the forms that it took. (For instance, one race, winged, was perpetually migratory, around and around its world. None of its institutions, mores, attitudes, beliefs were adaptable to surface dwellers.) Humans, despite every divergence, had a basic likeness to their hosts. Proof lay in the affinities which developed between individuals of the two kinds.

From scientific study, from literature, from friendship, Betans could hope to learn what it meant to be *that* kind of male and female, and how to be it. This would not happen in a single generation or a single century; what insight was gained might take a thousand years to transform civilization; the end result would surely be no copy, but uniquely Betan. Yet here could well be an approach to understanding. The lodestar for which so many had searched for so long, blind in their pain, could well be Sol.

Fidelio had begged it of Joelle: "Teach us your ways of love."

Neither she nor Christine paid close heed to the weather. Sunset gales were sometimes dangerous, but Centrum was Earth-days above the horizon. Besides, those winds came out of the west. Rain this early was unusual but welcome, lifting the heat. If any fell, afterward their clothes and footgear would quickly dry. They walked on bearing their private storms.

But at last Chris drew the older woman to her, for else the air would have ripped the words from her mouth: "I say, don't you think we'd better head back?"

Joelle looked around. The sky was inky. Lightning forked, thunder banged. Gray rags of cloud flew beneath. Spindrift blew stinging off a sea that reared, trampled, crashed, exploding its darkness into white foambursts, grinding the shingle together with a noise as of mighty millstones. She could not see far, but to the end of sight, bushes moved in brown, gold, red waves; trees were flailing; torn-off leaves and fronds whipped past, away into murk. The wind roared and yelled. It closed around her and thrust like a chill, turbulent billow, like the solar tidal bore that had drowned Alexander Vlantis. And still it strengthened.

"Yes," she called. "Shelter in the car. Not try to lift before this is over."

They turned about. Now the rain smote, first in spears, then in axes, then in a hammer whose single stroke went on and on forever. It torrented over the hard-baked soil, clutching at feet, until that began to dissolve in mud. The women slipped, fell, crawled half erect, clung to each other for help, and staggered on. The tempest filled Joelle's skull with blast, shriek, yowl. Thunder shook her bones.

This is impossible! a walled-off part of her cried. *In eight Terrestrial years, twenty-five Betan, we've met nothing of this kind... before evening... never!*

The holothete within her responded passionlessly: *What are twenty-five years in the duration of a world? Given sufficient time, anything that can happen will happen. Probably a massive cold front, sliding down from the arctic on a freakish path, has driven the terminator storms ahead of it. You should have checked a meterorological report before you left. But do not feel guilty. Only when you are in rapport with your machine can you think of everything.*

The wind rose and rose. Lightning turned the rain to mercury, then lightlessness boomed down anew. Now the hail came. Stones bounced across the land and whitened it. They hit flesh, bruised, drew blood which instantly washed away. There was no breasting that barrage. The humans turned and groped west, backs to it, seeking for a lee.

A shadow loomed ahead, a tree to huddle behind. They lurched around it, blinded, deafened, embraced.

A whip-thin branch flayed open Joelle's scalp. She fell to her hands and knees, down in the mud and tumbling water. A flash showed her the limb wrapped around Christine's neck.

It let go, it let her fall too. Quadruped, Joelle crept to her. Scarlet welled from Christine's mouth. She reached upward, into the hail. Joelle crouched, trying to be a roof. Christine's hands dropped, her eyes rolled back, lightning glimmered off their blankness. Joelle put lips to lips.

No use. A fractured larynx is swiftly fatal.

Joelle knelt under the tree with Christine's body in her arms.

XII

AT THE PROPER MOMENT in her orbit around Demeter, *Chinook*'s main engine awoke. For a few seconds, her electromagnetic shield against cosmic radiation was switched off. It came on again, rapidly building up a high positive potential on the hull, as soon as the plasma jet had reached dynamic equilibrium. At a standard one gravity of acceleration, which was about her upper limit when reaction mass tanks were full, the spaceship spiraled free and lined out for the T machine. Since it was at the L4 point, in the same path around Phoebus as the planet but sixty degrees ahead, the journey—with turnover at midpoint followed by braking—would theoretically take seventy-three hours, in practice a little more.

When everything was in order, Brodersen ordered all systems left on automatic and all hands to the common room. On his way there from the command center (which his mind, remembering cruises along Juan de Fuca and northward through the stern glories of the Inside Passage, still called the bridge) he felt Earth weight drag at him, a fourth more than what Demeter gave. He made sufficient interplanetary trips annually that he knew he'd adjust to this before long, together with watches set according to the Terrestrial day; but every time, his body was a smidgin slower about it. Passing down a companionway and a circular corridor, a yielding green carpet underfoot but otherwise bare gray and white paint, he wondered if he might not be thinking of himself as starting to get old, were it not for Caitlín.

Apart from furniture and recreation equipment, the common room was equally bleak. On notice as short as he'd given, nobody could have brought decorations or done anything else to add a touch of cheer. Yet when he saw her, the chamber came radiant.

From her backpack she had taken a brief crocus-colored dress. It set her like a sun against the large viewscreen before which she stood enraptured. Demeter filled a quarter of that scene, dayside cobalt blue shading into turquoise and sapphire, swirled with virginal white that here and there gave ocher glimpses of land, nightside a phantom of moonglow. The brilliance dazzled stars out of vision until you looked away, toward the frame, and let your eyes make ready to receive their myriads. "Glory, glory," he heard her croon, "and how could you not be a mother of life?"

"Easily," he couldn't help saying.

She jumped around, laughed for joy, and barefoot sped toward him. The added load on her seemed unfelt. *Well, she does abolish gravity*, flitted through him before the beloved mass collided and clung. She smelled of very recent soap and scrubbing, but also of herself, and an odor of sunshine lingered in the loose hair. Breasts strained against the barrel of his chest. The kiss went on.

"Whoa, whoa, horsey," he muttered when they came up for air. "The others'll be here in a clockblink."

"The Others?" She had such range of tone, with her grin to see as well, that he heard the capital letter. "Is it peeping Toms they are? Maybe they'll learn somewhat. Maybe we can trade technical information."

"You know I mean the crew, you spinhead." He disengaged. "Things'll be complicated aplenty without them finding their aged and supposed-to-be-revered captain in your clutches."

"Should they find him in someone else's clutches? You cannot suppose they'll take me for your maiden aunt. I disqualify on two counts at least."

His gladness flickered out. "And that'll bring on worse than envy, I'm afraid. Especially— Later, I'll explain later. But look, Pegeen, macushla, I realize this is a grand adventure to you. Except it's not. It's an ugly business. It's too goddamn likely to turn into the kind that gets remembered as ,'More fun, and more people getting killed—'" Fist smote palm. "You could be among 'em, oh, Christ, you could."

Sobered, she answered low, "Or you. Aye. If you want me to bounce less, I'll try my best, for you." Impulse returned, to send her fingers along his head and the blocky line of his jaw, caressing the slight bristliness. "But faith, Daniel, pessimism fits you badly, the fighter born that you are."

"I'm a realist, or trying to be. You live in a universe that's good and cheerful, same as yourself. I love you for that. You brighten mine up for me no end. Reality, though, reality doesn't give beans for our notions." Brodersen felt his ears warming, heard his words stumbling. He needed a way to phase out his sermon, and snatched at what seemed handiest. "Let me give you a for-instance. When I came in, I caught you claiming Demeter has to be...uh...viviferous because it's beautiful. That don't follow. Every planet I've seen is beautiful in its style, and nearly every one is dead and always has been. You make life out to matter more than it does."

She bridled a trifle. "Are you thinking I've not dealt with pain and death, and me a paramedic? Nor ever sat contemplating a fossil and—" She broke off. A crewman came through the door.

The rest were close behind. Brodersen shook hands, introduced Caitlín to those who had not met her earlier, exchanged "How've you been?" with each, urged beer or soft drinks from the cooler upon them, and at length got them seated in a row before him, his girl demure at its end. He hitched himself up onto the pool table, swung his legs, unlimbered pipe and tobacco.

"Okay," he began in English, which his followers used as a mutual tongue oftener than Spanish. "First off, let me say I can't figure how to thank you, and better not try. We shouldn't be too hard on those who didn't elect to come along. There probably aren't any absolute rights or wrongs in this affair. A person has to choose; and could be, when the chips come down, we here'ull wish we'd chosen different. I think not. But regardless of what happens, may I sing high soprano in the Grand Khan's harem if ever I forget your loyalty today."

Not simple loyalty, he thought. *They're too smart and free to be any man's dogs. I'd not've signed them on if they weren't what they are. Only, what are they? Do they themselves know? Risking your neck against hostile stars is not the same thing as risking your honor against duly constituted public authorities. Nine out of fourteen refused. I don't suppose among these five I'd find two identical motivations. Can I guess what the drives are? I can't flat-out ask. No telling what that might provoke. However, the information is almighty important, ¿no es verdad, old son?* His gaze raked them.

Stefan Dozsa, mate and electronics officer. Cocky as usual.

Philip Weisenberg, engineer. Calmly watchful.

Martti Leino, assistant engineer. Glowering from Caitlin to Brodersen and back again.

Susanne Granville, computerman. Intent, hunched forward in her chair, look never leaving the captain.

Sergei Nikolayevitch Zarubayev, gunner and principal boat pilot. His usual sober mien had lightened when Caitlin gave him an energetic hello kiss; they happened to be friends of old.

Stop dithering. Bend on the spinnaker!

"My wife's explained to you what kind of a chowder kettle we're in," Brodersen proceeded, "but under the circumstances—written communication and fake chatter, right?—probably she couldn't go into much detail. I'll quack on about the subject as long and as tee-jusly as you want, the bunch of you today or individually later on. For now, though, let me just summarize."

He ticked points off on thick fingers. "The robot observer at the gate, that you know about, reported what I swear has got to've been *Emissary* coming back. She was escorted on to the Solar System—where else?—and hasn't been heard from since. A couple of you who chanced to be around heard me grumble out my suspicions. Afterward some elementary research pretty well confirmed them. When I braced the governor, she fed me a steaming dish of moose turds, raisined with hints about awful things rampaging through the galaxy, and ended by slapping a house arrest on me and a gag rule on Lis. Well, I snuck out, and here we are.

"This is not exactly what you had in mind, when you volunteered to train for *Chinook* and then stand by in your regular jobs for me, hoping you'd get a crack at going to the stars. My compliments to your brains. You've seen the route we've got to go beforehand, and that if we don't, nobody will.

"I suppose Lis made clear to you what I suspect. This isn't the Union government as a whole acting, it's a faction within. Simple publicity should blow the conspirators out of the sky, if we don't allow 'em time to armorplate their arrangements.

"I aim to go to Earth and contact various people I know, mainly the Rueda tribe. That'll be under wraps, to avoid touching off possible alarms. Meanwhile you can take it easy aboard ship; officially you're nothing but a crew ferrying *Chinook* to her charterers. And maybe that'll be the whole game, far's we're concerned. Maybe my contact can take it from there. I'd sure like that.

"If not, though—well, my wife warned you, didn't she? I've

no notion of what'll happen. I'll play the cards as they fall, and if I make a bad bet, you go broke too." He jabbed the stem of his pipe toward them before filling the bowl. "I dunno if laws are left on the books about piracy. We could be forced to that.

"Listen, if this is more than you bargained for, do me a last favor and tell me, will you? I'll give you a formal discharge, I'll enter in the log that you protested, I'll keep you under the very mildest restriction, and I'll let you off at the first place safe for everybody concerned. Okay? Speak."

He tamped down tobacco and got it lit while he waited. Silence stretched.

"I didn't figure you would," he said in due course. "The offer stays open while we travel peaceful. Once action commences, if any does, that'll be too late to resign. Understood?"

Will I shoot whoever gives way under fire . . . out of these, my friends? Yes, I'd have to, and invoke space law at my trial, unless it turned out this whole safari sprang from a terrible mistake of mine. In that case, I'd rate the treatment my fathers handed out to bandits.

Ventilation whirred. The smoke gave his tongue a soothing love-bite. "End of speech," he finished. "Questions? Comments? Catcalls?"

"Yes." Martti Leino leaned forward, a motion that splashed beer from the mug he gripped. Harshly: "What is . . . Miz Mulryan doing aboard?"

Expected. Brodersen studied him before replying. Lis' youngest brother did not resemble her, showing more of the Ladogan side of their descent: short, broad, snubnosed, a slightly Asian outline to his face, with sleek black hair and tilted blue eyes. His normal cheerfulness was quite gone.

"She hid me after I'd escaped," Brodersen said. "Without her, I'd've had to stay someplace inhabited, and might've been recognized. Mainly, she's to be our medical officer."

"Her?" It was an open sneer.

"She's on the staff of St. Enoch's—well qualified to treat anything that might hit us, like injuries. Also, she'll double as quartermaster." Brodersen nodded. "Oh, she'll have her work cut out for her."

Leino glared at Caitlín, who sat hands crossed in lap and gave him a small, conciliatory smile. "Yes, you'll find plenty for her to do, won't you?" he snapped.

"Hey, easy," Weisenberg advised him.

Brodersen straightened and put the soldier-aristocrat's whipcrack into his words: "That will be enough, Mr. Leino. If you have a complaint against a person, including the captain, enter it formally. Otherwise accord your shipmate the respect she's entitled to."

The young man bent back in his chair as if slugged in the stomach. *I came down on him pretty hard, didn't I?* Brodersen realized. *Even if I did get mad on Pegeen's account, I shouldn't've.*

"Easy, easy," Weisenberg repeated. "No harsh words from anybody, please. We can't afford them. Miz Mulryan, you are welcome among us." Furrows sprang forth around his smile. "I wasn't looking forward to taking a share of the quartermaster's job."

"I thank you kindly, sir," she breathed, and let her glance rest on him a seconds more, aglow. He was medium tall, gaunt, craggy-featured, his Adam's apple large, his eyes small and brown under tufted brows. By habit, he wore a Scotch bonnet on his close-cropped white hair, maintaining to those who inquired that he did hold the rating of ship's chief engineer.

I thank you too, Phil, the captain tried to project. It was probably unnecessary. The Weisenbergs and Brodersens were old friends.

Susanne Granville patted Caitlin's shoulder. "Yes, welcome," she said in her French-accented English. "You will understand, spacemen 'ave a 'orror of untrained personnel—true, Martti? But these duties, I am sure you can learn to 'andle them. If I can 'elp, tell me, I pray you."

That's damn good of Su, when she's so homely and Pegeen's so gorgeous, passed through Brodersen. He checked himself. *What the hell am I thinking? Su's good people, that's all.*

Zarubayev raised his hand. The gunner was a big man, strongly built in a rawboned fashion; shoulder-length blond hair and a beard, both unfashionable on Demeter except in his Novy Mir home region, surrounded a Tolstoy countenance. "What about combat drill?" he demanded.

"Huh?" Brodersen grunted.

"You have said we should be prepared to fight if we go to the stars. 'Just in case' was what you said. Therefore we have built-in weapons like *Emissary*'s plus a stock of small arms. Now you speak of a possible clash. Piracy was what you said."

"Wait a minute," protested Stefan Dozsa.

"No, let him go on," Brodersen told the mate.

"Skipper," Dozsa replied in his own accent, "I did not object to the idea, simply to the language. I learned as a boy, government is the natural enemy of the people. If we accept its semantics, we have lost half the battle. We are not pirates, we are liberators."

Caitlín stirred. Alarm tinged her voice: "It's fanaticism you are talking, sir. My country remembers too well, too well."

Dozsa laughed. He was a stocky dark man with almond eyes in a wide and rather flat face. "Call us private police, then. Or evangelists. Or lunatics; that is most likely the best. But not pirates. Pirates hope to make money."

"Speak your piece, Sergei," Brodersen urged.

"I think we should have instruction and practice with small arms," Zarubayev stated. "Doubtless everybody aboard can shoot, but only you and I, Captain, have served in the Peace Command and know techniques of combat—space combat, too. We can instruct. There will be days to the T machine ahead, days more from the Solar gate to Earth, and who can tell how much beyond? Time to drill in a few basics, a little doctrine."

"Well . . . um-m-m—" Brodersen shifted his haunches around on the pool table. "We are not looking for trouble."

"Some training can do no harm," Dozsa said. "On this trip, most of us will not have much occupation. I would be happy for a thing to help fill my offwatches. What of the rest of you?" He cast a look toward Leino, who sat frozen. "Perhaps it helps unify us better?"

Discussion broke loose. After agreement to the proposal and details thereof, more matters arose. Two hours had passed when Brodersen dismissed the crew. Those not on duty could have stayed in the common room, but none did. On his way out, Weisenberg murmured, "I'll see what I can do about Martti, Dan, but it's really up to you; right?"

"Whoof!" said Brodersen when he and Caitlín were alone.

She took both his hands. "Poor dear. Sure, and it's no sport being a captain, is it, now?"

He lifted a corner of his mouth. "You'll find it's not exactly hilarious being quartermaster either, sweetheart. The job's more than cook and steward, though that's aplenty. You issue, you keep inventory, you see that stowage preserves the trim of the ship. . . . I'd better begin teaching you right away."

She slipped close. "Is the hurry that absolute?" she hinted.

"I'm afraid it is," he answered.

She sighed. "Ah, well. Later." Gesturing at the nearest viewscreen: "Out yonder is always a later, while we live, is that not so, my heart?" He made no reply, being too caught in the sight of her against those stars.

XIII

I WAS A GREAT proud salmon, but had no words for greatness or pride; I was them. My flanks were the blue of steel, my belly the white of silver, but all that I knew of metal was a hook that I had bitten upon and then torn my flesh free of. I was one with the water, and had always been. In my hatchling days it rippled and whispered about me as I huddled in gravel while the shadow of a pike slid across yellow shards of sunlight. Later it flowed, bubbled, caressed, enfolded, as I thrust myself downstream toward the sea. When it grew salt, it stung to life a knowledge which I had had in the egg, and I leaped in my joy, upward through a cataract of brightness where the air laid a sharp edge across my gills. Then for years outside of time I prowled the sea, chased, overtook, sank teeth into struggling sweetness, and exulted.

But at last there came drifting a fragrance which yearned, and I swung mightily homeward.

We were many, we were many, breasting a river that roared against us while coming alive with the gleam of our bodies. We were prey now ourselves, we died and died, but surely each death was in the same jubilation as the living had. I won through. The life within me clamored.

Beneath the peace of an upland pool, I scooped with my tail, in the gravel that once had sheltered me, a place for my own young. I did not understand that that was what they would be—I would have eaten any that I encountered—but still, then I loved them. And now he sought me, he. It was the farthest upstream moment of my being.

Before long I was ready to die. Then the Summoner came and took me into Oneness. I was Fish.

XIV

DEMETER DWINDLED swiftly in view, from a world to a globe to a small blue sickle to a point of brightness among countless more. Folk settled into their round of duties. Those were mainly just standing watch on the *qui vive*, when *Chinook* ran on full automatic like this, except in the case of the quartermaster. While she happily busied herself in the galley, preparing the first meal of the trip that wouldn't merely be taken from storage for heating, Brodersen sat in the captain's quarters with nothing to do but be accessible.

The inner, private cabin was of comfortable size and furnishing: double bed folded up to give ample deck space, chairs, closet, dresser, cabinet, shelves, table, data and communication terminals, sink, hotplate, miniature refrigerator, screens for both exterior and interior scans. Faintly murmuring, ventilators kept the air in motion, fresh despite his pipe; at the present stage of its temperature-ionization cycle, it had an evening flavor. The pale gray, blue-trimmed bulkheads were bare of pictures, the shelves of books, the whole room of almost anything personal, since there had been no chance to bring more along than he and Caitlín carried on their backs. Nevertheless it could come alive whenever they willed, for a goodly percentage of the entire culture of mankind was in the ship's memory bank.

Brodersen knew he ought to catch a nap, and a proper nightwatch of sleep after dinner. He'd been long in action. Overstrung, he was unable to. Tobacco alone didn't allay that, and in space he was very sparing of alcohol and marijuana. He decided to renew old acquaintances. Pressing the levers on his chair arms, he emptied the suction cups which held it in place against acceleration changes, and shifted it over in front of the terminals, where his weight re-anchored the legs. Having punched for a display of reference code and studied that a moment, he started Beethoven's Fifth on the audio retrieve and Hokusai's "Thirty-Six Views of Fuji" on the visual at intervals he would manually control, and settled back. *Maybe later some Monet, or even some van Gogh*, he thought, *or maybe no pictures but...m-m-m-...a little Kipling? Haven't read* Soldiers Three *for years*.

This was about as esoteric as his taste in the arts got. He considered himself basically a meat and potatoes man, though not one who scorned fine food—such as Caitlín and Lis, like most sexy women, could well prepare—or other high subtleties. His parents had seen to his getting a solid education, but his mind stayed quite pragmatic until he joined the Peace Command. Then the wish took him to make sense out of what he experienced, around Earth and on beyond. This led him to read rather widely in history, anthropology, and related disciplines, which in turn raised his awareness of the great creators. His first wife had encouraged that interest in him, his second was still doing so.

"I'm not an intellectual," he sometimes remarked. "I prefer thinkers." Yet he had endowed a chair of humanities at the Universtiy of Eopolis. The species needed to preserve, to understand and cherish its own heritage...in the face of the Others, of the whole cosmos.

He was beginning to feel neck and shoulder muscles relax when the door chimed. *Damn! Hell! Also curses.* The captain is never off call. He heaved his mass up, over the deck, into the outer cabin. It was small, strictly an office except for elaborate electronic links to the command center. Seated behind the desk, he punched the admit button. The door retracted, giving him a glimpse of the corridor that ringed this level where people dwelt.

Martti Leino stalked through and, as if remembering a planned procedure, snapped to a civilian kind of attention. "Requesting a private interview, sir," he clipped forth.

Oh, oh. Well, I knew this'd come. "Sure," Brodersen said, and closed the door. "Only since when has crew of mine needed to get fancy with me, let alone my own brother-in-law?" He waved. "Pick a chair. Any chair."

The young man (thirty-seven, Demetrian) obeyed jerkily. Red and white pursued each other across his countenance. His breath was ragged. "You look like the prophet Nahum with a hangover," Brodersen observed. "Slack off. Since you don't smoke, care for a drink?"

"No."

"What's wrong?"

"You know what." The visage before him staying quietly watchful, Leino forced out: "Your, your female!"

He's not out of control, not quite, Brodersen realized. *Good. I'd hate for him to call her something that left me no choice.*

He drank pungency from his pipe while he chose words. His voice he kept soft. "Do you refer to Miz Mulryan? For your information, she's nobody's female but her own. If you think different, just try pushing her in any direction she hasn't already picked to go."

"She's . . . openly . . . moved *in* with you!"

"Whose business is that but ours?"

"Lis', you bastard!" Leino shouted. He half rose, fists doubled, sank back, and snapped his jaws together.

"Of course. When I said, 'Ours,' I meant 'ours.' She knows, and doesn't mind."

"Or is she too proud and loyal to say out what she feels? I've known her longer and better than you have, Daniel Brodersen."

Longer, aye, the captain thought. *Better? Could be, too.* Though the family on the farm under Trollberg was large, seven children, Lis the first, Martti the fifth: still, an enormous surrounding wilderness, shared work and pleasure and discovery and sometimes danger, had knit it close. For whatever deep-lying reasons, the bond between those two was always especially strong. When he came to Eopolis to study nuclear engineering, she was newly divorced and they shared an apartment. She went to work for Chehalis, made herself more and more valuable as well as attractive to its chief . . . and amicably refused his propositions, which was fairly unusual, until at last he married her. Because she wanted it, this brother was best man at the modest wedding.

"Let me remind you, I've been her husband nigh on ten years," Brodersen said, mildly yet. "Don't you imagine that'd give me a few understandings of her you don't have?"

"Ten years—seven, Earth—is there not a saying on Earth about the seven-year itch?" Leino's grin was of the challenge kind.

"Do you imply some casual pickup—?" Brodersen checked his anger. The sardonic confession stirred within him that he had had several. No need to make it aloud. He leaned forward, arms on desk, pipe in right hand with the stem aimed at his visitor and wagged a little.

"Martti," he said, "listen. Listen close. You've evidently not encountered the fact it's possible to love more than one person at a time. I'd lay odds you will; but no matter now. What matters between us two is this. Your sister approves of the relationship. She and Caitlín Mulryan are dear friends." *I exaggerate a bit, but surely only because the three of us haven't so far gotten together often enough. Surely they are good friends, and better will follow.* "If you won't take my word, I give you leave to inquire of her after we return. Okay?"

Leino swallowed. "No. She'd bravely lie—" he fell into his home dialect—"for toward you whom she gave her oath; for to hide her wounds from me."

Brodersen locked eyes with him. "You've known me somewhat yourself. Do you seriously think I'm the sort of guy who could deliberately hurt his wife?"

Leino bit his lip. *He tries to be fair-minded*, Brodersen thought. *He's harking back.*

Upon graduation, Leino too had become a Chehalis employee. If anything, that was nepotism in reverse, trained professionals being in chronic short supply on Demeter. The sole possible favoritism Brodersen had shown in return was to assign him to a few projects in space—exploration, prospecting, establishment of mining bases on an asteroid and a comet—on which he, Brodersen, went along. He wouldn't have done it if Leino weren't competent. Humans get pretty closely acquainted under such conditions.

The captain pursued his advantage: "Neither Lis nor I feel this is any unfaith. Use your imagination. There are a million different unfaiths one monogamous spouse could practice on another, and too many of 'em do. Petty cruelty. Neglect. Shirking your share of the load. Simple, correctible, annoying slobbishness, year after year. Dishonesty, in some mighty basic ways. On and on. You're right, your sister would not sit still for betrayal—real betrayal.

"So calm down. You've had a surprise, nothing worse. You'll get over it."

"The humiliation," broke from Leino. "Publicly parading your mistress."

Brodersen's pipe was going out. He sat back, puffed the fire awake, formed a chuckle. "In this day and age? Why, I'll agree Lis and I are exceptional. We do our best to keep our private affairs private."

"Your affairs?" Leino flared. "How'd you like it if she did the same to you?"

Brodersen shrugged. "She's a free adult. I don't expect she'll ever betray me either. Anyhow, Caitlin's aboard on account of an emergency—we might not be under weigh without her help—and none of us, them or me, none of us is much good at being a hypocrite."

That, he thought, *as far as regards myself, may be my own biggest piece of hypocrisy to date. Well, a totally sincere man is a monster.*

The reflection was fleeting. It ended when Leino leaped to his feet, hands clenched on high, face contorted, and yelled, "Mean you, you swine, you'd corrupt Lis too? I give not a shit what comes of you, but before God Who shaped her, you'll keep fingers off her soul!"

Instinct made Brodersen answer, "Silence!" at an exact loudness. "Be seated. That's an order."

Spacefarers learn early that a shipful of lives can depend on instant obedience. Leino folded. Save for the ventilator and his gasps, the office emptied of sound for a time which Brodersen measured, until he said evenly:

"Martti, brother of Lis, hear me. You spoke of her pride. You admire her intelligence as well. Then what in the universe makes you assume she could be corrupted? She's simply chosen to fare a little different way from what you'd have her take.

"If you worry about her faith and morals, why didn't you object when she divorced her first husband? She pledged him on a Bible, remember; he's from the Holy Western Republic."

Leino stared open-mouthed.

"Because you knew that in spite of his impressive brain, he's an overbearing, inconsiderate, narrow-minded son of a bitch," Brodersen went on. "If she ever decides I'm as bad, she'll ditch me too, and you'll cheer, won't you? I aim to make sure she never does decide it. However, what's divorce and remarriage except polygamy in time instead of space?"

He let his question sink in before he continued:

"Don't get me wrong. I respect your principles. Where you come from, they work. Tried and true traditions; the family above self; the house presenting a solid front to the world—shucks, that's what I grew up with too. I'm not saying it's mistaken, either. For all I know, it's the absolute truth. I'm only saying it's not the only idea people can live by, or do. And you, Martti—not patronizing, merely stating a fact—you've not been much exposed to alternatives. You came to Eopolis, that calls itself cosmopolitan, straight from the backwoods. Well, Eopolis isn't cosmopolitan. It's a clutch of hick towns, alien to each other, huddled in the same few square kilometers. You've never seen Earth. Lis has. Besides, you've worked hard the whole time, often in space, which has limited your human contacts still more. Repeat: I'm not saying you should change your philosophy. I am saying you haven't had a proper chance to learn tolerance—real tolerance, down where it counts, about things close to people you care for. Try that, my friend."

"God's law—" Leino whispered.

Brodersen, who had been an agnostic since puberty, shrugged anew. "Never mind about God. Let's settle with the Others first." He returned to the attack. "Not prying at you, I seldom noticed you missing your sleep to make divine service after a late poker game or whatever. And I have heard you brag a bit about what you've done among the ladies, and seen you squiring around one or two who've got reputations. Not to mention those seasonal bacchanals in your home country."

Leino flushed. "I'm still a bachelor."

"And of course you figure you'll marry a virgin. And it won't harm her afterward if you step out occasionally, as long as you're discreet." Brodersen laughed aloud. "Martti, I've been in the Uplands a fair amount. I've told you they remind me of home. Let's not play peek-a-boo, huh?"

—The words went back and forth for half an hour. Leino's quieted as they did.

In the end, Brodersen summarized: "Okay, you don't approve, and I didn't expect you would on such short notice, but you agree our mission's too important to hazard for the sake of a personal brannigan, and Caitlín's important to it. Correct?"

Leino gulped—he had come close to tears—and nodded.

"Well, that's as much as she or I could reasonably ask," Brodersen said. "For your own sake, though, plus ours, I will make one small request. Strictly a request, you understand."

Leino's fingers strained together on his lap.

"If you can," Brodersen continued, "don't hold her at arms' length, stiff and formal. Remember, Lis doesn't. Be a little friendly. She'd sure like to be your friend. And I'd like for you both to be. After all, I've explained it's no overnight romp between us; I'm trying to think years ahead." He smiled. "Give her half a chance and you'll enjoy her company. For instance, you appreciate ballads. Well, she's a crackling hell of a balladeer."

"I am sure that is true," Leino said.

."Find out for yourself," Brodersen urged. "You'll have lots of time, even after we start those military drills. Ninety percent of derring-do consists of waiting around for something, anything to happen. Caitlín can liven those hours no end."

Afterward, alone, he mused around his pipe and a shot of Scotch he allowed himself: *So we make one more monkey compromise that may hang together for a short spell: in order that our undertaking—forget our daily lives—may go on. I wonder, I wonder, must the Others ever do likewise?*

XV

IF YOU KNEW precisely where to look, the T machine gleamed as the tiniest spark amidst the stars—aft, for *Chinook* had made turnover and was backing down upon it. Susanne Granville had, however, set the viewscreen in her cabin to scan Phoebus. Dimmed by the optics to mere moon brightness, so that corona and zodiacal light shone at their natural luminosities like nacre, that disc still drove most of the distant suns out of a watcher's eye.

"A last familiar sight," she explained to Caitlín. "The gate will be strange to me. I 'ave never guided a ship t'rough, except in training simulations. You see, we 'ad . . . figured? . . . yes, we 'ad figured on several re'earsals between 'ere and Sol before we started for anywhere new."

"Is it needed you are at all?" Caitlín asked. "I was taught the passage pattern is exact—no dance measure, nor even a march on parade, but like a chess piece jumping from square to square—and any autopilot can conn a vessel the way of it."

"That is true nearly always, and in fact the autopilot does. But the permissible variation is small. Exceed the tolerance, and we will enter another gate. Where we go then, God only can tell, and I do not believe in God. Quite possibly we reach some point in interstellar space, no machine on 'and, vacuum around us until we die. Certainly no probe from Sol ever came back." Susanne shivered the least bit. "It is a wise rule that a linker must be in circuit during transit, ready to take over wiz flexibility and judgment if anything unforseen 'appens. . . . The tea is ready. What would you like in it?"

"Milk, if you please. No, I'm forgetting, we've none fresh. Plain the same as you, and my thanks." Caitlín let her hostess pour and serve, out of ship's ware. Her own green gaze wandered.

She found little but the grandeur in the screen. Like everybody else, Susanne had embarked in haste. Aside from the office attached to the captain's, quarters differed merely in their color schemes, this room being rose and white. Otherwise nothing save the aroma from pot and cups distinguished it.

Double occupancy would have lent an extra touch, and it had been laid out with that capability in mind; but the computerman seemed likely to stay solitaire. Short, skinny, stoop-shouldered, long-armed, with slightly froglike features from which thin black hair was pulled back into a pony tail, she looked older than her twenty-eight Earth years. A high voice and a dowdy kimono didn't help. One tended to concentrate on her eyes, which were beautiful: large, thick-lashed, lustrous brown.

"I would 'ave brought a better tea if I 'ad the chance," she apologized. "What you make for our table from the standard rations, I am cook enough myself to appreciate. Per'aps when I 'ave leisure you could use 'elp from me?"

"Och, doing for this few is no job," Caitlín said. "Though if it's the recreation you're wishing, why, it's glad I'd be of your companionship."

"I t'ought we should get acquainted," Susanne proposed timidly. She took a chair facing her guest's. "This trip may become long or dangerous."

"Or both. And we the two women aboard. Besides, you can tell me about the rest of our crew. Devil a chance I've had to know any man besides Sergei Zarubayev better than to greet or else ply him with technical questions. Dan's kept me too busy at learning my duties."

Susanne flushed. "'E can explain people best. 'E 'as the, the knack for them. I am not ... outgoing."

"Regardless, you can give me an extra viewpoint. Furthermore, when we are free together, himself and I do not yet squander time on briefings."

Caitlín's grin faded when Susanne reddened more and sipped noisily. Reaching over, she patted her hostess' knee. "I'm sorry. Pardon my tongue. I'll try to stay as little shameless as happiness may allow me."

"You and 'e, you are in love, no?" The words were barely to be heard.

"Aye. Songbirds, roses, and hundred-year-old whisky. But fear not for his marriage. Never would I threaten that, for he loves her too, and she him, and a dear lady she is."

Susanne stared from cup to the sun and back. "'Ow did you meet?"

"Through Lis, the gods would have it. Doubtless you know she's active in the Apollo Theater, organizing, fund-raising, smoothing ruffled feathers—especially those feathers! Well, I've been on the same stage once in a while, to play a minor role or sing a few songs. Lis gave a cast party at her home.... You've not chanced to attend a performance I was in?"

Susanne shook her head. "I do not go out much."

Caitlín softened her tone. "They do say as linkers have interests more high than ordinary folk."

"No, simply different, and simply when we are in linkage. Uncoupled, we are the same as anybody else—" Susanne raised a palm and met the steady regard of the other. "Veritably, the years of 'ard training, the work *lui-même*, they 'ave an influence. It is often true what you 'ear about us, we are extreme introverts. The profession attracts that type." She attempted a chuckle. "Exceptions occur. A minority of us are normal."

"I wouldn't be calling you anything else, I think," Caitlín assured her. "Shy, maybe, the which I find a charm, brash hussy that I am. Your accent in English is pretty, too. You are from the south of France?"

"No, my parents are. I was born in Eopolis. You know *La Quincaillerie*, the big 'ardware store on Tonari Avenue? That is theirs. Well, I was the sole child, and unsociable, and all their close friends French, so—" Having by now set her cup down on the nearby table, Susanne spread her hands wide.

"Dan bespoke you as coming from Earth."

"'E 'as seen my curriculum vitae, but of course my girldom—girl'ood—why should 'e remember? My parents did send me back to study when I was ... sixteen, Terrestrial ... and tests showed me 'aving talent. Demeter 'as no facilities for making linkers. I lived with my aunt and uncle, and after I 'ad graduated worked for a firm in Bordeaux, until after six years away I got 'omesick and returned. Soon Captain Brodersen 'ired me."

Silence descended, large and clumsy. Caitlín kicked it to pieces:

"My turn, if you're interested. [The computerman nodded, anxiously eager.] Though I've less to tell than you. I was born in Baile Atha Cliath—Dublin, you'd say. My father being a prosperous physician, he could send his children to famous places on holiday, including your area, Susanne. But mostly I'd rather be tramping of the byways in Eire: a bad, rebellious colleen, I fear, who felt worse and worse put upon till at Earthside age nineteen I applied for emigration. The Irish quota was almost empty—we have half our land to fill again after the Troubles—and they snapped me right up. On Demeter I've been ever since." She sighed. "Ochone, how I long to walk the green, green country once more and kiss my parents. Despite our clashes and the hurts I gave them, their letters have been wistful."

"I am surprised you keep your *patois* this many years."

"Well, Gaelic is our main language, you know, and then too we have the way of striving to keep our identity within the Canton of the Islands, and Europe on top of that, and the World Union on top of that." Caitlín changed intonation. "I can talk Eopolis English when I want. Or British, don't y' know, or braid Scots, or daown-east Yankee, or Southe'n. . . . A ballad collector learns."

"You live in Eopolis?"

"Yes, in a riverside cabin on Anyway Bank, together with a mongrel dog, a pair of scuttlemice, a tank of rainbow moths, a horny old she-cat, and a variable number of kittens. And I work as a paramedic. When I am not adrift elsewhere. Which will be enough about me, I'm sure— You're looking at me most oddly, Susanne."

"Anyway Bank is a bad district," the linker mumbled.

Caitlín laughed. "It's a polyglot district, cheap and raffish and fun, but bad it is not if you make friends and keep your wits about you. What's left of my virtue has been worse endangered in the orderly room of St. Enoch's or fashionable homes on Anvil Hill than ever on the Bank."

"You travel about the planet, you said?"

"Aye."

"'Oo takes care of your pets when you are gone?"

"A grandfatherly ragamuffin by name of Matt Fry. How he got on a transport ship I'll never be knowing, nor anyone else. He does not tell the same story twice, and he had no special skill to justify his freight save that he's the most enchanting rascal born since Falstaff. I at least could promise to qualify in medics, for my daddy had given his girl a head start. Well, Matt is sweet and understanding with the animals, and he keeps the place clean and unburgled, and asks no more than the doss itself, plus

whatever bottles I leave behind me, none of them ever full."
Caitlín shook her head. "I wish I could give him shelter the
whole year, but we'd neither of us 'ave privacy, and then my
gentleman friends—" She halted. "Bad cess to me, I've
embarrassed you again. Can you forgive me?"

"No, no, no," Susanne stammered through her blushes. "No
offense. I did t'ink . . . you and Daniel—no, like you say, the
privacy—*allons*, we change the subject, no?"

"Best we do," Caitlín agreed soberly. "My tongue is too
loose. An Irish failing, like drink. Dan keeps after me to curb it."

"Talk and drink, I believe those are species problems, not
national." Susanne spoke fast, directing conversation away
from the personal, gaining confidence as she did. "I 'ave never
met an Irish before you, I have read some of your people's
works, and screened some of their dramas, and watched
documentaries. . . . Per'aps on this trip you can show me their
land?"

"Faith, I'd love to."

"And then I will take you t'rough Provence. More, if we get
time. But first we go to Ireland, because of your parents."

"Grand! Which do you prefer, a modern city—they tell me
Dublin is exciting these days—or historical monuments and
lone, lovely countryside? We may need to be choosing one or the
other."

"The countryside. Cities on Eart', they are too much alike.
Every countryside is unique."

"In ours it rains," Caitlín warned, "and drizzles, and rains,
and mists, and rains, and might snow a little. I've forgotten what
the season will be."

"*Cela ne fait rien.* I would still like to see. Our French
campagne, it is too civilized now, agridomains, parks,
communities, and in between a few spots they keep quaint for
the tourists."

Caitlín smiled sadly. "Hurry then to Ireland, for from what I
hear, she's fast going the same way. Glad I am that I knew her
wild, and that Demeter will stay herself while I live." She
hummed a bar or two of music.

"What was that?" Susanne asked.

"Oh, it's said to be an old lullabye. I set words of my own to it
not long ago, after my mother wrote to me from Lahinch where
she was holidaying."

"The words? Would you sing?"

"When ever did a bard refuse?" Caitlín laughed. "It's mercifully short.

> *Luring tourists to us,*
> *Luring tourists nigh,*
> *Luring tourists to us,*
> *Charging them the sky-y,*
> *Luring tourists to us,*
> *Crooning melody,*
> *To the Stone of Blarney,*
> *That's an I-irish industry.*

Thereafter the two of them grew more and more lively.

XVI

WHEN *Chinook* was approximately a million kilometers from the T machine, watchship *Bohr* established laser contact. Notification of her clearance for Sol had already been beamed here. What remained was a formality or two, and the sending ahead of a small automatic "pilot fish," which would tell the guard at the far end of the gate that a vessel was coming through and the usual safety measures were to be put into effect. Procedures were completed while *Chinook* maneuvered for approach to the first beacon she must pass.

That was not the outermost one. The path she would follow wove among seven glowing globes. It was not similar to the Phoebusward track around the Solar engine, which had ten beacons. Many minds had speculated about the reasons for those variations. The alien spacefarers had probably found some answers, Brodersen thought.

He sat by himself in the command center. The odds were overwhelming that he would be the merest passenger during transit. Cybernetic systems ought to handle everything. If they failed or looked about to fail, Su Granville at the computer, Phil Weisenberg and Martti Leino in the engine room—under her direction—would take over. Nevertheless he felt obliged to be on station, and without Pegeen to distract him, much though they both wanted to experience the hours together. Brodersen never wearied of watching. Visually, approach to a gate was less spectacular than many things in space. But he would think of what the sights meant, and try to comprehend that beings existed who had made this be, and feel his soul drown and soar in awe.

Each passage was slightly unlike the last, since beacons were always changing their configurations to match the wheelings of stars through the galaxy (and who knew what further protean

138

aspects of the universe?). The shifts were too small for senses to notice in less than decades, they were easily compensated for, and in any event, a ship had a certain amount of tolerance. If she veered off a particular course by a few kilometers, she'd still arrive where she was supposed to, albeit the exact time and position at which she appeared might not be quite what they were meant to be. Even so, space law rightly prescribed a slow tracing out of a path, with ample margin for error.

After all, a bad mistake would throw you into the unknown. Assuming that a complete transit pattern involved two or more beacons, seven of them gave you 5913 possible destinations. (Robot probes had verified that assumption, departing from here as well as from the Solar System, never to return.) In addition there were infinitely many paths which did not go straight from marker to marker, each of which would also take you somewhere. (Robot probes had verified that likewise, until the authorities decided they'd lost too many.)

Brodersen knew that a particular track would bring him to wherever the alien ship had gone—and *Emissary*, which afterward returned in order to vanish into a different kind of trap. Like the rest of the public, he had not been told which track it was. (At the time, he had agreed that secrecy was a sensible policy.) A machine must lie at the end of that gate. One of the human probes must have appeared there earlier. But if the aliens noticed it, they would have no way to tell who sent it from where.

Like most people, Brodersen took for granted that many, perhaps all of the remaining beacon-to-beacon courses likewise led to T machines. The trouble was, once you'd gone through, what was your route back? You'd blunder blind through gate after gate till your supplies ran out, unless you found an advanced society which could help you. *Emissary* had set off in that hope, but *Emissary* knew that such a civilization existed. Yet the next T machine might simply have been at a relay point in an otherwise empty place.... Sure it was that very few tracks led to races that were knowledgeable in these matters. The Phoebean System, for instance, had been devoid of sentience, let alone spacefaring civilization, until the Voice guided men there....

Hours passed.

Mostly *Chinook* fell free, and he floated loosely harnessed to his seat in the exhilarating ghostliness of zero gravity. Then when she reached the prescribed distance from a marker, gyros, softly whirring, swung her about; jets kindled; for minutes he had a slight weight; again he drifted. The silence was vast. He could have used the intercom to talk with Pegeen, but that would have been open for the whole crew to hear. Nobody else had anything to broadcast either, as visions swung majestic across the screens.

A sphere against blackness, moon-sized to the eye, shining green as Ireland until it dwindled from sight . . . the T machine at their closest approach, a foreshortened cylinder reaching over a few degrees of arc, white with a hint of pearly sheen athwart the stars, a spine-walking sense of how much mass how tightly gripped in upon itself were here a-spin how furiously . . . a sphere whose color was not in the visual spectrum . . . the Milky Way, the nebulae, the galaxies beyond our galaxy. . . .

And now heaven was altering enough for him to notice: this bright star and that bright star moving closer together or farther part, at last flitting and weaving over the dark like fireflies, as *Chinook* went ever deeper into that field which the monstrously whirling monstrous mass created. . . .

The time was long and the time was nothing until a siren called, "Stand by!" Brodersen's pulse leaped. He caught the arms of his chair. The ship turned heavily, came to rest, hung an instant. Force grabbed him. The final maneuver along any track was a sharp acceleration straight toward the machine.

He felt no jump, no warp, nothing except free fall when the jet cut off. In his viewscreens, the universe appeared momentarily to stagger. It steadied at once; the effect was an optical illusion due to persistence of vision. Everywhere around, he saw titanic serenity; a cylinder, dwindled by remoteness to a bit of thread, which was not the cylinder he had been seeing; a disc like that of Phoebus, but whiter, fiercer, which was the disc of Sol.

Chinook had passed through.

He resumed his captaincy.

"Aram Janigian, commanding watchship *Copernicus*," the face in his outercom receiver said, heavily accenting the Spanish. "Welcome, *Chinook*."

"Daniel Brodersen, commanding. Thank you," was the equally ritual response. "All's well aboard."

"Good. Your position and vectors are acceptable, no immediate correction required."

Familiar though it was, Brodersen felt impressed anew by the fact that a ship always emerged with the same velocity relative to the second T machine as she had had relative to the first at the instant she jumped. Somehow energy differences between stars were compensated for within the transport fields—unless some conservation law that man knew nothing about was in operation.

"Here is your update," Janigian said.

It went directly from computer to computer, starting with the exact local time. A readout showed Brodersen that he was within two hours of his ETA: pretty good. Solar wind conditions, notices of craft elsewhere in the System, etc., etc., followed. When that was done, Janigian delivered selected items personally. Port Helen, of the Iliadic League, was closed by a strike; a shipment of cometary water and hydrocarbons, inbound for Luna, had been granted A priority; an asteroid from interstellar space, swinging by on its hyperbolic orbit, would make close approach to Mars on 3 February; pending further notice, a sphere of one million kilometers' radius around the San Geronimo Wheel was interdicted to unauthorized persons and carriers—

Brodersen started, fetched up against his harness, and bounced back. "Huh?" he exclaimed. "How come?"

"A scientific project that doesn't want gas contamination; or so I understand," Janigian said, bored. "Why do you care? You're cleared for Earth."

"Um-m . . . I'd hoped to visit the Wheel, as long as I'm here," Brodersen lied fast. "Reviving happy memories. What is this project?"

"I don't know. I'll have the complete announcement fed into your bank if you wish. Perhaps you can arrange permission."

"Thanks. Please go on."

The briefing completed, the farewell courtesies exchanged, the vectors calculated, *Chinook* set out at one gee. She would need between four and five Terrestrial days to round Sol and reach Earth. It should be a totally routine voyage.

Brodersen tapped for a readout of the prohibition. Having glowered at it, he unsnapped himself and paced among the instrumentalities, blank surfaces, and star-crowded screens of the command center. Eventually he activated the intercom. "Captain to chief engineer," he said. "Phil, would you come up here?" A part of him imagined Caitlín's disappointment that he had said nothing to her. Later, later—to her and them all. First he needed a consultation with the top technical expert aboard, who was also his oldest friend aboard.

Weisenberg sauntered through the door. The furrows in his countenance lay easy; he rarely registered excitement. "What's what, Dan?" he asked in his drawled English. His parents, Neo-Chasidim, had moved to Demeter to escape persecution in the Holy Western Republic.

"You were listening, weren't you?" As was customary, Brodersen had put his conversation with Janigian on the intercom. "Okay, check this business on the San Geronimo Wheel and tell me what you think it smells like."

Weisenberg placed his lank frame, joint by joint, into a chair before the terminal. Silence followed. Brodersen felt sweat prickle forth on his skin and caught a whiff of it.

"Well?" he snapped at length.

Weisenberg looked at him. "It is rather noncommittal, isn't it?" he said.

"Noncommittal, hell! Who do they expect will take seriously that goose gabble about turning over a public monument, for months, to research that trivial?"

"Anybody who isn't paranoid, Dan. Foundations do underwrite odd undertakings; and the monument in question is monumentally unimportant to just about everyone alive."

Brodersen slammed fist against bulkhead, hurtfully hard. "All right, I'm paranoid! You too. The whole gang of us. For good reason. *Emissary* is being held somewhere, if she and her crew haven't already been destroyed. Doesn't the Wheel seem logical?"

Weisenberg nodded his white head. "Well, yes, if you insist, it does. No vessel would likely pass near the closed zone. If any did, she'd have no cause to turn scanners that way at full magnification, and identify a modified *Reina*-class ship orbiting close." Long fingers rubbed a long chin. "Where is the Wheel currently?"

Susanne had gone off duty, or Brodersen could have had that information straightway upon inquiring. As was, he fumbled out his demand on a keyboard. He and Weisenberg peered at the visual display which accompanied the numbers. "Yeah," he said. "Not far off inferior conjunction with Earth. Which gives it an extra recommend as a prison."

From his chair, Weisenberg considered the skipper, who

stood crouched above him. "You mean we should swing around and have a peek," he said softly.

"What else?"

"Why, we proceed to Earth as per our flight plan and alert the Ruedas as per our own plan."

"Chancy," Brodersen growled. "It'll take time for them to make an excuse to send off a boat, and go through all the preparations and paperwork. Meanwhile anything could happen. If nothing else, Aurie Hancock's going to get suspicious about me sooner or later—and I'd bet on sooner; she's a smart old bitch coyote. At present, we've got the jump. If that is where *Emissary* is, we can bring the story to Lima—pictures—why, we can make a public statement and broadcast that will kick the whole miserable conspiracy to shivereens!" He ended on a roar.

"Easy, easy," Weisenberg cautioned. "The detour will add two-three days' travel time, you realize. Suppose we see nothing. How do we explain ourselves when we reach Earth?"

"Oh, we'll write a story en route," Brodersen said impatiently. "Like, well, a freak meteoroid hit that damaged our communications so we couldn't report it, but went into free fall till we'd made repairs. Improbable as a snake on stilts, yes, I admit that. But not totally impossible, and we can fake the traces, and besides, Aventureros can persuade the board of inquiry to treat it as a trivial incident.

"Or doubtless we can dream up a better gimmick. We'll have days." Brodersen swung away from the terminal, around the deck, hands clutching wrists behind his back, footfalls banging. Whenever he passed by a viewscreen, his brow was crowned with stars. "We'll consult the rest, of course, but I'm sure they'll agree. In fact, I'm going to order an immediate change of vectors, toward the Wheel."

"No," Weisenberg said. "Wait a bit."

"Huh?" Brodersen jarred to a halt.

"Till we're far enough from the T machine that the watchship can't notice we're moving wide," the engineer explained.

Brodersen snapped his fingers. "Right you are."

"You're right too, pal. We've got to take the chance. This might be our last possible way to reach the Others." Weisenberg still sat quietly and did not raise his voice; but in his eyes appeared a light which the Baal Shem Tov would have recognized.

• • •

Rain had blown in from the sea to take Eopolis unto itself. Aurelia Hancock, Governor General of Demeter for the World Union, had opened the two windows near her desk that she might breathe the freshness. Cool damp enfolded her and graced her nostrils, together with sounds of water falling, striking, gurgling, odors of wet roses and grass and gingery thunder oak. The sight, framed in pale daphne panels, was of silver-gray that slanted out of blue-black, down onto darkened verdancies and reds. Beyond lawn and fence, cars passed shadowlike. The far side of the street faded into mystery.

Her phone yanked her from it. "Your call to Miz Leino is ready."

"Uh!" she heard herself grunt. There had been no response when she tried an hour ago. Having put the instrument on "persist," she had riffled through news compendia, fallen into reverie . . . and not even smoked, her palate reminded her. Her calves tingled, also, and her sacrum protested. *I've been in this chair too long*, she realized. *At my age, you turn to lard fast if you don't move.*

"Connect," she said, while her mind wandered on: *I've got to get more exercise. Play tennis again—regularly—I may as well admit I'll never make myself go through a lot of dull daily gymnastics alone. But who's to play with? Jim?* They used to, she and her husband. *Tennis wasn't all we played, either.* He was too far gone into the bottle these days: nothing disgraceful, charming as ever, in him it took the form of indolence, but he plain wasn't interested in a cure. *Then who?* The idea of her fat knotty-veined legs capering around the court opposite some obsequious junior official was uninviting. And be damned if she'd beg for an arrangement with any colonial woman member of the club, after the snubs she and Jim had been getting. And here came Elisabet Leino into the screen, slim, sun-tanned, happy in her house and no doubt in her bed, looking politely hostile.

"How do you do, Governor Hancock," she said, not inquired. "I'm sorry I missed you earlier. I was working in the conservatory and didn't hear the chime."

Or were you stalling me for a half-plausible hour? The tappers report that mostly you do delay answering. Aurie fastened a smile on her face. "Why the formality, Lis? We're old enemies across the card table. And in civic affairs, we've been allies."

Eyes that were slightly slanted and wholly ice-blue scorned hers. "You know why, Governor Hancock."

Aurie gathered her spine together. Fingers found a cigarette. "As you will. If I haven't made things clear by now, no use trying. May I speak to your husband?"

The Athene visage did not stir more than its lips. "No."

"What?" For an instant, it was as if the rain outside flowed upward.

"He is ill."

Attack! "Really? I don't believe a doctor has visited your place."

"Do your agents record every detail about us?"

Aurie started the cigarette and inhaled its rain-defying acridity while she assembled her retort.

"Miz Leino, if you prefer that form of address, your husband must have explained to you what the situation is. When I requested his cooperation and he declined, I had no choice but to put him under temporary restriction and you under temporary surveillance.

"Since then, certain phone conversations—yes, we are monitoring. Once the emergency is past, you have a Covenanted right to sue for damages. Meanwhile, we're monitoring. Two phone conversations indicated he was staying put as he's supposed to. It happens, though, the second of those calls came when you'd left the house and evaded the agents assigned to watch you."

She drove into the woods, parked her car, entered the bush, and lost her city-bred shadowers. Hours later, the tap recorded an exchange between Dan Brodersen and Abner Croft. Hours after that, Lis Leino returned to her car and went home.

Were both of those talks with Croft faked? Ira Quick has passed on to me a confidential memo about such a system. Leino could have had her daughter take a call; the kid needn't be aware what was happening. And my detectives have not yet managed to prove that Abner Croft exists.

Aurie thrust her intent forward. "And now, my dear," she said out of her teeth, "looking over routine documents, I've suddenly discovered that *Chinook* cleared for Sol days ago. I was never informed. The law doesn't require that I be. But *Chinook* is Dan's pet ship, and Commissioner Two Eagles is a good friend of yours. You understand, I'm sure. I must speak to Dan."

"He's ill, I told you," Lis said, abominably cool. "He needs sleep. I will not rouse him."

"Then will you admit police officers to confirm he's there?"

For the first time, Lis colored. "Absolutely not. Get your God damned warrant."

"I'll issue it myself," Aurie warned, "and if he's absent, charges may be brought against you too, Miz Leino."

Arrogance: "Proceed, Miz Hancock. I will be consulting my attorney." Blankness.

Aurie slumped. Outside, rain rushed and twilight thickened.

He's gone, she knew. *He slipped free somehow, and boarded his spaceship, and reached the Solar System.*

How to overhaul him? Or how to repair the harm?

Inform Ira.

She should set that in motion this instant; but for a span, her hand could only bring the cigarette up, to parch her inner lips, and down again. *Ira*, was going through her, *beautiful Ira Quick, you made so clear to me how our first human order of business is social justice, and how the Others and the seeking of them are—like Milton's Lucifer, did you say?—Beautiful Ira Quick, I'll do what I can for you.*

XVII

A MESSAGE rode a carrier beam up from Eopolis to a comsat, which passed it on to the big transmitter orbiting Demeter farther out. Thence it crossed interplanetary space to the T machine, near which *Bohr* received it. The first part was a name and two addresses on Earth, followed by URGENT OFFI-CIAL; the rest was in cipher. Obediently, the watchship's communications officer put the tape that had recorded it into a pilot fish, which passed through the gate to the Solar System and homed on *Copernicus*. The officer there sent it off on a tight beam to a relay station which shared the orbit of Earth and this T machine, ninety degrees from either, and which passed it to the planet. In that vicinity, a series of electronic complexities took place. Eventually—after milliseconds—a telephone chimed and lit up in both of Ira Quick's offices, Lima and Toronto. Nobody was present at night, nor had he left word where he could be reached. (As a matter of trivial fact, he was enjoying a postprandial cognac with a pretty and ambitious young statistician whose person he would enjoy later on.) Getting no response, the phones filed the message, as directed, in a special playback bank for which only he had the combination.

It happened that he was in Toronto. He had gone there upon his recent return from the Wheel, taking his family along since it seemed he would be on hand for some time. The necessity was deplorable, of seeing to the national side of his career after overmuch concentration on the international. Winter in central North America felt nastier every year, as if to refute the experts who said Earth was *slowly* heading into a new ice age. (To cope with that would require an immense government organization. Yet still infatuates of the Others would let people, effort, and resources pour forth uncontrolled to the stars!)

On the morning after his pleasant occasion, a blizzard

147

shrieked down from the tundras and blinded the city in flying white. Commitments demanded he go to his headquarters. Not even full-length hologramy with stereo sound was always a substitute for shaking the hand of a humble constituent or lunching with an important one. From the hotel he could easily have shuttled underground to the Churchill Building; but first he must seek his place in the suburbs for a change of clothes. He'd considered renting a room downtown against these frequent contingencies, but decided not to. If word ever got out, there might be jokes about it.

His wife gave him breakfast and no questions. He gave her a nice big kiss before he left. She deserved it. Alice McDonough was not only a niece of the man who reunified Canada after the Troubles, and thus a nexus of priceless political connections; she was attractive, an excellent hostess, the mother of his three sons, and devoted to him . . . or, at least, possessed of the decency to keep her outbursts private between them.

His car battled its way toward the capitol complex. Wind yelled and buffeted it, snow streamed around the canopy, cold crept in past the heater. He felt irrationally glad to enter the parking garage; the storm roused primitive terrors in him. Greeting his employees as genially as usual, he proceeded to his inner office and switched the giant viewscreen from a direct look outside to a recording of a Hawaiian beach.

Now the environment felt good: warm scene full of blue and white and surf-boom; comfortable chair; broad, solid, fully instrumented desk; carpet soft underfoot after he'd doffed his shoes; autographed pictures of celebrities, original cartoons, honorary diplomas, certificates of membership, framed letters, each a sign of esteem and affection. The work ahead of him, if less important than what he did for the Union, had its own fascination. Last night lingered piquant in awareness. "Ah-h-h," he murmured, smiled, and activated the phone playback.

A red light flashed. What the hell? He jabbed the number sequence required. The screen lit with his name and Aurelia Hancock's return address. His heart lurched. He pressed for the next frame, saw gibberish identified by a number, and brought in the appropriate decoding program. Plain English appeared.

Dear Ira,

I pray this isn't terrible news, and you get it in time to do whatever you judge best. You remember about Daniel

Brodersen, don't you? Reference: [More numbers and letters. Quick could have summoned the file of correspondence forth, but felt no need. It remained vivid in his mind how he had approved Hancock's suggestion of shutting that troublemaker up.] Well, I've discovered he's escaped and is on his way to Earth. [Details followed up to the present, the insolent silence of Elisabet Leino and the weasel of a lawyer she'd retained. It didn't seem practical to arrest her, she had too many friends, but Aurie had threatened her with the Emergency Powers Provision, the Dangerous Instrumentalities Act, and the Finalist precedent if she infringed any more.]

I checked, on pretext of surveying traffic patterns, and found *Chinook* went through the gate exactly according to her flight plan [appended]. She ought to be at or near Earth when you get this message.

I don't know for sure what Brodersen intends. Maybe he doesn't either. It's a safe bet, though, he'll try to contact his former in-laws the Ruedas and get their help.

Ira, dear Ira [she wasn't his type of woman physically, but he'd found her responsive to heavy flirtation, which had helped bind her undoubted competence firmly into his cause], I can't say how sorry I am for letting this get by me, or what I'd give to be able to make it good. I'll do anything you order me. Meanwhile I'll sit as tight as possible. I'm certain you can handle the problem, same as you can handle every other, but it makes me cry that you have the extra work and worry.

Sincerely,
Aurelia

Quick took pride in his cool, swift reaction. He intercommed for word on the ship; his staff would obtain that for him promptly and discreetly. Then he reviewed the letter and its addenda with care, sat back, stroked his beard, and considered what to do.

First, refrain from panic, from any outward fuss. Second, put full-powered surveillance on Brodersen and each member of his gang from the moment they landed, or from this hour if they had already done so. (What a damnable uncertainty! The time when a vessel emerged from a gate, as measured at that end, bore only a loose relationship to the time when she had entered it at the other end, presumably because of variations in the path she followed around the T machine. None had yet arrived ahead of her pilot fish, but some had been very close behind, and some as much as three days late.) He could commandeer the North American secret service—or, rather, several well-chosen agents thereof—through the same channels as he'd used to get cooperation about *Emissary*.

Yes, watch Brodersen and see what happened, what might be learned. But the instant any of them tried to get hold of the Ruedas, grab him and his whole bunch. A warrant for their arrest was among the contents of Hancock's message. They could join the prisoners in the Wheel, to share whatever disposition was made of those.

Quick turned to other matters. After an hour, his chief of staff called in. Chauveau looked worried. "Sir, about the *Chinook* spacecraft," he said. "She's overdue, and hasn't sent any word, either."

"What?" Quick clutched the arms of his chair. "Isn't Traffic Control interested?"

"I didn't know their exact routine or whom to query at the Astronautical Control Board, and it took a while to find out. Seems that when a vessel enters the Solar System, the watchship beams her flight plan to her destination—in this case, Earth—but that simply goes into the data bank. They think anything more would be complicated and unnecessary, because a ship forced to change plans can always notify one of the stations that take emergency calls.

"Well, this person I got hold of retrieved the record for me, which said *Chinook* ought to have made Earth orbit yesterday. Next she checked with Traffic Control, then with its Iliadic opposite number, and—well, in short, boss, nobody knew anything. My contact is quite concerned, but I managed to make her wait—hinting at a special mission which may have developed a slight hitch—wait before alerting the Safety Division. She won't for long, I'm afraid."

"Good man," Quick said with an extra dose of warmth. Through him flared a hope. *The one-in-a-million accident, that's never happened yet, did happen, and destroyed them.* He rallied his wits. *No.*

"What shall we do, sir?" Chauveau asked.

Quick's mind sprinted. None of the staff knew why he was concerned. To pursue the matter as hard as was needful, he must give out a story. He had one prepared by now.

Donning his most serious demeanor, he said, "Jacques, this is strictly confidential, and perhaps I shouldn't tell you at all. But I trust you, and I want you to feel motivated. You know about discontent growing on Demeter, complaints, formal protests and petitions, a couple of actual riots." *Mainly, colonial businesses object to paying taxes to their mother countries and the Union—claim they're getting almost nothing in return—as if they weren't still part of humanity and obligated to help their less fortunate brethren.... No need to preach the gospel to yourself, Ira Quick! And I must admit a few gripes are legitimate. The government has not been as solicitous of their welfare as it should be.* "What's not been publicized is the development of out-and-out revolutionary sentiment, gradually moving from seditious talk toward action." *Not strictly a lie. I am anticipating what I fear may someday come true if the right people don't stay alert and in control.* "Oh, among a tiny minority so far, of course. But you know what damage a few terrorists can do.

"Governor Hancock has warned me that the owner-captain of *Chinook* may be involved and may have come here for no innocent purpose. She approached me rather than anybody else because we are close political associates, you know, and she relies on me to proceed cautiously. Remember, she has no firm proof against this Brodersen. He *could* be honest. False arrest would provoke more antagonism back there, as well as violating his rights."

Quick combed fingers through his beard. "His behavior does look suspicious, though, eh?" he finished. "Let's start by finding out where he is."

"I'd better put you in touch with Assistant Commissioner Palamas, the person I spoke to on the Board," Chauveau said.

"Yes. While I talk to her, establish standby connections with—" Quick named them. A few had helped him take the initiative of sequestering *Emissary*. More knew nothing about that, but one way or another could be persuaded to exert their influence in useful directions, without requiring much elaboration of his story. They trusted him, or owed him for past favors, or would be glad to put him in their own debt. Between them, they wielded considerable power.

His conversation with Palamas proved satisfactory. She'd instigate a search, System-wide if necessary, and report the results straight back to him.

After that, however, the hours set in like gnawing rats.

Those reaches out yonder, hundreds of millions upon hundreds of millions of kilometers, were not exactly patrolled. Here and there—on ships, moons, asteroids, manmade stations—were powerful radars or other instruments such as multiplying spectrometers, mostly for scientific purposes. They could be pressed into service, but that could not be done in a fingersnap, the more so when goodly fractions of an hour often must pass between message and response. And then they must sweep across distances more enormous yet, through degree after degree of arc, while time bled away.

Quick had a gut-cold idea where *Chinook* probably was. He hadn't dared do more than suggest it to Palamas, hinting that the studies going on at the San Geronimo Wheel were more important than the government had indicated and it would be too bad if an ion trail disrupted them. He could but hope that somebody out in space would agree, and would be in a position to check. It would certainly not be wise to communicate directly with Troxell.

Somehow he lasted out the day, shook the humble hand, congratulated the scholarship winner, conferred about strategy for the next election over a lunch that he even noticed dimly was excellent, coped with assorted desk business, kept a drumhead affability stretched across his face. At seventeen hundred hours he called Alice to say he wouldn't be home that evening either. "Working late, may be all night," he explained.

"Yes," she said tonelessly.

Her look pains me. I am a compassionate man. "Truth," he said. "Call me back later if you don't believe it."

"Why?" she sighed.

He frowned. "Are you getting depressed again, dear? I've told you over and over that simply because my job requires me to move around a lot, you shouldn't stay in the house and mope. You need to develop outside interests, activities—"

"You told me not to join the Galaxy Club, they're too much a pressure group for interstellar exploration. I was loyal and didn't. Now I've reached my limit of things you do want me to belong to."

"Hey, let's not start fighting."

"Oh, no. My problem is I love you." Her voice still sounded flat and tired. "And the kids. I think they need some protection I can give them. Have you ever speculated what kind of love relationships the Others have?"

Pricked, he snapped, "I've heard fifty thousand speculations about everything conceivable concerning the damned Others—and claims of contact, creeds, crankeries, bad songs, worse writings, never a bloody thing constructive, never anything but avoidance of our proper human business."

"Goodnight, Ira," she said and broke the circuit.

He rolled his eyes ceilingward. "God, give me strength, if You exist," he declaimed, "and if You don't, do it anyway, huh?"

Preparations soothed him a trifle, as they might a dog turning around before lying down in the grass. This wasn't his first vigil here, and the place was equipped for it. In theory he could manage everything from his house. In practice that required interconnections—for example, to special data systems—which would be expensive to install and imperfectly secure. He sent out for dinner, made the couch into a bed, loosened his clothes, settled full length in the embrace of a lounger, and considered what entertainment to screen. Maybe a classic book he'd always meant to read or a classic show he'd always meant to see? No, he was too tightly wound. Either mindless relaxation or else an affirmation, playing back one of the noble speeches by the founders of the Party—or, wait, why not a couple of his own addresses, to study the form and possibly find details to improve? He reached for the retrieval control.

His phone chimed.

He was halfway out of the lounger before he had brought himself back down into calm. And still he sweated and shivered underneath.

"I've finally heard," Palamas said. Background indicated she was calling from her apartment or whatever it was. "They appear to have located *Chinook*, approaching the Wheel from the far side."

Brodersen, *may his figurative soul burn forever in mythical hell*, guessed—"What precisely is your information, please?"

According to her answer, the probability looked high. A metallic object of about the right size had been detected at the edge of the forbidden zone. It was inbound, currently under low acceleration or none. A couple of days earlier, a Solar weather monitor had happened to record a jet trail outbound along what would be an appropriate path. The facts all pointed to *Chinook*'s having made for the vicinity of the San Geronimo Wheel, coasting by, using enough boost to swing around and get aimed sunward again, coasting once more (*for a better look*), presumably soon to accelerate for Earth at a full gee and arrive with whatever yarn her crew had concocted. *No, arrive with a broadcast that thousands of receivers will pick up, as soon as she's in range.*

"I expect we can reach her," Palamas said. "Lasers might miss, but if her radio is open as regulations require, she ought to hear a strong signal."

"No—I mean, hold on." Quick marshalled words. "I do appreciate your efforts, Miz Palamas, and won't forget them. But this matter is more critical than I'm free to tell you. I'm afraid I must call further on your patience."

He leaned nearer the pickup. "This has to be done as secretly as possible," he said. "Nothing must leak to the news media, not a hint, not a whisper. Basically, I'm invoking my ministerial powers under the Covenant of the Union. That spaceship will be ordered to head straight for the T machine and return to the Phoebean System, maintaining outercom silence, under the severest penalties for noncompliance.

"Do you understand me, Miz Palamas? The severest penalties. You and I have a long night's work ahead of us. I have to notify the appropriate people, confer with them, get the arrangements made. You have to call your superiors, refer them to me, take for granted that their consent will be forthcoming while you start space units scrambling to enforce my order. Do you read me well, Miz Palamas?"

"I . . . think I do . . . Mr. Minister."

"Good." Quick flashed a taut smile. "I repeat, your service in this emergency will not be forgotten. Now let's take a few minutes to discuss exactly what all this means and how we can best operate."

She was middle-aged and dumpy; a check during the day had revealed she was placidly married and a registered member of the Constitution Party; but Quick had gotten eager cooperation out of harder cases than that.

The fear in him began to melt. Brodersen & Co. were fugitives from the law on Demeter, accused of conspiracy against public order. He had the warrants that said so. He also—given support in the right quarters—had authority to dispatch them back through the gate, incommunicado, subject to a nuclear warhead at the slightest sign of rebellion. Meanwhile he'd alert Aurie and she could prepare to take them in charge.

The details and contingencies were endless, of course. For instance, no vessel was anywhere near the Wheel except for *Chinook* herself and empty *Emissary*. Brodersen might attempt something desperate. No matter how smoothly the business went, Ira Quick had no limit of work to do, and afterward no limit of trail-covering and explaining away. He would need strong help, yes, on the highest level.

Moreover, this crisis made him see with full clarity that he and his fellows had stalled too long, too weakly merciful, about the final disposition of *Emissary* and her personnel. The time was overpast to act, for the sake of humanity.

That knowledge was unexpectedly exhilarating. Quick practiced a fighting grin. *By heaven, Brodersen*, he thought, *I've got you corraled, I'm about to saddle and mount and break you ... but thanks for the challenge!*

XVIII

WHEN THE DIRECTIVE reached *Chinook*, her captain's first response was to issue a command of his own: "Cut the engine; five-minute phasedown." A siren hooted warning. Crewfolk hastened to secure loose objects and find handholds for themselves. Meanwhile thrust dropped steadily until the ship fell free, under no acceleration save that of the distance-dwindled sun toward which she was bound.

Caitlín arrowed from their apartment into the office where Brodersen was. She had quickly and gleefully mastered weightless motion. Trouble could not altogether sober away from her face and body the joy of flying. The slim, coverall-clad form shot through the doorway between, banked off two successive bulkheads with a hand and a foot, reached the desk, seized a crossbar on its edge, came to a halt with an effort that sent blood surging to cheeks and bronze locks tumbling about them, and, floating, stretched across to plant a kiss on the man's mouth.

"Easy, hey, easy," he said. His own massive frame sat buckled into a chair. "We got a decision or three to make, fast."

She turned grave. "What is it hauled you in here?"

"That call from Stef," he said unnecessarily. The mate, on watch in the command center, had received the message and summoned Brodersen to the private line.

"You've thunder on your brow. What's wrong, my life?"

"You'll hear when the rest do." His arm brushed her and nearly tore her loose as he reached for the intercom switch.

Temper flared. She reached to slap back at him. "Would you be shoving me about like a dead thing?"

"Damnation," he half snapped, half pleaded, "we may have to make for the Wheel, and every second we're a couple of hundred kilometers closer to passing by it."

Instantly contrite, she did not waste time apologizing, but stroked fingers across his head. "Captain to crew," he declaimed. "Attention. We've received word from Earth—long-range 'cast, and they must've gone to a lot of trouble to locate and identify us. It's got a government call sign. We're wanted on Demeter on, quote, 'grave charges of conspiracy against public order and safety.' We're to proceed straight to the T machine. No, not quite straight. They specify the flight parameters. We'll come nowhere near enough to anyplace to make our announcement, with the outercom equipment we've got. Besides, we're forbidden to speak to anybody, except an official vessel that contacts us first. We're warned that watchships have been assigned to enforce all this by, quote, 'the strictest means appropriate.' The writ is in the name of Ira Quick, Union Minister of R & D, and invokes nothing less than full emergency powers."

He drew breath. "In short, brethren and sisters, the enemy is onto our game, faster'n I feared, and we're ticketed for the same oblivion that *Emissary* is in, or worse. What to do about it?"

"Jesus, Mary, and Joseph!" had burst from Caitlín before she steadied herself, clung white-knuckled to the bar, and regarded him through eyes gone emerald-hard. A babble came over the intercom. "Quiet!" Brodersen shouted.

When he had it, he said: "Either we go along like good little taxpayers or we take counteraction of some kind. But counteraction will have to start right away, I imagine. That's how come I stopped thrust. Which don't gain us much time, though. Think fast, people."

"We should be meeting together, the way we are not only voices to each other," Caitlin protested.

"Yeah, but I told you, our sunward speed—"

"Could we not be cutting it the while, aye, and aiming toward that Wheel of infamy? If we do decide to be meek after all, then they'll not know on Earth what we did beforehand, will they, now?"

"By God, you may be right. Hold on, everybody." Brodersen tugged his chin as he reflected aloud. "Let's see...killing our present vector and applying one for rendezvous...yeah, I'd guesstimate we can maneuver for two-three hours before radars that're a.u. distant from us can spot the difference...finite signal speed, large probable error...and besides, the way we're supposed to go lies in that general direction—Yes!" He slapped

his desktop, a gunshot noise and a violent countermotion of his
harnessed body. "I'll bet my left ball against your virginity,
Pegeen, we can lay a course clear to the Wheel, such that none of
'em yonder, no closer than the orbit of Mars, can tell we aren't
working toward the path they want us in."

His tone approached a roar: "Stef and Phil! Start us braking.
Half a gee. That won't commit us beyond redemption in a couple
of hours."

"Had we not best beam a message to Earth at once, to say we
will obey?" Zarubayev asked.

"Sure, sure," Brodersen agreed. "The order specifies the form
of our reply. Nothing but the number one-oh-one, addressed to
a particular Astro Board official but with no identification of us.
They really are leaning into the secrecy, aren't they? Okay, Stef,
put it out on the laser.

"Su," he went on, "do you savvy what this is about? Before we
can plan, we need more facts. Hook yourself up and compute if
we can reach the Wheel while looking, from the inner System, as
if we're just angling toward the prescribed track. That is, how
long might we reasonably be occulted by it? Take account of
every station which may be fingering us, but don't forget to
figure in how much the radar disc of the Wheel may be enlarged
by its radiation shield. Can do?"

"Wiz probability only." Granville's reply was cooler than
anyone would have awaited who did not know her well. "No
guarantee."

"Shucks, all we ever do in this universe is play odds. How
long will you need?"

"'Alf an hour, per'aps, mostly for to search out the data."

"Good. If your answer is positive, we'll start boosting
whichever way you figure is optimum for getting to the Wheel
unbeknownst. Then we'll meet in the common room and
wrangle. I favor a rescue operation for the *Emissary* people. You
may disagree," Brodersen told his crew at large. "Put your
arguments together while you wait. Think hard. Pray for
guidance, if you're so inclined . . . but think!"

Afterward, in his mind, he rehearsed what they said—not
actual words, which were scattered in fragments, spoken into
each other's mouths, disorganized as words always are when

several human beings try to reason together—but a kind of synopsis, an attempt to frame the different spirits wherein they left the gathering.

Sergei Zarubayev, glacier-practical: "What choice has the cabal left itself except to kill us?"

Stefan Dozsa, roughly, his fist punishing his knee: "And they will continue in the government. They may well *become* the government. So it goes from despotism to tyranny."

Philip Weisenberg, ashiver with emotion he seldom showed: "This looks like our first chance, man's first chance, to find the Others. Will we let it be the last?"

Martti Leino, furious: "No! God damn you, Daniel Brodersen, haven't you gotten the family you're supposed to be responsible for in enough trouble already?"—but later he yielded, sullenly, in part because he was alone, in part because Dozsa gibed at his courage till the skipper stopped that.

Caitlín Mulryan, aloud and ablaze: "What do you mean, saying I must stay inboard whilst you make your raid? I'll have you know—" and she too needed calming down before she gave reluctant consent to his tactics.

Susanne Granville, softly: "Why would I 'ave come along, my captain, if not to follow you?"

Himself: "Maybe I overplayed my hand, making for here. I do honestly think not. I did underestimate the opposition—mainly, I suppose, Aurie Hancock. But it stands to reason they'd've acted as fast and decisively if we'd gone straight to Earth; and we'd've had far less room for maneuver; and for sure we'd not have the evidence we do, that *Emissary* is back.

"Well, 'twill be mighty easy to send her off toward Sirius, manned by the corpses of her crew, and not much harder to dispose of us. I'm not saying this will happen, but I am saying 'twouldn't surprise me. You want to sit idle under such a risk?

"If we can snake Langendijk's band out of yon jail—I'm personally convinced it is a jail—'What then?' you ask. I don't know, except that then we've got the real clinching proof. The pictures we've taken of *Emissary* through the scanners we might have faked, but how can we have faked the people? And, you know, they may have picked up some useful capabilities wherever they've been.

"We mustn't count on that, of course. I've developed a couple of alternative battle plans which I'd like to sketch out for you.

They're strictly tentative. We'll have to see how the bones roll. We're not playing poker any more, you realize, we're shooting craps.

"If you accept my notions, I'll next have to try and find out if there is any possibility of us pulling off a whizzer at the Wheel. Maybe there isn't."

Weisenberg cut insignia out of sheet metal, Caitlín did a little retailoring, and Brodersen was attired like a rear admiral in the space corps of the Peace Command. Alone in the command center, he waited for the outercom to establish contact for him.

Silence enfolded his head, somehow deepened by the low weight which settled him in his chair. He heard the breath in his nostrils, felt the collar at his throat. Stars glistered multitudinous in the screens, the Milky Way gleamed around its lanes of darkness, the Solar disc stood pharaonic between wings of light. High magnification in one display showed him his target, spokes and rim slowly turning as if to grind an unknown grist. The captive ship was not in that field and he didn't reset the scanner toward her, for he had seen and made a record; he had seen.

Leino's initial protest rose while he waited, to move spookily around within him. *Have I the right? I'm committed now, but should I ever have begun? It could be that Quick and his bunch are trying to protect us from something ghastly.*

Ha! his rational and his willful selves responded together.

Well, but should I have stayed home anyway? the ghost wondered. *Less on account of Lis, though she's who Martti was thinking of, than Barbara and Mike.* Their own dear fetches came to snuggle in his lap; he could nearly feel the warmth and scent the gentle odor that only small children have. *It's not as if Demeter won't be ample for their lifetimes. In fact, an opening to the galaxy 'ud mean all sorts of revolution, maybe good—I believe that but might be wrong—or maybe bad, but nothing for sure any longer . . . the kind of surety their father ought to make for them. . . .*

He stiffened. *Horse shit!* he flung forth for an exorcism. *Must I tramp over this ground again? The Union isn't stable, no country is, the real for-certain hell is brewing on Earth itself, and Demeter's a hop through the gate from here. But everywhere around is a universeful of newness, new homes, new knowledge, new ideas. The single thing it hasn't got is absolute security. No part of it does. The closest we can come to that is through opportunity.*

Hoy, the buzzer. End of sermon, huh?

He pressed accept. The telescreen presented the image of a young man, in civilian garb but of disciplined bearing. Nonetheless, astonishment registered. Brodersen's anxieties went down a notch. Obviously they'd received no word at the Wheel.

"Peace Command special mission," he said. "Matthew Fry, admiral, commanding transport *Chinook*." His pseudonym he borrowed from Caitlin's housesitter. As for his ship, a fictitious designation was unadvisable; *Reina*-class craft were too few.

About three seconds passed while light waves bore his statement across space, plus reaction time at the far end, plus the time for a reply to arrive—eleven heartbeats; Brodersen counted them, and at the back of his brain felt pleased that they were no more. "Sir, you—pardon, sir," the young man gulped. "We had no inkling anyone was anywhere near us."

What I reckoned on. Why should you keep a lookout? And why should Quick notify you? That might cause you to wonder a bit. Nor will his radars show if we go the whole way to you, because you'll be occulting us for hours.

I did fear that you might've overheard the radio message to us. But again, you had no cause to be listening. Any communication to you will go on a nice economical laser beam, your orbit being exactly known.

"You weren't supposed to have that information till now," Brodersen said. "Connect me with your chief: sealed circuit."

Time. "Sir, he's off duty, asleep. Can it wait?"

Brodersen had been alert for such a chance to learn more. He put on his martinet expression. "Insubordinate, are you?" he barked. "State your service, rank, and name."

Time. It was hard to browbeat a person through a transmission lag like this. However, a top-deck PC officer was impressive, especially in space where he held almost life-and-death powers. "Pardon, sir? I, yes, of course, I'll buzz Colonel Troxell at once."

"I required your service, rank, and name. You will give them to me."

Time. He in the Wheel blanched and said helplessly: "North American secret service, Lieutenant Samuel Webster, sir."

So that's who I'm dealing with. Yeah, Quick's North

American. It figures. "You'd better learn to snap to orders if you don't want to get busted, Lieutenant Webster. Well, I won't put you on report. Get me the colonel."

Time. "Yes, *sir!* Thank you, sir!"

More time passed, minutes. Brodersen wished his image allowed him to light his pipe.

A burly man, hair hastily brushed and tunic hastily thrown on, appeared in the screen. "Troxell speaking." His gaze probed. "Admiral, uh, Fry? Welcome, sir. You catch us unprepared, I'm afraid, but we'll do our best." The closing of his lips which signified that he was through talking had a military snap.

"Very good," Brodersen said. "First, you will maintain total outercom silence except to this ship. If you happen to get a message, I want to know what it is and dictate your reply. I'll give you the reason shortly. Second, I want to raise my acceleration to a gee, which will let me dock at the Wheel in five or six hours. Is that feasible?"

Time. "Well ... yes ... but—Admiral, as a routine matter I'd like to see your orders."

Not unexpected. "Will you transmit me yours, Colonel?"

Time. "What? Pardon. Kindly explain."

Brodersen chuckled as he supposed Admiral Fry would. "You're operating under extreme security. The North American secret service isn't noted for passing confidential documents around carelessly. Neither is the Peace Command. We'll put both our Omega spools in your reader when I arrive, and compare." Scanning for transmission would automatically wipe the encoded information.

Time. "Your mission's really that secret?"

"Since it relates to yours, yes. Colonel, brace yourself. You've been guarding the members of the *Emissary* expedition. Are you ready to add a follow-up load of nonhumans?"

The effect was as powerful as Brodersen had hoped. (Otherwise he might have turned tail then and there and tried to convey his news to another spacecraft or two, an isolated asteroid base or two, before the watchships hunted him down—poor though the chances were that that would do any good.) Troxell's doubts vanished. They had been feeble from the outset, for he had no grounds for suspecting that anybody outside the government and the *Faraday* crew had any intimation of the facts.

Still, Brodersen must work warily, though with unlimited brass. In effect, he, holding two pair, was seeking to bluff out a full house. Pretending to knowledge he did not possess, he must get it from Troxell under guise of telling his own story.

As for that: After *Emissary* returned, the PC had planted an extra guard on the Phoebean T machine. A strange vessel did emerge. She was boarded and her crew made prisoners without resistance. Having already leased Chehalis' well-equipped but idle exploratory ship, the PC took them and their essentials away for safekeeping. To forestall any speculations, Fry declared when he entered the Solar System that his destination was Vesta, and went spaceward of his true goal before doubling back toward it.

Troxell believed. No fool, he nevertheless was predisposed to believe. Brodersen had anticipated that. The warders of the Wheel—twenty-one total, as he learned by feigning a slight misunderstanding—must be of more or less Actionist ideology. Else Quick, studying dossiers, doubtless getting depth-psych examinations made of volunteers "for a confidential assignment of utmost importance," would not have picked them.

Soon Troxell was eager to talk. He needed to justify himself, he who had been penned in for these many weeks with his prisoners who were also his accusers. Brodersen listened patiently, encouragingly to all the antistellar theses. For a minute he was tempted to deny that the detention was proper, an act decided upon by the Council. But no. A few sentences can't overturn a man's faith.

Meanwhile his heart slammed, skin chilled and tingled, soul hallooed, behind a hard-held calm—for in between chunks of the lecture, he caught mentions of truth. The *Emissary* crew had been eight years at the far end of their gate. They had lost three members. Carlos and Joelle were alive. They maintained the aliens were friendly and anxious to begin cultural exchange.

They had an alien with them.

Brodersen could hit on no safe way to find out what the creature looked like. He gathered that it could live under Terrestrial conditions, was of approximately human size, and claimed to be the sole representative its race would send unless mankind freely chose to establish relations—"And later they dispatched a ship of their own regardless, huh?" Troxell said. "How dumb do they suppose we are?"

"Well, they may have found reasons to change their minds," Brodersen temporized. "It has to be investigated, and you've got the only people with experience of them.

"Besides, maybe more important, the Council has decided

that we must have far better intelligence of them before we can allow anything to happen. I hope our arresting this group will drive the point home and we won't need to take more drastic measures. You well realize, Colonel, we can't have public hysteria either. Hence the secrecy."

Time. "Yes, of course, Admiral Fry, no argument. Let's discuss arrangements, shall we? What precautions have you in mind?"

—Eventually the conference ended.

Full Earth weight had resumed as *Chinook* drove onward. The Wheel had grown in sight enough to notice. When outside communication went on standby, the crew became free to load the intercom with jabber. Brodersen knew he must get them properly organized. The venture would be precarious at best.

He stood up, stretched and eased, stretched and eased, till the hardest knots were out of his muscles. *Hell take hurry*, he decided. *Oh, I'll brief them and drill them as well as I can. But that's not awfully well; won't fill more than an hour or two. First we should rest.*

First I will go back to Pegeen. It could be our last while together.

XIX

ON DELICATE THRUSTS of her auxiliary motors, *Chinook* aligned herself with the open hub of the Wheel. Flame-tinged vapors gushed across night and dissipated. That made possible a rapid bleedoff of the enormous electrostatic potential which shielded her against cosmic rays. When she was well positioned, gliding in on a carefully monitored trajectory, a gyro within her began to turn. Her hull gathered spin until it was rotating slightly faster than the station. By then she was quite near.

Her people sat still to avoid motion sickness from radial weight variations and Coriolis force. Brodersen drew comfort from the steady tones of the control officer ahead. His cover yarn account for *Chinook*'s absence of insignia other than a registry number and his flamboyant company emblem, as well as the presence of an energy gun turret counterbalanced by a missile tube. Just the same, they might have grown suspicious— perhaps on Earth, to send a warning hither at the speed of light. But evidently not. His heart slugged, though, his jaws ached from being clenched, sweat trickled cold along his ribs and reeked. More than a quarter of a Terrestrial century had gone by since last he was in combat.

The spaceship drifted into the hub at a few meters per second. She was very little off center. (That had better be the case. A vessel her size had scant clearance.) Soft-surfaced roller bearings upon them brought *Chinook* to a halt, bow projecting out the front end, stern and focusing tubes out the rear. Her spin became identical with that of her surroundings at the instant when her main personnel and cargo locks were opposite the correct entry ports. This caused the Wheel to gain angular momentum, but the change was minuscule. After a sufficient number of dockings had significantly affected rotation, a jet in the rim would reduce it.

Since this visitor had no freight to discharge, only a gangtube reached forth to osculate the exit for the crew. A reserve tank filled it with air. Equalized pressure activated a sensor which flashed a green light and beeped. *You may come on through.*

Brodersen ran wooden tongue over sandy lips. Yet otherwise, as of old, he was abruptly cool, too busy to be nervous. "Okay," he told his men. "Remember our doctrine and signals." He blew a kiss to Caitlín, who stood behind them, a submachine gun in her clasp. Susanne was elsewhere, linked to her computer and, through it, to the whole ship, which would respond to any command she gave. Limited input restricted her to a few basic actions, but Brodersen was glad of even that much backup.

Caitlín touched lips to the muzzle of her weapon and dipped it in his direction. He turned from the glory of her. "Good luck," he wished all his folk, and went ahead.

Centrifugal force, equal to about one-tenth gee, put the airlock under him, but the airlock contained rungs. Beyond its outer valve, the gangtube offered him another set, closely spaced because it was accordion-folded to minimum length. Fluorolight cast odd shadows among the pleats. He bounded down. Low-weight had a magic of its own.

Emerging, he took a short fixed ladder to a balcony-like platform intended to help the unloading of baggage. Thence a second ladder went to the deck; but he stopped where he was and looked. This was the moment before he charged or fled.

Five meters high, a broad corridor arched out of sight on either hand, convex above him, concave below. He saw doors along it which shut off disused facilities. A hatchway led to a spoke, passageway to the rim. The hall was drably painted and carpeted; the draft from ventilator grilles came loud, with a faint smell of oil, a sign of recent neglect.

Men clustered beneath him. Save for Troxell, who was in business tunic and slacks, they wore coveralls. Each had a holstered sidearm: slugthrower, not stunner. Brodersen counted. Twenty-one. A measure of optimism lifted in him. *The stunt's worked so far. They're here, the lot of them, including the communications and control officers, maintenance technies, quartermaster—*

It was what he had gotten the colonel to agree to. Lock his present captives in the auditorium. (Brodersen had ascertained where it was located.) Bring his entire following to meet the newcomers and help them escort the nonhumans (who might conceivably use nonhuman capabilities in attempting a break) to a safe place.

"Greeting, sir," Troxell called in English. His bass echoed the least bit between bare panels. "Everything in order?"

"Aye," Brodersen said.

"Come on down."

"Wait a minute. I want a man at my back."

"Huh?"

"Can't be too cautious, can we? Very well, Sergei."

Zarubayev appeared, bearing a tommy gun. He sprang to join his captain. The agents showed surprise. Bearded, long-haired, dressed like them, the Russian jarred on their expectations.

Here we go. Brodersen whipped forth his pistol. Zarubayev's gun swept downward. "Not a move!" Brodersen shouted. "Hands up before we shoot!"

"What the hell—" Troxell's roar cut off when Zarubayev's weapon chattered. The warning burst whanged nastily off the opposite bulkhead. The warders froze.

"Hands on heads," Brodersen commanded. "Quick!—Okay, boys, come on through."

Weisenberg and Leino joined him. They bore automatic rifles, and bundled on their backs were more firearms.

"Stay as you are and nobody will get hurt," Brodersen said. "But whoever acts funny will die. Is that clear? He will die."

Inwardly he begged that that not happen. Those fellows were doing naught but their job. He'd encountered some like them, though, when he truly wore the uniform of the Union, whom he'd helped kill. The commitments on either side had been irreconcilable.

His glance flicked right and left. Zarubayev was smiling, as if he enjoyed this. Maybe he did. Weisenberg stood tense, his mouth stretched out of shape, though his piece never wavered. Leino's face was wet and strained, helmeted in dank hair, and he breathed hard, but he didn't seem frightened either. *And me, well, they used to call me the Great Stone Phiz,* Brodersen remembered.

Back at the airlock, Dozsa and Caitlín were his reserves, guarding a line of retreat. He wondered how they looked. It was no picnic carrying out a paramilitary operation with amateurs. He'd assigned posts as thoughtfully as might be. Zarubayev, though Demeter born, had grown restless and spent a few years in the PC, interplanetary corps, before he went to work for Chehalis; he'd seen no fighting but had gotten plenty of drill and maneuver. Leino, raised in the wilderness, was a champion marksman. Weisenberg could make any tool a part of his body, and a weapon is a tool. All three had ample space experience. Dozsa did too, but not with arms and seldom outside a ship. *Pegeen— Yes, I did what I could in the time that I had. Whether I gauged well, we're about to learn.*

Rage racked Troxell's visage. "Are you crazy?" he yelled. "What is this piracy? Do you imagine you can get away clear, you sons o'bitches, you—" He choked.

"Take it easy," Brodersen answered. "I told you we mean no harm unless you force us. Listen. Our aim is to free the *Emissary* crew. They're being detained under false pretenses. You've been hoodwinked. Ira Quick is a crook, and you'll see him on trial before long."

"Prove it!" an agent challenged.

Brodersen shook his head. "As Antony told Cleopatra, I am not prone to argue. The newscasts will inform you. Today you'll follow orders.

"Move over there, by that door marked 14." He pointed. It was well clear of the spoke entrance. "Bunch together. I want you in easy range of this guy." He jerked a thumb at Zarubayev. "He'll watch you while the rest of us go spring the prisoners. Then we'll disarm you and lock you up. We'll leave you a hand drill or a hammer and chisel or whatever we figure you can use to break free in an hour or two, after we're gone. Do you understand? We'd hate to harm anybody. We're not bandits, we're trying to set right a terrible wrong that threatens the Union. Consider yourselves under citizen's arrest, obey us, and everything will be fine. But I repeat, we'll shoot if we must.

"Move! Keep those hands on your scalps. Move!"

They shuffled from him. He was aware of the scuff, of panting and trembling and muttered maledictions, of sweat and glares. "Stop," he cried. To Leino and Weisenberg: "Proceed."

They ignored the ladder and jumped, falling like autumn leaves. He followed. The impact was light in feet and knees. The hatch was two bounds off. It stood open. Brodersen waved his partners through. When they were gone, his free hand grabbed a rail, he swung himself into the companionway.

A pistol crack whipped him to a halt. Twice. Thrice. It stabbed his eardrums. He twisted about where he stood. The bunch of agents was breaking up like a glob of dropped mercury. Men scampered off or flopped to the deck, drew their guns, and fired. Zarubayev's raved, a couple of bodies below crumpled, then he reeled back. Blood spouted from his neck and belly.

Brodersen blazed into the foe. Through him there flashed: *A fanatic, a devotee, a hero . . . must've hunkered down a bit when two or three others hid him . . . yanked his rod out and let fly . . . knowing he'd almost surely miss, but he'd trigger a fusillade—I'll never know who it was—*

He heard Troxell bellow, saw the survivors retreat, when Dozsa reached the platform, crouched above Zarubayev, and sprayed the corridor with metal. It wailed as it ricocheted, through the rattle of explosions. Troxell's party disappeared up the curvature of this world.

He won't continue a fire fight under these conditions. Pistols are too inaccurate, especially here . . . low weight, Coriolis vectors, the sighting wrong—

Two men sprawled dead, their shapes gone graceless, their features hideous. Three more were badly wounded. One dragged himself away, legs trailing, one stared at a shattered kneecap and whimpered, one sat slumped against a bulkhead, going into shock. Zarubayev's blood dripped off the platform, slow and scarlet, slow and scarlet. Dozsa snarled at the edge. Caitlin stood by him now, wild of countenance, cursing in a torrent, but swinging her weapon steadily back and forth.

What Troxell will try to do is block us from freeing the prisoners.

Brodersen's paralysis broke. It had only lasted a few seconds. "Hold the fort!" he shouted. "Keep well covered! We'll be back!" He swarmed along a short circular staircase to the elevator.

Weisenberg and Leino were there. The senior engineer had obviously had to restrain the junior from rushing up to join the battle, which would have been useless or worse. They were still wrestling. "Let's go," Brodersen said, and pushed the button for it.

The elevator was little more than a steel slab at right angles to a belt which carried it. Three more served the same passageway. Between them, easy to step onto, were ladders, liberally supplied with resting places. Those were for emergency use. The shaft extended almost nine hundred meters. Staring into its bleakly illuminated depths, Brodersen saw it converge in perspective on an atom-small terminus, and dizziness touched him.

Weisenberg sagged down onto a bench and stared at the floor. "Eli, Eli," he mumbled, "that this had to be."

Leino, on his feet, gripped the rail as if to crumple it and shook his rifle aloft. His Upland speech came raw: "They fell on their own deeds, they swinehounds."

"We're not done with them yet." Brodersen's response was mechanical. Most of him howled, *I led Pegeen into this, Pegeen.* "I feel sure they hope to catch us at the auditorium."

Weisenberg glanced up, instantly alert. "Can they?"

"Dunno. You heard what I managed to worm out of Troxell concerning the layout here. I didn't dare push too hard."

"Jesu Kriste," Leino groaned, "this thing crawls."

"It's meant to," Weisenberg told him. "Change of gravity and air pressure. You need time to adapt. Whichever the enemy takes won't be any faster. And they retreated spinward from us. The auditorium is antispinward from here. We'll have a slight jump on them."

"Yes, and just the three of us have them outgunned," Brodersen added. "Sit yourself, Martti. Recover your strength."

He set an example, after choosing a rifle from Leino's load, but his mind gave no cooperation. *Pegeen. Lis. Barbara. Mike. The stars.*

Once as a boy, on a sail cruise through the San Juan Islands, he'd developed a galloping earache. There was nothing to do but endure until the drum broke and relieved the satanic pain. That took a couple of hours. This five-minute ride felt longer.

But then it ended. He led the way in a rush, up a stairwell which continued past the hatch to the deck. For the hundred-odd meters he could see until curvature blocked vision, the corridor lifted before him like a ramp. Though he was never climbing while he pounded through its hollowness, Earth weight dragged at him. Breath surged rough in his gullet.

A double door beneath a photomural, Armstrong on Luna— He'd expected to shoot out the lock, but the fastening was a mere latch, a steel bar between two brackets that must have been hastily welded on after he called from space. He cast it loose and flung the portal wide.

Ranked in their hundreds, seats confronted a stage as empty as they were. Nearby, the *Emissary* explorers rose in amazement. Most were sloppily clad, they blurred together for Brodersen as he sped toward them, until he saw Joelle— *Judas priest, her hair is gray, she's skinny, well, eight years*—He saw the alien, chimerical cross between an otter, a lobster, a seal, a duck, a kangaroo, an alligator, a porpoise, no, none of those really, nothing he could name, nothing his vision was ready for, a brown blur—"We're springing you!" he bawled. "We're your friends! We're getting you out of here! Joelle, do you know me?"

"Freedom, freedom, freedom!" Leino chanted.

A tall man stepped out of the group. Brodersen recognized Captain Langendijk. Weisenberg ran to meet him. Brodersen and Joelle stopped, stared, held out hands toward each other.

Weisenberg and Langendijk halted. "This is a rescue," the engineer said between gasps. "You're unlawfully held—we've come to set you free—make the truth known—we've met resistance—may have to fight our way back to our ship—here, arm yourselves—"

"Dan," Joelle marveled. Her eyes were enormous, ebon, in the ivory face.

He collected his wits. "Hurry along," he wheezed, and caught her by the wrist. She in turn gestured at the nonhuman, which moved toward her.

A man joined them. "Daniel!" he exclaimed. *"Por todos los santos—"* Carlos Francisco Miguel Rueda Suárez. He had grown bald.

A hefty blond woman followed. Brodersen recalled fleetingly the name Frieda von Moltke. The rest milled, bewildered. Brodersen started back up the aisle he was in. It wouldn't do to get blockaded.

"Hurry, hurry!" he shouted. Once beyond the doors, Weisenberg and Leino could pass out the stuff they carried. After that, let Troxell beware. His engineers were at Brodersen's heels, yelling, waving. Still most of the captives dithered. Langendijk urged them on, but they weren't soldiers, nor bound by the heart to these wild invaders. Clamor and weapons roused an instinct to hide. They needed a few minutes for comprehension.

Brodersen re-entered the corridor. His right hand gripped his rifle, his left Joelle. The alien tagged close behind her. Leino came immediately after. Weisenberg paused in the doorway to beckon at the laggards. Von Moltke took the chance to work a tommy gun loose from the bundle on his back. Rueda Suárez started to do likewise.

Down the bend of the deck came Troxell and his men. Their front rank carried by the legs a couple of large tables, tops facing forward—shields.

Brodersen could never afterward quite remember what

happened. A new fight erupted. He and those with him backed down the hall; they zigzagged, they knelt, they dropped, they ran further, they kept shooting, and somehow none of them was hit. Somehow the enemy was gone when they reached the next spoke.

He guessed their fire had been too heavy, allowing pistols too little chance to be effective. Or the agents had run low on ammo. Or both. Troxell would have kept enough to hold trapped the *Emissary* people who'd not moved out at once. A return to the auditorium would be suicide.

Joelle shook Brodersen back to full awareness. "Listen, Dan, we must go to a particular storeroom. Fidelio—the Betan—the alien here can't eat our food. We have supplies for him."

"Huh?" he said. "No. Too risky."

"Not if we hurry," Rueda snapped. "Almighty God, Daniel, Fidelio's our link to his entire race!"

"Okay," Brodersen decided. "Lead us. On the double."

The storeroom wasn't far off, nor was it locked, and the rations were packed handily for carrying, apparently mostly freeze-dried. Burdened, the party sought the nearest shaft, piled on the elevator, and rode it to the hub.

They said almost nothing on the way. They were stunned. Brodersen counted: himself, Joelle, the alien, Weisenberg, Rueda, Leino, von Moltke. Four saved; well, that was plenty, if they could bear witness at Earth. If not, he'd be footnoted in history as a desperado who got killed in a raid he attempted for an obscure purpose.

The elevator delivered them. They sped down a hall that was sharply rounded. There was the platform. There stood Pegeen, Dozsa, Pegeen, Pegeen. She cheered. Brodersen did not see Zarubayev, who must have been carried inboard. She could have done that in this scant weight. Did he live? That question must wait its turn. Troxell would soon find a course of action. They'd better be gone before then.

Brodersen's company scrambled up the ladder and into the ship, followed by him. He made for the nearest intercom unit. "Su, get us the hell on our way," he rasped.

Valves closed. The engine awoke. At low acceleration, *Chinook* withdrew from the machinery around her and regained open space.

Fingers plucked Brodersen's sleeve. He looked about and saw von Moltke. "If you please, Mr. Captain," she said with a hoarse accent, "I hear your gunner is a casualty. I hear too your armament is like on *Emissary*."

"Yes," he said, stupid in his exhaustion, "yes, it is."

"I was a gunner in *Emissary*," she reminded him. "I can check details by your engineers. Let me shoot out the transmission dishes on the Wheel and the ship. Best I disable the ship too. Then they cannot tell Earth about us." As he hesitated: "I doubt they haff called, but they will soon unless we prefent. If we prefent, no harm to them. They must sit quiet till somebody worries and sends a speedster to check. Meanwhile, howeffer, you are carrying out what plan you haff. Correct?"

"All right," he said, "I authorize. Coordinate it with Phil, Chief Engineer Weisenberg, that is, and with our linker, Granville," while he longed for nothing but Caitlín.

Minutes later, a slicing energy beam made the San Geronimo Wheel mute. It did no further damage; but a missile left *Emissary* a whirl of fragments. That hurt.

Two more felonies, Brodersen thought. *We'd better build us a damn good case for deserving an executive pardon.*

Never mind now. The immediate objective is just to survive.

No. Above and before that, sleep. He barely managed to put affairs temporarily in order and start the ship on a course he deemed proper before he stumbled to bed.

Sergei had died. Caitlín held Brodersen close.

XX

Again at an earth gravity, *Chinook* made for the T machine. On the route prescribed, the trip would take six Earth days.

"Our best bet is to conform for the time being, while we try to work out a strategy," Brodersen had explained. "Else they'll come after us, and a watchship has more legs than we do. We for sure can't outrun a tracker missile."

Von Moltke had probably saved him and his following from that, his mind added. News of his assault would have provided the perfect excuse to order this vessel blown out of existence. That would not by itself relieve Quick and company of the embarrassment created by the *Emissary* travelers left behind, not to mention whatever questions were occurring to Troxell's outfit; but presumably they could cope. They would certainly try to cope, and even failure on their part might prove lethal.

As was, while *Chinook* remained at large, bearing the possibility of exposing the whole affair, Langendijk's faction should be safe from everything worse than continued imprisonment. Indeed, from a tactical viewpoint it was good that Brodersen had not succeeded in releasing them. Now the cause of—liberty?—did not have all its eggs in one highly breakable basket. Half by chance, his operation had worked well.

No. It didn't. Men are hurt, men are dead. The agents among them are bad enough. I can live with that—their fighting us was almost criminally reckless; maybe being penned up for weeks drove them a little crazy—but Sergei is dead, my own man, my friend.

He had awakened beside Caitlín, for a moment conscious only of her. Then the memory rolled over him. His shuddering breath roused her, to embrace and murmur to him for a long while. "It's a war we're in, Daniel, my darling, and men have ever

174

fallen in war. Yours is just, a strife like what they waged against tyrants and foreign overlords again and again on Earth, and us today the happier for it. I knew Sergei too, aye, better than I've told you. He joyed in the universe; but if he must leave it, proud would he be that this was why." Thus did she slowly give him back his heart, until he could rise and go about his work.

Later, though, entering their quarters to fetch something, he found her seated silent, the marks of crying upon her. When he asked what the matter was, she said in a near whisper that she was making a song and wished to be alone.

She was absent, on duty, when he met with Joelle Ky, Carlos Rueda Suárez, and the nonhuman. Presently he would arrange a general gathering at which his entire band could hear the tale of *Emissary*. However, he must not delay getting a skeleton of the facts for himself, to aid him in planning, and this was most rapidly done when a minimum of people were on hand. Despite his gratitude to Frieda von Moltke, he did not invite her, for their lack of acquaintance might slow down the proceedings. Carlos was a cousin of Antonia, Brodersen's first wife. Though he was a child when she died and had not often met his in-law, they shared considerable background. Brodersen had first encountered Joelle on business nineteen Earth-years ago; since moving to Demeter, he'd looked her up whenever he revisited the mother planet, and for the past decade—

Never certain exactly how he felt about her, she being unlike any other woman ever in his life, he was shocked anew when she entered the office. They had birthdays within a month of each other, but suddenly she was fifty-eight, long gone in a place whose strangeness must have helped grizzle the locks he remembered as blue-sheening black, line the brow he remembered as serene, thin the flesh to a cloak tightly drawn over bones which remained as exquisite as before.

He bumbled to his feet. "Joelle," he said out of a lumpy larynx, "hello. It's wonderful having you here."

She smiled. That and her voice hadn't changed either; both were pleasing and a little remote, like compositions by Brancusi or Delius. "Thank you for everything, Dan. I'm so eager to learn precisely what 'everything' means—certainly an enormous lot—" They clasped four hands and might have kissed, but Rueda came through the door and, in Peruvian style, hugged the captain.

"Daniel, Daniel, how magnificent!" His Spanish almost

warbled. "Our rescuer, our warrior—I've been talking to some of your crew—Do you know, when I was a boy I idolized you. And I was right. By God, but you are a *man!*"

Stepping back, he reassumed proper aristocratic dignity. Brodersen studied him for a second. A ghost of Toni lingered in Rueda's straight-lined, short-nosed countenance and hazel eyes. Of medium height, he had laid a small paunch onto his slimness while he was away, and Brodersen understood how he must resent that trace of early eld: doubtless worse than being left with a mere brown fringe of hair. At least his mustache was the same.

Then the nonhuman arrived and overwhelmed all other impressions. The chances were that he (she? it?) had no such intention, Brodersen decided. If anything, the attitude of the creature looked diffident, though how could you tell? But the sight—he'd need practice before he made complete sense of those contours—the gait—the smell that was like a seashore, only not really—

"May I give you a formal introduction to Fidelio?" Rueda said, smiling. The alien extended the lower right arm. Brodersen shook hands. He'd done the same with a tame gibbon once, in Asia during his PC hitch, and been startled; the ape's thumb was laid out wrong and had no ball to it. Fidelio's clasp made the gibbon's brotherlike.

Brodersen met the eyes, which resembled the eyes of no animal on Earth or Demeter, and forgot about handshakes. It roared in him: *This is an intelligent nonhuman being. This is, this is. I'm living the dream that always was in me.*

"Fidelio," he stammered, "welcome. *Bienvenido.*"

"*Buenos días, señor, y muchas gracias,*" coughed and whistled out of the fanged mouth. Suddenly Brodersen laughed aloud—not at anyone or anything, simply laughing, his mirth reborn.

"Come on into the cabin," he urged after he was through. "What can I offer everybody? Does Fidelio mind if I smoke? We may as well be comfortable."

Two hours later, they shared an embryonic idea of what had been going on around Sol, Phoebus, and Centrum.

Rueda could no longer sit. He paced the room, back and forth, making gestures like karate chops. Blood had withdrawn from his features, turning the olive skin gray, and he stared at the

narrowness enclosing him as his ancestors had stared across
sword points on a duelling ground.

"It must not be borne," he declared. "It will not be. They
subvert the Covenant, they would close the star gates, *ay*,
kidnapping and murder are small among their crimes. Daniel,
Joelle... Fidelio.... Never fear we may do wrong fighting them.
We cannot."

Cross-legged in an armchair, pipe bowl hot in his clasp and
smoke mordant on a scorched tongue, Brodersen said, "I guess
that's axiomatic, Carlos. The question before this assembly is
where we go from here. And how. And whether."

Joelle had chosen a straightbacked seat opposite him and
had scarcely stirred except to talk, for the most part giving a
dispassionate account of Beta. Her hands lay quiet on her lap.
Fidelio sat beside her on a tripod of feet and flukes and likewise
moved little, save that his whiskers trembled. "You must have an
idea or two, Dan," she said.

"Yes!" Rueda jerked to a halt and stared at the captain. "You
were always bold, but never heedless."

Brodersen scowled. "Maybe I have been, this time around.
Or maybe there've been too goddamn many jokers in the deck. I
was, well, kind of childishly hoping you from *Emissary* would
have brought back a wild card we could play."

Joelle's lips quirked upward, barely enough to be seen. "If we
had that, we wouldn't have languished in the Wheel."

"No, but—" Brodersen shrugged, drew on his pipe, laid it on
an ashtaker, and met their gazes head on. "Okay," he told them,
"naturally my shipmates and I have discussed several schemes.
None of them appeal much, but see what you think."

He ticked them off on his fingers. "We can defy the bastards
immediately, veer off, scoot around the Solar System. We can't
prowl forever, but we do have a lot of delta V before our tanks go
dry. Food stores are ample for years, and air and water recycling
can go on as long as fuel for the migma cells holds out, which is
years more.... Oh, of course Fidelio's limited to—what? Several
months?—but we wouldn't be out in space that long anyway.

"You see, the watchships can hunt us down. An accelerating
craft is a difficult target, and we can doubtless shoot out some of
their missiles, but they'd swamp our defenses in the end.
Meanwhile they'll've kept us far from Earth or any settlement.
That whole effort might turn out to be impractically large and
visible for the opposition—they can't afford publicity which they

haven't doctored—but I wouldn't count on it. Bear in mind, they've got a grip on enough of the levers of power to have already done things like jailing you."

"Ah, but wait," Rueda said. "We can beam our word, can't we? I suppose your radio transmitter is like ours, not designed to get a message across an astronomical distance. Probably no one would be tuned in anyhow. But the radios are limited precisely because the lasers can reach far."

"Two problems there," Brodersen replied. "First, a message like that to Earth or Luna or the satellites gets picked up by a comsat, you know, and passed on from there to its destination. What you may not know, because it hardly ever makes any difference, is that the program includes censorship. Only certain classes of official communications may go in cipher. Everything else, a computer scans, and if it spots a reference to a 'flagged' subject, the message goes to a human, who decides whether or not it's harmless. The system dates back to the Troubles, and even I have to admit it's not all bad. For instance, it was what trapped the Finalists before they were quite ready to set off their atomic bombs. But you can bet your bottom sol that when Quick's bunch started planning what to do in case *Emissary* returned, a very early order of business for them was to quietly get control of it—put in the right programs and personnel so they can intercept whatever may threaten disclosure.

"Second, we *might* be able to get through to somebody else, like a ship or on an asteroid or a Mars base or something. I say 'might,' because most such have very limited receiver facilities— we'd have to get fairly close—and only ships are certain to be listening constantly for input. Well, we might, regardless. But if that somebody heard us, would he believe? And if he did, would others believe him? Never forget, we're not up against a maverick like me, we're bucking some of the biggest and most respected political figures alive . . . who got to be that way, most of them, because they're masters of propaganda and public relations.

"All in all, I figure the direct attack has a very poor chance of succeeding. Odds are that we'd be killed before we could accomplish anything.

"What else have we considered? Well, when we're near the T machine, we're bound to be in communication with its watchship. Actually, under present circumstances, more than one watchship will likely be near. We presume the officers and crews for the most part are not villains, are simply following orders which may well be puzzling them a bit. If we tell them our story—show them Fidelio—do you see?

"The trouble here is that the cabal must also have thought of this, and battened down hatches. Else they wouldn't have told us to go there, huh? They may not know we have Fidelio aboard, but they do know we've seen and photographed *Emissary*. That's dangerous enough for them. My guess is, one ship will have a couple of key officers who are in on the conspiracy. The moment we start to tell tales, she'll throw a barrage at us. Explanations afterward are cheap. We are visibly armed, and I'm sure there is indeed a warrant out for us on Demeter. It wouldn't be hard to claim that in the best judgment of those officers, we were about to open fire ourselves.

"The third possibility is, we go through the gate to Phoebus and see what's at yon end. Maybe they're less well prepared, less equipped, and we can break free or do something else worthwhile. I've actually considered—since we've got you here, your knowledge—I've considered trying to run the pattern that'll bring us to Centrum from Phoebus, and asking for help at Beta. But it's a pretty wild notion, because the guardians aren't likely to grant us much leeway.

"In fact, what worries me about making the transit we're supposed to, is . . . well, Demeter being thinly populated and relatively isolated, news isn't hard to control. It'd be simple to scrag us. For instance, as soon as we're well away from the T machine and the regular watch crew, the ship escorting us could fire a missile. Afterward the world would hear about the tragic accident which destroyed *Chinook*. I'd hate to believe this of Aurie Hancock, but it is possible. Otherwise we'll be interned indefinitely. The Phoebean System has plenty of sites for a secret prison camp. I daresay we'd be joined by the rest of your crew.

"And that's the extent of our thinking to date. My own instinct says we should tentatively plan on returning to Phoebus and doing whatever seems best when we get there, though keeping our eyes and our options open until then. I may well be wrong. I'd sure be glad of any suggestions."

"Whew!" Brodersen finished. "What a lecture! I could use another beer. Anybody else?" He rose to go to the fridge.

"Hold," Joelle said.

"What?" He checked his stride.

Seldom—when a problem was unusually arousing, or when

things got really good in bed—had he seen a light such as kindled her countenance. "Dan," she told him, her voice ashiver, "we can go straight from Sol to Centrum."

"What?" he yelped.

"Yes." She sat forward. "The Betans, they've been exploring the gates for a thousand years. They've gone beyond trial and error. They don't have a complete theory; nothing compared to what the Others know—"

"The Others," Rueda murmured.

"—but they have achieved some comprehension," Joelle went on. "Take three places, three stars if you want, A,B,C, with known gates—T machine guidepaths—from A to B and from B to C. Then the Betans can compute a direct route between A and C."

It was like a nova burst in Brodersen.

"Not with absolute certainty," Joelle was saying. "They haven't measured the local curvatures of the continuum that well. But the probability of success is high. Surely higher than for the schemes you've described."

"And—and—" Brodersen groped through splendors. "We can go to the Sol machine...make like starting for Phoebus...then lie, bluff, threaten, or whatever, till we're so far into the transport field that we're nearly an impossible target.... We'll come out at Centrum. Go to Beta. Come back leading a Betan armada."

"Whose only offensive weapon need be the truth," Rueda said. Whether or not he had heard about the physics earlier, the idea was new to him also. He too stood transfixed by revelation.

Brodersen snatched the beer glass which had stood by his chair and swung it in circles over his head. "By the honor of the house!" he roared out of his youth. "We'll do it! We will!"

"The computation is difficult," Joelle warned. "Fidelio and I will need to conduct research, and I'll need to apply holothetics. You do have holothetic capabilities aboard, don't you?"

The flame in her now was like nothing he had ever seen. *I shall return to what I am*, radiated forth. Heat and cold fled across her cheeks. *I shall again be One with the All.*

Rueda rested an intent look upon her. It was as if Brodersen could read the Peruvian's mind. *Will you become, for us, what the Others refuse to be?*

•   •   •

They would give Sergei Nikolayevitch Zarubayev a spaceman's funeral, launching his flag-shrouded body from an airlock, on a bier driven by a signal rocket, while his shipmates stood by and heard their captain read the service.

First Caitlín took the obligation as medical officer of washing him and laying him out in his cabin. From four bowls which she filled with oil, and wicks of string afloat upon bits of wine-bottle cork, she made lights to burn at his head and his feet. The fluoros she turned off; and she called for a wake for him.

She met a little surprise, a little objection—barbarous custom; the civilized thing was to gather afterward, with coffee—but Brodersen, Dozsa, Granville, and von Moltke understood, though it was in none of their own traditions, and made the rest agree. (The skipper felt that he and his people needed to get drunk, in this pause between battles, and Sergei would have appreciated being the occasion of it.) They held the party in the common room. Su and Stefan had decorated it somewhat, making paper flowers and the like. Hard liquor and pot appeared, besides the usual refreshments; viewscreens brought in the universe for a larger ornament; music Sergei had favored and ballet he had loved rollicked in playback. Folk stood around and remembered him.

After several hours, Martti Leino left. By then, a kind of liveliness had entered. Arms around shoulders, Brodersen, Weisenberg, and Dozsa were tunelessly belting out "Ford of Kabul River." Von Moltke and Rueda snuggled in a corner. Granville and Ky held a serious conversation. Fidelio observed the exotic race.

Leino walked down the circular hall to Zarubayev's quarters. The door stood open. He heard a few notes, hesitated, frowned, and went on in.

As bare as the rest, this room was draped in shadow and yellow lamplight. Zarubayev lay on his bed, attired in his uniform. Hair and beard glowed through dimness; otherwise his face had gone empty. The flames around him threw off a clean odor and the tiniest warmth. Caitlín sat beside him. She wore a blue kaftan, the best gown she had along. Her locks streamed unbound. In her left arm she cradled her sonador while her right fingers drew from it sounds like a muted woodwind.

She stopped when Leino entered. "Oh," she breathed.

"What—" He tightened. "Never mind. I am sorry I interrupted."

"No. Wait. Don't go." Caitlín made to rise, saw him unbrace a minikin bit, and sank back down. "You came to say farewell. I'd not stand in the way of that."

He bunched his fists and hastily released them. "You don't, Miz Mulryan."

"You've no kindness for me."

"Hoy, this is nil time for hakkerie."

"I meant no more than this, Mr. Leino: if it's alone you'd be with your friend, I can well come back later." She did get up.

Startled, he exclaimed, "Stop. Please. I knew you kenned him before, but not that you . . . cared."

She smiled most gently. "Aye, he was the quiet lad, was he not?" Stillness; then, low: "Even when showing me, this voyage, how to handle firearms in combat, he took none of his many opportunities to grow familiar, though he well knew I'd have liked it. For he saw me now as Daniel's woman, not his captain's but his friend's. The which gives away much about him, doesn't it?"

He flushed. "When did you first meet him?"

"Before I met Daniel. He came to the hospital, injured, as you may recall. We bantered amidst his pain. The world thought him humorless, but that was not true. Oh, he spun me the wildest yarn about the trouble he was having, him a Russian who did not enjoy chess. . . . After he got well, we met when we could, until I started spending my whiles in Eopolis with Daniel. We were never deep in love, Sergei and I, but he meant an oceanful to me."

"And to me," Leino said slowly, staring at her where she stood in front of the dead man. "We were on jobs together in space, the kind where you trust your life to your partner. On Demeter we'd go backpacking, sailing, partying—" His talk trailed off.

She nodded. "What happens between man and man, no woman will ever truly understand; but precious it is."

Half drunk, he threw at her: "What about man and woman?"

She turned to brush fingertips across the countenance which had been Zarubayev's. "That's worse to find words for, however long and hard the poets have tried." Her glance went back to Leino. "Indeed Sergei and I shared more than simple pleasure." Again it sought him who did not move. "They never realized," she said, nigh under her breath. "They took him for dour when he was only shy; but oh, the fun in him when once he felt at his ease! They took him for being practical as a machine; but I recall a night we brought a telescope outdoors, and after we'd lost ourselves in the forever, he began to speak of the Others. He believed they cannot be ignoring of us as they seem to, but most have a care and compassion we are too small to feel—"

She broke off. "Well," she said, "you don't want me to maunder, you want to give him his sending from you. Goodnight, Martti Leino."

"No!" He lifted a palm as if to block her. "Please stay. I didn't know anyone else was so near to him." He rubbed a wrist across his eyes. "Forgive me. May I ask what you were doing in here?"

"Nothing to mention."

He insisted: "You were singing."

She squared her shoulders. "Well, yes, I was that, a song, as we do in the Irish countryside. But it would be wrong to put on a show when such is not the way of my fellows aboard. Goodnight."

He stretched an arm in her path. "Please, Miz Mulryan— Caitlín—please don't go."

Her green gaze met his blue. "Why?"

"Because, oh, I told you, we share a heavy loss and . . . they're singing Kipling songs in the common room—What is yours?"

She dropped her lashes. "Merely an *ochlán*. A dirge, you'd say."

"Would you do it over?"

She regarded him for a moment before she decided. "Aye, since it is you who wish. He would have himself."

They sat down on either side of the bed. The lamps flickered, shadows moved inward, ventilators whispered. Faint, rowdy sounds which drifted in from the wake did not seem out of place. Caitlín's fingers evoked the "Londonderry Air."

Oh, would the stars might mourn for this our comrade,
    Weep tears of light across a riven sky,
Or that the rain which falls upon his homeland
    Were bidding him a long and last goodbye,
Or at the least, a blossom drop to kiss him
    From off a tree where springtime breezes blow:
For then we'd not be all alone in grieving.
    The world would sorrow too, the world that he loved so.

But silence reigns among the suns and planets.
    The leaves are dumb, the weather's deaf and blind.
We've only us to keen for this our comrade

And know that he was bright and strong and kind.
Ochone, ochone! He's gone like any sunrise.
Ochone, ochone! He laughed while he was here.
Ochone, ochone! He is no more forever.
What's left for us lies still, yet still is very dear.

XXI

I WAS A CROW. My first dim dreams ended in hunger when the universe went void. Angered, I tapped at its shell until this broke apart; and there was the day. My eyes filled with dazzle. I opened my mouth to it and yawped for food. Wings overshadowed me, a beak large and hard thrust into my gape, love poured thence to my inside. Soon I was aware that naked others were crowding me, so I crowded back and demanded as loudly as they did.

Plumage grew on us, and we spent much time happily admiring our own glossy blackness. But before long our parents shoved us from the nest. After the first beautiful terror and wild flapping, I learned how the wind would upbear me and what power lay ready to be unfolded in my wings. I took the air unto me, soared, swooped, glided, rejoiced. The sky was mine, and the whole earth below it ripe for raiding.

I belonged to the flock, of course, and had my place in the ranking and my occasional duties, such as watching out for hawks or men when we sought the lands beyond our woods. I never wished things were otherwise. Crows have *fun*. We chattered, intrigued, shouted our mirth, went off on expeditions, persecuted owls, found goodies to eat and sparkly things to bring home, were endlessly entertained by the antics of alien creatures, lorded it over the treetops. In the depths of leafless cold, we could still peck a living out of the snowcrust. But oh, the green and rustling summers! Oh, my female and our darling small chicks!

I grew old at last, weak, slow, though my knowledge of this was misty. One day a fox caught me on the ground. I broke free of his jaws, but blood spattered out of me until I could fly no more. Finding me a thicket, I sprawled on damp mushroomy soil, shut away from the sky, panting, while darkness blew ever stronger through me. Then the Summoner came and, still alive for a while, I departed that country wherein I had been Bird.

XXII

A CHIME SOUNDED through the cabin Joelle had taken. "Come in," she called.

Brodersen did, closing the door behind him. Framed by the impersonal chamber, he seemed doubly big and vivid. It blazed up in her that she wanted him.

Stop that nonsense! she ordered herself. *He's busy, preoccupied, see the haggardness, how the powerful arms hang at his sides, the gray eyes look more downward-slanting than ever. Furthermore, I will shortly begin my proper work, the wonder of Oneness will possess me and nothing else will matter.*

Nevertheless desire continued to thrill faintly along her veins. Eight years, no, nearer nine, and Brodersen had been that last lover, when he visited Earth— She'd not found celibacy difficult on the expedition, when every waking hour was charged with discovery. The risk of a man getting emotionally involved and pestering her when she wanted to carry out a project (as had happened a couple of times at home) was an overly high price for the rubbing of an itch that came infrequently anyway. *Of course, at last I did pay. Christine*—Chris lay buried on Beta. Dan was here, two meters from her.

"I stopped by to check on how you're doing," his deep voice said.

"Quite well, thank you," Joelle replied above her pulse. "We're certainly fortunate that you were foresighted enough to keep this ship completely stocked."

"Foresighted, hell." He grinned. "I was champing at the bit, and figured that if anything broke my way—like you coming home early—I should be ready to take off myself before some bureaucrat found a reason to refuse me clearance."

He glanced around. "Just the same, we got caught pretty flatfooted," he said. "And you folks from the Wheel are worse off. Uh, about changes of clothes for you. Pegeen—Caitlín Mulryan, our quartermaster, you recall, she'll be happy to lend you a couple of things—you're about the same size—and she'll make more out of spare cloth we've got along when she gets a chance, for you and whoever else wants. She's a good seamstress. You might be thinking what sorts of garment you'd prefer."

Joelle shrugged. "You know I don't care, provided it's comfortable. But thank her for me, please. I'll try to remember to do so in person, but you also know how forgetful I am about everyday matters."

"What more can you use? For instance, most of us keep a small private stock of food and drink. I imagine you'd rather not eat every meal in the mess."

"Oh, if they don't mind me often being a poor conversationalist, I don't mind sitting at a public table. I shut the noise out.... But it would be nice if I could offer you—offer a guest refreshment." She gestured, noting how awkward the motion was. "Won't you sit down? And, well, I didn't acquire any dislike of a pipe while I was gone."

"I noticed that at the conference, and was glad." He took a chair. She brought another to face it. Fetching out his tobacco pouch, he went on, "I can't stay but a minute or three. Got to arrange for making the salt water bath you say Fidelio needs. We have the chemicals, I'm sure, and the metal or plastic or whatever for a container, but we'd better make some recycling arrangement too, in case this trip stretches out longer than I hope it will."

"Isn't that a problem for your engineers?"

"Yes, but first Fidelio has to explain exactly what the requirements are. That'll be slow, even with Carlos to help, he knowing some of the Betan language. No, languages, right? You're the expert in those, but I gather you're due for a computer session. I think I can help discussion keep moving. Not to mention forty million other things that need attention before I knock off."

"Do call on me if you encounter serious linguistic problems. By the way, would you consider modifying a set of encephalic attachments for Fidelio, so he can link in with me? He's a holothete."

"Huh? I'd no idea."

"It appears to affect the personality less among Betans than among humans." Silence closed in while she tried to say what she wanted to say. Breaking the barrier in a rush: "Dan, it's wonderful seeing you again. More than being liberated. *You* were the man who did it."

He became busy charging his pipe. "No, we did, the team of us; and Sergei— We may not have done you a favor. You're headed into danger."

"Were we in no danger in the Wheel?"

"Yeah, true . . . I guess. . . . I have to keep shoving away this nightmare notion that we're dead wrong in what we're trying to do. That I'm putting lives at hazard for naught."

She managed to lean forward and drop a hand on his knee. "Don't fret. Politics always confuses me, but you've a feel for it and a knowledge. I rely on your judgment, as you'll have to rely on my calculations. Have faith in yourself, Dan."

"I'd better," he said dryly. His fingers remained at work on his pipe. "Well, are you set to make that analysis, Joelle?"

Have I grown too gaunt and gray for him? She withdrew her touch. "Yes. It'd be easier, perhaps more certain, if Fidelio and I could operate as a holothetic unit and take a complete theoretical structure from a memory bank. However, I did master the physical principles the Betans have found apply to the T machines—those were right down my alley, as you'd put it—and he and I have finished ransacking your ship's data collection for exact parameters of local space-time. The information appears to be sufficient. I expect I'll need a preliminary run-through today, then tomorrow work out the guidepath in detail."

He got worry lines between his brows, the way he'd done when first they met, he an Aventureros engineer consulting her about a thorny design problem. Oh, he'd fallen into such awe of her intellect, though really she doubted it was better than his—differently configured and oriented, but not intrinsically better—except when she was joined to her machine. He'd found excuses to meet her later on, which led to outright dinner dates after he was widowed and had moved to Demeter and made occasional trips Earthside. She enjoyed his company as she enjoyed a gust off the sea. Eventually, impulsively, she let him into her bed, and was astounded. . . . How young those worry lines made him look.

"Supposing we do reach Beta," he said, "will they help us? You and Carlos emphasized how they don't want to interfere, how careful they've always been about respecting less advanced species."

"Humankind is special to them, though," she assured him. "We'll have extensive explaining and persuading to do, I admit. But when we of *Emissary* described our history and sociology, what little we could convey, they found it no more grotesque than what they'd encountered among other races. Their leaders do believe we can help them through their psychosexual crisis."

"So they'd—m-m-m—what?"

"Make an appearance in the Solar System, I imagine, invincible, but simply protecting us while we broadcast the facts to Earth."

"And they offer us a fabulous bargain, you said. Their technology in exchange for franchises to exploit Jupiter and Saturn, which we can't anyway. Right?" Brodersen struck fire to tobacco, peering at her across it. "Of course, that will destroy the Actionists, and every party like theirs. Quite aside from the scandal, I mean. The whole philosophy will be killed."

"How?"

"Why, it's obvious. As fast as we acquire that same technology, we'll skite off through every star gate the Betans have mapped, as well as mounting our own program to chart new ones. The sheer profit to be made, in countless places and ways, must beggar the imagination. Else why would the Betans bother with our giant planets? So even before we start large-scale emigration, the balance of economic power will shift away from Earth. It'll also shift away from governments, unions, giant corporations, toward small outfits and individuals. There goes the tidy world welfare state the Actionist types hope to build. I daresay Quick foresees as much."

Joelle frowned, striving to comprehend. "But that isn't logical, Dan. Presumably welfare measures serve a need. If the need comes to an end, who would want to continue them?"

Brodersen laughed the ringing laugh she knew. Smoke burst from his mouth. It smelled masculine. "Dear, you're doing it again. Assuming people are logical. They aren't. The welfare state—any state—is an end in itself. It's the way for a few to impose their will on the many. And Judas priest, how those few do want to! Need to." He puffed on his pipe. "Talk with Stef Dozsa if you're interested. His country's been through the mill, over and over. Holy Roman Empire, Mongol Empire, Ottoman Empire, Austrian Empire, Soviet Empire, Balkan Empire.... No, maybe you shouldn't. That history's made a rabid anarchist of him. Harmless in his case, but if he converted you—well, under your stiffish exterior, Joelle, you've got a lot of wildness bottled up. I know."

You do, Dan!

Brodersen stirred. "My personal weakness is I ramble," he said. "I'd better stop boring you and carry on in my proper job."

"You weren't boring me," Joelle answered with effort. She felt the heat in her face and breasts. "You never did. Were always rather fascinating, in fact, I suppose because we're so unlike."

"Yeah, we are. Well, anyhow." He rose.

She did too. "Why don't you come by this evenwatch after we're both off?" she suggested. "I could indent for some food and wine. Remember how you used to do the cooking? I'm still terrible at that, but... I'll bet you've improved."

"Not much." He looks at his toes. "Besides, I— Happens I have a date. Sorry, but it's not the kind a person breaks."

"May I ask what?" she said through the hurt.

"Caitlín and I have an anniversary. Demetrian calendar; comes oftener that way." He raised his eyes. "Didn't you know? I thought it was obvious.... No, we're not married, I'm still with Lis and have no plans to change, but Caitlín—well, she and I are awfully close."

"I see."

He caught her hands. "Joelle, uh, she's not jealous. I mean—oh, hell it's fine having you here, and— Not propositioning you, but if you'd care to—later—"

She made herself smile, lean forward, touch lips to his. "I might. We needn't be in a hurry, though. And don't you feel obligated." *Because I fear that is what you feel right now, obligated. Caitlín is like a fair-skinned Chris.*

Besides, I'll soon be transhuman. "All right, Dan. So long."

Small, plain, humble, though never servile, Susanne Granville waited in the main computer room. She had turned on the viewscreen, scanner aimed at Sol, and sat watching. Dimmed but magnified, the disc was a turmoil of spots, flares, fountaining prominences, within coronal nacre. Music sparkled. Joelle recognized Nielsen's *Fynsk Forar*. Music, like architecture, was one of the few formal human arts she thought she responded properly to. She and Susanne had talked about it for an hour or more during the memorial party for the gunner.

"Hello," she said. "I didn't expect to find you here."

Susanne jumped up. "I knew you would be running a final check on the software, Dr. Ky, and wondered if I might be of assistance. Just in case, I excused me from 'elping the quartermaster [*Caitlín Mulryan*] make dinner."

Oh, yes, Joelle did not reply. *How often I've met this. You are the mere linker, I the supreme holothete. Your eagerness is to know you've been of use to me. Like Chris, like Chris.*

You'll see me in my linkage, that you are not capable of, ascending to a heaven you can never reach but which you have glimpsed in fragments. I will touch the Absolute, I will be in the Noumenon, I will know Final Reality, not as a mathematical construct, but immediately, in my brain and bones.

O Susanne! she thought. *I wish I might kiss and comfort you, as I could not Chris, as I could not Eric.*

Her mind veered (and this irritated her, made her twice eager to get into circuit, where such undisciplined things did not occur) to ask how much she was originally attracted to Brodersen because his mother was a Stranathan and he had visited that family many times as a boy. Eric Stranathan was of it, Joelle's first and most unforgotten lover, son of the Captain General of the Fraser Valley, himself a linker.

It was they together, Joelle and Eric, who were the earliest to learn that the gulf between linker and holothete was not one of degree but of kind, unbridgeably wide. For no clear reason, her recollection fled back to a dull lecturer in a stuffy hall, at a convention in Calgary . . . but the reason was clear; that evening she'd met him.

XXIII

The Memory Bank

"THE HUMAN BRAIN, and hence the entire nervous system, can be integrated with a computer of the proper design," the speaker was droning. "We have long since progressed beyond the 'wires in the head' stage. Electromagnetic induction suffices to make a linkage. The computer then supplies its vast capacity for storing and processing data, its capability of carrying out mathematico-logical operations in microseconds or less. The brain, though far slower, supplies creativity and flexibility; in effect, it continuously rewrites the program. Computers which can do this for themselves do exist, of course, but for most purposes they do not function nearly as well as a computer-operator linkage does, and we may never be able to improve them significantly. After all, the brain packs trillions of cells into a mass of about a kilogram. Furthermore, linkage gives humans direct access to what they would otherwise know only indirectly.

"For present, practical purposes, its advantages are twofold. (a) As I remarked, programs can be altered on the spot, in the course of being carried out. Formerly it was necessary to run them through, painstakingly check their results, and then slowly rewrite them, with possibilities of error, and without any guarantee that the new versions would turn out to be what we most needed. Once linkers and their equipment come into everyday use, we will be free of that handicap. (b) By the very experience, as I have also suggested, the linker gains insights which he or she could have gotten in no other way, and hence becomes a more able scientist—including a better writer of programs—when working independently of the apparatus, too."

Good Lord! Joelle thought. *Do we really have to endure this?*

True the conference was an important political as well as scientific event. The military secrecy in which she had been raised was beginning to lift; here in Calgary, people could freely discuss developments which had been hidden for decades or worse; the public was entitled to information, in popular terms, during the opening ceremonies.

The trouble was, no words could describe being in linkage: creating n-dimensional spaces, and time-variant curvatures for them, and tensors within, and functions and operations that nobody had ever before imagined. You fashioned a conceptual cosmos, learned that it was wanting and annulled it, devised another and another, until at last you saw what you had made and, behold, it was very good. Each time the numbers rushed through you to verify, and you knew how much reality you had embraced, it was an outbursting of revelation. The Christian hopes to be eternally in the presence of God, the Buddhist hopes to become one with the all in Nirvana, the linker hopes to achieve more than genius—is there a vast difference between them? Yes: the linker, in this life, does it.

In days, hours, fractional seconds. Afterward he or she cannot entirely comprehend what happened. The high moment of love also lies outside of time; but we understand it better, when at peace, than the linker understands what the linker has known.

Joelle's gaze roved. Hey, wasn't that a handsome young man a dozen seats to her right! Why hadn't she seen him earlier! Well, she wasn't given to noticing people. War orphan, brought up from infancy in the pioneering holothetic program, lately released into academe as the Troubles faded out, a virgin who didn't know what to do about the opposite sex and wasn't sure she wanted to—

"—while linkage to macroscopic machinery has not proven cost-effective, the case has turned out to be otherwise for monitoring and controlling scientific instruments. For this it is inadequate to supply the operating brain with numbers such as voltmeter readings and nothing else. For example, a spectrum is best considered—rationally appreciated—when the operator sees it and, simultaneously, knows the exact wavelength and intensity of every line. Through appropriate hardware and software, this can now be done. Subjectively, it is like sensing the data directly, as if the nervous system had grown complete new input organs of unprecedented power and sensitivity.

"Workers elsewhere have experimented with that. The principal thing Project Ithaca [in which Joelle was raised, a part of it] did was to take the next step. What is the *meaning* of those data, those sensations?

"In everyday life, we do not apprehend the world as a jumble of raw impressions, but as an orderly structure. Yonder we do not see a splash of green and brown; we see a tree, of such-and-such a kind, at such-and-such a distance. Although it is done unconsciously, yes, instinctively, since animals do it too, nevertheless we may be said to build theories, models, of the world, within which our direct perceptions are made to make sense. Naturally, we modify these models when that seems reasonable. For instance, we may decide that we are not really seeing a tree but a piece of camouflage. We may realize that we have misjudged its distance because the air is more clear or murky than we knew at first. Basically, however, through our models we comprehend and can act in an objective universe.

"Science has long been adding to our store of information and thus forcing us to change our model of the cosmos as a whole, until today it embraces billions of years and light-years, in which are galaxies, subatomic particles, the evolution of life, and everything else that our ancestors never suspected. To most of us, this part of the *Weltbild* has admittedly been rather abstract, no matter how immediate the impact of the technologies it makes possible.

"In order to enhance laboratory capability, Project Ithaca began work on means to supply a linkage operator directly with theory as well as data. This was more than learning a subject, permanently or temporarily. Any operator has to do that, in order to think about a given task. And indeed, outstanding accomplishments came out of the Turing Institute here, pioneering ways for the linked computer to give its human partner the necessary knowledge. Project Ithaca greatly improved such systems, and its civilian successors continue to progress. We call them holothetic.

"The work has had an unexpected result. Those operators whom Ithaca trained from childhood, linkers who today are adults advancing the art in their turn, are more and more getting into a mode that I must call intuitive. A baseball pitcher, an acrobat, or simply a person walking is constantly solving complex problems in physics with little or no conscious thought. The organism feels what is right to do. Analogously, we have for example reached the point of manipulating individual amino acids within protein molecules, using ions directed by force-fields which are directed by a holothete, in a manner that perhaps only the Others could plan out step by step. Likewise for any number of undertakings. Direct perception through holothetics is leading to comprehension on a nonverbal level.

"This is doubly true because our theoretical knowledge is far from perfect. Quite frequently these days, a holothete senses that things are not going as intended, that something is wrong with the model—and intuits what changes to make, what the real situation is, as we so often do in our ordinary lives. Later systematic study generally confirms the intuition.

"My colleagues will be discussing various aspects of holothetic linkage. This introductory sketch of mine—"

When the dullness was outlived and the audience moving toward drinks, Eric came over and introduced himself. He had been noticing too.

In a canoe on Lake Louise, they shipped their paddles and idled. The water danced blue, green, diamond. Around it, above forest, mountains sheered aloft into silence. Ever so slightly, the boat rocked with each motion they made.

She dipped a finger over the side and watched how ripples spread. "Electron interferences make a moiré too," she mused. "It's wonderful finding the same here. I never paid attention before." She looked at him and savored. "Thank you for bringing me." A little scared, she let her eyes drift elsewhere. "Electrons do it in three dimensions. No, four, but I haven't perceived that . . . yet."

She had made similar remarks to him after they'd attended the ballet in Calgary. Over coffee and brandy she had told him how sublimely Newtonian *Swan Lake* and *Ondine* were, when to him—he said—they were sublimely sexy. Still, he, a linker, found as much mathematics as melody in a Bach recital, or admired above everything else the subtle perspectives in Monet. (Looking at the same 3-faxes, she pointed out interactions of colors to which he said he believed critics of the past couple of centuries had been blind.) Today, for whatever reason, she saw unease stir in him.

"Look, Joelle, don't get lost in abstractions— Wait. Please. Let me explain what I mean. Sure, you and I work with data, set up paradigms, compute resultants, sure. Fine. Fine job. But let's not let that interfere with what we, well, find in places like this.

In our private lives especially. This—" he waved a hand around the horizon—"is what's real. Everything else we infer. This is what we're alive in."

She regarded him for a long while, during which he glowed. That night they became lovers.

He Canadian, she American, in an era when military governments were paranoid after the Troubles, before their countries federated and joined the World Union... he and she were separated for more than a year. Meanwhile holothetics was evolving exponentially, from a mere improvement of linkage to a wholly new order of perceiving and existing.

She sensed her growth away from him, and it hurt, but she could no more resist what she was becoming than a fetus in the womb can. By the time he had finally arranged to come join her at the University of Kansas for R & D purposes, she knew what he must learn and had completed the necessary arrangements.

When he arrived at her office, they made love. Then they made a sandwich lunch and talked. At last she leaned over and kissed him, lingeringly but tenderly, almost as if she bade goodbye to a child. "Let's go!" she said. As she led the way to her laboratory, her stride became triumphant.

Down there, she warned, "Words are no use here. You must experience for yourself. We're about to become more intimate than ever in bed. Enormously more."

Quasi-telepathic effects had been reported, when a passive linker in a holothetic circuit not only received the same data and theory in his brain as the active one did, but "felt" that latter's ongoing evaluations. "You, uh, you'll slave my unit to yours?" Eric inquired. "According to what I've seen in the literature, that doesn't convey a particularly strong or clear impression."

"Everything isn't in the current literature. I told you I—we—all right, *I* am making whirlwind progress. I've acquired a, I don't know, an insight, a near-instinct, and the feedback between me and the system, the continuous reprogramming at each session—" She tugged his sleeve. "Come along. Get to know!"

"What do you have in mind?"

She frowned the least bit. "That'll depend partly on you, how you're taking what happens. We'll begin with you and the 707. Just think in it for a while, get settled down. Then, through the cross-connections, I'll phase you in with me and my computer. That will have to be strictly input to you, no access to effectors, or you might ruin some delicate experiments. I'm going to look in on them, you see. My help is called for often enough that we have constantly open channels between them and my system. Genetics at a lab right on this campus; nuclear physics at the big accelerator in Minnesota; cosmology in Sagan Orbital. I hope I can lead you to a hint of what I'm doing these days. I'll know, because you will have an output of a kind to me. In effect, I'll be scanning your mind. Yes," she said into his stupefaction, "I've reached that stage.

"Afterward—" She threw her arms around him and kissed him. "Let there be an afterward."

He responded, but she sensed he sensed that her tone had been kind rather than prayerful.

He lowered himself into the proper lounger, set it at the reclining angle he liked, let muscle and bone go easy, before he pulled the helmet down over his head, adjusted and secured it, put his wrists through the contact loops, tapped fingers across a control plate and checked out the settings. While linking herself likewise, she saw the olden thrill shaking the fret out of him.

"Activate?" he asked.

"Proceed," she answered.

"I love you," he said, and pressed the main switch.

Thereafter she felt and thought what he did, with a minor part of her awareness.

Momentarily, senses and intellect whirled, he imagined he heard a wild high piping, memories broke forth out of long burial as if he had fallen back through time to this boyhood swimming hole and moss cold and green upon a rock, that hawk at hover and the rough wool of a mackinaw around him. Then his nervous system steadied into mastery. Electromagnetic induction, amplification of the faintest impulses, a basic program which he had over the years refined to fit his unique self, meshed; human and computer became a whole.

"Think," she said, and Joelle knew his response: How could he not, when his was now a mightier genius than any which had been on Earth before his day?

"Words are no use here," she told me.

They were fully cognizant of their environment. Had they wanted to, they could have examined its most micrometric details, a scratch and a reflection on polished metal, the shimmy

of a needle across a meter, mumble and faint tang of oil in the
ventilation, back-and-forth tides in the veins. But she sensed
that even she no longer entirely mattered to him. He had a
perceptual universe to conquer.

In the next several milliseconds, while he cast about for a
problem worth tackling, a fraction of him calculated the value of
an elliptic integral to a thousand decimal places. It was a
pleasant semi-automatic exercise. The numbers fell together
most satisfyingly, like bricks beneath the hands of a mason. *Ah,*
came to him, *yes, the stability of Red Spot vortices on planets
like Jupiter, yes, I did hear talk about that in Calgary.* The sweep
hand on a wall clock had barely stirred.

He marshalled a list of the data he thought he would need and
sent a command. To him it felt like searching his normal
memory for a fact or two, except that this went meteorically
faster and more assuredly, in spite of drawing on banks which
were hundreds of kilometers away. The theory reached him,
formulas, specific values of quantities, yes, that particular
differential equation would be an absolute bitch to solve; no,
wait, he saw a dodge; but was the equation actually plausible,
couldn't he devise a set of relationships which better described
conditions on an aborted sun—?

An ice-clean fire arose, he was losing himself in it, he was
getting drunk on sanity.

Eric, she called: no voice, no name, a touch.

He must wrench his attention from Jupiter, with a vow, *I'll be
back.*

Eric, are you ready to follow me?

It was not truly a question, it was an intent which he felt. It
was her. At dazzling speed, as neurone webs adapted to each
other's synapse patterns, she merged with him. The formless
eddies that go behind shut eyelids were not shaping into her
image; rather he got fleeting impressions of himself, before her
presence flooded him. Was it her femaleness he knew as a secret
current in the blood, a waiting to receive and afterward cherish
and finally give, a bidding she chose not to heed but which would
always be there? He couldn't tell, he might never know, for the
union was only partial. He had not learned how to accept and
understand most of the signals that entered him, and there were
many more which his body never would be able to receive. That
became a pain in him as it was in her.

Eric, in this too you are my first man, and I think my last.

Forebrains, more alike than the rest of their organisms, meshed. Besides, Joelle had practiced cross-exchange on that level and developed the technique of it with fellow linkers, until she was expert. Communication between her and Eric strengthened and clarified, second by second. It was not direct, but through their computers, whose translations were inevitably imperfect. Impressions were often fragmentary and distorted, or outright gibberish—bursts of random numbers, shapes, light flashes, noises, less recognizable non-symbols, which would have frightened him were it not for the underlying constancy of her. What touched his mind as her thoughts were surely reconstructions, by his augmented logical powers, of what it supposed she might be thinking at a given instant. The real words that passed between them went in the common mortal fashion, from lips to ear.

Nevertheless: he took her meanings with a fullness, a depth he had not dreamed could be, there on the threshold of her universe.

"Genetics," she said aloud. That was the sole clue he needed. She would guide him to the research at this school. Knowledge sprang forth. The work was on the submolecular level, the very bases of animate being. She was frequently called on to carry out the most exacting tasks, invent new ones, or interpret results. Today the setup was in part running automatically, in part on standby; but she had access to it anytime.

Her brain ordered the right circuits closed, and she was joined to the complex of instruments, sensors, effectors, and to the entire comprehension man had of the chemistry of life. Receiving from her, Eric perceived.

He got no presentation of quantities, readings on gauges whose significance became plain after long calculation. That is, the numbers were present, but in the experience he was hardly more conscious of them than he was of his skeleton. He was not looking from outside and making inferences, he was *there*.

It was seeing, feeling, hearing, traveling, though not any of those things, for it went beyond what the poor limited human creature could ever sense or do, and beyond and beyond.

The cell lived. Pulsations crossed its membrane, like colors, the cell was a globe of iridescence, throbbing to the intricate fluid flow that cradled it in deliciousness, avidly drinking energies which cataracted toward it down ever-changing gradients. Green distances reached to golden infinity. Beneath every ongoing fulfillment dwelt peace. The cosmos of the cell was a Nirvana that danced.

Now inward, through the rainbows, to the interior ocean. Here went a maelstrom of . . . tastes . . . and here ruled a gigantic underlying purposefulness; within the cell, work forever went on, driven by a law so all-encompassing that it might have been God the Captain. Organelles drifted by, seeming to sing while they wove together chemical scraps to make stuff that came alive. As the scale of his cognition grew finer, Eric saw them spread out into Gothic soarings, full of mysteries and music. Ahead of him, the nucleus waxed from an island of molecular forests to a galaxy of constellated atoms whose force-fields shone like wind-blown star-clouds.

He entered it, he swept up a double helix, tier after tier of awesome and wholly harmonious labyrinths, he was with Joelle when she evoked fire and reshaped a part of the temple, which was not less beautiful thereafter, he shared her pride and her humility, here at the heart of life.

Her voice came far-off and enigmatic, heard through dream: "Follow me on." He swept out of the cell, through space and through time, at lightspeed across unseen prairies, into the storms that raged down a great particle accelerator. He became one with them, possessed by their own headlong fervor, the same speed filled him and he lanced toward the goal as if to meet a lover.

This world outranged the material. He transcended the comet which meson he had become, for he was also a wave intermingling with a trillion other waves, like a crest that had crossed a sea to rise and break at last in sunlit foam and a roar—though these waves were boundlessly more shapeful and fleetly changeable, they flowed together to create a unity which flamed and thundered around an implacable serenity—*Bach could tell a little of this*, passed through him, for he had his reasoning mind too; that was a high part of the glory—*but he alone could, and it would only be a little*—

The atom awaited him. Its kernel, where energies querned, was majestic beyond any telling. Electron shells, elfinly asparkle, veiled it from him. He plunged through, the forces gave him uncountable caresses, the kernel shone ahead, itself an entire creation, he pierced its outer barriers and they sent a rapturous shudder across him, he probed in and in.

The kernel burst. That was no disaster, it was an unfolding.

The atom embraced him, yielded to him, his being responded to her every least wild movement, he knew her. Radiance exploded outward. The morning stars sang together, and all the sons of God shouted for joy.

"Cosmology," said Joelle the omnipotent. He fumbled to find her in a toppling darkness. She enfolded him and they flew together, up a laser beam, through a satellite relay, to an observatory in orbit beyond the Moon.

Briefly he spied the stars as if with his eyes, unblurred by any sky. Their multitudes, steel-blue, frost-white, sunset-gold, coal-red, almost glittered the night out of heaven. The Milky Way rivered in silver, nebulae glowed where new suns and planets were being born, a sister galaxy flung her faint gleam across Ginnungagap. But at once he leagued with the instrumentality which was seeking the uttermost ends of space-time.

First he was aware of optical spectra. They told him of light that bloomed from leaping and whirling gas, they told him of tides in the body of a sun—a body more like the living cell than he could have imagined before—and of the furnaces down below where atoms begot higher elemental generations and photons racing spaceward were the birthcry. And in this Brahma-play he shared. Next he felt a solar wind blow past, he snuffed its richness, tingled to its keenness, and knew the millennial subtlety of its work. Thereafter he gave himself to radio spectra, cosmic ray spectra, magnetic fields, neutrino fluxes, relativistics which granted a star gate and seemed to grant time travel, the curve of the continuum that is the all.

At the Grand Canyon of the Colorado you may see strata going back a billion years, and across the view of them a gnarly juniper, and know something of Earth. Thus did Eric learn something of the depths and the order in space-time. The primordial fireball became more real to him than the violence of his own birth, the question of what had brought it about became as terrifying. With it, he bought the spirals of the galaxies and the DNA molecule with energy which would never come back to him, and saw how it aged as it matured, even as you and I; the Law is One. He lived the lives of stars: how manifold were the waves that formed them, how strong the binding afterward to an entire existence! Amidst the massiveness of blue giants and black holes, he found room to forge planets whereon crystals and flowers could grow. He beheld what was still unknown—the overwhelming most of it, now and forever—and how Joelle longed to go questing.

Yet throughout, the observer part of him sensed that beside hers, his perception was misted and his understanding chained. When she drew him back to the flesh, he screamed.

They sat in the office. Her desk separated them. She had raised the blind on the window at her back and opened it. Shadows hastened across grass, sunlight that followed was bright but somehow as if the air through which it fell had chilled it, the gusts sounded hollow that harried smells of damp soil into the room, odors of oncoming autumn.

She spoke with all her gentleness. "We couldn't have talked meaningfully before you'd been there yourself, could we have, Eric?"

His glance went to the empty couch. "How meaningful was anything between us, even at first?"

She sighed. "I wanted it to be." A smile touched her. "I did enjoy."

"No more than that, enjoy, eh?"

"I don't know. I do care for you, and for everything you taught me about. But I've gone on to, to where I tried to lead you."

"How far did I get?"

She stared down at her hands, folded on the desk in helplessness, and murmured, "Still less than I feared. It was like showing a blind man a painting. He might get a tiny idea through his fingertips, texture, the dark areas faintly warmer than the light—but oh, how tiny!"

"Whereas you respond to the lot, from quanta to quasars," he rasped.

She raised her head, challenging their shared unhappiness. "No, I've barely begun, and of course I'll never finish. But don't you see, that's half of the wonder. Always more to find. Direct experience, as direct as vision or touch or hunger or sex, experience of the *real* reality. The whole world humans know is just a passing, accidental consequence of it. Each time I go to it, I know it better and it makes me more its own. How could I stop?"

"I don't suppose I could learn?"

She knew he cherished no hope. "No. A holothete has to start like me, early, and do hardly anything else, especially in those formative young years." Her eyes stung. "I'm sorry, darling. You're good and kind and...how I wish you could follow along. How you deserve it."

"You don't wish you could go back, though, to what you were when we met?"

"Would you?"

He could never truly summon up what had happened this day. However—"No," he said. "In fact, I dare not try again. That could be addictive. For me, nothing but an addiction, and to lunacy. For you—" He shrugged. "Do you know the *Rubáiyát?*"

"I've heard of it," she said, "but I've had no chance to become cultured."

He recited:

Why, if the Soul can fling the Dust aside,
And naked on the Air of Heaven ride,
*   Were't not a Shame—were't not a Shame for him*
In this clay carcase crippled to abide?

She nodded. "The old man told truth, didn't he? I did read once that Omar was a mathematician and astronomer. He must have been lonely."

"Like you, Joelle?"

"I have a few colleagues, remember. I'm teaching them—" She broke off, leaned across the desk, and said in a renewed concern: "What about us two? We'll be collaborating. You're strong enough to carry on, discharge your duty, I'm certain you are. But our personal lives— What's best for you?"

"Or for you? Let's take that up first."

"Anything you want, Eric. I'll gladly be your wife, mistress, anything."

He was quiet a while, seeking words—she supposed—that might not hurt her. None came.

"You're telling me that you don't care which," he said. "You're willing to treat me as well as you're able, because it doesn't greatly matter to you." He raised a palm to check her response. "Oh, no doubt you'd get a limited pleasure from living with me, even from my conversation. If nothing else, I'd help fill in the hours when you can't be linked...until you and those fellows of yours go so far that you'll have no time for childish things."

"I love you," she protested. A pair of tears broke loose.

He sighed. "I believe you. It's simply that love isn't important any more, beside that grandeur. I've felt affection for dogs I've kept. But—call it pride, prejudice, stubbornness, what you will—I can't play a dog's part."

He rose. "We'll doubtless have an efficient partnership till I go home," he ended. "Today, though, while something remains of her, I'll tell my girl goodbye."

She sought him. He held her while she wept. But when at length she kissed him, her lips were quite steady.

"Go back to your link for a bit," he counselled her.

"I will," she answered. "Thank you for saying it."

He walked out into a wind gone cold at evening. She stood in the doorway and waved. He didn't turn around to see. Maybe he didn't want to know how soon the door closed on her.

XXIV

THE NEWCOMERS were naturally much in demand aboard *Chinook*. It was thus a small surprise to Weisenberg when Rueda Suárez invited him to stop by for a drink before dinner. Entering at the agreed time, the engineer heard a folk song from the Andean altiplano throbbing at low volume and saw that the leader was screening a page of verse.

Rueda followed his glance. "García Lorca," the Peruvian said. "I am pleased to find the data bank here is well stocked: my favorites, him, Neruda, Cervantes, everyone, not to speak of music."

"Well, we planned against possible years of being away, the same as you did," Weisenberg answered. "Moreover, like you, we hoped we'd be showing some of the human culture to nonhumans."

"Years... in your case, sir? Are you not married?"

"Yes, with five good kids. But the youngest is starting in the university, the rest are entirely on their own. Sarah was slated to come along on the expedition, quartermaster. Of course, when we had to scramble as we did, I wouldn't let her." Weisenberg chuckled, though pain stirred beneath. "More accurately, I didn't tell her—I skipped out, leaving a message—because a person needs a nice safe black hole to shelter in when Sarah gets her Jewish up."

"I see. Won't you sit down? What would you like? I drew a ration of each type of liquor in the stores.

"Scotch, then, thank you. Neat; water chaser." Weisenberg folded his leanness into a chair. Rueda poured the same for both and settled opposite.

"I thought we should get a little acquainted," the host said. "In forty hours we will be at the T machine, and God alone knows what will happen. If Daniel's scheme succeeds and we reach Beta, we still have a long, hard effort before us. If it does not, we may well be in instant danger of our lives. We had better know the ways in which we can depend on one another. And . . . perhaps you can find duty for me. I feel useless, I worry, I drink too much." His smile was rather sour. "Frieda might keep me occupied, but she's exploring the new men around her."

Weisenberg took a smoky sip. "Can't you ask the skipper for a job?"

"I hate to add to his burdens. Besides, you are our general technical expert. If you could give me a suggestion for me to make to him—do you see? You and I may communicate better than most. I heard you spent years in Perú, working for Aventureros."

Weisenberg nodded. "I studied nuclear engineering in Lima. There was no school of it then on Demeter. Afterward, yes, I did take a job with your company. That was what got me hooked on being in space. But I loved the city too. It's beautiful, and gave me many glorious moments. I was there when the Covenant was signed!"

"Why did you return, if you don't mind telling me?"

"Oh, mainly for my parents' sake. It was not easy working groundside, though raising a family kept me reasonably cheerful. When Dan started Chehalis, I jumped into his employ."

Rueda stared at his tumbler, drank, and stared again, as if it held an omen. "Space," he murmured. "Yes, we must each of us be obsessed with space, no? Why else would we be here? I think I was first caught in boyhood, on a cold and brilliant night at Machu Picchu. The stars above the Incan ruins were like a host of angels."

"Or of Others," Weisenberg said as softly.

Rueda gave him an examining look. "Are you among those who make the Others into God?"

"No, not really." The conversation was becoming intimate fast; but only forty hours of peace remained. "However, I went to Neo-Chasidic rabbinical school in Eopolis. A man can bear the marks of that his whole life, no matter if the faith has gone."

"Well, I am a Catholic of sorts, I think, but I must admit those years at Beta made me wonder a lot. Until then, I'd almost taken the Others for granted. But when the Betans, with their fantastic capabilities, turned out to be mortal and troubled, the same as us—mystified and awed by the Others, the same as us—yes, it upset a great deal in me." Rueda grimaced. "I was a political conservative too. Now I see how things I never dreamed of have been infecting government, and that faith also shakes." He knocked back his whisky. "It continues possible to believe in the power, wisdom, and benevolence of the Others. May it always continue possible."

Having taken a sip of water, he lifted the liquor bottle off the table beside him and made an offering gesture toward Weisenberg. The engineer shook his head. Rueda glugged forth a refill for himself and started on it.

"I am not a cultist about them," Weisenberg said. "For instance, I do not believe they are working secretly to guide us and the whole universe. Maybe they are, but their Voice denied it, also to the Betans. By and large, I'm agnostic about them, and will stay that way till we get some direct information, which may well be never."

"Still, they are important to your soul," Rueda observed.

Weisenberg nodded anew. "Fundamental. Especially when I'm watching the sky in space. Though they probably do not play at being gods, it does seem impossible—well, impossible for me to accept, at least—that they're indifferent to us . . . that they let us use their gates merely because we can't hurt anything of theirs, and show us a single path to a new planet in idle kindliness, like a man feeding pigeons bits of a sandwich he isn't going to eat. No, obviously they did, somehow, study us closely before ever Fernández-Dávila left Earth. Can they since have lost interest in us?"

"They may have gone elsewhere," Rueda said. "Remember, nobody, including the Betans, nobody has seen a ship of theirs."

"Maybe they keep their ships invisible. Maybe they don't need ships. It does not make sense they would abandon those T machines—think of the investment of energy and resources—or, I'm certain, that they would abandon us. I can easily imagine they keep out of our sight. We could be overcome by their presence, crushed. But damn it, they must be benign. They must *care*."

"This is a big galaxy. Apparently millions of intelligent races, or billions. Could they spare the time?"

"If they can build T machines around—how many suns?—they can follow what happens on the planets."

"Like God? 'His eye is on the sparrow.'"

"Oh, the Others hardly have infinite powers. We might not be able to tell the difference, though."

Rueda turned grim. "They're not doing much in the way of helping us, aboard this ship, are they?"

"They never passed any miracles for individual benefit that I heard of," Weisenberg admitted. "I've tried and tried and failed and failed to guess what their relationship is to us, how their concern expresses itself. I'm only convinced to the marrow that they do care—that the Voice didn't lie when it said they love us."

It was time to prepare yet another meal. Caitlín entered the common room on her way to the gallery, and stopped short.

The alien...the Betan...Fidelio stood, or sat, or squatted, or poised before one of the big viewscreens, staring out. Interior lighting dimmed the sky for her eyes, but she saw the Milky Way stream past his head. He was alone.

"Oh," she blurted. "Good day to you."

Though he didn't glance around, he answered in a hoarseness that whistled, *"Buenos días, señora Mulryan."*

Caitlín went to Spanish. "Do you know me, then, already, not even looking?"

"My race has ears more keen than yours." Without practice, a gifted hearing was necessary to follow most of what Fidelio said. But he spoke fluently and grammatically. It was just that nature had never quite meant him to utter sounds of this kind. As if realizing he might have been too curt, he went on: "Each individual has a distinct odor, too. This is something else you are not evolved to notice. However, your eyesight in air is much better at long range than mine, and I can only helplessly admire your tactile sensitivity." He turned, now, in a single fluid motion—light gleamed along his fur— to confront her.

She strode across the deck until she stood before him. "I like your smell," she said. "It brings me back to my homeland, and me a child at play where the sea made the shingle grind together like millstones...but it's different enough, too, that I am also a child at dream on the same shore, seeing fairyland in the clouds....Pardon. You could not understand that."

"Perhaps I could. My folk too have myths and phantoms, which are strongest in the young."

She laid hands across his webbed and clawed paws, because

his own hands were further back, gripped their knobbliness, and said gladly: "I was sure of it. But I didn't know you would be so learned about us. To recognize a word like 'fairyland'!"

"My work has been with other sapient species. That aids me in guessing what might matter to yours." The altogether blue gaze grew intent upon her. "I own to being surprised at your immediate comprehension of me. My accent seemed much too thick for everyone who is not off *Emissary*."

Caitlín disengaged and shrugged. "Well, I collect songs in several languages."

The big brown form reared up, the whiskers quivered. "Do you mean that you sing, yourself? And not formal music, such as the expedition's people played for me, but an ordinary kind?"

"Why, did they never sing?"

"Yes, once in a while, but—" Fidelio hesitated. "I remarked that my race has comparatively discriminating ears."

Caitlín grinned. "I know what you are trying to be tactful about. Well, if nonetheless you got interested in our music, from recordings—I'd never call myself an outstanding performer, but—"

"Good day," said a new voice.

Fidelio had no need to see who spoke. Caitlín did. Joelle Ky stood in the main doorway.

"Oh, good day, señora!" Caitlín made haste to give her a soft salute. "Can I be doing anything for you?"

"No. I happened by." The holothete held her lean form as rigid as her tone.

"We were starting a chat—"

"This is the first member of this crew with whom I can freely talk," Fidelio explained.

"Won't you join us, Dr. Ky?" Caitlín asked timidly.

"No," the other woman said. Her countenance was likewise frozen. "What could I contribute? Do carry on, Señorita Mulryan. Dinner can wait. No doubt it's more important to widen Fidelio's experience of ... humanity." She strode from sight.

Caitlín stared at the space where she had been. The Betan's query jerked her attention back to him: "Is there conflict between you two?"

"No. I never—that is—" Caitlín drew breath. "After all, we have barely met, she and I. Of course, I knew about her, and was in awe, and hoped—" She half sighed, half shuddered, then squared her shoulders. "A conflict is possible anyhow," she admitted. "Captain Brodersen has told me a few things. She may resent my closeness to him. But I'm sure this is completely foreign to you."

Did Fidelio hunch over, as if defensive? "Have you not understood? We want this kind of thing *not* to be foreign to us."

"Well, yes—" Caitlín stammered. "I suppose—I've heard— It's stunningly strange, but—" Tears glimmered forth, though they did not go past her lashes. "What you hoped would be an opening to love has become one to hatred and dread. Oh, my poor dear!"

She rallied. "We're bound for what's better," she said. "Dan Brodersen will see to that. Meanwhile, it would be wise if you come to know humans besides the few who went to your planet. We do differ very much. Surely some among us can help you. Also, getting acquainted will lift everyone's minds off the loss we've suffered and the desperate action a few days hence." Again she took hold of him, this time by the hands, since he had reached those out. "Let me be your guide. I can interpret, yes, and arrange small get-togethers and try to keep things cheery. We all need that."

"Many thanks," he replied. "You are kind."

Still he stood bent, and his words came mechanical. Caitlín observed him closely, against the unpitying stars. "You were glad for a moment," she murmured at last, "but that has fled you."

He made a noise that might correspond to a sigh. "It is nothing you can do anything about, señorita. And if we win free, it will soon be cured."

"Do you care to tell me what?"

"I am a holothete, like Joelle Ky, and long out of the . . . the state of communion. You have heard it becomes vital to us, or at least to our happiness." Fidelio lifted his head. "No matter. It is no worse for me than for her."

"But you are among aliens!" Caitlín cried. "And we have the equipment aboard, but it could not fit you, could it? Why you must be miserable!"

She flung herself against the massive, warm body and hugged him. He touched her in shy response.

"Listen, Fidelio," she said when they separated, "you've the spirit to see brooding is useless. You can set your trouble aside for a bit. You were doing so when we got interrupted. Let's go back to where we were then. Music. You'd like to hear our songs, and I'd be overjoyed to hear yours." Briskly: "Now I must prepare the food, but there's no reason why we can't be singing the while."

He stirred, straightening. Life returned to his voice. "Yes, please, let us. Could I assist you in your work?"

For the first time since they left the Wheel, she laughed.

"What is it?" he asked.

"Oh... thank you.... Maybe you could carry a few things. But I was remembering a primitive cottage in Ireland, and seeing you at the kitchen sink wielding a dish towel."

As if a weight had fallen off her, Caitlín danced toward the galley. While she did, she commenced his education.

> *La cucaracha, la cucaracha,*
> *Ya no quiere caminar—*

"Ah." Frieda von Moltke's breath came warm and musky. "That was good. You are very good."

Martti Leino opened his eyes to the round, wide-nosed, full-mouthed countenance below his. He was not tall; she was; she had readily been able to kiss him on his lips and inside them till it began to crest in her. Then she roared, and it was like riding an earthquake. Her arms and thighs still clasped him. Sweat glued strands of yellow hair to the slightly florid brow and cheeks; he felt the same moisture against his belly.

"You too," he said. "I had fun, and I surely needed some. Thank you."

She laughed. "We are not done yet, my friend. Howeffer, what about a beer first? And do you mind if I smoke?"

"No. I don't myself, but no." He rolled off her and propped himself on his pillow at the headboard. Her feet smacked the deck. She was heavy: not fat, save for the huge breasts; solid. Crossing her cabin, she took a cheroot from a box—the ship was stocked for a variety of minor vices—and put it between her teeth before she dealt with the bottles.

Returning, she paused at the bedside. Her regard of him grew speculative. "Martti," she asked, "why did you close your eyes after we began?"

He moved them from her. "Habit," he mumbled.

"I think not. We could haff turned the lights off if you wanted. You were using effery sense, until— Did you decide to pretend I was somebody else?"

"Please!"

"Oh, I am not offended if so. We are not in luff. I don't want to pry, either. I am just curious."

He kept silent. She handed him a flask, which chill had already bedewed, and lit her tobacco. Smoke eddied acrid. She joined him, sitting up, flank against flank.

"I like you much, I belieff, Martti," she told him. Slyly: "I expect you will compare well with your shipmates. Stefan Dozsa is nice but—hasty? Maybe not promising. I am not sure of making the other two at all. Weisenberg acts thoroughly married when we talk, and Brodersen has his mistress, who is far prettier than me."

Leino scowled. "Yes, he does."

Once more Frieda's gaze grew thoughtful. "She is a delightful person. Gifted; she was singing a few of her own songs while she took measurements to make me some decent clothes. And she runs a splendid galley. And seems to handle the rest of the quartermaster job well. What else?"

"I can't say." Leino spoke fast. "I haven't known her long. Yes, she is quite a girl." Abruptly, twisting about to confront her: "Tell me about yourself, Frieda. Everybody's been lost in talking about Beta and Earth politics and things like that. Now we have hardly any time left before—Well, what has your life been?"

The gunner shrugged and blew a smoke ring. "I haff knocked around."

"Tell me."

"If you will then tell me your story."

"Mine isn't much," Leino said. "I'm such a young fellow—I'm beginning to find out how young—You've seen more."

She collected bottle and cigar in her right hand, that the left might rumple his hair. "You are cute, Martti."

Relaxing into her pillow: "Well, an outline, if you want. I was born in East Prussia thirty years ago, except for me it has been thirty-eight. My family was not rich, but we remembered across a couple of centuries we had been Junkers, and later furnished officers for the Soviet Empire, and after it broke up— *Ach*, the mansion our ancestors owned was in sight of our home. My father was a guerrilla in the Troubles. I joined the *Freiheit Jugend*; we neffer had to fight, but we held us ready. At last I took a *Wanderjahr* before I enlisted in the Peace Command. They gafe me space training. When *Emissary* began to recruit, I applied and was accepted."

"Not exactly a homebody, you," Leino said.

Wistfulness flitted over her. "I would like to marry, and get my immunity refersed, to haff children while my parents can still enjoy being grandparents. If they are alife . . . and we may be headed into death ourselfs."

"Yes, it's hard waiting helpless, isn't it?"

"Oh, that is the usual fate of humans. You wait for the medical lab results or the jury's verdict or how the next shell will fall on a battlefield or—whateffer." Frieda sucked her cheroot into an Aldebaran redness at its end. "What is terrible here is, we may be mankind's last chance for truly reaching the stars. Our enemies will not stop if they wipe us out, *spurlos versenkt*. They will fear the Betans or somebody might come, and for that reason work to get control, until they can openly put weapons at the Sol and Phoebus T machines for keeping a hermit kingdom. It is too possible. My folk remember the Soviets."

"Unless the Others intervene," Leino said. "Is that altogether a daydream? Did you get the least clue in *Emissary*?"

Frieda's expression sharpened. "No. What sign besides the Voice did the Others effer giff us . . . or the Betans, or any uff those races the Betans know?" She swigged her bottle dry, dropped it clunking to the deck, and struck fist upon knee. "Martti, I do not like thinking about the Others. We did for eight years. They haunt the Betans, more than Christ haunted Europe—oh, I could feel when I began learning language and helping in our studies, I could feel. I told you I come from a country full uff remembered dreams and nightmares both." Violently: "Forget the bloody Others! We make our own destiny!"

"Well, yes, maybe." His answer was subdued. "I've wondered myself. I'm a Christian—not awfully good, I'm afraid— That's made me wonder about their effect on us. Oh, doubtless they are nothing more than a species ahead of us in science and technology. Brains likewise, I suppose, but do brains count for that much? I wouldn't be surprised but what our holothetes are as intelligent as them; or more, even. If they are angels, as our pastor in my home town thinks they might be, or if they're simply free from original sin, then why did they let the Troubles happen? And the heresies, the wild cults that center on them? Could they actually be damned, or be outright demons? I don't know, I don't know."

Surprised, Frieda said, "Let us leaff religion be." She was silent a minute or two. "Can I punch for music, Martti?

Beethoven, I wish—the First Symphony, while he was still happily learning from Haydn and Mozart. I want to hear happiness."

"Sure," Leino said, and stroked her.

She came back to him amidst a gamboling of harmonies, to put aside her smoke and snuggle close. "This is excellent background for fucking, too," she said.

"Uh, wait," he demurred. "I need a rest."

She reached for him. "I am certain you will find you haff more capability than anybody showed you before." Pause; calculation; stab: "Caitlín Mulryan can do likewise, or I miss my guess." Seeing him wince: "Neffer mind. A joke. You are a dear sweet man. Let us enjoy this short while before we enter the gate."

Again he closed his eyes.

XXV

TODAY IRA QUICK held off Toronto's winter by a recording, played on the giant viewscreen, of York Minster. It was not static but moved slowly around the delicate façades, soaring and intricate vaults, glowing windows of that loveliest of medieval churches. Tuned down to bare audibility, yet losing none of its might, a Gregorian chant gave background. The show was a reminder of what man, Earthbound and alone, had achieved: the heritage now menaced by inhumanness. It strengthened him in his resolution.

Simeon Ilyitch Makarov, premier of Great Russia, sat across from his desk. He had flown here incognito at Quick's urgent request. "You are the most powerful individual in our group," the North American had said, "and the two of us are the most determined. We're at a crisis point, I'm afraid; we have to confer and decide. I shouldn't be more specific over the phone, scrambler or no. And I can't come to you. All my present lines of communication center on this office."

Arrived, Makarov lit an atrocious cigarette, inhaled hard, and demanded in accented Spanish, "Well, what have you to report?" He was a stocky individual with a walrus mustache and thin gray hair, his garb unfashionable and rumpled, a survivor of combat in the civil wars which had sundered his country, his existence ever since consecrated to its eventual reunification.

"No knowledge you don't already possess. You're as well aware as I that *Chinook* is approaching the T machine, scheduled to arrive in about three hours. That's why I must stay put. Someone has to give new orders in case something unforeseen happens." Quick slapped his palm down. "Christ! Transmission time of more than twenty minutes!"

"Yes, our group agreed you are best positioned to take that responsibility. Why do you suddenly want me to share it?"

"You do in any case, Sr. Makarov." Quick frowned. "There is one new development, I hope unimportant. I learned about it while you were on your way. I've been kept personally informed about the San Geronimo Wheel. The fact that a pet research project of mine is supposed to be going on there is sufficient excuse. Troxell doesn't send any details by laser, of course, but he is supposed to beam a periodic 'All's well' signal. It's overdue."

"That could be bad!"

"Or it could be plain carelessness. He's grown less than punctual; the isolation, the strain are getting to him and his men. I don't think I should send an immediate inquiry—too conspicuous, makes me look too concerned—right when *Chinook* demands my total care." Quick paused before he added weightily: "And yet analysis of radar data shows the ship used quite a peculiar, uneconomical boost pattern to get onto the path we required. It had her effectively in the radar shadow of the Wheel—given that astronomical distance, plus the electromagnetic shielding—for hours."

Makarov grunted as if struck. "Why did you not tell the rest of us at once?"

Quick sighed. "I only found out lately. Please understand, sir, we, I *must* proceed with caution. As is, too many people are involved. If I call for information on a top priority basis, they will speculate why. If I lay stress on a particular question, they will speculate further."

"Hunh! I've gotten things better organized in Great Russia."

"That's a major reason why you are so valuable, so critical to our effort," *you barbarian tyrant.*

"Precisely how much information has leaked, what kind, and to whom?"

Quick spread his hands. "'Precisely' is an impossible requirement. I am, as I said, not dealing with a handful of disciplined men like yours, whose silence is guaranteed. I've done my best to keep you *au courant*, as well as I can follow events myself."

"Yes. I do, though, have many different matters claiming my attention. Suppose you summarize for me, whether or not you have already described a specific item."

Is he playing with me? Or is he, underneath a peasant shrewdness, basically a dullard? This isn't what I need him for today.... I do need him. I must oblige. Maybe, several years hence—" Quick arrayed the facts in his head and began:

"Our original group knows the full story, of course. That includes those subordinates we have co-opted." Among them were the entire crew of the watchship *Lomonosov*, most of them newly assigned, which had gone ahead to wait at the Phoebean T machine for *Chinook* to arrive. They were either veterans of Makarov's, who entered space service after the wars but remained devoted to their old leader, or else technically trained covert agents of his. Quick had had to admire how swiftly the premier arranged this when appealed to. The Astronautical Control Board had been grateful to have the arrangement made on its behalf, especially at such short notice. Now *Bohr* need not leave her station to escort the vessel of wanted men off to detention.

"I had the crew of the *Dyson* interviewed by a psychological team. The pretext, which the psychologists themselves bought, was trying to find out how spacemen react to peculiar occurrences. Apparently none of them suspect the truth, though they do wonder about the incident. No serious problem, I'd say." *Dyson* was the watchship at the Solar portal when *Emissary* returned to the Phoebean System. Quick almost wished he had a God to thank, that Tom Archer, captain of *Faraday*, guardian craft as the other end of the gate, was smart as well as loyal. He'd sent a pilot fish ahead, asking *Dyson* to come through and lend emergency assistance; then he shepherded *Emissary* in the opposite direction. Finding no one at the Solar System exit, as he had hoped, he instantly led his captive off to a safe distance and got in touch with Quick. By the time *Dyson* returned, the minister had a message ready for the puzzled captain— apologies and all that, but it had suddenly proved necessary to transfer a certain load in secrecy, for it was not the kind of thing that extremist elements on Earth or Demeter ought to know about.

"*Faraday* is much more difficult, but I needn't repeat that, need I?" Archer and his mate were sworn to the cause, but it had not been feasible to hand-pick the rest of that crew. Those persons had inevitably rejoiced at the reappearance of *Emissary* and had made a fuss over leading her into quarantine not as a public health precaution but as if she were an enemy. After consultation with his masters, the captain told his men, in effect, "It turns out she may really have brought back something dangerous—maybe not, but the government wants to investigate thoroughly and cautiously, and meanwhile does not want public hysteria. So to make dead sure of preserving security, we're off to Hades on a scientific assignment." Fast and versatile, watchships often did serve as exploratory vessels; and the outermost world in the Phoebean System did have curious features about which the planetologists would like to know more. "Yes, this will keep you from the families and friends you expected to see before long, but orders are orders. They'll be reassured we're all right. And we'll collect fat pay for the extra duty, remember that." —*Faraday* would not stay out there forever.

"Troxell and his agents may be a larger hazard still," Quick proceeded. "No matter how carefully we chose them, they've been exposed for weeks on end to some damnably persuasive prostellar arguments. If one or two of them should be converted . . . they could ruin us the same day they set foot back on Earth.

"Those are the obvious people to worry about. We have plenty of less obvious. They run the whole gamut from my assistant Chauveau or Zoe Palamas, for example, whom I've fed forebodings about incipient rebellion on Demeter, down to technicians in space stations who were asked to locate *Chinook* and transmit the command to her that she return home.

"Sir, the situation is precarious and worsening. I'm less and less able to stay on top of it by myself. I must have strong help. Of our whole group, you can best supply that."

Makarov stubbed his cigarette viciously before he sent it down the ashtaker and reached for another. "What would you have me do, this exact hour?" he growled.

Quick sighed. "If I knew that, sir, I probably wouldn't have had to call on you. The truth is, though, what will happen soon is unpredictable. If matters go wrong, I may well be unable to maintain secrecy alone. Nor was I ever used to doing so to this extent. Your advice, your connections, your action— Do you follow me?

"Suppose everything does proceed as we hope. [*Chinook* comes to the T machine, obediently maintaining outercom silence. The regular watchship is *Copernicus*, the hastily dispatched special one is *Alhazen*. Crews of both have been warned that the travelers are wanted on Demeter on criminal charges and must be presumed dangerous. Additionally, Broussard of the European Confederacy has seen to it that the captain and gunner on *Alhazen*, though not privy to the facts, are men who can be depended on to obey his command to shoot when in any doubt; his national government will protect them afterward before the board of inquiry.... However, suppose *Chinook* passes through to Phoebus without incident. There *Lomonosov* waits to conduct her off. When remote from *Bohr*, *Lomonosov* sends a boarding party which secures the Demetrians, interrogates them, communicates with Governor Hancock, and waits for further instructions.]

"We still won't know for a while exactly what the Brodersen gang has done or can still do. We may get a nasty surprise. For instance, they may have propagandized the Wheel. We had better be prepared to respond fast and decisively.

"For now, though, what if trouble comes in the next few hours, in any of a hundred unforeseeable ways? What then? I repeat, sir, events are moving too rapidly for us. We've had to improvise, we're overextended, our cover stories are full of gaping holes, too many people—from Hades to the Wheel and back—will shortly be asking too many questions. What shall we *do*?"

Makarov blew smoke. It stank. "That will depend on what the reality is," he said. "You are right, I had best keep vigil with you."

After a moment he added, "The absolute reality is always death."

Quick sat straight. *I half feared this. Did I also half wish for it?* "I don't quite understand," he faltered.

"Do they not have a proverb in English, 'Dead men tell no tales'?"

Yes; and how many graves have your executioners filled, Makarov? Quick's mouth was turning cottony. He felt cold, though the office was well heated. "We have . . . our group has . . . discussed extreme measures, true. But strictly in case of dire need."

"You have been telling me the need has become dire—whether you know you have or not."

Quick clutched the arms of his chair. *Attack!* "Perhaps you should be more specific, sir."

Makarov waved his cigarette. "Very well." His tone stayed matter-of-fact. "I have given thought to this, you realize, and have sounded out others in our team. If you were not included, no insult. Your actions, yes, your leadership demonstrate you are fundamentally a realist.

"We can have *Chinook* and her crew destroyed. We can send

a trustworthy detachment to dispatch the personnel in the Wheel, including Troxell's.

"*Faraday*—I am not yet sure. We can have *Lomonosov* destroy her at Hades. Later we can explain these losses as a sad set of accidents, coincidentally happening in close succession. Well, there is no haste about *Faraday*. If possible, I prefer we spare her, since her crew is primed with hints of monsters from the stars.

"Ideally, we arrange the scene at the Wheel so it appears the monsters, who had enslaved the *Emissary* crew, took over the quarantine station as well. Yes, and when Brodersen arrived on his private investigation, they lured him to them, captured him and his men, departed in his ship for their planet. Fortunately, they betrayed themselves to the alert *Lomonosov*, which blew them to pieces."

Despite having entertained similar notions—*as fantasies, as fantasies*—Quick felt it incumbent on him to whisper, "Do you seriously imagine we could get the whole human race to swallow such a piece of sensationalism?"

"Enough of it, probably," Makarov said. "Nothing a government claims is too preposterous for most of its citizens.

"Bear in mind, I do not say this strategy is feasible. That we must find out. For example, will Stedman cooperate fully? His nerve may fail him when he imagines facing his God. If he or somebody else becomes unreliable, what can we best do about them? In any event, how do we explain and justify the fact that so many in the Council, in higher echelons everywhere, were not notified and consulted at once? What evidence can we manufacture, what particulars can clever men invent for us?

"The advantage of creating invaders from the stars is that we can then easily attain our objective, a guard at both T machines to wipe out any alien ships the instant they appear. Public opinion will support this, yes, require this, and an end to exploration. But we do risk failure and exposure.

"Maybe the safest course is to destroy *Faraday* with the rest and make everything look accidental. Or, hm, we could throw some of the blame onto terrorists. In that case, we must find a different political route, more slow, toward our goal.

"The whole point, Sr. Quick, is that whatever we do, it must not be done timidly. We must have the balls to accept great hazards. Believe me, the danger in shilly-shallying is grossly greater.

"Yes, I must certainly stand by you in these next hours," Makarov closed.

"You're saying terrible things," Quick protested. "Why, some of those you'd kill have been freely helping us."

"I have heard another English proverb," Makarov retorted. "'You cannot make an omelette without breaking eggs.' Is an excellent saying.

"In the past I have found it necessary to sign death sentences of followers who had been valuable. I judged they were beginning to follow me too independently; or they had questionable associates; or— Well, I had a state to rebuild from chaos. How could I investigate every single case?

"For our separate reasons, Sr. Quick, we deem it vital that the human race stay home, carry out its natural tasks, and shun outsiders . . . at least until it is properly organized to cope with them. Vital. Now in days before cell therapy, what woman hesitated to have a cancerous breast cut off? That harmed her beauty, but she had no choice if she would live, did she?

"Furthermore, Sr. Quick." Makarov leaned forward. "Furthermore. *You are committed.* Our whole little organization is. We had an ideal, we stumbled toward it, we made missteps as people always do, and today we are close to ruin. Is our ideal not correct regardless? How well can we continue to serve mankind from a prison?

"Prison it will be, if any strong hint of the facts ever comes out. Publicity will lead to investigation. Subordinates of ours will seek to save their own hides by tattling on us. *Chinook* is forcing us beyond the limits of any legal technicalities. We are quite clearly conspiring to violate the Covenant rights of her crew. We have already violated them, by deliberately causing a groundless warrant to be issued for their arrest. From this will spring countless further charges of malfeasance in office. We will be locked away for a long, long time—unless we strike the right blow at once, and strike it hard!"

A part of Quick recalled an essay he had read years before, on how intellectuals are chronically fascinated by violence as an instrumentality—drawn, repelled, drawn back, as they might be to the idea of sexual relations with a barely pubescent girl or with a sentient nonhuman; it is a kind of xenophilia, and when a conflict of which they approve (and they approve of most) does erupt, they take the lead in cheering on the warheads and calling for more soldiers to feed the furnace. At the time he had thought what reactionary nonsense this was. Later, cultivating his fair-mindedness, he had had to admit there might be a limited amount of truth to the thesis. *Yonder son of a bitch is right in the present context. You can't make an omelette without breaking eggs. Why, you can't maintain an orderly everyday society without breaking an occasional head.*

And, Christ almighty, he must indeed go forward. Otherwise—arrest, indictment, trial? An actual jail sentence? A rehabilitative psychiatrist (squat, plump, blue-jowled, fleshy-nosed) probing the psyche of Ira Quick, which his grubby breed would never understand in a geological epoch? Release after he was aged, aged, to whatever drabness he could find in the wreckage of career and social life? His boys, wife, friends, mistresses, the whole world naming him kidnapper and murderer, he who had striven for nothing but human betterment?

I am well known as being fast on my feet.

Quick ran tongue over lips. "Sir, I don't necessarily agree with either of your proposals." Ah, good, how calmly he spoke despite the thick hammering inside him. "Nevertheless, when a statesman like you speaks, I listen. Would you care to explain in detail?" He felt his brave smile. "We do have to pass the time while we wait."

The voices around the cathedral image were marching to their triumphant conclusion.

XXVI

Chinook WAS OVER a million kilometers from her goal, decelerating, when the first communication struck her. Brodersen took it in his office.

The screen showed him an angular visage speaking British English: "Vincent Lawes, commanding watchship *Alhazen* on special duty. You are *Chinook* of Demeter, are you not?" It was scarcely a question. "Give me your captain."

"You have him," Brodersen answered. "What can I do for you?"

The seconds ticked away while light beams flew forth and back again. Caitlín, seated beside Brodersen, gripped his forearm, which was bare. He was acutely conscious of that warmth and pressure, of her hasty breath and faint sweet woman-odors.

"Now hear this well, Captain Brodersen," Lawes said. His tone was harsh and a tic jumped near his right eye. "You are wanted on serious charges. Your ship is armed. My orders are to see that you pass through to the Phoebean System to be taken in charge there. I am to consider you dangerous and take no chances with you. None. Do you understand?"

"What procedure shall we follow?"

Time. "You will maneuver as usual, except under direction from us, not *Copernicus*. In fact, you are to have no contact whatsoever with *Copernicus*. You will beam every message at us, and in English. *Copernicus* has been directed off her usual orbit. She'll keep on the far side of the T machine from you as you make transit. To contact her, you'd have to broadcast—and in Spanish, since nobody aboard her knows English. We will detect that. Any untoward action of yours can provoke our fire. I repeat, do you understand? Make sure you do, Captain Brodersen."

"My, my." The Demetrian clicked his tongue. "You are tight in the sphincter, aren't you? How come? What harm in a little chat?"

Time. Caitlín chanted, a whisper—a Gaelic curse, Brodersen thought.

"I have my orders," Lawes replied, scissoring off each word. "Among other things, you stand accused of trying to disseminate technological information which would endanger public safety. Without questioning the dutifulness of the *Copernicus* personnel, I am to see that you send no word to them or anyone else. Needless to say, they are not to tune you in. If we become engaged with you, they will join us."

"I see. M-m, how about yourself, Captain Lawes? Our side of the story is pretty interesting. We've quite a bit we can show you, too."

Time. The sole surprise, if it was that, was the appalled vehemence of Lawes' "No! Absolutely not! At the first sign of any such attempt, I'll switch off. If you persist when I call back later, I have discretion to attack."

"Okay, okay. What else?"

Time. Brodersen muttered to Caitlín, "They've sure got to him, haven't they? Prob'ly by more than an appeal to his loyalty. He's an officer of the Union, after all, not of Europe. Bribe, blackmail—"

"Your path and vectors are incorrect for a transit," Lawes said. "Explain."

"Yeah, I was coming to that. We've developed collywobbles in the main control system. Acquired a wrong momentum and have to compensate. Instead of making straight for our first base, we're applying parameters which will bring us to zero relative velocity near Beacon Bravo. From there, we'll move to the proper location for a standard approach. I have the figures here, if you'd like me to transmit them."

Discussion went into technicalities for several minutes. At last, reluctantly, Lawes said, "Very well. We will be tracking you continuously, remember. Stand by for possible further instructions. If nothing suspicious happens, I will re-establish direct communication at nineteen-thirty hours. Is that clear?" Receiving his acknowledgment, he blanked without a goodbye.

Brodersen leaned back. "Wow," he said. "For a while there, I wondered if he would shoot. His finger's awful twitchy on the trigger. But of course, at this distance, Frieda can intercept whatever he might send—I presume."

"It's desperate our enemies are, I'm thinking," Caitlín said.

"Right. And the more desperate people get, the more dangerous. Us included." He turned to smile at her. The darling face drew close to his. "Well, we've three to four hours before things get spiny. Better rest up, macushla, if you can."

She ran fingers down his cheek. "I've a more interesting idea, my life."

"Huh? I—Look, I've got to make the rounds, jolly the troops, check everything out—"

"If those responsible have not their departments in good shape by now, you're too late," she said firmly. "They do, though. I've sounded them out in ways the Old Man cannot. The morale of most is flying banners; the rest are at least of stout heart. Aye, we might hold an assembly, for a few rousing songs of revolution and freedom. But that's best done as late before our plunge as may be." She grinned. "Thus you've better than an hour free, Daniel Brodersen, and sure I am you've the wit to pass it in style."

"Uh, well, uh, look, frankly, I'm so full of worries, I doubt—"

She stopped his lips with hers. Her hands roved. Presently she laughed. "See? *That* fret of yours was for naught." Springing to her feet, grabbing his wrist: "Come along, me bucko. No use to struggle. You're doomed."

Stars blazed in every viewscreen of the command center. The dimmed image of Sol hung like a burning moon, Earth hidden from sight behind it. Elsewhere a globe glowed wanly golden, the sign at which the ship had halted. In another direction, the cylinder that was the T machine whirled, its mass and might brought by a tiny distance—about fifty megameters, hardly more than the circumference of a terrestroid planet—down to a bit of jewelry adrift in heaven.

Brodersen floated alone, harnessed, listening to his blood. Those tides went more easily than he had expected. He would not have taken a fear suppressant in any event, for he needed each millisecond he could shave off his reaction time, but he had figured on being strung tight. *Pegeen is heap good medicine*, he thought.

If only she could be here. She wouldn't distract him ... willingly. He just wasn't sure that in her nearness he could remain the complete robot he ought to be. It was plenty hard curbing the knowledge that soon she might die.

And Stef poised at detector and communicator consoles in the electronics shack; Joelle as holothete and Su as linker were parts of the ship, her pilots through the shoals and breakers ahead; Phil and Martti occupied the engine room, though likely they were condemned to do no more than sweat; Frieda had the armament center, with Carlos—who had learned something about it earlier—to give partial assistance. That left Caitlín to comfort Fidelio. Tuning briefly in, Brodersen had heard her swapping music with the Betan.

A blink and beep sent his attention to the outercom. Lawes' haggard countenance jumped into its screen. "Watchship— there you are. Are you prepared?"

"More or less," Brodersen replied. "We've still got problems. I do hope the apparatus doesn't suddenly run wild. That could send us off to Kingdom Come, you know."

Time lag here was imperceptible. Dozsa had reported *Alhazen* as being a few thousand kilometers off. Magnification could have made the lean shape visible, but Brodersen saw no cause to bother. "I ... hope the same ... for your sake," Lawes said. "Proceed according to your declared flight plan. I'll stay in touch. ... Proceed!"

"Yes." Brodersen addressed the intercom. "Captain to crew. You heard the man. Get busy." He saw Lawes flush and clench teeth, as if twice convinced this was a pack of pirates.

Weightlessness yielded to a small, varying sideways drag and a sense of Coriolis twist, as *Chinook* rotated from her gyros. That stopped; for an instant she orbited; full thrust awoke and she darted forward. Acceleration crammed Brodersen into his seat.

It took a minute for Lawes' instruments and computers to determine what was going on and inform him. "Hold!" he screamed. "You're aimed wrong!"

"God damn it, I know," Brodersen snapped in his best imitation of a person fighting dismay. "I told you we're having troubles. Hang on, don't bother me."

"What are you *doing*?"

"You think we want to go off on a random path and disappear forever? Get off my back. I've got to see about stopping us."

"I'll give you a short chance, Captain." Lawes clamped his mouth shut. Brodersen and his followers exchanged words which they had rehearsed.

The ion drive cut out, as it must if *Chinook* was to tread the measure Joelle had calculated for her. Falling toward the next point of inflection, she turned her nose again. A radar could spot the movement if it was set to do so, but he gambled that that wouldn't occur to Lawes for a while.

"Navigation estimates we can stay on this trajectory for six hours without getting too far into the field," he said. It was true. "The engineers expect they'll repair the breakdown well before then."

Lawes squinched eyelids close together. "I want to know more about it. Why didn't you call in sooner?"

"Weren't we supposed to maintain silence? We aren't actually criminals, Captain. We're law-abiding citizens, anxious to get home and clear our names. How the hell we ever got accused of anything, I faunch to learn. . . . All right, if you wish, I'll screen the pertinent parts of our log and the CE's notes."

Those were works of art, Brodersen judged. Nevertheless he was fumble-thumbed about presenting them. His job as skipper was to talk, nothing else—dish out the blarney as long as possible—keep his adversaries in play, while Joelle and Su and the laws of physics drove his ship onward.

He had a mere twenty minutes or thereabouts of plausibility until the next acceleration fell due. His pilots would go at top speed, no safety margin to speak of, since every margin around them was beset. . . .

A renewed boost.

"Stop, *Chinook!* Are you insane?"

"The controls are insane, that's what."

"I can't believe this any longer."

"Ask your own CE to study the information we sent. Have him study it real hard." Brodersen won that debate also.

The drive had stopped and he hung as if at the bottom of a dream. Sweat off his face bobbed around in globules. Pegeen might likewise become glitter strewn among the stars. His underwear absorbed perspiration but left him chill and gamy. Time extended.

Lawes reappeared in the screen. "My engineer says your material does not make sense," he snapped. "It's superficially plausible enough that it must have been concocted. You're attempting to escape."

"Escape into what?"

"Never mind. Brodersen, you will reverse immediately or we shoot."

He's reacting on schedule, he is. "Wait, Captain Lawes. Wait half a tick. You're about to compromise your mission and jeopardize your career. Take heed while you can."

"What are you raving about?"

"I'm not raving. Please note I'm speaking very carefully." *As slow and wordy as I gauge I can get away with.* "Curb your own emotions and listen. You can spare a few minutes for saving your ass and maybe your superiors', can't you?"

"Well—" Lawes swallowed. "Go on. Speak to the point."

"I will. Okay, we lied to you, we bought ourselves time to get this far. It was necessary. The fact is, there's a lot more behind our arrest than a miscarriage of justice. Want to hear?"

"No! I have my orders!"

"It mightn't be safe for you to know, eh? Well, from our viewpoint, we've zero to lose. If we go to Phoebus, the way things are, we're dead. Jumping off into the galaxy, we have the teeniest chance of finding help somewhere. We don't count on that, of course. But we'll have several extra years of life while our supplies last. I don't think this will bother your bosses much. If anything, they should be glad to get rid of us so cheaply."

"My orders say, either see you off to Phoebus or kill you. If you don't return at once, you'll not get an hour of those years you mention."

"We're armed too, Captain. We can block your missiles for a bit. Meanwhile we'll broadcast—in Spanish, visual, at full power. Can you be certain they won't tune in aboard *Copernicus*? Or chance to catch it on a different spacecraft? We've wattage aplenty to be received ten million kilometers off. It's a story which will bring down some big people. In cases like that, little people get carried along. . . . I wish you would let me talk to you, Lawes."

"No." Torment. "Have you anything further to say before we start shooting?"

"Why, yes. I have this suggestion." Brodersen thrust his whole personality forward. "Call Earth and ask what to do. We'll be zigzagging on, sure, but you're aware of how long a proper transit pattern takes, and we'd much rather come out in a planetary system, at a T machine, than in the middle of interstellar space. The best guess is, this means we have to pass from beacon to beacon—the more, the likelier—and swing straight inward from the last. You've time for a call. Meanwhile, unless you shoot, we'll stay quiet."

"Well—You have no right to bargain!"

"I am bargaining, though. Hear me. What I wish you'd do is direct your message not to the office you're supposed to, but to your own high command. Lay the matter before them. You'll find them astonished at what's been going on."

"We're under security."

Brodersen sighed. He'd expected nothing else. "Okay, as you choose." Louder: "But *call!*"

After more argument he won his point. The screen blinked and he collapsed, breathing hard. It would take about three-quarters of an hour for an interchange, via the relay satellite, between here and Earth. By then, at her headlong pace, *Chinook* should be deep into the transport field.

Stars exulted. He stirred and said through the intercom: "You heard that, boys and girls? We're this far along. Rejoice."

A few small cheers replied. Caitlín struck a ringing chord from her sonador and declared, "You carried us, Daniel."

"No, you all did," he answered. "Hey, Pegeen, I love you."

"Wait till I get you to myself again," she said.

Joelle is listening— By tacit agreement, conversation died away. Occasional words went around, most of them functional. Tastes in music varied too widely for a shared concert. Folk at their posts remained in their lonelinesses. Brodersen relived his latest passages with Caitlín; the first had rated twelve on the Beaufort scale, the second had been as gentle as that final union, close to dawn, in the cave beneath Mount Lorn.... He even dozed for a spell. The ship roused him, changing direction, squandering chemical auxiliaries as well as expending nuclear fuel in order to keep hard on her way.

He was bobcat-alert before the response from Earth came due.

Dozsa's voice delivered it, a shout: "Missiles!"

The decision was, "Kill," Brodersen realized. *Quick, or whoever is at the other end, is afraid we may have a plan.*

He must sit with nothing but fingernails in his fists. Survival had ceased to be any affair of his.

At high accelerations, crossing the gap in a couple of minutes, though they changed vectors at varying intervals to confuse counterfire, the torpedoes homed on *Chinook*. Nobody aboard was spacesuited. If a nuclear warhead exploded near the hull, that was that.

Brodersen spied the exhaust streaks, silver and narrow. Sensors locked onto the tubes. A computer extrapolated.

Zarubayev had fine-tuned the system. Fire sprayed across darkness as energy-gorged laser beams found their targets. An "All clear" jubilated, telling humans they would not die in the next few seconds.

The ship trembled. Von Moltke had launched missiles of her own. This was her ultimate job, to outguess a living opponent.

Chinook was not only much bigger than *Alhazen*, she carried throw weight out of proportion. Watchships weren't really intended for battle. Their weapons were partly a relic of the Troubles, partly a concession to vague fears... which Quick's faction strove to entrench....

The vessel surged around Brodersen, plunging toward her next way station.

Twinkles in heaven— "Gunner to captain," von Moltke intoned, "they stopped our barrage."

"They were meant to, this first time," he reminded her. "A lesson. Stef, have you got contact?... Okay, put me through."

His intention was to repeat his original threat, negotiate for the escape of his command. He did not, repeat and repeat *not*, wish to kill more men who were doing what they'd been assured was their duty.

The stars were beginning visibly to crawl in the viewscreens. Soon he'd be in such warped space-time that no rocket would have a prayer of tracking him down. Of course, any signal he transmitted from there would be hopelessly garbled. Well, everybody would be satisfied, sort of—

"Missiles!" Dozsa bawled. He spat an oath and rattled off RA, dec, approximate vectors. They had to be from *Copernicus*.

Judas priest, this was my worst fear, that Quick's influence would be strong enough to compel Janigian's honest crew—

"Missiles!" Those came from *Alhazen*, one, one, one, one, as fast as the tube could launch them.

"Captain," von Moltke said starkly, "I do not belieff we can strike that many in a flock."

Granville's wail: "No, I compute we cannot. *Mon père—*"

Joelle, like steel striking steel: "We can reach the next beacon and accelerate straight inward before they arrive."

Brodersen surged against his harness, even as weight returned. "No!" he bawled. "We'll end up anywhere—" Knowledge smote home. "Carry on."

The ship blasted. Almost, he imagined he saw the T machine grow before him, whirling and whirling.

He did see the first few splashes of flame, as Frieda parried. Then Sol was gone from its screen. The stars were an altogether different horde. The sun was not white nor yellow nor the blood-orange of Centrum, but ember-hued and shrunken. Tawny beneath colored bands, thrice the width of Luna seen from Earth, stood a planet. Frighteningly close gyred a great iridescent cylinder.

Brodersen let himself tumble for a minute into a night that roared.

Winter fell downward, white around the tower in Toronto.

"Well," Quick said at last. "They're gone."

"You are sure?" Makarov demanded through a choking haze of smoke. He lacked the scientific education to follow each detail of what had just come in.

"Yes," Quick told him. "Whatever scheme they had—if they did— I suspect they were in fact running off at random, except for trying to ... to maximize their probability of— Oh, how can you estimate it? ... Never mind. They were forced to make their gate entry from the spot where they happened to be. They are gone, Makarov. I beg your pardon. They are gone, Premier Makarov. Like the thousands of probes our species wasted, searching for new guidepaths. We can forget about them."

Makarov hunched his bulky frame. "You are quite certain?"

"Yes. Absolutely." Quick sagged and covered his eyes. Exhaustion shuddered in him.

"Ah." Makarov puffed. "Good. What a simplification."

Quick looked back up. "Hm?"

Makarov smiled. He seldom did. "A factor less in the equation, perhaps the least known factor, do you see?"

I see you're a mathematical illiterate, went through Quick.

He gathered strength together. A civilized man had better stay the equal of a barbarian war lord. "Right. We'll have the personnel of *Alhazen* and *Copernicus* interrogated, of course, but apparently they heard nothing they shouldn't. This leaves us *Lomonosov* for any special missions we decide on—plus a welcome breathing space, I'd say."

"We do not sit and pant much," Makarov warned. "In the bright light of the new situation, we act. First, after notifying our major collaborators, I think we should send *Lomonosov* to the Wheel. If they find no undue complication, they dispose of those who are there, including Troxell's group. Afterward we have leisure to make complete arrangements. Is this agreed?"

I've had an inferno's worth of hours to agonize over the moral issues, Quick thought. *A time finally comes when the civilized man must attack alongside his ally of expediency, or be left behind and have no voice at the peace conference.* "Sir, let's sleep on it and then talk further, but at the moment I am inclined to believe that in principle you are right."

XXVII

CAITLÍN FLOATED by herself in the common room. A handclasp on a table edge held her against air currents that made a cloud of her unbound hair. She had turned off lights, the better to see out the viewscreens. Like big windows, they gave her the encompassing universe.

In most, stars crowded as ever before, the same god-hoard of gems in a crystal-black bowl, so many that she could not see how heaven was altered; nor did the argence of the Milky Way pour through channels greatly different from those above Earth or Demeter. In one direction the T machine was visible, but barely, a needle lost among vastnesses. *Chinook* had moved well clear of it before assuming a stable orbit around the planet.

The strangeness stood to right and left of her. Right was the sun disc, one-sixth the width of that which shone upon her birthland. Its red glow needed no stopping down; she could look straight at it, suffer nothing but after-images, and discern a faint, ocherous corona. She found no zodiacal lens, which turned the sight doubly foreign.

Left was the giant world. The ship happened to have emerged opposite the dayside, and at her distance would need a pair of Terrestrial years to swing once around. Hence the globe stayed nearly at full phase, broad and bright enough to shine all else out of the screen which revealed it. Unaided vision noticed how spin had flattened the disc. Tones of amber shaded subtly into each other, below cloud belts that were deep or pale orange streaked by blue-green and auburn. The shadow of a moon was like the pupil of an eye. Where night sliced off a crescent, it was not wholly dark, but a faint sheen wavered.

Mingled luminances turned the room into a cavern of soft lights and lairing shadows, a place of mystery and silence.

The stillness did not break the moment Martti Leino entered.

233

He checked his flight in the doorway when he spied Caitlín and hung for a minute, staring at the slender, frosted form, before he almost barked, "Hello."

Tresses swirled in radiance and darkness as she pivoted on her arm. The free hand brushed a lock aside to clear sight for her. "Oh. The top of the morning to you," she hailed, though in a hushed voice.

"Morning—well, yes, our clocks do say eight hundred—as close to a morning as we'll ever know," he blurted. Immediately: "I was looking for you."

"Were you that? Why?"

He shoved from the doorframe, arrowed across to the table, caught it and let his body stream free like hers, directly across from her. This close to him, her face was clear in the shinings from outside, while shadows brought forth the sculpturing of it. His speech stumbled: "I noticed what trouble you were having at breakfast—"

"Aye, weightlessness is grand until one must clean up and stash things, then it becomes a polka-dotted bitch." While supplies did include plenty of squeeze-tube rations and other materials intended for these conditions, housekeeping for nine humans and a nonhuman got complicated even when the quartermaster was experienced. "Well, my ancestors outlived worse. Only think, I might have been a maidservant in a Victorian Protestant home! I'll be learning the way of this."

"You shouldn't have to cope alone, now that Su will be too busy. I—I can help, Caitlín."

"What? Will yourself not be in hourly demand?"

"No. I'll get jobs, of course, but— Oh, true, every spaceman's trained to assist in some kind of research, and when we've no proper scientists along— Well, the studies that our best qualified people can carry out won't need much support from me. Phil Weisenberg can generally handle the setting-up and so forth. I've talked with him and he agrees I can probably be more useful, most of the time, helping you . . . if you want," Leino finished, dropping his glance.

"Why, that's dear of you and I thank you." She reached to clasp his shoulder. "May the roads you take be always soft beneath your feet."

"We, we have to help each other . . . be as kind to each other . . . as we can," he mumbled. "Don't we? While we live? There will never be any roads really for us, roads we can walk on, ever again."

She smiled. "Sure, and you're not losing heart already, are you, Martti, lad? When we've only just snatched our lives back to us and won free?"

"Free?" His gaze swung wildly about, he gripped the table edge with needless force, till his nails whitened. "Locked in a metal shell, blundering blind through space as long as our food holds out, no longer, if we don't go crazy first—" He wrestled for control.

She stroked his head and made comforting noises low in her throat. At last he could say with simple despair, "You do know, don't you, we're lost? Fidelio's confirmed his folk have never been here. We'll grope from T machine to T machine— In a thousand years, spending billions of probes, the Betans found how to go between a couple of score stars... and no Others, nobody to help... Caitlín, we're done for."

She shook her head, still smiling through the hair that streamed athwart stars, and answered quietly, well-nigh merrily, "I'll believe that of me when they lay the coppers on my eyes, and maybe not then. But suppose the thing that you say is the worst, Martti, darling."

He jerked violently. "Och," she breathed, "you're in bad shape, so you are. If you're to help me, let me help you first. Hold still."

In a deft maneuver she released the table, drew alongside him and slightly behind, caught his left arm in her left hand and pinned his legs between her knees. He uttered amazement. "Easy, lad, easy," she said. "I must be anchoring myself if I'm to give you the good strong back rub you need." Her right hand went over him. "Aye, a rat's nest of Charlie horses, as my father would say were he less dignified and more Irish. Peel down your coverall to the waist."

He trembled as he obeyed. "Relax," she urged. "Let go. We'll drift loose, but sooner or later we'll fetch up against a wall—a bulkhead—and meanwhile I can be loosening of that poor latissimus dorsi for you."

Kneading, she chuckled. "All my own invention. Free fall sex made me wonder about free fall massage, the more so when himself often is tensed—No, easy, I told you, easy."

Looking about her as she worked: "Suppose we shall indeed go lost for some years, until our food is no more and each of us much choose how to die. I do not admit this is the case, mind you, but suppose it is. What a grand fate!"

"Huh?" he exclaimed. "You can't be serious."

"I am that. Oh, it will be hard to give up mountains and seas, sunshine through rain, a hearthfire at evening. But think, Martti, dear. Look. The glory yonder, and we making ready to *know* it—then more Suns, more worlds, more beauties and marvels, maybe at last a new Demeter for us, though if not, why, then at the end our few years out here in the universe will have held more than most centuries ever did before." Her hold upon him tightened, her working hand grew eager. "Be glad in your life!"

Intended for the unknown, *Chinook* bore a superb panoply of scientific instruments. But save for the two computermen, no specialist in any of their uses was aboard. Sufficient technical knowledge, including the knowledge of how to look things up, existed among the travelers that, largely under Weisenberg's guidance, they could find ways to learn something about the realm wherein they were stranded. However, that might prove to be fatally little.

Then Joelle made her announcement to captain and engineer: Fidelio had the skill. His race had explored many planetary systems, no two alike. Its professional spacefarers included a cadre trained in making and interpreting an enormous range of observations, against the day when the next robot probe would return with the news that it had found another gateway back. He had been one such, as well as a xenological officer who spoke for his ship when she visited aliens. The combination had gotten him picked for *Emissary*.

"His technique involves holothetics, as you should expect," she cautioned. "We'll have to modify a unit for him to use. The way was developed on Beta, and between us we remember fairly well what it is. But you realize a certain amount of cut-and-try is necessary. Furthermore, our equipment is crude by his standards."

"Could we build him the right kind?" Weisenberg asked.

"If you were thrown back in time to Galileo, could you build him a hundred-meter orbiting reflector?" she gibed. "Oh, I daresay a few minor improvements here and there will be possible for us in due course, especially in software. At present, though, we must get what data we can. You go do the obvious things, determine masses, take spectrograms, et cetera. You have to do them anyway. After Fidelio's linkage is ready, he can tell you what kind of additional information he and I will need, particularly information fed into us directly and continuously.

"Let us alone to consult. Go about your business. I'll tell you what else to do and when."

Brodersen lifted a brow without saying anything. She recognized his "My, isn't the air kind of thin on top of that high horse?" expression from of old. *He never used it on* me *before!* went through her like ice. *He was always too respectful of my mind. What's changed him? The stress of this expedition? That* Caitlin *adventuress?*

The question persisted in her through the days that followed. Not that she was obsessed: except by work, like everybody else. Nevertheless it came back into her awareness again and again, most sharply when she was trying to sleep.

This was often difficult. She had never taken naturally to weightlessness. To her, the pleasure of floating and flying was slight compared to the tedium of long daily times at the exercise machines lest her blood go stale and her very bones dwindle. (The rest talked or sang or watched shows, that kind of thing. She cared for none of it. Theoretically she could have retreated into her head, where mathematics and the memory of the Noumenon dwelt, as she frequently did at leisure. But the dull, sweaty exertions were too nagging.) Worse, just as she was on the edge of dreams, more and more she would rouse with a gasp from a sense of falling into a fathomless pit. Then she must drift in the dark at the end of her leash and try for calm. Thoughts rolled forth which she did not want.

Why do I care that Dan no longer cares? He was never more to me than an animal, smarter and stronger than most, excellent in bed, yet only an animal, to fill some of those hours when I was being only an animal. If my body wants use, he intimated he'd oblige—probably not now, he's probably too harassed and uncertain, but eventually. Or I could turn to ... Rueda, I suppose. A man of the word like him would see past my post-menopausal gray hair, and doubtless be quite an artist. Never mind dignity. Sex is a mere bodily need, like defecation.

Is it? Eric, Eric!

Hold. Wait. It isn't even a need. I've gone close to nine years without and hankered little and seldom.

Is the fear of death making me feel lonely? We are going to die out here. The odds against us finding our way back are ... no, not incalculable ... ridiculous. ... But if we take reasonable care, given reasonable luck, we ought to have, oh, ten years until the food is gone. With no geriatrician aboard, I could be dead of bodily failure earlier than that.

Besides, I learned long ago not to fear death. Having looked straight into Reality— There is no "I" to dread the loss of. There is a temporary association of mitochondria, eukaryotic cells, intestinal flora, and the like, the whole symbiosis shading off into the world around it that begot it, serving no end except the perpetuation of the genes within. Were the immortality of my "person" offered me, I would not want it. Too petty, amidst atoms, eons, and galaxies.

Indeed, I should welcome this unparalleled chance to explore, experience, learn. That I cannot report my findings to my colleagues is regrettable. However, from my viewpoint it is the loss of a very trivial satisfaction compared to what awaits me in the next decade.

Then why do I want somebody holding me? Why is it so long till mornwatch and my work?

Work was absorbing despite every exasperation of zero gravity and Murphy's Law. The aim was to adapt *Chinook's* holothetic system for Fidelio. First came the mechanical part, a helmet to fit his skull and attachments for the rest of his frame. This was easy. Thereafter came the electronics, circuits built and adjusted to resonate with a nervous web that was the consequence of several billion years of separate evolution. This would have been a major research project if it had not already been one on Beta. As was, most of the requirements were known. Just the same, Su Granville and Joelle herself must spend hour upon hour writing programs and then in linkage, whenever Weisenberg had supplied a new fistful of data from his instruments. Leino helped somewhat, and the others did what jackleg jobs they could as occasion demanded. Else they were engaged in astronomy and space physics. Because they had to be kept fed and their clothes and bedding laundered, Caitlín put down her eagerness and did that for the cause of survival. Often at mess or during exercise periods she sang to them. That was almost the only recreation that anybody got.

Hardware available, the true challenge came: to create the basic program by which Fidelio would integrate himself with the computer. Even among humans, each holothete was a unique case. Fidelio was not human. Furthermore, Betan computer technology had considerable differences from Terrestrial. (Yet oddly enough, insofar as comparisons were possible, it did not seem that holothetes of either species had a deeper or broader insight than those of the other. Betan machines possessed numerous superiorities, but, linked into them, Joelle had functioned more or less the same as at home. Did brains have equal limitations? Or did the Ultimate itself?)

Again, and in a still higher degree, the task would have been hopeless had it not been accomplished beforehand on Beta, when mutual linkage of members of the two races was seen as desirable. Joelle and Fidelio were simply trying to duplicate something from *Emissary* which they remembered fairly well...except that there was nothing simple involved. Instead there was a whole new computer language—practically a new semantics—plus an elaborate program for translating to a language the *Chinook* machine could handle, plus a program of translating back, plus an open-ended set of special instructions. Joelle and Fidelio had the fundamentals in their heads and knew in a general way how to reconstruct the details, by brute-strength logic, calculation, and experiment.

Not as an analogy but as a metaphor: The problem was like that which would face a Peruvian called upon to interpret between a Chinese and an Arab, when he is rusty in both their tongues, the former stutters, and the latter is a deaf-mute.

Without linkage, the problem would have been insoluble. Susanne would hook herself up and check tentative programs for inconsistencies and inadequacies, when she wasn't needed for the ongoing research elsewhere. Joelle and Fidelio would then try them out. This was hard on Joelle; she would perceive Reality distorted, bleached, fevered, and afterward have nightmares, in which she most commonly saw Eric's rotted corpse. She would wake, tell herself Fidelio wasn't complaining, though it must be worse for him, and go back to work. To enter the pure Noumenon again was always healing.

Chinook lay for a pair of weeks in orbit around the planet which humans had given no name.

"Everything seems ready, female of intellect," he said when he had given the assembly a careful examination. He used the speech, throaty and whistling, that his people did in air. It was much easier for him than Spanish. "Let us make a trial and, if we find we are on a strong tide, go straight ahead to sense the wholeness of this volume-where-we-swim."

She felt a smile at the idiom. It faded as she looked at him.

Half a sea creature, he was beautiful in free fall. Long and richly brown, his body undulated from prowlike muzzle and lapis lazuli eyes to the end of the powerful, precisely controlled tail; each digit of the six limbs knew what it did, and its motion flowed. His tang as of iodine nigh overwhelmed her with memories of beaches on Earth, surf and wind, sunlight and gull wings. How wrong that he was caged in this narrowness between two computer stacks, that meters and switches were before him instead of living underwater fronds, that his sight was bounded by painted metal instead of moving green depths and, overhead, a splintered radiance.

She pulled her attention away and, keeping a grip on a handhold, punched the intercom button. "Su," she called. "This is Joelle. Come." It might take the linker a few minutes to get shut of whatever she was doing.

"To go back to the deeps below the deeps, that will be like returning to the shore after inland years," Fidelio breathed.

"I know," Joelle said. The same ardor was in her. Holothesis shared with a Betan had dimensions no human partner could offer, among them the knowledge that her dissimilarities to him gave him an equal heightening. Together they had speculated whether the Others might not be several distinct races who formed groups that were permanently linked.

"It has been dry . . ." Fidelio's voice trailed off. He was not really capable of self-pity.

Pain on his behalf clenched. Her free hand sought his nearest arm, the upper right. The claws on that paw could have shredded her, but she felt simply warmth and velvet. "Oh, Fidelio," she whispered.

Your food stores are good for less than a year. You will die among glabrous, tailless, four-limbed trolls who can't unaided swim a single day; no wife will hold you that you may suckle her for the last time as you sink; we do not know how you ought to be mourned.

His un-Earthly gaze captured hers. "I would ask this of you, Joelle," he said calmly. She expected him to shift his glance at once, for a Betan stared hard only at someone who had angered him or at someone whom he loved and was offering his faith to. He kept looking. The blood beat in her ears. "Be warned, it is no ripple, it is a wave."

"Yes, if I'm able."

"Now that I can use this equipment, let me be the holothete whenever we need a single one, as long as I remain."

For you have nothing else left, do you, Fidelio? She let go the handhold in order to clasp his arm doubly. "Y-yes."

"You can carry out searches of your own when I float at rest. In a while, the system will again be yours entirely."

Her eyes stung. God damn it, she wasn't about to cry, was she? Joelle shook her head; the drops flittered glittering.

"Is this not acceptable?" Did he sound resigned? How could she tell? "*G'ng-ng*, I understand, female of intellect. My request ebbs."

"No, no!" The force of her reaction dismayed her. *Overwrought, short on sleep, the forebrain functional but the rest going into oscillation. If I don't take care, I'll have hysterics.* "You . . . misunderstood. I didn't mean a negative. Of course you take over. Any time, any time."

"You let water flow, Joelle. You are sorrowful [wounded? without vital nourishment? cast on a sharp-shelled reef?]. Have I done that?"

"No. You—no. Fidelio, we can link together!"

"Often, I trust, beginning today. I scent a splendor before us. But Joelle, dear mind-mate, more often—" He was stammering, she thought, and she saw the tendons grow tense behind his claws. "Alone in the All, I can raise Beta from it, wife, co-husbands, children, grandchildren, friends, the living and the dead alike, not mere memories but perceived realities in space-time; I can *feel* that they exist. It will be nearly as good as embracing them."

He stopped. Blurrily though she saw him, she sensed his astonishment. "You did not know this, Joelle? You have never done it yourself? No words will serve to explain. Well, I think I can show you, teach you, before I go down. I must certainly try. It is very fine that I can make you a gift."

She cast her body against his, held tight, and wept.

Susanne came through the door. "'Ere I am," she said; and: "Oh! *Pardonnez-moi! Vous me pardonnerez!*"

Awkward in free fall, she tried to withdraw. Joelle, twisting her neck about (cheek brushing along the pelt of her mind-mate, who had gently laid his two lower arms around her while the talons of the upper left stroked her hair) saw the linker sprattle in the doorway like a large black spider. When Fidelio, with whom she begot new comprehensions, was soon to die, but before he died might lead her to Oneness with Eric and Chris and himself and— "Get out!" Joelle screamed. "You ugly little bitch! Go!"

Susanne fled weeping.

"What has come loose?" the Betan asked anxiously.

Nobody, nobody should see me like this...except you, you're not human, you've my fellow holothete.... I'm being irrational. I was unfair to that linker. I must apologize. No. How can I explain? Anger: *Why should I explain? Why must I alone forever be rational?* Bewilderment: *Why have I kept remembering Eric, these past weeks? He's no more than a linker either. Less than that, the last I heard—settled down, long married, become a not particularly important administrator in Calgary.*

Joelle gasped for air. "N-n-nothing, Fidelio. I'm tired and— Hold me close, let me rest a while. Then I'll get a sleeping pill," *from our medical officer, that Mulryan woman; well, she may have the grace not to try sympathizing,* "and...afterward I'll be in better shape to...oh, Fidelio!"

Susanne sought her cabin, saying no word to anyone, apart from informing Caitlín that she wouldn't be in the mess for dinner.

Next mornwatch she entered the computer center expressionless. "I'm sorry I yelled at you," Joelle greeted her perfunctorily, in English. "I was feeling distressed on Fidelio's account. He's an old friend."

"I understand, madame," the linker replied with care; and they went about their mutual business.

Actually Susanne had little to do beyond monitoring, to make certain the union of Joelle, Fidelio, computers, and instruments did not start going subtly agley. It did not; the bugs were finally out of the system. The two holothetes joined awarenesses as two lovers who know each other well join bodies, and became more than the sum of themselves, and let the universe pour through them.

Much they already knew from observations and deductions made by their shipmates. The bearings of neighbor galaxies showed this region to be approximately five hundred light-years from Sol in the general direction of Hercules. That information made various bright stars like Deneb and objects like the Orion Nebula identifiable, which in turn defined the position more precisely. (As if it mattered. A single light-year is an abyss wherein imagination drowns.) The sun was a red dwarf of type M, mass 0.02 Sol, luminosity 0.004 Sol. It had five planets, none of them in the least Earthlike, all seemingly barren—except, perhaps, this largest, around which the T machine and *Chinook* were orbiting at a distance of some twenty-four million kilometers.

That world was a giant, ninety-two percent the mass of Jupiter, attended by a dozen moons. Its mean distance from its primary was 1.64 a.u., a bit further out than Mars is from Sol. Like Jupiter, it had a vast atmosphere, chiefly hydrogen, secondarily helium; lesser components included ammonia, methane, and more elaborate organic compounds. Also like Jupiter, it was hot from contraction; the upper air was thin and space-cold, but lower down it thickened and warmed, until water became a vapor and storms raged that were the size of lesser planets. Most of its bulk was liquid, though sheer pressure, despite temperature, kept solid a metallic core equal to about five Earths.

Spinning around once in ten hours and thirty-five minutes, it generated an immense magnetic field which trapped charged particles from the sun. However, the latter was so feeble a radiator that these Van Allen belts were nowhere near the Jovian intensity. No human could safely linger long in them; but, given her electrostatic defenses, *Chinook* could drop down through them and climb back up without those aboard getting a dosage to worry about.

She would have a reason to.

Joelle and Fidelio would have lost themselves in sun, moons, ambient magnificences and subtleties, every uniqueness. Hardly had they settled into the wonderful kaleidoscope, however, when a thing tugged at the fringes of their consciousness. They dismissed it a while, explored a vortex, found out why an inner globe rotated widdershins, established that this whole system was older than Sol's; but the thing would not go away. Almost impatiently, they brought their double mind to confront it. Hertzian emission from the world they were circling, yes, surely, what else would you expect?

The fact leaped forth.

Lightning, synchrotron effects, a hundred separate sources were putting forth radio energy yonder. Each had its set of patterns, which the holothetes understood in the way that a ballet dancer understands how another is executing a *pas seul*. But one small element was like a flute, defiant and variable amidst the uproar of a gale at sea—

Perhaps in a decade of concentrated effort, unaided humans would have made this discovery. The holothetes realized instantly that here was nothing which unliving nature could produce: therefore, that they were overhearing the discourse of beings which were alive and intelligent.

Afloat in the common room before his crew, the planet splendid at his back, Brodersen said into a hush: "Yeah, I do believe we should go look."

"The hazard is too great," Joelle objected. "We're safe in orbit. We can keep signalling."

"Till we start starving?" Dozsa snorted. The effort to get a response had been his. "We could, you know."

"Really?" Caitlín asked. "And why should that be? Have you not been sending on their wavelengths, and a mathematical signal they cannot mistake?"

Dozsa smiled through the weariness on his broad features. "You've been too busy to hear the news, no, my dear? Well, the basic problem is the sheer size of that world. And, yes, the natural background at those frequencies, the noise level. Without holothetics, we might never have strained the information-carrying fraction out. It's a mere by-product of broadcasts. The natives, whoever they are, have no reason to listen for calls from outside, I am sure. We must use a tight beam, to get a power they cannot miss picking up and identifying. But then we touch just a very small area." He gestured at the tawny globe. "The whole of it is *huge*. And the broadcasting sources aren't fixed, they appear to be constantly moving around."

"I'd like to know how that's done," Brodersen remarked, "or how electronics is possible there."

"At any rate, I have been making the attempt on the—off chance, do you say?" Dozsa went on. "Although mainly to pass the time while others collected more planetological data. The probability of our striking a receiver which happens to be tuned to the precise right band is—" he released his handgrip for a moment to shrug the more eloquently—"about like the probability of our guessing the path around that T machine which will get us back to the Solar System."

"Besides," Rueda pointed out superfluously, "we're under a time limit. Exercise will not maintain our health indefinitely in free fall. We must soon have weight. Our reaction mass is limited, and if we go into spin mode, that's irreversible; we'll lie in orbit forever."

"Therefore, either we quit here and jump through a random gate, or we make an effort to contact the natives," Brodersen summarized. "I vote for sticking with what we've got till we know it's useless." He could give tactical orders to be obeyed on the spot, but in a loneliness like this, a captain who did not consult the strategic wishes of his followers would not long remain captain. "There is thinking, technologically sophisticated life here. And it's a life that maybe rates high with the Others, since they didn't put the T machine in a Lagrange position, but right in satellite orbit before God and everyman." He paused. "The dwellers could be Others themselves."

Silence fell, until Caitlín whispered, "Marvel on marvel, dear darling, if that be so!" Planetlight shone golden in her eyes.

"The conditions there," Joelle protested.

"*Williwaw* should be able to meet them," Brodersen replied. "She was tested out at Zeus—robotically, of course, because of the radiation, but still, she could take everything that hit her." The biggest attendant of Phoebus was actually larger than Jupiter by the mass of a few Earths or Demeters. "I figure a crew can stand several hours at a crack. Sure, it'll be hazardous, but I've seen worse hazards and I'm still around to lie about them."

He got scant argument.

When it was done, Brodersen said, "Okay, next question. Who goes with me?"

Caitlín snapped her head "up," but it was Rueda who exclaimed, "With you? What are you talking about?"

"Since it will be risky, we'll send a minimum crew," Brodersen told them. "Pilot, co-pilot doubling as communications officer, and—well, they'll both be busier'n a one-armed octopus, so I figure a third as well, to be lookout and whatever else is required."

"I!" Leino and Frieda practically shouted.

Weisenberg cleared his throat and said louder than he was wont: "Hold on, everybody. Hold on. Let's talk sense. Which you are not doing, skipper, if you really mean it about going down yourself."

"Huh?" Brodersen grunted. "I'm qualified for co-pilot, at least. Do you suppose I'd send men into danger I don't go into?"

"Dan, that's chemically pure horse shit." In Weisenberg's mouth the vulgarism had shock value. "The captain does not do such things. He has no right."

"True, true," Rueda put in. "You are too important to our survival."

Brodersen flushed. "Oh, come on!"

"No, you come off—off that nonsense," Weisenberg snapped. "Aye, aye, if something happened to you we'd elect a new chief and carry on. But we'd not carry on as well, would we, now? You're no superman, Dan. You do have a talent for coordinating people's efforts, though. Besides, you tote around a lot of knowledge about your responsibilities, the kind of knowledge that never gets written down."

A murmur of assent answered him. He thrust his Rameses face in the direction of it. "We've got to be cold-bloodedly rational about this," he said, rapid-fire. "Those who go must be competent to go, and at the same time be those whose loss wouldn't cripple us. Besides Dan, we have three who can pilot the boat, and we need two. Stef, Carlos, Frieda, right? Which two?" His hand chopped off their yeas. "Shut up. Think straight. Carlos could readily replace Stef as mate. But you could too, Frieda, with a bit of strain, and you're the only gunner we've got. That's a real specialty. I'm not saying we'll run into a fight out here. Most likely we won't, unless against nature; but that might require placing a ray or an explosive exactly where it's needed. True? True.

"Very well, Stef and Carlos pilot. They can squabble between them who gets top billing."

His glance darted back and forth. "Who'll be the third? Certainly not either of our holothetes. Nor Martti or me—shut up, I told you, Martti! I'm the CE and he's my assistant and backup. Without proper maintenance, and repair at need, this ship is dead. Who's left? Su and Caitlín. Su has much better technical training. But gravity on that planet is about two and a half times Earth normal. You're not strong, Su." His lips creased momentarily upward. "Tough, I'd say, tougher than you have the reputation of being; but not very strong in the muscles and not too fast in the reflexes either. Caitlín—"

"Wait a flinkin' minute!" Brodersen roared.

"No!" Leino yelled.

"Do you *mean* that?" Caitlín cried. She released her handhold, kicked off, arrowed to Weisenberg, and cast her arms about him. The impact knocked him loose and they drifted away together, gyrating, while she gave him kiss after kiss and outrage boiled around them.

XXVIII

GUIDED BY HER HOLOTHETES, *Chinook* dropped easily down to a synchronous orbit which kept her above the region her boat would seek out. That put her below the radiation belts. Indeed, the field warded off most of the particle flux that she encountered in free space.

Conveyor and cranes swung *Williwaw* clear and the daughter vessel blasted free. "O-o-oh," Caitlín breathed, a sound like a prayer. She had watched approach on the viewscreens and been awed, but now she was out in flesh and bone before a terrible splendor.

Optical systems in the control cabin opened on one entire hemisphere and elsewhere on large sections of heaven. The planet filled almost half. When she looked its way, there was nothing else to see; amber and gold, the inward-flooding light bore every star out of vision. To the right, unutterably distant, red bands along the rim of the world deepened into purple and thence into the cosmic blackness. The sun stood yonder, a tiny coal. To left was the nearer edge of night, a dark which lived with faint sheens, remote flashes, and orange streaks that were high clouds catching dawn-glow. Between stretched the daylit face, bright zones, richer-hued bands, in a thousand shifting shades, they themselves ever changeable, streaming, undulating, forming whirlpools, tides, rivers, an endless dance, majestic and joyous.

The boat murmured and throbbed. Recondensing jet vapor made a ruddy fog-bank aft, small to see—it dissipated as fast as it formed—but soon veiling *Chinook*'s globe from sight. Weight held the farers steady in their seats. Though less than a gee, acceleration was considerable, in order to get them down shortly after local sunrise. Rueda's exchange of information with the ship was a dry obbligato, unreal-sounding.

He ended it as if in relief. Thus far everything was satisfactory. For a while he sat quiet, like his companions. Radiance made a halo of his baldness. At last he said softly, "Mother of God, a man might die quite happy after this."

Dozsa grinned, not too mirthfully. His accent thickened. "If you wish. Me, I have a wife and children at home. Here is the kind of experience I like to *have* had."

Rueda looked surprised. "And still you came along?"

"What else? I agree we must go search, and I am best qualified." Dozsa was piloting, since besides past practice, he was a martial arts enthusiast, trained into strength and speed. "Don't get me wrong, Carlos. I am not afraid. In fact, I relish the challenge. But I will relish it more in retrospect." He crossed himself. "Or in the afterlife, if God does not will we succeed. Our death ought to be clean and quick."

"Aye." Caitlín was barely audible. "A shooting star in a sky like that—sure, and there are many harder fates, there are."

"One feels near to God on this mission, no?" Rueda said, almost as muted. "But He is not the kindly old Father the sisters told me of in school, nor the just Lord our priest called on."

"He is those and more," Dozsa replied. "Caitlín, you pagan, even you must be hearing Him out of your childhood."

She shook her head. Braided, her hair was a chiaroscuro around it. "No. Perhaps they were too Catholic in Ireland for me, a part of their seeking to rebuild after the Troubles and keep the faith after the Others . . . and I a rebel born. I've no anger in me any more, though."

Dozsa smiled. "Well, let's not argue. We have not the energy to spare. If you don't mind, I will include you in my prayers. Most likely I shall be thinking a few."

Rueda looked behind him to where she sat. "What do you believe in, if I may ask?" he inquired.

"In life," she said.

They fell silent, watching the planet draw closer, night recede across it and brightness grow. Presently a fresh set of demands for readings and confirmation of flight plan details rattled forth. Having complied, Rueda added, "That was unnecessary, my friends."

Brodersen's voice replaced Joelle's. It was almost unrecognizable: "My fault. I insisted. You're really okay?"

"Never better, my darling," Caitlín made bold to answer, "save for not having you here. And this cabin is rather cramped for sports anyhow. Make up our bed before I come back. It needs it, you will be remembering."

"Pegeen, please—"

"I'm sorry." She reached toward the loudspeaker as if toward him. "You fear for me. But would I not be fearing for you, were you bound off like this? Ah, don't be selfish, be glad for me on such a grand adventure."

"I'm... trying...."

"No, more than an adventure. Magic they never dreamed of in Tír na nÓg. Do you know, I was thinking we'll need a name for our planet, do we win to its people. We can scarcely pronounce theirs, whatever it be."

Brodersen hesitated. "And?"

"I thought of Danu, the mother goddess of the Tuatha de Danaan, they who became the great Sídhe."

"Done, by thunder!" he decreed.

Williwaw entered perceptible atmosphere more abruptly than above Demeter, for this air was compressed hard by gravity. Her path and vectors had been computed with that in mind. She got continuous guidance from Joelle, holothetically linked to instruments whose operators Fidelio had told what to probe for. Else her mission would have been suicidal.

As was, in the first hour Dozsa used himself to limits beyond what he had been sure were his. Rueda was nearly as busy, handling communication back and forth, often helping steer. The cabin soon stank from their sweat. It filled with monstrous roars, shrieks, rumbles, whistlings. Their own weight hauled at the humans, two and a half times what their race was evolved to bear. Every finger grew heavy, an arm was a burden, necks strained to keep heads positioned, guts sagged, hearts toiled, ribs ached from breathing, mouths dried out and throats went raw.

That would not have happened on a test centrifuge or aboard a watchship under full thrust, where a person could sit or lie at ease. Danu raged. Stratospheric impact made the boat shudder, bounce about, buck like a mustang. Deeper down, at low relative speed, she encountered winds to send her tumbling. If not skillfully met, they might have torn her wings off. Designed for Earthlike worlds, she was aerodynamically poor on this one. Nor did skill alone compensate, when the whole sky was strange.

More than once, Joelle herself was taken by surprise, as some violence erupted which she had not had the data to predict. However swift her response, it must be spoken, which ate seconds. From a Betan mother ship she could have piloted directly, could virtually have been the vessel. Dozsa and Rueda, though, must cope however they were able, till they got a word to help them.

Twice they passed through storms. Blindness clamped down, until lightning turned flying cloud wracks incandescent. Thunder followed; it was like being inside a cannon. The gales racketed and snatched. Each drop through turbulence ended with spine-jarring force. Roll, pitch, and yaw flung bodies against harnesses. Once hailstones crashed against the hull, once a Noah's rain engulfed it.

Throughout, Caitlín watched. She could do nothing else, except now and then tap a shoulder and point to a thing in the distance that looked sinister—mountain-tall cloud, vortex of turbulence, snake's nest of lightning, or a wildness for which humans had no ready word. Otherwise she refrained from bothering the men. She watched, she sent her whole being outward, she laughed for happiness.

Williwaw won through. Occasionally it seemed doubtful she would, despite computations giving her favorable odds, but she did. Reaching the altitude whence the broadcasts originated, more or less, she found peace. Here the air was thick and warm and had no haste. Thermal currents welled from below to help upbear her. The autopilot could take over. She lazed through a broad circle and began a broadcast of her own, taped signals on various Danaan wavebands. A beam carried Rueda's dull tone aloft: "We are safe. Repeat, we are safe. Give us a few minutes to rest, and we'll report."

Like Dozsa, he slumped, chin falling on chest. Caitlín leaned forward to touch both men. "Oh, my poor tired dears—" She stopped, for she grew aware of what was around her.

Without light amplification, she would have been blind. Given it, she saw widely. The foreignness was such that she needed a while before vision could truly register; but an onrush of beauty came at once.

Above, heaven was indigo at the horizon, lightening to violet at the zenith. Single clouds wandered there, faerie shaped, colored for a Colorado sunset. The sun itself stood high in a rainbow ring. Below, a cloud deck lay like an ocean, but no ocean that men had ever sailed. Its reach was imperial; it had peaks, canyons, smoky plains, great slow cataracts, infinitely intricate yet never twice the same. Aureate, it was touched with reds, streaked with blues and greens and browns, shadowed where it plunged into mysteries.

A flock went by afar. Were they winged, were they finned? They were gone too fast to see; but they had gleamed.

There came a lulling sound from outside, from the calmly flowing wind.

Caitlín reclined her chair and let aches begin to drain away. The heaviness upon her was only like a strong, over-kindly hand.

After a while the humans recovered enough to talk with their ship, take readings, record views, and talk some more. A while after that, certain Danaans arrived.

Caitlín saw them first. Her partners were busy again, not as frantically as on the descent, but worriedly. Communication to space had cut off. The speaker gave nothing but crackle, buzz, chaos, no matter what Rueda tried. Somewhere above them, in that serene-looking heaven, some electric event had somehow made the upper atmosphere opaque to every frequency at his command. This was not a possibility, or at least a likelihood, that the holothetes had foreseen. They were not gods, they had had less information to go on than a Betan expedition would have gathered, and besides, every world in the universe is unique. Dozsa feared the trouble portended an equally sudden change in the air. Dense as it was, its pressure close to the limit of what the hull could withstand, might not currents go through it, Gulf Streams of gas whose borders were roiled and dangerous? Without overmuch hope, he sought hints from instruments and from the feel of the boat.

Thus they might well have missed the newcomers, gone by entirely, had Caitlín not been on the alert. She cried out—sang out—and pounded their backs while her other hand pointed, tuned screens to magnification, pointed afresh. Rueda whistled. "Marvelous," he said. "Make for them, Stefan."

Dozsa scowled. "I'm not sure," he replied. "Under these conditions, to break our holding pattern—"

"Down, you *amadán*!" Caitlín shouted. "I swear they are what we came here for!"

"How can you tell?" the mate demanded.

"Do you mean to say you cannot?"

"Well... well—all right. I suppose if we don't investigate, we'll have had our trouble for nothing."

Caitlín rumpled his sweat-gummed hair. "Now you talk the way Dan would be wanting."

Between buoyancy and updrafts, stalling speed for *Williwaw* was low. Downward bound, Dozsa slowed her as much as he dared, or maybe a little more. The sight before her sprang into clarity, and dazzled.

By the woman's count, nineteen forms, traveling by twos and threes, had risen from the clouds beneath to converge well ahead of the vessel, a kilometer lower but precisely on its projected track. They were the size of sperm whales and had the same basic torpedo shape, the same blunt snouts—in which the mouths (?) were set foremost, circular, closable by sphincters—and flukes at the after end—though these were fourfold, both horizontal and vertical, and seemed to be flexible control surfaces rather than propellers. Short tendrils and long antennae encircling their muzzles doubtless held, or were, sense organs. From their middles bulged a pair of intricate muscular structures, out of which sprang smooth, narrow wings that exceeded the body in length. Forward of these were two arms (or trunks, since they appeared to be boneless) ending in what humans could only call hands.

The coloring was exquisite: royal blue on backs shaded to sapphire beneath, while the wings were ashimmer like diffraction jewels, each movement of their pliant surfaces an interplay of chromatic waves. Glory exploded when the creatures began to dance for the spacecraft. They swooped, they soared, they planed, they turned, they glided within centimeters of each other, they arced off across kilometers, a wheeling, weaving, fountaining measure which seized the mind and drew it into itself as great art ever does, or love.

"They have music for that," Caitlín foreknew. "Carlos, can you be tuning in their music?"

Rueda tore loose from his own rapture and worked with the sonic receiver. Presently he had eliminated the boom of the boat's passage, damped the wind-sounds, and brought in the song. From sea-deep basses to ice-clear sopranos, and below and above those pitches humans can hear, tones filled the cabin. They were on no scale known to children of Earth; if they gave the men any clear first impression, it was of unshakeable power; but Caitlín said while tears stood in her eyes, "Oh, the joy in them, the joy! You cannot hear it? Then look how they frolic."

"I'd better concentrate on keeping us aloft," Dozsa said. Despite his gaze straying to the half stately, half genial harmony of movements around him, he swung *Williwaw* through a tight curve.

"It's welcoming us they are," Caitlín said. "If they are in truth the Others, och, I always knew those must be happy folk."

"Eh, wait, my dear," Rueda cautioned. "It's a superb spectacle, but you're jumping to conclusions. Those could simply be curious and playful animals, like dolphins cavorting around a watercraft."

"With hands? They use their hands better than hula dancers."

"Where are clothes, ornaments, tools, any sign of artifacts?"

"They need none right now. Hush. I think I may be in the way of starting to understand that music."

"You'd better hurry," Dozsa warned. "I can't safely continue this maneuver. I'll have to go back to a larger radius pretty soon. The trouble is, our stalling speed seems to be more than the top they can manage."

"As one would expect," Rueda said. "Nature designed them for . . . Danu. Man did not design this boat for it. Besides, she's nuclear-powered, while they run on chemistry—I'm sorry, Caitlín, you wanted quiet."

"No, go on, if you've a thought," she said. "I just wanted to listen, not dispute. I'll save an ear for you. Science too is a set of arts."

Rueda smiled lopsidedly. "I'm no scientist. A Sunday dabbler in it at most. . . . We are getting this scene on tape, aren't we?"

"Aye, of course."

"Good," Dozsa said bleakly. "Life like this on a world like this. It'll give us much to talk about in the years ahead."

The pageant went on. Humans spoke amidst its melodies, staring at its motion, as they flew between red dwarf sun and sea of cloud.

"I think they must be live lighter-than-air ships," Rueda ventured. "Those giant bodies are mostly gas bags, inflated by their own heat. Vents help them rise or sink, the wings catch winds, and probably there's a jet arrangement as well, using a bellows or—I don't know; but the atmosphere's dense enough at this level to make it practical. They breathe hydrogen instead of oxygen, naturally, but I suspect they're otherwise not so unlike us, they're also made of proteins in water solution."

"Where do they come from?" Dozsa wanted to know. "What made them evolve? How did life start in the first place? Where does the food chain begin?"

"How many years and research organizations will you allow me for those questions, my friend? If you want my guess, I'd say the 'primordial ocean' is down under the clouds, where the air gets really dense and chemicals can concentrate—orginally on colloids? Remember, this planet is like Jupiter or Zeus or Epsilon. It radiates more than it receives. That means a thermal gradient to drive biochemistry, especially when the sun is weak. Energy comes more from below than above. I daresay our altitude here is marginal for life, like Antarctica or the sea bottoms of Earth."

Dozsa scowled at the dancers. "Intelligence developing when the whole ecology floats? How would it? No stone for tools, no fire—"

Rueda nodded. "That's why I confess to doubts about those otherwise delightful animals."

Caitlín straightened in her harness. "Wurra, wurra, where have you two parked your imaginations?" she challenged. "Can you not think of growths adrift for use, like kelp and fish bones, only better? If you must have a thing that answers to fire, what about enzymes that catalyze reduction of organic compounds? And do we know what made apes turn manward on Earth, let alone dogmatizing about the subject on a foreign planet?"

Rueda stroked his mustache. "True. However, I decline to believe in the possibility of electronics without solid materials, minerals, being available. Yes, conceivably the Others know tricks with pure force-fields. But how does one get from here to there? Not in a single bound! Native Danaan sentience might develop, it might get as noble and artistic and intellectual as you please, but by itself it has *no* way to build a scientific-technological civilization." His laugh came brittle. "*E púr si muove.* We've detected transmitters." He sagged. Weariness flattened his voice. "Never mind. I'm afraid this gravity is getting to my marrow. I can't think very well. How I hope something more happens soon."

Dozsa nodded. He had no reason to repeat what they knew. Their stay was sharply limited in time. Muscles might adapt to high weight, but the cardiovascular system, the entire fluid distribution of the human body, could not. Blood was pooling in the lower extremities; the laboring heart grew less and less able to supply the brain; seepage out of cells would bring edema; eventually the damage would be irreversible.

Meanwhile the hull was not impermeable. At this pressure, molecules of hydrogen were leaking through metal. The mixture would at last become explosive.

"Well, we planned on remaining till near sundown." Dozsa sighed. "Probably we were too optimistic. Distances must be great everywhere on Danu. Those people, if they are intelligent, must be those that happened to be close by. The others—the Others—"

"The true Others would have arrived sooner, is that what you are saying, Stefan?" Caitlín asked.

Again he nodded.

"It's right you are, I fear." She looked back outward. "But how lovely they are here, how full of bliss!"

Dozsa returned *Williwaw* to her former height and path. The dance continued. The visitors watched and recorded as best they could.

The ember sun passed noon. More Danaans came.

There was no longer any doubting their sapience. The dance dissolved, and those took over who had brought equipment. Some had curious objects hung on their titanic persons, some guided vehicles of various shapes (platforms? birds? chambered nautiluses?) from which projected devices (telescopes? cobwebs? interlocked rings?). They did not attempt to meet the spacecraft, but came to rest well beneath her and adjusted their apparatuses.

The radio receiver brought in ordered sounds, in the same wide range as earlier tunes but plainly speech.

"Give me five minutes," Rueda muttered, and got busy with a reflection spectrometer which had been preset for him aboard *Chinook*. Dozsa held the boat in a steady wheeling at a steady speed, though an afternoon wind was rising to drone around her structure and thrill through it. Aches, exhaustion, the drag of gravity were forgotten.

"How do we respond?" Caitlín inquired out of exultation; and immediately: "Och, aye, a notion, if you've none better, boys."

"The mike is yours," Dozsa said. "What have you in mind?"

"A patterned signal, to show them we wish to communicate. Why start with mathematics? They know full well that we know the value of *pi*. But if we can recognize their music for what it is and enjoy the same, faith, they can ours." Caitlín reached down to the webbing on the side of her chair. "Well that I thought to bring my sonador."

She inserted a program and touched the keyboard. *Eine Kleine Nachtmusik* tumbled forth. "They offered us mirth," she explained. "Let us offer it back."

A screen at high magnification showed the Danaans reacting. At least, they moved about ... to confer?

"Ha!" Rueda said. "I expected this." He tapped the spectrometer. "Those vehicles, most of those gadgets are metal. Tell me how that was mined, on a planet whose surface is hot liquid hydrogen."

"It wasn't," Dozsa declared. "It came from outside."

Seen against purple heaven and a tower of cloud, two Danaan carriers linked together. One of the pilots withdrew on mother-of-pearl wings, the other remained. Suddenly he (?!) and the machines were hidden behind great sheets and curtains of light. Outward and outward they flared, every color, a created aurora. It wavered about for a short while, as if uncertain. Then—

"Jesus, Mary, and Joseph," Caitlín whispered. "They're replying to Mozart."

She must show the men how this was true, how the lambencies matched the notes (in no simple fashion, but even more truly as the unseen artist strengthened a grasp on the intent of an Earthling centuries dead) until spectrum and scale became a single jubilation. Her understanding of the fact was not strictly scientific, demonstrable by any standard analytical technique; it was the kind of insight that came to Newton and Einstein.

Later sendings and transformations confirmed it. Attempts at television exchange failed; evidently the electronics were too unlike. Only music and radiance could say, back and forth: "Hello, there; we love you."

The short day drew toward a close. Caitlín stayed ecstatic, while her companions grew slowly grim.

At last:

"We must go," Dozsa said. "We have no choice."

"We'll be back." Caitlín spoke as if in dreams.

"No, I hardly think we will," Rueda told her with compassion. "Haven't we agreed? It's death to linger, down here or up in orbit. Oh, yes, we may be wrong about that, but what can we do except proceed on our best guesswork . . . and haven't we agreed?"

She bowed her head. Twilight closed in; it was golden. The Danaans waited below for her next message.

Rueda leaned around in his seat to clasp the hand Caitlín lifted to him. "Those are not the Others," he reminded. "They cannot be. I guess that they are a . . . a favored race. One that the Others come to openly, maybe because they're happier, kindlier, more creative than most. If that's right, then the Others give them metal things, for them to realize the better what they are—born artists, and who knows what else? But not scientists. Not engineers. They can't help us. And we, we can't survive long in these parts, unless we put *Chinook* into spin mode and make her unable ever to leave. And how often do the Others visit these adopted children of theirs? Maybe they will next week, but maybe they won't for a thousand years. How can we tell?"

"Aye." Caitlín squared her shoulders against the weight upon her. "Our best bet is to seek onward." She laughed shakenly. "We've seen this much of what the universe holds. Ho for the next world!"

Dozsa bit his lip. "If possible," he said. "We're still out of touch with *Chinook*. We'll have to fight our way alone, unguided, up to clear space."

Caitlín cast regret from her. "Go, lad, go," she urged. "You'll make it. We'll yet be seeing wonders more lofty than here."

XXIX

I WAS A CHIMPANZEE, born where forest met savannah. My earliest memory was of my mother holding me to her. The warmth and odors of her flesh mingled with the sharper fragrances of hair, and with the smells of soil and growth everywhere around us. Leaves glowed green-gold overhead, sunbeams slanting between them to fleck the ground whereon she sat. My lips sought through her crisp shagginess until they found a teat and gladdened me with belly comfort.

Later I ran free and noisy in the band, save when an elder bared teeth. Then one cringed respectfully back. The Eldest, He, was like the sky over us all, which sent rain and sunlight alike, and sometimes roared and flashed till we squalled in terror: for He did lead us to safe trees and delicious fruits, He did lead us in that grimacing, howling threat-dance which made the leopard slink off.

I learned where to find bananas and birds' nests, insects and grubs. Later I learned how to moisten a stick and probe it into the anthills which loomed under the savannah blaze. I began to stand my share of lookout while we drank at the river. Further grown, I became the only female who joined our occasional hunts, when we went after a small animal, caught it, tore it asunder, grew wild from its meat and salty blood and crunchy bones. A craziness more pure was to spring, swing, soar from branch to branch, become speed and air, clasp and let go the tree as a lover.

The first who mounted me was He. His grip was python-strong, He growled and thrust, the scent of Him whirled me away. But afterward when my seasons came upon me, I liked best another among the males, the gentlest. We would groom and nuzzle through long, lazy, lovely whiles, or sit hand in hand on a bough looking out over the moon-white plain.

There was everything to wonder at, sun, weather, a butterfly, elephants, lion roar, flower aromas, the creatures that came in bright shells and stepped forth on two long legs, the distant twinkle of the fires they made at dusk.... We peered, prodded, snuffed, nibbled, listened, hooted our merriment or chattered our anger or mutely marveled.

Greatest of wonders was whenever my waxing heaviness departed in pain and left a baby to cling to me. It would grow up and leave me at last, or it would grow still and I would carry it around, hurt, puzzled, till it turned strange; but always would come new babies, new love.

Once the male I liked best wanted me when He did too, and defied. But he was soon thrashed and, groveling, offered his rear. It was a different male who at last brought Him down and became He. A later morning, when we stirred awake, we found the body which had so long dominated us lying at the edge of our glade. A breeze played with its grizzled fur. The ants were busy. The vultures came. We went away, for somehow fear had touched us.

After a crocodile got my special mate, I drifted into a different band. Rank by rank, I rose to be first among its females. We ordered ourselves in less clear and less conscious wise than the males, but we knew who ruled over whom. Indeed, now in my ripeness I had no more dread of them, from Him on down. They came and went on their foolish errands; we endured; and the band was really ours—was mine. I took the choicest food and resting places among females, but I also often kept watch over children, not just my own, and herded them back from danger.

Less and less often did my seasons come upon me. Less and less eager for movement, I took to staring outward from the troop, into shadows or rain, across open land, upward at night to the stars, full of a feeling that more lay yonder than we had wind of.

Suddenly, from darkness, the Summoner came. I was borne off and became One, as it were with dawn and lightnings. The tree among whose limbs I leaped was the tree which bears the worlds. I would be returned to live out my chimpanzee days, unharmed, but would ever be haunted by joy I could not really remember. I was Mammal.

XXX

WANING FROM HALF PHASE, the red sun ever closer to its illuminated crescent, Danu remained sublime to the eye. Opposite, a pair of moons stood forth among the brilliances that filled the firmament.

Martti Leino could not bear to watch. Alone in his cabin, he hung tethered, for his hands were clasped white-knuckled together except when he smote the bulkhead and rebounded, his legs kicked at nothing except when they trailed helpless. Tears bobbed glittery around his head.

"No, God, Lord, no," he croaked. "Please. You know not what You do if You let her die—" Horrified: "Forgive me! Lord, I spoke ill there. But save her. You can. You will, nay? Please—"

He drew lungful after lungful of air till his head spun, his limbs tingled, but he could at least say in a flat voice, in Finnish: "Martti, boy, you are developing a classic case of hysterics. Do you know that? Very well, stop. It isn't helping Caitlín a bit. Offer an orderly prayer if you wish, but don't tell God His business, and do be about yours.

"Ow-w-w-w!" he howled and writhed about.

He was halfway back under control when the door chimed. "Hoy?" he asked aloud, stupidly. The chim repeated. "Come in," he hiccoughed. The chime sounded again. He remembered he had locked himself in, to be undisturbed after he began to tremble. Well— Slipping his leash, he kicked toward the entrance, misgauged and fetched up against a table, and went through a set of rookie mistakes before he got the latch released.

Frieda von Moltke entered, checked her flight at the jamb, had a good look at Leino, and secured the door behind her. Since he merely gaped, she took the initiative: "Hell and damnation, you are worse off than I expected."

He closed his jaws. "What do you want?" he managed.

260

She clasped him by the upper arms. They drifted off, a slight rotation making the room wobble slowly around them. "I saw how you were getting frantic," she said. "You went away. Good, I thought, maybe a drink, a tranquilizer, a nap; he calms down when nobody watches. But you were gone too long."

He turned his face from hers. "They are gone too long."

"Yes, communication broken for hours, and now they must be blasting from the planet, if they are still alife, without guidance, yes. It is very bad for us if we haff lost our boat."

"Jesu Kriste, believe you that matters?"

She gripped him harder. "Martti, dear, listen. My family were soldiers from as long ago as we haff chronicles. They knew what it is to lose a friend. *Ich hat' einen Kameraden . . . ja.* You mourn. But you go on."

He knotted his fists. "If you think—simply a friend—"

Frieda nodded to herself. She checked their flight as they passed a chair, hooked an ankle behind it to hold them, kept him by her left hand, and used her right to cup his chin. "You are being no use to anybody, you know," she said mildly.

"Yes? Who is not? The whole crew is waiting, only waiting. What else can we do?"

"We can hearten us, to be ready for tomorrow," she said. "We can comfort each other. I came to you for that. Cry if you want. It will not make you small. I saw my father cry more than once, when we went to lay flowers in the cemetery for his old guerrilla corps."

"Frieda, Frieda," He clasped her, buried his face in her bosom, and shuddered. She stroked him.

"ATTENTION!" the intercom boomed. "All hands! Listen!"

Both heads snapped that way.

"Listen." Brodersen's tones came raw, gulped forth, as if he was weeping. "Message from *Williwaw*. They, they, they're okay. Bound back to us. Arriving in two-three hours. They didn't find any help for us, but . . . they're alive! Well! They're coming back!"

"Ya-a-a-ah!" Frieda screamed, and grabbed Leino's whole body against hers. He floated like a rag doll, mouth working. Between sounds she did not know, she heard: "Lord, I thank . . . Christ, I thank. . . ."

After a few minutes Brodersen made a calmer announcement. Joelle could talk the boat home, and he personally would handle the chores of docking. Everybody else might as well

sleep. The three from *Williwaw* would certainly be needing to. In
about twelve hours, or however long it took, there'd be breakfast
call, followed by a general debriefing. Then probably *Chinook*
would boost back to the T machine for another jump. That
would take more than an Earth day. Meanwhile they could
throw a proper wingding to celebrate. "Good night. A real good
night, ain't it? A real good night."

(*Chinook* entered the shadow cone of Danu, and half of
heaven was blotted out.)

"We celebrate right away," Frieda laughed, and kissed Leino.

He jerked back. "What do you mean?"

She widened her china-blue eyes. "Why, what do you
suppose, luffer? We are both glad."

He thrust clear of her. Floating off, he held denying palms in
her direction. "No. Not right. I will thank the Lord."

"Oh, yes. Afterward—"

"Get out!" he yelled. "You slut!" He struggled. "No. I'm
sorry. I didn't mean that. But—well—please go, Frieda. You
mean well, but please go."

She regarded him for several seconds, and went.

Brodersen had restlessness to work off. (Pegeen, Pegeen.)
Usually at such times he did exercises, but that would now have
been intolerable. Therefore he made a tour of inspection.
Everything was in order, he knew it would be, but the gesture
helped him, gave him a sense he was doing what he could for the
worldlet that would most likely be his and Caitlín's till they died.
Not that he was its God—Judas priest, no! (The juxtaposition
tugged a brief smile from him.) He merely needed to give
whatever he was able.

Goodbye, Lis, he thought as he flew down silent corridors.
*Goodbye, Mikey, boy. You ought to do all right, and you may
not even remember me. Goodbye, Barbara, dear darling. You
may.... Why do I worry most about you, Babsy? You'll grow to
be like your mother, a free-standing woman who can shove the
world up its own south pole if it dares to threaten you.*

*I'll miss you, my kids. I really don't want you to miss me, but
it'd be nice to believe you'll remember me kindly.*

He rounded a corner, catching the metal to swing himself
about. *Lis—God damn it, Lis, I love you!*

I love you too, Pegeen, and how the hell can I measure

between the two of you, and why should I? Lis sits forsaken; but she can have another man if she wants, or men, and live out a long and full life. Pegeen is here; but chances are she'll die young in space along with the rest of us, and I'm not worth that.

Brodersen mustered a grin. *I do not feel guilty. I was in a war, and this was how things worked out, and if I made mistakes, the opposition did too. It's a shame what's happened, but Lis and Pegeen both would whop me in the chops if I started whining about it. They'd tell me just to keep on trying.*

Triumphantly went through him: *Pegeen's alive. I'll see her again in a couple of hours.*

The broad door to the common room appeared. He knew no reason to check inside, but did anyway. As he passed through, he heard sobbing.

He snagged a table whereon miscellaneous games were played, felt the reaction surge through his muscles, and hung anchored by his fingers. The viewscreens showed a total eclipse. Danu—which Caitlin had named—stood monstrous, not quite black but mysteriously ashimmer and ringed in crimson, while elsewhere the stars blazed and a visible pair of sickle moons went by. Mumbling ventilators underscored the stillness. The normal, health-reinforcing temperature and ionization cycles had brought a chill to the air, with a subliminal smell of night.

The inkblot shape of Susanne Granville huddled in a corner. She clasped a chairback while her free hand covered her face. The brightness from heaven was enough to be merciless.

Brodersen kicked off and speared through the cold. "Hey, Su, what's wrong?"

"Oh! *Monsieur le capitaine....*" She snatched for breath while he halted by the same chair. "I am sorry. It is no never-mind," she coughed.

"Aw, come on." He realized anew what a sweet person she was, how much he liked and, yes, respected her. Almost shyly, he laid an arm across her shoulders. "You got troubles, Su."

"I ... I *am* sorry.... I should 'ave gone to my cabin—"

"But?" He held her a little closer.

"It is empty there. 'Ere is the galaxy for to see." She sank her head on his breast.

In a short while she lifted it—he discerned her homely countenance by starlight—and confessed, "I, I make the apology, Daniel, good friend. It is wrong I cry when they come back safe, no? But—" Her eyes, her really beautiful eyes, caught his. "One thing. You 'ave n-n-no need for 'urrying about this. You 'ave more urgent matters. But—" She gasped. "We are lost in eternity. Tell me, please, when you 'ave time—what can I *do*?"

"Ah-h," he murmured, scenting that she also was a woman (without desire, when Caitlín was scheduled soon to disembark, but with a sudden extra affection), "you're left out of the linkage, right?"

"Not forbidden. 'Owever, Fidelio and Dr. Ky, they do everyt'ing—" He felt her tense in his arms, saw in the ring of the Milky Way how she mastered her lips. "What is left for me, Daniel? 'Ow can I 'elp you?"

He made kindly noises, and eventually took her to her cabin, where he gave her a sedative and a brother's kiss before he left. As the door closed behind him, he wondered what the devil he could find for her.

XXXI

ON AUTOPILOT, which observation had shown to be safe, *Chinook* accelerated toward the T machine. En route, her crew had a party. Brodersen recommended going all out, no stinting of booze or pot or anything else. First Caitlín, assisted by Susanne, made a tableful of canapés, and Weisenberg turned out some new ornaments for the common room, colorful objects of metal and plastic, in his machine shop.

"Ladies and gentlemen," the captain stated when his folk were gathered, "we have before us the serious business of getting drunk—stoned—high as a kite, boiled as an owl. I refer, of course, to the International Standard Kite, flown under one gravity in air at STP, and to the International Standard Owl, whose condition is determined by encephalogram after it has consumed one liter of hundred proof Scotch."

"No, Irish," Caitlín required, and lifted her glass of the same to his. *"Sláinte go fáil leat."* They grinned at each other. Though she had ached from high weight and battering flight, she had seldom given him a finer time than when she awoke after arrival, unless maybe he compared subsequent times.

"Here's to our noble selves," Brodersen toasted the company.

Most of their responses were nominal. He considered them. The viewscreens held splendor, Danu's dayside receding in the sky but still large, the sun like a ruby, stars and the galactic river and stars. Nobody watched—not that that was the purpose, but it seemed as if they were turning their backs on the cosmos.

Carlos Rueda appeared cheerful. Frieda von Moltke had made him royally welcome. However, tonight she played more to Stef Dozsa, though he was pretty dour. Phil Weisenberg wore a calm, polite smile. Su Granville had gained back a little morale from helping Caitlín; nevertheless, beneath her face Brodersen discerned woe. Joelle Ky had taken a chair offside and was devoting her attention to Fidelio—almost ostentatiously, which wasn't her style. Martti Leino had, plain to see, not been sleeping well and, no matter how he tried, could not keep his gaze of Caitlín.

He's in love with her, Brodersen thought. *Understandable. Maybe she ought to—Or maybe not. I don't know. It could raise more trouble than it ends, he's such an intense kind of guy. . . . And what should I do about Joelle? She's got something eating at her too. I'm not sure what.* He laid an arm around the girl beside him, felt her supple slenderness, inhaled her fragrance of youth. *I hate to give up any time I might spend with Pegeen.*

He laughed.

"What's funny, my heart?" she asked.

"Nothing," Brodersen said in haste. *Ha! There I was, taking for granted I'm such a God's gift to suffering womankind that a night with me will instantly make Joelle purr. Joelle!* "Uh, how about some music? From you, I mean. Now that we have you back." He brushed his mouth across the wonderful softness of her cheek; and practically felt Leino's look stab him; and no doubt Leino wasn't the only one. *I'd better stop flaunting this that I have and they don't. Only how can I?*

"Well, if people want." Caitlín paused. "No, instead of a recital, what do the lot of you say to a dance? Sure, and there's naught better for loosening sadness."

"We're a tad short on women," Weisenberg pointed out. "Four. Ah, well, Fidelio and I'll be the wallflowers."

"Three," Joelle said. "Leave me out."

"Shucks, no," Brodersen requested. "Why?" When she sat obstinate, he went over to her, leaned close, and whispered, "You always enjoyed ballroom dancing when we were together. What's gone wrong?" Her gaze upon his seemed doubly dark. "We need you. The disappointment at Danu was a stiff blow. If we don't cheer ourselves up, we'll be too goddamn low to cope. Please, Joelle."

"What about Fidelio?" she answered in the same English. "Nobody worries about his feelings."

As if she had overheard, Caitlín called, "Och, we don't need exact partners. A square dance, a jig—yes, Fidelio too. Why not? They must jump about for fun on Beta." She chuckled. "Faith, it's very special this will be. The first interspecies dance in human history."

Brodersen queried the alien about it in Spanish. He was surprised at the eagerness of the positive response.

"Then it's settled," Caitlín said. "Let's be seeing how best we can unsettle it. Give me a few minutes to work out steps to suit us." Taking up her sonador, she programmed it for accordion-like sounds and played while she skipped about the deck. Her yellow dress billowed out from the swift slim legs, the bronze hair tumbled free.

Somehow the sight, followed by instruction, did break the mood that was upon them. When the actual dancing began, to music from the data bank, persons even laughed—at first at their own unpracticed clumsiness, as when Rueda tripped over Fidelio's tail; later at jokes and japes, lame though most of those were. Blood pulsed warm again; light sweating made them smell each other as flesh; stamping feet, clasping hands, driving rhythms set them wholly aware they were alive.

After a few rounds, they began to drop out for drinking and talking and different recreations. A ping pong game got under weigh. Caitlín sang her "Midsummer Song" for Weisenberg, Rueda, Susanne, and Frieda. Later on, couples formed in more leisurely dances. (Brodersen and Susanne were decorous, Dozsa and Frieda anything but, other combinations varied. Leino grew alcoholically gleeful when Caitlín was in his arms, and Joelle pressed hard against Brodersen.) It became a good party.

Around the middle of it, Caitlín found herself telling the rest: "Aye, we're lucky, that we are. You've seen the tapes from Danu. If you did not thrill, we might as well bung you out the airlock, for you're already dead. And they are nothing beside the reality. I had that, but I'll not be selfish, I'll give you your turns at the next marvel, and the next and the next. If we never come home, still the gods will have bestowed more adventure on us than ever our kind had before." She struck a ringing chord from her instrument. "And who says we will not? The universe is ours, and I see no bounds for us at all, at all."

"Haven't you been composing a ballad on that theme?" Brodersen asked, a trifle muzzily. "Seems to me I've caught you at it in odd moments since you returned." He had not pursued the subject then, for she didn't like to talk about art in progress. That took away the *mana*, she said. Besides, she had immediately turned his mind elsewhere.

She nodded. "Yes, I have."

"Is it finished?" Leino blurted. "For everything's sake, Caitlín, let's hear it!"

"If you desire," she said. A burst of applause replied. "Well, now, it's not about us, you understand, but about the future, when humans all fare freely as we are doing today. For they will, they will."

She hitched herself onto a table, sat swinging her bare feet, and made a strong guitar of the sonador. The Milky Way in a viewscreen crowned her uplifted head.

> *A bugle wind is blowing.*
> *It's time that I be going*
>   *From summer clouds*
>   *In gentle skies*
>   *Where light comes lancing through,*
>   *From nights of moon and dew.*
> *However far I wander,*
> *My song will yearn out yonder,*
>   *A note, a tune,*
>   *A melody*
>   *In memory of you.*
> *The stars are stark that shone so soft*
>   *Above our darling land;*
> *But I must fare away, aloft,*
>   *And hope you understand.*
>
> *Where unknown suns are burning,*
> *Their living worlds are turning.*
>   *A dance from dawn*
>   *To day to dark*
>   *On mountaintop and sea*
>   *Goes everlastingly.*
> *Though, ignorant, we blunder,*
> *So death may drag us under,*
>   *A note, a tune,*
>   *A melody*
>   *Till then will sound from me.*
> *What miracles abide out there,*
>   *What wise and foreign mind,*
> *What enterprises man may dare,*
>   *We can but go to find.*

Yet still, in all the wonder,
The tolling of the thunder
    That quickens in
        Those virgin skies
            When first they know our ships,
            A longing strikes like whips.
I'll sing while founding nations
Among the constellations
        A note, a tune,
            A melody,
                Remembering your lips.
And when at last your runaway
    Comes back from the abyss
Of starful dark to common day,
        Forgive me with a kiss.

Hours later, Weisenberg explained he was an old man, and
made a not altogether steady way to his bed. Fidelio soon
followed. (Did every sentient race need a periodic retreat into
dreams?) Frieda led Dozsa off. Brodersen took Joelle into a
corner, where they sat down and spoke quietly and earnestly.
Leino engaged Caitlín. After he had made a point of ignoring
Rueda and Susanne for a time, though she kept talking to them,
the Peruvian smiled wryly and suggested to the linker that he
and she refresh their drinks—after which he nudged her, his
hand on her elbow, to the viewscreen where Danu glowed, and
they drew chairs side by side. Lights were dimmed; most
illumination came from without, soft and shadowy. A speaker,
also turned down, gave forth Bach's Brandenburg Concertos.

"Listen, will you?" Brodersen's pipe chopped through an arc.
A pungent cloud trailed after. "You've been treating poor little
Su goddamn shabbily. She's bleeding from it. We can't afford
that, not in any of us."

"What would you have me do?" Joelle retorted. "I admit I
yelled at her once when she'd done no wrong. I apologized
afterward, didn't I? What else am I obligated for?"

"Well, stop shoving her out of her job. Assistant quartermaster isn't enough. Caitlín's told me—uh, this is strictly
confidential—she's told me how she's had to pretend she can't

handle any number of tasks, to make Su feel needed. That's hard on Caitlín; she has her own pride. Anyway, there are pretty narrow limits to what's possible along those lines."

"Are you asking me to make work likewise? Dan, I can't. She'd see right away what I was doing and be twice wounded—wouldn't she? Besides, I can't deprive Fidelio. It was plenty bad when I took over the guidance of *Williwaw* because his Spanish was too heavily accented." Joelle caught Brodersen's wrist. "I promised him he could handle every computation which was feasible for him, from elementary linkage on up. He has nothing else left, Dan; and he'll soon die."

He regarded her in silence, the haggard features, the sculpturing beneath that had not changed. "You know," he said at length, "you aren't really the steel-jacketed intellect you claim to be."

"Did I ever? Not on purpose, I swear."

"N-no, I guess not." He pondered. "Suddenly, after all these years I've known you . . . Joelle, I begin to think you're the most innocent person I've ever met."

She leaned against him, not with the deceptive smoothness of Caitlín or the heartiness of Lis but with the jerkiness he remembered; she had never learned nuances. "And . . . you . . . aren't exactly tough inside . . . either, are you?" she stammered.

Rueda and Susanne traded recollections of Europe. They had many cathedrals and museums to share. The real pleasure came when they learned also they had small inns and cafés mutually. As she bespoke those, she grew vivid. She had visited Perú as well, but only seen the standard places. He relished telling her about others.

"If we get back—we might, you know, we might—I'll take you there," he promised.

"You are very kind," she said.

He spread his palms. "No, I'd enjoy it. To be quite frank, until this evenwatch you seemed, well, rather colorless to me. I am delighted to discover how wrong I was."

She flushed and dropped her glance.

Seeing that she had grown confused, he turned more serious; that mood was easier for her. "We're in the same boat too, aren't we? Both of us essentially superfluous—at best, spare parts."

She turned toward Danu. "No, you went planetside."

"Precisely because I am an expendable. It's by no means certain I'll be needed for anything similar again. Or if I am, we've days and weeks to fill in between those occasions—we two—no?"

She winced. "'Ow?"

"We must figure that out." He snapped his fingers. A new idea kindled him. "See here, Susanne. What this ship does not have aboard is trained scientists. Laboratory- and field-type, that is. What she does have is a data bank holding most human knowledge; not to mention Fidelio, who'd doubtless like to pass on his education. Why can't we make ourselves into experts?"

She lifted her eyes. *"Nom de Dieu!"*

"We'll have to think a great deal," he rushed on, "and study, and experiment, and— You a chemist, perhaps, I a planet-ologist . . . or whatever useful talents we find are ours. . . . Su," he hurrahed, "we've work ahead of us!"

Leino had gained the boldness to tease Caitlín where they sat. "About that latest song of yours," he said. "I thought you were dead set against any notion of sex-specific roles. But your verse describes 'man' going into space. Shame on you."

She wrinkled her nose at him. "For your information, me bhoy, 'man' in that context does not mean 'adult human male' but 'humanity.' Why should the lines not be from a woman outbound, and him left behind?" She pretended to brood. "Oh, I'll get back at you for this, Martti Leino, so I will. Only wait for my next song."

"I'm sorry," he exclaimed. His features stretched into lines of pain. "I didn't meant to offend you."

She took his nearest hand between both hers. "No offense! Honestly. Don't be that vulnerable, love."

He bent his neck and muttered, "I am, to you."

She brought her right hand to his head, along temple and cheek and jawline and ear to the back of it, where her fingertips moved through his hair. "Ah, it's a sweet lad you are."

He grew incoherent. His free fist hammered his thigh. "Caitlín, I—I resented you—I'm Dan's brother-in-law, you remember, and Lis— But you aren't what I thought. You're lovely. You *give*. You're adorable." He grabbed for breath. "Pardon me. The whisky was talking."

"Were you not, then?" she asked tenderly.

"What's the use?"

Caitlín moved to embrace him. Across his shoulder she spied Brodersen, his own arm around Joelle. They exchanged a look and, after an instant, swab-O signs which nobody else saw.

Susanne and Rueda were the last to leave. They had been conversing too animatedly to stop, until finally nature required yawns. He escorted her to her door.

"Goodnight, Carlos," she said. "Good mornwatch, rather."

He heard the nervousness in her tone, bent, and kissed her hand. "Goodnight, Susanne," he said, and departed.

As per program, *Chinook*'s autopilot set her in orbit at a distance from the T machine. The transition back to weightlessness woke some individuals who had been sleeping off their carouse. More experienced ones merely shifted dream-gears.

Brodersen was in his office, running computations— *Williwaw* had expended a hell of a lot of reaction mass on her trip, and he wanted an estimate of how much more such he dared allow—when Caitlín came through the doorway. "Well, hi," he said, gladdened. "How'd things go?"

He saw the trouble that rode her, unbuckled from his chair, and catapulted himself to grasp her. She grasped back. "Hey, honey, what's wrong?"

"Och, I don't know, I don't," she said against his shoulder. They floated together. "Tell me first how it went between you and Joelle."

"Oh . . . all right. Two or three bouts. Nowhere near as good as with you, macushla, but all right. I don't expect it'll repeat often. Frankly—no turndown of her—frankly, I hope it won't. I'd a lot rather have you."

"And I you." She shivered.

"Wait, you don't mean to say Martti hurt you?"

"No, no, no. He was clumsy drunk but tried to treat me like a glass princess. He could do nothing else, though, Dan, nothing. No matter what I did. This past hour too, after we'd slept and the liquor was mostly out of him. He wept. You'll not be letting him know I told you this, will you?"

"Of course not."

"Do you think I should keep on? He told me no; but she's a rotten mistress who can't help her lover overcome—" Caitlin felt Brodersen go tense. "No, maybe I'd best leave him in his grief for a time."

"I suppose the same. Tell me I'm not just being greedy."

"You aren't, my dearest, you aren't."

He laughed and hugged her. "Well, Pegeen, I am the captain of this Flying Dutchman, and I can dictate schedules. Okay, we take an extra rest before we pick up our duties.... M-m-m-m."

XXXII

As the ship drew deeper into the field that made the star gates, and the sight of Danu blurred into shining shapelessness, Brodersen wondered if Caitlín said a wistful goodbye to the world that had enchanted her, that she would surely never see again. Or was she too caught up in her ardor of exploration? How he wished she could be here in the command center beside him, where he sat idled. Was there really a good reason for her not? Well, yes, in her role as medical officer she ought to be standing by in sickbay where she was, just in case. Yet any "in case" was apt to be immediately lethal to everybody.

Low weight came on a whisper of chemical rockets, for a few minutes. *Chinook* moved toward the final beacon. It was silvery in hue. Fidelio had strongly suggested touching every base before making the jump. All those markers taken together must have a purpose, must lead to other T machines, whereas it was possible—even likely—that the builders had not found reason or time to establish a construct at the end of every shorter guidepath. Many of those might give on empty interstellar space, as a purely random course around the cylinder almost certainly would. True, the order in which you went by the signal points made all the difference. Nine of them, the total around this transport engine, gave more than a third of a million destinations. Had the Others themselves visited each one?

Chinook went on the simplest and most obvious route, from the outermost inward along those zigzags which involved the minimum total expenditure of energy. It *ought* to lead to something—if the Others appreciated engineering elegance—if they weren't constrained by external factors—

Well, if nothing lay beyond this gate, the castaways would simply have to settle down to life in the void. Zero gee could only be tolerated for so long in a stretch, then weight became essential to health. Under continuous boost, reaction mass would presently give out. So it would be necessary to put a spin on the ship, with a large radius in order to minimize centrifugal variations and Coriolis effect.

Foreseeing that need as a possibility, designers had included provisions against it when they worked out their modifications of the *Reina* class. The hull could be split in two, its forward and after halves separated. That involved a lot of work, only part of which could be done by explosive seams, but the capability was there. A cable (of whisker filaments, for the tensile strength) would connect them still. Under the impetus of the lateral jets, they'd move a couple of kilometers apart, and the same motors would set them rotating. Earth-normal pseudogravity would thereafter prevail inboard. The cable would carry power from the reactor to the living quarters. And another Wheel would go whirling off through space: another prison.

Brodersen grimaced, not for the first time, at the prospect of carrying out such a job with his inadequate crew. It was a sizzling hell of a lot more complicated than it sounded. Merely balancing masses in the hemispheres, let alone scrambling around outside in spacesuits—

We'll do it, though, somehow, if we must, he vowed. *And junk that rattlebrain word "prison," huh? Pegeen will be here!*

To die at last.

He made a gesture of thrusting away, and hauled his attention outward. The cylinder gleamed near. He wondered how it felt to Joelle and Fidelio, perceiving directly through the instruments while they piloted the vessel through forces that negated space-time. He'd never know. That experience lay beyond words; it was mystical, maybe transmystical. He'd better stick to practicalities. Both holothetes were in linkage because they themselves had no idea what they would emerge into, what they might instantly have to understand and do.

And here comes the beacon, hard off our port bow.

The siren whooped warning. The hull swung about and plunged. *Chinook* passed through.

First he stared wildly around after a T machine. The heart drummed in his breast. He saw it afar, a staff laid across blackness, and the breath gusted from him in a shout.

Next he grew aware of how much blackness there was. No

stars shone behind that rod. Well-nigh every line of sight was empty of all but night. In one burned a lurid blue-white spark, at the middle of a pearly haze which spread out on either side like wings. Elsewhere, well apart, he discerned faint points of light and a few small, cloudy glows. Motors off, the ship fell silent through the dark.

"My God," Brodersen mumbled. "Where are we?"

Action snapped to life in him. He got on the intercom. "Captain to crew. Report by stations." Shaken voices told him nobody had come to harm, yet.

Joelle spoke last, as if in dreams. "Fidelio and I think we know already what's happened. It is very strange—" Abruptly machine-like: "We need more data. Accelerate at about forty-five degrees to our present radius vector around that sun you see, inward. Commence the planned observational programs and be prepared for further instructions."

"Aye, aye," Brodersen said. A small part of him wondered why his obedience was so automatic. The Joelle he recalled, who liked him and indulged his wish for her company—even for what little of her knowledge he could comprehend—but always remained at heart aloof: she was no more. What he had embraced a few nightwatches ago was an oldish woman, yes, spinsterish, pathetically eager for him at first, then wistful in her stiff fashion, and helpless-looking after she fell asleep. Since, she'd busied herself discussing contingencies with those who'd man the instruments, spent most of her spare time in her cabin, and been shortspoken at mess—embarrassed, he speculated, though he couldn't figure out why she should be.

However, her brain is still good, and right now its enhanced beyond my poor imagining.

Weight returned. Brodersen knew at least a trio of grounds for building up speed. Doppler measurements; improved sampling of ambient conditions, such as solar wind; cameras detecting planets as streaks across the background of the stars. *But where are the stars? This system holds nothing for us.*

Until sure that everything was okay, he ought to stay put in the command center. However, unless an emergency came up, he was supernumerary. He fiddled with controls and peered at meters, trying to learn what he might.

The blue-white fierceness which Joelle had called a sun was *really* brilliant; the optics stopped its radiance way down. It was giving *Chinook* illumination comparable to what Sol gives Earth, but even at high magnification the disc showed tiny, suggesting it was far and far distant. By selective scanning and amplification, he managed to find a lesser companion, yellow, nearly lost in the glare.

The fuzzy patches scattered around heaven turned out to contain points of light enmeshed in luminous mist and intricate filaments. They must be Orion-type nebulae, close by, where new suns were forming out of dust and gas as he watched. For the most part, what had appeared to be individual stars were in fact star clusters, widely separated.

Reports from the astrolab started arriving. Beyond range of ordinary viewscreens, but plentiful within the reach of the observatory equipment, were more nebulae. In a particular direction was a huge region, invisible to the eye, violently radiating in the infra-red and radio wave length. Throughout the entire sky was no trace of the familiar external galaxies, though it held sources of similar radiation.

More and more of these results, as the hours wore on, were reached under Fidelio's management. He told the humans what to look for, and they found it. He must have a damn good idea of what kind of place *Chinook* had gotten into.

Brodersen puffed his pipe. He believed he could guess the answer himself. It boomed through him like the toning of a great bell.

Su being co-opted to do scutwork for the researchers, Caitlín was preparing dinner solo. Hitherto no one had had more than a sandwich, hastily snatched on station. She'd gotten the Old Man to decree that a decent meal under relaxed conditions was necessary.

In the ordinariness of the galley she sang while she worked, cheerful songs from unpretentious corners of Earth. When she began carrying things out into the mess hall, her music faltered. That chamber adjoined the common room; the doors between were rolled back; from the big viewscreens beyond, primordial blindness leaped out at her, the blue star ablaze at its core.

"You do give a lovely light," she murmured. "I've seen the same in glacier crevasses and once a nuclear furnace. But what does it shine on?"

She stopped in her tracks. Joelle had entered the common room. After a moment's hesitation, she nodded greeting. Caitlín went out to meet her.

"Hello, there. Why are you not in linkage?" the younger

woman asked. "Food won't be ready for an hour, and I was thinking that then I'd need a crowbar to pry you loose."

In face and body, Joelle grew rigid. "I am not required any longer."

"O-ooh, I see. Fidelio wants to be alone." Caitlín reached out, caught the other's shoulder, and squeezed gently. "Leaving you the more alone."

Joelle yanked free of the clasp and made to turn around. Caitlín touched her and said, "Please, have I offended you? I'm sorry. I was never meaning it. You came in here to see the view where it's best, is that not right? Don't let me drive you out."

Joelle halted. "You weren't."

"I fear I was, me such a hoyden. I simply felt sad and— But why should I ever feel sad for you that I admire so much?" In a rush: "Dr. Ky, if it's worried about Dan you are, don't be. My faults outnumber the stars, but jealousy is not among them."

The chance phrase took them both aback, brought both their gazes outward into night. In the muteness that followed, a drift of curry odor seemed doubly lost.

Joelle said at last, harshly, still staring away, "Thank you. You understand we have had a relationship before, don't you? Very well. I don't wish to continue the discussion."

"Aye, how petty we are, and our trouble, in this universe."

Joelle came close to sneering. "You were eager to quest further, weren't you? Well, Miz Mulryan, what do you think of what we've come upon?"

"How can I give you an honest answer when I don't know what it is? You'll be telling us in due course, and it will be grand to learn."

Joelle's expression softened a trifle. "No secret. Doubtless several people have already realized, while you've been too busy to hear them talk. Don't plan on staying long. The captain will soon insist on a report, then order us back to the T machine for a new jump. Fidelio and I are keeping us going meanwhile, partly on the microscopic chance we'll find some trace of something that may be helpful, but mainly for . . . for his sake. Fidelio's. It *is* fascinating."

Caitlín reached for her again. "And you barred from it." She didn't venture to complete the gesture, but dropped her arm.

"I'll play the data back later for myself."

"Not the same, is it?"

Joelle's look lost itself in the blue star. "No telling where we are in space," she said low. "Besides, that's really a meaningless phrase... under these circumstances. Let's call it somplace in the embryo galaxy, and date it from ten to twenty billion years before we were born."

Air whistled in around Caitlín's teeth. "We've come through time?"

"Why not? *Emissary* did. Ships going between Sol and Phoebus do to a lesser, variable extent. For all we know, the Danu that *Chinook* found may be millennia in the past or future of the Wheel that *Chinook* raided—though from a relativistic viewpoint, I'm being very imprecise in my language.

"What theory we have says that a transport field cannot take you any farther back in time than the moment of its own generation. But I hardly imagine that Danu exists yet. Therefore, either the T machine around it is... was... will be extremely old, or else that field meshes somehow with the field of the machine here. The second seems much likelier.

"And in any event, the Others must have originated even earlier than this." Joelle smiled without humor. "We're early enough, however, aren't we?"

"Aye," Caitlín whispered, "if the stars haven't yet been made."

"Few so far. Not many atoms more complex than hydrogen and helium. The gas clouds are still collapsing inward to form the galaxies. The suns will condense from them—"

"—like dewdrops from dawn mist." Caitlín's being glowed.

"—and higher nuclei form within those—"

"—air for our breath, iron for our blood, gold for a wedding ring."

"—but the process has scarcely begun. What you see yonder is a young star. It's so big that it could take shape with a single companion, out of a Bok globule, rather than as part of a cluster within nebula—a type O supergiant, fifty thousand times as luminous as Sol. If we were much closer, its radiation would kill us. It hasn't long to live on the main sequence: a few million years at most, till it erupts as a supernova. For a short while it will be as bright as the entire galaxy was—is—in our day... before its remnant sinks down into a neutron globe or a black hole. The heavy elements created in that explosion will be blown into space; they'll become part of the later generations of suns and planets.

"The star has a smaller companion; have you seen? It will be affected. What we'll get, if humans and Betans know any astrophysics, is a recurring nova, nothing like the supernova but casting elements into the universe also.

"I daresay a situation similar to this has already occurred elsewhere, freakishly early in cosmic history, perhaps inside a nebula. There came to be enough local concentration of carbon, nitrogen, oxygen, all the necessary materials, that planets could coalesce on which life could arise, even then, before there was even this hint at a galaxy to come. Perhaps one or more of those life forms evolved into the Others."

"Possibly," Joelle finished, "a small part of what makes you and me up is being made there, in those stars, right now."

Caitlín smote her hands together and said, "No wonder the Others would make a gate to come see!"

"Doubtless." Joelle sighed. "I'd hoped they might have a scientific station. That's why we continue moving slantwise to the T machine, instead of heading straight back. But I don't believe any longer that they have. It would be somewhere nearby if it existed, would it not? After all, everything, including materials for the T machine itself, would have to be sent through from the past. That's a huge enough undertaking for anybody, demigods or no. Surely they have competing claims on their attention. And when the giant blows up, it'll wipe out whatever is in orbit around it, unless maybe the T machine itself can survive. No, I daresay the Others just come through occasionally in ships, or whatever they use, to take observations. The interval could be thousands of years."

After a minute she added, "If they do have an installation, in spite of my guess, it's elsewhere. We haven't a prayer of finding it, in a system laid out on this vast a scale. No, we'll hang around for a day or two, probing, peering, broadcasting—a forlorn hope if ever there was one—and finally try another jump."

Because of how she stared at the star, Caitlín asked her, "You'd be happy here yourself, learning, is that not so?"

"Not feasible." Joelle smiled lopsidedly. "We'd run out of mass and have to change over to spin mode, which would terribly hamper any studies. Worse, we'd always wonder what opportunities we'd missed. We must go on." Again she hesitated. "That's frightening." As if to get it out before she could strangle the impulse: "Hearten us, Caitlín, will you?"

The quartermaster flushed, her lashes fluttered, her voice lost steadiness; never before had the holothete seen her that shy.

"Can I? Me, I, I'm nothing but a bard of sorts. You're a doer—Dr. Ky—an understander, a Druid. Our lives rest on you."

"No. On Fidelio, the way things are . . . at present. And you understand what I cannot— Excuse me." Joelle swung about. "I remember something I'd better do." She left with hasty strides. Seen from behind, her shoulders trembled.

XXXIII

JUMP.

Again heaven was full of stars. For a heart-stopping instant Brodersen could find no T machine among them. After he did spy it, made tiny by distance, he became able to look around him and wonder.

A sun disc hung out there. About the same size as that which Earth saw, it was distinctly greenish—an oath of amazement exploded from him—and heavily spotted. According to a meter, the luminosity per unit area exceeded Sol's by some thirty percent. The corona was immense around it, and ruddy; without magnification, he saw flares and prominences like fire geysers; but no zodiacal light appeared, though he spotted down brightness and amplified weak sources to the limit of his screens.

Having taken reports, he ordered *Chinook* to accelerate in the orbital plane of the transport engine and research to commence. Then he scratched his head and plaintively addressed the intercom: "Hey, what's going on? I didn't know the main sequence included green stars."

The holothetes didn't reply. They were too immersed. After a minute, Su Granville's diffident tones reached him: "I t'ink I can guess. Green is not an impossible color, but the range of surface temperature for it is so narrow that we seldom 'ave observed it."

"Is that why the Others are interested in this one?"

"No, I suspect it is simply leaving the main sequence and 'appens to be going t'rough a brief green phase."

Hydrogen burned away at the core, the nuclear reactions moving outward— "Wait. Doesn't it become a red giant?"

"Yes, in due course. But at first it shrinks and grows very much 'otter. That shortens the peak wavelength. Expansion 'as now begun, but needs time yet for to cool the surface, redden the light, while the total output increases more—" She went into dismay. "Oh, you know the elementary astronomy! I am sorry."

"Don't be, Su. I should've figured this out for myself."

Once assured that nobody had detected anything dangerous, Brodersen left the command center. He couldn't resist peeking in at the various investigators and asking questions, but left before he turned into a nuisance and sought Caitlín. She stood in the common room, surrounded by the views it offered, marveling. As he entered, she sped to him, threw her arms around his neck, and kissed him with cyclone force.

He responded. When they came up for air, she crooned, "Oh, Dan, Dan, what we're seeing! What we'll learn, aye, and do!"

"I sure would like to do something," he grumbled. "This being useless gets on my nerves."

She cocked her head. Her grin grew mischievous. "Well, Captain, you could be dealing justice to a poor deprived quartermaster. Yonder sight makes me horny."

"Good Lord! Does any sight *not* do that, ever?"

She disengaged herself and took him by the elbow. "Later, you can help me cook."

Reports came in through the hours.

The ship was thousands of light-years from Earth, to gauge by the altered outlines of the Milky Way and bearings of neighbor galaxies. Identifiable astronomical objects were not noticeably changed, including monstrous S Doradus. Hence the date, reckoned from the hypothetical beginning of the universe, was the same as at home, give or take a few million years. *Chinook* had returned from the distant past.

Doppler readings on the T machine, combined with radar ranging of the sun, gave the latter a mass above Sol's. On that basis, theory gave it an age on the order of ten billion years. More precise measurements would be needed to refine that figure. Clearly, however, it must belong to an early generation. This was confirmed by a paucity of dust around it and by the weak metallic lines in its spectrum. However, it contained more heavy elements than might have been expected. Perhaps it had formed in the vicinity of a recent supernova burst. (Could that have been the detonation of the blue giant the humans lately beheld? They speculated mightily and futilely.)

It had planets. One moved at more or less the same distance as the T machine, a little over an a.u., a little less than ninety degrees ahead. The globe was Earth size and bore oxygen in the atmosphere.

There was no telling where the Others had originally placed their device, except that presumably it was not in a sixty-degree position. Maybe it had once been straight across from the living world, like the ones at Sol and Centrum and stars elsewhere known to the Betans. If so, it must have exhausted its station-keeping capability at last: for now it orbited as subject to perturbation as any natural heavenly body.

Brodersen shook his head and clicked his tongue. Anything he could utter was inadequate anyway. "Well," he said, "I guess whatever interest the Others had here died out long ago. Unless they care to watch the system itself die."

Soon Dozsa's receivers cast a dazzling doubt on his conclusion. A source at the terrestroid planet was emitting a radio pattern which, though simple and repetitive, must be of artificial origin. A beacon, a message? For *Chinook*, absolutely a summons.

It was a three-day flight.

Those who could do astronomy were kept busy supplying Fidelio with data which he integrated into an ever more complete picture. They were much too slow for him. He spent most of his hours in holothesis nevertheless, probing his stellar environment through direct instrumental input, considering it, or perhaps oftenest contemplating the Ultimate in that way of his which gave him a sense of those he loved being real within a space-time which unified him with them.

Meanwhile the engineers checked *Williwaw* out after the stresses of the Danu trip, treated her to a thorough overhaul, adjusted her as best they could for predicted conditions, and replenished her mass tanks from the ship's supply. Brodersen lent a hand whenever he was able. They had no room for a larger work party.

Rueda and Su were left with more leisure than they wanted. Joelle was almost completely at loose ends.

Waking very early in the second mornwatch, unable to get back to sleep, finding no solace in books or music, she rose, threw on a coverall, and left the barrenness of her cabin. She'd go borrow the galley to brew herself some tea, which she had neglected to draw as private rations, and thereafter, while the Betan rested, get into her own linkage. It was awkward to do unassisted, but she'd be damned if she asked for help. That would be downright humiliating when she was unprepared to accomplish anything of value and merely intended to submerge her being for a while in the hearts of atoms and stars—in what was well-known about them, nothing else. It wasn't even as if that state were an addiction which must be satisfied. After all, she'd experienced it in fullness quite recently.

Fullness. . . . Everything has gone empty.

The corridor underscored her feeling when she emerged into it, a hollow length of metal curving away on either side, lined with shut doors, air chill and rustling. When one of the doors, Frieda von Moltke's, slid back, Joelle started, nearly frightened.

Martti Leino stepped out, waved before he closed it, and as he turned around saw the holothete. Likewise surprised, he blurted, "Good morning, Dr. Ky. How are you?" His hair was tangled and his clothes carelessly redonned.

"Insomniac," Joelle said, because it must be obvious. "And you?"

Leino looked smug. "Well, I haven't slept much either. Was going for coffee in the galley, I've run out in my quarters. Would you care to join me?"

Joelle changed her mind about tea. Why should her face grow hot? "No, thanks, I want to walk about." She left him.

Is that floozy servicing every man aboard? she thought. *If so, why should I gave a damn? What's it to me? At least she seems to have wiped the hangdog misery out of Leino he's been carrying around these past days.*

What caused it? I had the impression he paired off with Mulryan the nightwatch after the party, but no, he seems to have been avoiding her since. Did he think he was going to get laid, and instead get refused? A quarrel— But she's been speaking kindly to him at mealtimes, though she rarely hears better than monosyllables in reply.

I don't know. Nobody tells me anything. Perhaps because I never ask. I don't know how to. Or much of anything that involves people.

Eric made me wholly human for a short while—made me, wholly human—but then I went too far beyond him into a Reality too enthralling. I became Cartesian. A few subsequent lovers who were holothetes had bodies attached to their minds, but merely attached, as far as I was concerned. The rest were hardly more than bodies, conveniences, pets at best.

Did that leave me vulnerable to Chris, beautiful sweet Chris?

To love is to be vulnerable, I suppose. Argh! Nothing could have come of it. True?

As for Dan—

Her feet took her up a companionway toward the scientific level, where the computer room was. Metal enclosed her in narrowness. A phrase came back from her Tennessee girlhood. Though she might be part of Project Ithaca, at the frontiers of human knowledge, her foster parents had sent her to Sunday school. There the Protestant chaplain of the military reservation used to read from the Book of Common Prayer as well as the Bible. The whole scene came back, whitewashed walls, banal picture of Jesus blessing the children, windows open to clover smell and hum of bees, her class sitting, primly clad on straight wooden chairs while the big man's bass rolled over them. "—fast bound in misery and iron—"

You know, he looked and sounded a lot like Dan. He impressed me tremendously, at my small age. I wonder, in spite of his being pious, I wonder if he may have been as good in bed.

Stop that!

Joelle achieved a smile at her own expense. *Why? Is it blasphemous?*

No, she realized. *It's dangerous. I dare not get obsessed with Dan, as I fear I am tending. That would be Chris all over again. He's Mulryan's. Oh, she'll let me borrow him once in a while if I wish, and he'll be considerate, but I know he'll begrudge the time he could have been with her, out of these few years we have left. And that will feel so lonely, so lonely.*

I dare not admit Descartes (as a maker of symbols which have no more scientific meaning left in them than does the Last Judgment) was wrong.

Reaching the passage she wanted, she took a route which brought her by the astrolab. Its door stood retracted on a darkened interior and she heard speech. Surprised anew, she halted.

Carlos Rueda Suárez: "—Yes, I grant you the government of Demeter needs sweeping reform, and probably the planet as a whole needs more say in policies that affect it. But autonomy? Independence? Why, it isn't the germ of a nation."

Haven't I had vague designs on him? Joelle stood where she was.

Susanne Granville: "What do you mean by 'nation'? Is Perú homogeneous? The Andean Confederacy? Why cannot our

separate colonies make a little World Union of their own?"
Almost accent-free in Spanish, she did not speak timidly but
with spirit and, it seemed, a certain relish.

Rueda: "You sound like Daniel Brodersen."

Granville: "I have listened to him and learned."

Rueda: "And thought for yourself as well, I notice." A sad
laugh. "Why are we arguing? What can politics matter to us?
We're adrift in space-time. Quite conceivably Earth and
Demeter and the whole human race don't exist any more, if that
isn't a nonsense phrase. We'll never be sure."

Granville: "Maybe we will be." In English: "We ain't licked
yet, my friend."

Rueda: "Daniel again, I hear. Ah, well, Su, we've talked
about a great deal in these past hours, haven't we? Life and fate
and God and little things that are big to us—why not Demeter?
But when we're less tired."

Granville, softly: "You have reason, Carlos. Also, the view is
too lovely for disputations. Look."

Dan would rack me back for eavesdropping, Joelle knew. *I
could go around in the reverse direction, but he might want them
warned I've noticed them.* It was an effort to louden her
footfalls, halt in the doorway, and call, "Hello, there."

The room was full of shadowed bulks. Light from the hall
picked Rueda and Granville out dimly, where they sat at the
farther bulkhead, facing each other at knee-touch distance. A
single viewscreen behind them brimmed with clear darkness,
stars, Milky Way, the planet a yellow-green brilliance and near it
a golden point that was its moon. Caitlin had proposed naming
it Pandora, since no one knew what it might hold for them,
trouble or hope or both.

Rueda sprang up to deliver a courtly bow. "Ah, Dr. Ky.
What brings you here?" Neither he nor the linker seemed
flustered, though Joelle suspected the interruption annoyed
them.

"I . . . I wanted to inspect some readouts," the holothete said.
Why the devil do I feel embarrassed? "You two?" *Wait, I didn't
need to bark that question at them.*

"No secret. I thought everybody knew. Su and I have become
deadwood, or at most very marginal assistants. We've decided to
learn specialties the ship needs, but we've scarcely begun to
explore what we might be best at. So we came here to play with
the apparatus when it wasn't in demand."

And fell into conversation which went on the whole nightwatch. How warm your voices sounded. Joelle shivered a bit in the cold of a clockwork dawn. "I see. Well, good luck." She walked stiffly from them, toward her computers.

Orbiting Pandora at twenty-five thousand kilometers, the travelers of *Chinook* saw it big in a screen in their common room. Under the glare of the dying sun, which burned opposite, the shrunken oceans were aquamarine and continents stood forth as brownish blots, sharply defined. A few water clouds were tinted pale olive; larger were the buff-colored dust storms. There was no sign anywhere of ice or snow, but vast salt beds gleamed livid. Beyond one limb was the moon, scarred crescent, half the apparent size of Luna seen from lost Earth or Persephone from lost Demeter. Elsewhere shone the universe.

Floating in front of his crew, Brodersen growled, "Blast it, we've got to send a party down, or admit we're not serious about wanting help to get home. It may not look promising, but how can we tell? Beta wouldn't look promising either if we didn't know better. Right, Fidelio?"

The alien made a noise of concurrence. His eyes caught luminance from a world as foreign to him as it was to the humans.

Once Pandora had been of the proper mass at the proper distance from the proper kind of star to bring forth life. Plants freed oxygen into its air, conquered the land, drew a rich diversity of animals after them; the yeast of evolution worked through hundreds of millions of years until a creature existed that thought and wrought.

But now the globe was raddled with age. Wearied by tides, it turned on its axis in almost a month. Its nearer moon had drifted far off. Another, a small body on its own path, appeared to have been stolen away. Long since spent, radioactives in the core gave no more heat to drive crustal plates about and raise new mountains; erosion had worn the last ranges down to hills. Nevertheless huge drops occurred, where continental shelves tumbled down to the bottoms of dead seas, to crusted wastes and brine marshes.

Waxing toward extinction, the sun had already forced much of the atmosphere off into space by heating and by solar wind, against which Pandora no longer had a strong magnetic field for shelter. Water had followed. The drying oceans gave up dissolved carbon dioxide, and greenhouse effect sent temperatures soaring.

Though furious rainstorms might still take place in some regions, especially around sunset and dawn, most land was parched and its winds gritty. The tropics might be seared to death; at least, searchers found no trace of life in them. Sparse vegetation survived in what had been the temperate and polar zones. There, winters as long as Earth's and nights twenty-five times as long grew bitterly cold. Day was always an inferno.

And this would worsen for some two billion years, until at last the red giant filled the sky and devoured its child, before sinking down to black dwarf oblivion.

"We've identified what may be ruined cities," Brodersen continued. "We've positively spotted what could be a large ground base, which emits steady beeps, and we've inspected the broadcasting satellite, which is probably to simplify navigation for visitors after they come through the gate."

He and Weisenberg had flitted in spacesuits to examine the latter. It was a metal sphere about the diameter of *Chinook*, featureless except for pitting by micrometeoroids. (That suggested how ancient it was, in this system where few small bodies were left.) The men had guessed that transducers in the alloy turned solar energy into radio-frequency code. While effective, it didn't fit Brodersen's notion of what the Others would have done. More disappointing was the failure of any beings to come welcome the new arrivals or respond to repeated signals.

He thrust his jaw forward. "Well, you know this," he said. "The question before the house is what we do about it. I claim we should send *Williwaw* for a sniff-around. Somebody must call here occasionally, or somebody may be on hand, waiting to see what we're like. Agreed?"

It was.

He put on his most genial manner. "Fine, fine. Okay, next we decide who of us goes. First off, me. . . . Hold on! Listen!

"This is not a Danu situation. There the boat mainly had atmosphere and gravity to cope with—nature. Here the crew will have to disembark, or what's the point of the whole maneuver? We may need a soldier, a diplomat, a woodsman, anything. With due modesty, which is mighty little, I remind you that I've handled a lot of such-like jobs.

"Shut up, Phil! Could be you were right earlier about the captain being indispensable; but we've been shaking down since. I can name three or four of you who could take over from me and soon be running things as well. Besides, if I can't exercise my *machismo* once in a while, I'll go all soggy.

"I have spoken. Let's consider who else we can best send."

Debate converged faster than Brodersen had expected. Dozsa, again, for chief pilot; Rueda, again, for co-pilot and general backup (Su Granville looked still more anguished than when the skipper had appointed himself); Fidelio, for his experience with xenosophonts (the Betan gravely assented); Caitlín, this time for medical help should that be needed (Leino stood locked into silence).

Pegeen—oh, no, no! I really let things get out of hand, didn't I? She bounced about, caroling. *Pegeen, what if things go wrong on yonder hellball?*

XXXIV

Chinook DROPPED INTO a low orbit, canted in such wise as to make it easiest for *Williwaw* to reach her goal. The boat came forth, vapor gushed, she fell toward the planet. Its darkling shield swelled to fill the view; it was no longer ahead but below.

Strapped behind Dozsa and Rueda, helpless, Brodersen reached for Caitlín beside him and caught her hand. She gripped back, hard. The next minutes would be the tough and perhaps fatal ones. Intensively though the atmosphere had been studied from space, it was not familiar. It might have any number of tricks in it to send a craft flaming. There was no ground control to talk her down. The mother ship couldn't help, outside of brief and widely separated whiles, until she had climbed back up to a synchronous position. She had had to descend for the launch because of the radiation that seethed from the sun, against which the boat had no electrostatic protection.

Brodersen's palm was so sweaty he couldn't tell whether Caitlín was dry or not. She gave him a grin and a thumbs-up sign. Abruptly she twisted around to stroke her free hand across Fidelio, who squatted aft in a specially rigged harness. The Betan laid claws on her head for a moment, most gently: a blessing?

They pierced the sky. A thin whistle grew slowly to a roar, while impacts shocked through the hull and it often lurched. After a time, though, Dozsa glanced back, his own countenance streaming, and called, "Okay, we've made it."

Brodersen cheered. *Damn!* he thought ungratefully. *Why do we have to be cocooned in so I can't reach Pegeen to kiss her? Well, just you wait till we land, my girl, just you wait.*

On a long, heat-dissipating slant, *Williwaw* glided downward across the world. Brodersen stared, fascinated, eerily aware that he would set foot on it. (*How did Armstrong really feel? He was such a private man.*) A night sea rolled thickly under the small moon; a ghastly stretch of salt flats ended at an escarpment kilometers high; beyond lay the plateau which had been a continent; sunrise revealed it bare, ocherous, soil baked into brick, cracked and scored; a dust storm was momentarily blinding; along a dry canyon reared a few sharp, brightly colored tall snags above mounds of rubble. Had they been a city?

Dozsa started the airjets. Rueda navigated for him, at first by the sun according to calculations made in advance, eventually by homing on the transmissions from their destination.

As they traveled northeast, the land rose; the season helped too, fall in the northern hemisphere; temperatures dropped and more and more life came in sight. Scattered shiny-leathery shrubs and isolated large plants, vaguely suggestive in their grotesqueness of saguaros or Joshua trees, grew closer together; streams flowed into pools; a reddish sward strengthened from patches to ground cover; stands of dendriforms became a forest, whose gleaming brown-violet fronds rippled in the wind. Overhead, heaven was cloudless, purple rather than blue, with a tinge of green from the sun, which stood well-nigh motionless behind the spacecraft.

Fidelio spoke. Brodersen must concentrate to follow his hoarse, wheezy Spanish: "I think the seasons are more extreme here than on any of our planets, biologically as well as in weather. Nothing grows in the long nights, nor in the winter that is approaching, nor, I would suppose, at the terrible height of summer. Animals must needs be adapted to this. We have likely arrived at a time of ingathering and feverish making ready."

Brodersen started to say that this guess jumped far beyond the available facts, but decided not to. The Betans did have knowledge of a variety of worlds—nothing like Pandora, of course, but a couple were included which had some resemblances. Besides, at present his own interest in the local ecology was quite incidental to—

There the goal was!

Caitlín cried out, Brodersen and Dozsa muttered astounded oaths, Rueda crossed himself, Fidelio stirred and his iodine smell sharpened. Photographs taken from space conveyed little of the reality which was here.

A city certainly had existed, long and long ago. Remnants of walls still lifted in a few places above crowding wildwood, their vivid primary hues and soft pastels undimmed. Where turf decked glades, great blurry-edged blocks lay tilted, only half buried.

North of the ruins stood a complex of several buildings, seemingly intact. Dozsa swung the jets down and hovered to let his companions observe. At first the structures were hard to see as anything but gaudy masses; then the eye began to track the design and found a solemn kind of beauty. Hexahedrons upbearing colonnades fitted harmoniously into each other, around a central tower made of arches and spirals, crowned by a three-dimensional golden sunburst. An enclosed bridge soared between the outermost eastern and western edifices in an arc of bird's-wing delicacy that somehow also belonged.

Two kilometers farther north, wilderness stopped, debarred, forced to grow around what must be a base for spacecraft (and for what else?). Impressive though it was, and in spite of being the lure which had brought the voyagers here, this offered much less to vision. Mostly they saw a sweep of turquoise-tinted paving, close to four kilometers square. Hemicylinders (sheds? barracks?) fenced it, the same color, their curves elaborated by what might be entrances and scanners. Near the remote end of the field was a large, dove-gray dome. Lesser bubbles clustered about it. A complex metal web rose and spread above, doubtless pertaining to the radio transmitter and possibly to other equipment. Squinting at the flat surface, they made out broad circles traced in it by grooves. Were those hatches, leading to silos wherein ships might safely rest?

That fine detail was barely discernible, for a slight waveriness enclosed the whole ensemble, like a hemispherical heat-shimmer.

Tears ran quietly down Caitlín's cheek. "Glory be to Creation," she faltered, "another race in the universe that knows, thinks... and they not dead."

"What?" Rueda asked absently. He was at work trying to raise *Chinook*, which ought to be stationed in synch by now. "What do you mean?"

"Is it not clear, man? The countryside lies desolate, the cities fallen, save here where we see a bit of restoration—in the ancient style; for look, the port before us is not of the same architecture at all, at all. Who but the Pandorans themselves would come back and erect such a memorial, after they went through the gate to a young world?"

She had spoken in English. Brodersen put the question in

Spanish to Fidelio, who opined, "That seems reasonable, fellow swimmer, though a fang remains caught in its flesh. Why should they go to so much trouble for mere—*ang'gh k'hrai*—basking? Sentiment? Yes, for mere sentiment. Data storage can preserve every memory of the mother planet, for hologrammic re-creation at will, better than a few unused houses on this crumbling reef."

Dozsa took the boat out of hover mode and started her circling. "The answer to that," he suggested meanwhile, "is that the houses are not unused. They get visitors."

"Why?" Rueda asked. "What visitors? Tourists? Hardly, when nothing but fragments are left, aside from yonder bit of copywork. Fidelio's right, electronics can give more of Old Pandora. Scientists, then, keeping track of what's happening? They wouldn't need facilities this big and elaborate, I'm sure, especially with an astronautical technology that must be equal or superior to Beta's."

"Earlier I proposed a few thoughts on life cycles here," Fidelio said softly. "They were reasonable, yet they may well be afloat with no roots in truth. Dogmatizing about sophonts we have never met is whirlpool unreason. If ever we find out what these are like, the single certainty is that we will be surprised."

"To be alive is to be forever surprised," Caitlín said. "How good that is."

"Never mind now," Brodersen interrupted. "Let's first see whether we can make contact. . . . God damn it, Carlos, are they asleep up in orbit?"

As if summoned, the lean features of Weisenberg, acting captain, sprang into the screen. His usual calm snapped apart. "How are you?" he almost yelled. "Are you safe?" He relaxed a bit when he heard the report and saw the pictures, both direct and off tape. Joelle, enmeshed in holothesis, took everything straight into her brain. The rest of the crew watched at their posts.

"Doesn't seem like anybody's home," Brodersen finished with a sigh. "Well, we'll explore, and maybe get a clue to when the next ship is scheduled in, or figure a way to leave a note, or—I dunno."

Weisenberg frowned. "Someone's minding the store," he warned. "Or something is. Else that field would be covered by wind-blown dirt and brush taking root, not to mention animals making messes. Have a care how you approach."

"M-m-m, yeah, good point. We'd better keep ourselves in gear, though. Stay tuned for another thrilling episode."

After a conference inboard, *Williwaw* swung about and neared the base from above. She had a machine gun in either wing. Dozsa sent a burst. Nobody was present to be hurt or angered, and it was a simple, handy kind of probe. Rueda tracked it; Brodersen monitored a camera for slow-motion playback under magnification.

The bullets struck the diaphanous canopy. The tracers among them skittered fierily aside. Dozsa brought the boat around in a grab of swiftness and snarl of jets, and headed for clear sky.

No person spoke until they had examined Brodersen's record. Not a slug had penetrated more than a few centimeters before rebounding, flattened by the impact. "Hoo-ha," he muttered. "If we'd come sailing cheerily into that—Fidelio, have you any notion what it might be?"

The Betan made an indescribable gesture. "Conceivably hypersonic waves of ultra-high amplitude, heterodyned to form a quasi-solid shell. Conceivably a more subtle and efficient type of field, unknown to my people. Pandoran ships, descending, must transmit a signal that turns it off for them, but I disbelieve the signal is one we could hit upon by trial and error."

"Me too. Okay, what's next?"

Brodersen's question was rhetorical. From the beginning, they had expected to go out on foot—were determined to. Dozsa brought the flyer back down, low and slow. Midway between the base and the handsome complex, an opening in the forest seemed to offer a spot for a vertical landing and later takeoff. Dozsa descended ultra-cautiously, jets loud at their labor. Close scanning showed the ground did not yield under that pressure, save for the low ruddy growth on it. Nonetheless he kept wheels retracted and extended skids, which he could drop off if they got mired or otherwise trapped.

Williwaw came to a firm, level halt. The engines whined into a silence that rang in the ears. A popping in them followed, and a hiss, as air was bled out to equalize with the lower Pandoran pressure. Folk unbuckled. Caitlín beat Brodersen to the kiss he had promised himself.

"Well," he said after shaking hands all around elsewhere, "let's commence. Get your firearms ready." Taking an automatic rifle, he writhed past seats in the cabin, went down a ladder to the belly of the vessel, and operated the airlock. Through that he cycled as if into poison... which might be the case, no matter what spectroscopes related.

He didn't expect it. Chichao Yuan had died on Beta from a lethal dose of naturally produced gas, but that was a most unlikely happenstance, unprecedented in the Betans' own experience. Still less plausible was catching a native disease, fungal, microbial, viral, anything, when the two most similar biologies known to Fidelio did not even base their heredities on the same nucleotides. Ordinarily the expedition would nonetheless have proceeded more deliberately than this, sending remote-controlled machines out to collect samples for analysis in a segregated chamber before the first member ventured forth, and maybe quarantining him afterward. *Chinook*, however, lacked trained personnel. Therefore the skipper claimed the proud privilege of being guinea pig.

He swung himself out, to the ground, and stood as if in a dream. *Me, old Dan Brodersen, I have betrod a new world, the first man ever.* Feeling almost giddy, he stooped to touch the soil, grub some up, roll it between his fingers. It was warm and dry and smelled like... charcoal?

Heat smote him, savage as in the Sahara Desert. Parched, the air sucked moisture from nostrils till they stung, lips till they cracked. Though its rarity dulled hearing somewhat, a wind boomed loud, making branches creak and fronds rustle. He felt it like a breath from a furnace. Tarry odors filled it.

He peered around. Now that he was outdoors, the green glare changed colors more than he had awaited: on springy dull-red turf, murky boles and limbs rising three or four man-heights, deep-hued serrations that grew from them, shadowy reaches beyond where bushes cast back sun-flecks in mica-like glints, the skin on the back of his hand. The sky brooded Tyrian. A dozen winged creatures flapped across, bronze-bright. Midget flyers that could not be insects returned, after the alarm of the landing, to buzz about.

"Dan, darling love, how do you fare?" Caitlín's dread ripped from his walkie-talkie.

"Fine," he answered. "Honest. Calm down. Sit back, remember our doctrine of caution, wait till I'm sure."

I won't be sure, of course, he thought. *Never can be. Might be inhaling death at this minute.* He found that the idea didn't worry him, far-fetched as it was. *Then why do I hate the notion of letting Pegeen come out?*

I can't postpone that much longer.

Stumping around, he noticed for the first time how he weighed a little more; Pandora's gravity exceeded Earth's by a few percent. On a log inside the woods, he spied a cat-sized animal, and froze while he stared. It was a tailless quadruped with glabrous, pale-blue, shiny skin, a beak, three eyes—the third on back of the head—and a fanlike dorsal fin. Noticing him in turn, it folded that member and bounded off.

"Too fast for a reptile or lower-grade critter like that," Brodersen said when he had given a description over the radio. "Equivalent of a Terrestrial mammal? I dunno, but I expect I'd never have seen it if my shape and smell weren't too outlandish for instant recognition. My guess is, therefore, that's the basic animal shape here, four-limbed, three-eyed, beaked. The sail may be a cooling device; could have a sense organ built in too, I suppose."

The miracle of that small beast struck home in him. A whole evolution, an entire face of life itself. And Ira Quick wanted to keep humankind stanchioned in his sociological cattle stalls.

Brodersen continued. Partway around the glade, he stopped once more. This time, what he saw was a trail.

Underbrush was scant and presented no real obstacle. Yet a meter-wide strip of bare, hard-beaten loam ran straight into the forest: as nearly as he could gauge, straight toward the buildings that were his next goal. He stood thoughtful, in the blistering wind, before he continued his round. On the opposite verge, he found the same trail, equally linear, likewise vanishing from his view into the depths.

Game on Earth and Demeter didn't make that kind. When asked, Fidelio said the same was true on Beta. Well, Pandora could be different.

Brodersen led the way down the path, followed Indian file by Caitlín, Dozsa, and Fidelio. The party bore weapons, walkie-talkies, canteens from which they often swigged, light backpacks of assorted gear. Rueda stayed behind in the boat; he had objected strenuously, but such a reserve was essential and he was the logical choice. Save for wind-sough and an occasional croak or trill, the forest was quiet. "Trees"—they looked more like giant succulents of varied species—and "canebrakes" grew well apart, probably for lack of water, but their widespread foliage made a roof, so that shadows speckled by green sunbeams turned the surroundings just a little cooler than the open was. Now and then a creature droned or fluttered or scurried by; once the party glimpsed at a distance an animal as big as a pony, likewise bearing a dorsal fin; but on the whole, this was an unfruitful wilderness.

"Life swims upstream, until overwhelmed and sunk," Fidelio had philosophized. "When the sun of Pandora began to betray it, higher species must have died, unless the sapients took a few along when they fled. There remained lesser, simpler breeds; and evolution started over. The sun did not change too fast for them in the next few million years." He had drooped his whiskers, a sign of regret or pain. "It will. Another massive extinction; another rally; another and another, though I think each is more weak and starveling: until the end. When will Pandora lie wholly bare? In a billion years, perhaps."

A billion years, Brodersen remembered as he walked. *Counting to a billion, at a standard rate of four numbers per second, would take*—he had checked a minicomp—*almost eight years. A billion real-time years—that's a mighty long rearguard action to fight against the Norns.*

Though does any race of being ever fight anything else?

The walk was brief, through an afternoon that would linger for Earthdays. They came out beneath brazen heaven and saw the houses of unknownness.

Only turf, brush, and younglings of larger plants grew right around them. Clifflike, rainbowlike, walls lifted sheer until they became intricately recessed, colonnaded, intermingled. No doors or windows broke their smoothness. A portal did give on a courtyard. Brodersen took his followers through. Here also nature strove to return. Roots had not split paving or siding (yet) but low vegetation decked corners where dust had gathered and tendrils crawled up convoluted pilasters. A creature flew from a gallery; had it a nest there?

The newcomers paid scant heed. In the middle of the yard was a pair of statues.

The pedestals were stone, the sculpture in the same (?) perdurable material as the façades. Realistic tints lent a conviction that these were portraits. The entities represented were twice human height, which might be art but which Brodersen suspected was truth. Nudity revealed them as two-sexed (probably, Fidelio said; and Brodersen remembered reading about a plaque on the first things man had sent out of the Solar System). Bulky, short-legged, long-armed, stub-tailed bipeds, they had three eyes but flat beakless countenances. A blueness covered them that was not hair or scales or feathers.... The catalogue of their appearance could go on.

In four-fingered hands, one held aloft a hammer and unmistakable wood ax, one a sheet of hide or fabric which bore pictographs (or hieroglyphs or—). No matter how foreign the shapes, their stances bespoke tranquility.

After silence had lasted, Caitlín murmured, "Goodfate to you, people of Pandora."

"Or are they the Others?" Dozsa asked in as hushed a tone.

Brodersen shook his head. "Hardly," he answered. "The Others build moon-heavy machines out of star stuff for crossing the universe, space and time both. They wouldn't bother with this kind of thing."

"Could the Pandorans be apprentice Others?" Caitlín wondered.

Dozsa turned pragmatic: "Are these Pandorans? How can we tell?"

"I think they must be," Fidelio replied. "They have the four-limbed, trioptic anatomy. Features like the dorsal fin and beaks instead of jaws doubtless stem back to primitive animals from which the higher forms of the present epoch developed."

As if placental mammals died out, or evacuated Earth, and ages afterward new species arose whose ancestors were platypuses, Brodersen thought. *Or lizards or worms.*

"Well, let's poke around," he said.

There must be a way into the buildings, but none existed that the strangers could find.

"They return at intervals and clear away the weeds in this area," Brodersen posited. "Else it'd be choked."

"How often, though?" Dozsa demanded.

"To estimate that," Fidelio said, "we would have to know growth rates. Those would take us a year or two to learn. And then we would merely have a guess. Ten years? Twenty? You could establish yourselves here, the gravity would suit your bodily needs, but I do not imagine you could live off the country."

Caitlín winced and hugged him. He had less than one year. He gave her a moment's response before his whisker-dithering, tail-twitching curiosity took over again.

"Uh-huh," Brodersen said slowly. "It doesn't seem practical. I did think we might leave a message, maybe engraved on stainless steel set next to these figures. Symbols that read...oh...quote, 'We're lost, we plan to grope on through gate after gate according to such-and-such a pattern, but please come after us.'"

"Would they pay any attention?" Dozsa challenged.

"Would you not?" Caitlín flung back. He nodded. "But how shall we be making them understand?" she inquired of Fidelio.

"I seize no slightest idea," he admitted. "In eight years of intimate relationship with your expedition, we achieved a little comprehension back and forth. And it seems our two races are more alike than most."

He sat for a while on feet and flukes, a long, graceful mahogany shape among oven-hot high-colored walls. The claws and webs of an upper hand closed on his muzzle, the fingers of both lower hands were bridged. "No," he said at last, croaking and piping the Spanish that perhaps hurt his throat, "I sense nothing. Remember, if you do go on, you go on at the risk of emerging on emptiness. The Pandorans are not the Others. Unless they know the Others—why should they necessarily, more than your folk or mine?—even if they can translate your appeal, they would be sending a crew in your wake at the same hazard. Caitlín, female of love, would you order that?"

She stood dumb.

After another while, Fidelio said, "For my part, I am very willing to swim with the school. You may choose to stay, in hopes of help before your supplies are gone. My counsel, which could be wrong, is that you seek onward. But make your own judgment, dear friends."

"No!" burst from Caitlín, in English. "A selkie like him to be dying on this mummy world? If he cannot have the sea back, let him at least have stars!"

Brodersen smiled sadly and laid a hand on her shoulder. "You're too fast off the mark, honey," he reproached. "I wanted to say that."

They could do nothing more as they were, and the heat was

sapping them. Sunburn would hit them too, quicker and crueller than on Earth, if they didn't take care. "We'll quit for now," Brodersen told Rueda over the radio, "rest a few hours in the boat—you keep that air conditioner going, hear me?—and figure what to try next. Maybe we should snoop around the landing field in case we can learn something. Maybe we should rig ladders to reach these high-level arcades. Or maybe we should take off right away, though personally I'd rather not. Anyhow, we'll be along pronto."

"I'll have food ready for you," Rueda promised.

The party went out through the portal in no special order and started across the more or less open section of second growth that separated it from the virgin stand. The green sun scorched and glowered, the wind resounded.

Fidelio cried aloud. Not before had the humans heard surprise and agony in a Betan voice.

Brodersen saw shafts fly from the woods, short, thick, vaned at the rear, with triple-barbed metal heads. "Drop!" he roared, and hit the dirt himself. His rifle snarled, spraying the forest, ripping chunks off its suddenly nightmare stems, raking in among them.

A high ululation responded. Forth from the ambush sprang a couple of beings. Later Brodersen would learn that Caitlín had snatched the chance to turn her camera on them. For him, that was needless. He saw with total clarity and he would not forget while he lived.

They were bipeds, slender, chest-high to him. Their heads were three-eyed and beaked, their hands had three evenly spaced fingers, their feet were hooflike, their backs sprouted fins, their color was brown. They wore short trousers in whose belts were knife and tomahawk. One clutched a sort of crossbow. The other had been wounded; black blood ran from an arm.

They did not charge but bounded off right and left while they shrieked. Brodersen fired at the nearest. "Don't!" Caitlín shouted. "They're fleeing, frightened—Dan, they have minds!"

He let them go but gave the woods a fresh burst. Dozsa joined in. More than two savages had been in that attack. No retaliation came. *Scared the lot of 'em off,* Brodersen decided. *The pair who ran out were sheerly panicked. Maybe I nailed a few. Hope so.*

He released his trigger. A searing silence rolled over him, deepened by the wind. He rose to a crouch and looked around.

No sign of further danger met him. "Stand guard, Stef," he directed. "If you think you see a movement, any kind of movement, shoot."

He went over to Fidelio. The Betan lay in a lake of blood. His was purple. More pumped out of the wound which the quarrel had torn through his body between the upper and lower arms. It had already soaked Caitlín, where she knelt trying to stanch the flow.

She glanced at Brodersen as he neared. "No use," she told him dully. "I've not the equipment nor the knowledge nor the time. A major artery, a vital organ—" The flow was diminishing. Fidelio's harsh breathing was too, and he relaxing out of his death struggle.

Caitlín moved to lay his head on her lap. The blue eyes sought toward her. "Fidelio," she said in Spanish, "can you hear me?"

"Sí," rattled faint.

"Fidelio, we'll get home. And we'll help your people learn what they need to about our ways of love, though I think they've much to teach us of that."

"Gracias—" Brodersen could barely hear.

Caitlín stroked hands along his fur and sang very low:

Sleep, my babe, for the red bee hums the silent twilight's fall.
Aeobhaill from the grey rock comes to wrap the world in thrall.

She had sung it for Brodersen's children, the ancient "Gartan Mother's Lullabye." The melody was beautiful.

Alend van och, my child, my joy, my love, my heart's desire,
The crickets sing you lullabye, beside the dying fire.—

Brodersen left them alone and, taking every soldierly precaution possible, went to scout the thickets. He found no killed or wounded, though wet black spashes told him he'd hit oftener than once. Probably the band had borne its casualties away, as a troop ought to. He gathered a few dropped weapons for later examination and returned. By then, Fidelio was gone.

Having reported to an appalled Rueda, Brodersen commanded, "No you stay put. This space here's too small for a safe landing, especially when you'd have to work the boat alone. You ought to be secure enough. But if in doubt, scramble! *Williwaw*'s too much a key to everybody else's survival to jeopardize on our account." After a protest: "Shut up, mister, and obey orders."

He turned to Caitlín and Dozsa. "Okay, let's start. You in the middle, Pegeen. Keep alert. Fire on the slightest suspicion. We'll hold fast in the boat till *Chinook*'s ready to receive us."

She pointed mutely at the shape below her feet. He shook his head. "No. We can't, when we might be bushwhacked on our way. I won't organize a detail to recover him afterward, either. Wish we could, but—would you want your friends to endanger their lives for your corpse? I can't believe he would.

"Come along."

XXXV

THE SPACESHIP BLASTED, away from the planet, back to the T machine for her next leap. On the first evenwatch after mess, the common room lay unused. Nobody wanted to look at Pandora and its green sun, nor confess dauntedness by suggesting viewscreens be turned off. In pairs or alone, crewfolk drifted to their quarters.

Brodersen and Caitlín lowered their bed because only thus could they really sit next to each other, leaned against pillows and bulkhead. They had put on pajamas, which they seldom did, and poured stiff whiskies. Their adjacent hands were linked.

The liquor slopped about in his tumbler. He took a draught of its smoke and fire, and another, and saw his grip grow steadier. "Oh, God, Pegeen, oh, God," he groaned, "I lost a crewman again. *I* did."

"It couldn't be helped, darling," she answered. "Nobody blames you."

"Except me!"

She let him stare at nothing and gulp air for half a minute before she put her drink on a sideshelf, took him by the jaw, and dragged his head around to face her. "Now that will do, Daniel Brodersen," she snapped. "It's pitying yourself you are, the which is the lowest emotion there is."

He met her gaze, stern in a frame of unbound bronze hair, swallowed hard, and nodded. "Yeah. You're right and I'm sorry. It was a damnable shock, but I should have taken it like a man."

She put her arm about his neck. "No, dearest, don't feel at fault about that either. You've borne a load you can let go at last—must let go." She kissed him, long though tenderly rather than passionately.

When they were at ease, she sighed. "Truth to tell, I'd no great fret about you. Phil Weisenberg, however, I fear he's in a bad way."

"Huh? Well, he skipped dinner, but a setback like this could destroy anybody's appetite."

Caitlín bit her lip. "You didn't hear him when he called me to say he'd be absent. Nor did you see him when we embarked, or afterward while we made ready to boost.... Oh, aye, you *saw* him, but you can't have noticed; you'd too much else on your mind. He's being a quiet, efficient, polite robot."

Brodersen scowled. "That's rough news for sure."

Caitlín squeezed his hand. "Don't take on this worry yet, my heart. Let me see what I can do. You're old friends, I know, but I've a notion he'd not open to you simply for fear of adding to your burdens. He may find me safer."

"M-m-m . . . well, you do have a gift. . . . All right." Brodersen drank further. Abruptly, hoarsely, "Maybe you can guess why those devils attacked us."

Caitlín gathered words. "They are not devils, Dan," she then said. Her tone was gentle. "They are intelligent beings like you and me—still hunters, whose few scattered dwellings in the wilderness we did not see from above—but our ancestors were the same, not very long ago. Oh, glad I am we seem to have killed no one of them."

"After what they did?"

"Think. What are they? A race evolved from lower animals in the past few million years, after the sun changed."

"Yes, that's obvious."

"Think further, Dan. The older race had departed. They might come back on occasion, out of reverence or a sorrowful curiosity, but why would they establish that base, to hold a flotilla of ships, and raise those buildings in the ancient style, and set forth images of themselves? Why, unless to help their successors? Abolish the worst horrors of such an environment. Give the new beings what is useful—as it might be iron for forging boltheads for the hunt—but a piece of technology at a time, maybe once in a century, so they can grow into the use, not the misuse—" Caitlín laid a palm over Brodersen's mouth. "Hush, macushla; let me finish. I suppose the elders guide the whole younger culture in its development, or all of what different cultures exist on poor Pandora. I suppose too this guidance is even more slow and careful, not to wither the native spirit and genius but to let them flower. That would explain, would it not, the statues—reminders of the teachers who return after generations and reopen their school—teachers that I think do everything they can not to become gods.

"In the end, though well before the planet is much worse burnt, there should be a civilization ready and able to move out among the stars."

Caitlín smiled, sipped, brushed lips across Brodersen's cheek. "Does that sound reasonable, my sweet?" she asked.

"Well. . . . We can't do more than guess—" He banged his tumbler against his own shelf. "Why in hell's name did they shoot at us?" he rasped.

"How could they know what we were? We none of us looked like the teachers. We could be demons invading their holiest shrine. Or we could be two new kinds of beast, to kill as a precaution or to kill for meat. Fidelio said he thought this is the season of ingathering, against a frightful winter—for mates, children, everybody they care about. He might have died in the Wheel for evil cause. This was only because of a mistake, and because of love."

"We didn't foresee. The universe took us by surprise."

"It always will, Dan. You know that."

He nodded jerkily, drained his drink, set it down, and turned to her. "Pegeen, you make things good again—"

They clung to each other, nothing more. When she felt the tension going from him, she urged him with her arms to lie down. He closed his eyes. She kissed the lids. He smiled. She drew alongside him. Soon he was asleep.

She had taken but little whisky. Rising, she paced around barefoot, fingers tightly interlocked, a growing distress on her countenance. At length, after a glance at the man to make sure he was soundly at rest, she went to the private line intercom and punched a number.

Weisenberg's voice dragged from the receiver. "Yes?"

"I hope I've not waked you," she said.

"Oh, no. The hour's not late." A machine might have spoken. "What is it, Caitlín?"

"I'd like to see you if I may."

He hesitated. "Is it urgent? I am tired. I'd be dismal company."

"Company be blowed! Your job description does not include keeping me amused. I want to come around for a bit and talk. Kick me out whenever you wish."

"Well, if you insist."

"Thank you, Phil, dear. I'll be there in two quantum jumps."

She lingered only for a smile at Brodersen.

Rounding the corridor, she encountered Leino. Fully clad but unkempt, he prowled with a marijuana cigarette reeking in his fingers. He and she stopped on the spot and stood a few seconds.

"Good evening to you," she ventured.

His look went up and down and across her. The pajamas she wore were thin. "Where are you bound?" he demanded.

"I've business that won't wait, Martti, and beg your pardon for that." She started past him. He lifted a hand as if to take hold of her, but let it drop. She came to Weisenberg's door and went on through. He saw.

Having secured the latch, Caitlín paused a moment. A single fluoro lit the room, set to the minimum short of switching off altogether. The data screen, that could bring forth most of humanity's heritage, was dark. Weisenberg sat slumped in the dusk; his wrists dangled off the chair arms, his chin dropped nearly to the breast.

He raised his head by degrees. "Hello," he recited. "Can I offer you something?"

"Aye, but I think not liquor. Stay where you are, Phil." She released a chair and carried it over to seat herself opposite him.

He let his glance fall back down. "My apologies. I told you I'm tired."

"If you were healthy tired, you'd be snoring." She leaned forward to catch both his hands in hers, warmth around chill. "What's wrong?"

He forced each syllable out. "Don't you regret Fidelio's death?"

"'Regret' is a shabby word for this."

"Well, then, consider me in...in mourning for the second comrade we've lost." Weisenberg shivered a little. "I don't want to make a fuss. It's just I don't have your talent for—" He halted.

"For what?" she asked, mildly and inexorably.

He gulped. "Please...don't misunderstand....No insult to you, Caitlín, no idea you don't...feel...as deeply...maybe more....But you do have your...your talent....You'll compose a song and...exorcise...the worst pain...the way you did for Sergei...won't you?" He swallowed anew. "I'd like to hear it when you do. It'll help."

"No, Phil," she said. "I'll not be making any lament for Fidelio."

Startled, he looked up, straight at her.

"That wouldn't be right, you see," she explained. "I did not know him, not truly. None among us but the *Emissary* folk did: Joelle Ky best, I suppose, and how much she? Me, what can I tell of him? The bare, bleached bones of what happened. Nothing of *his*. I'll not give him a song that to me is mechanical. He was worth more than that."

"I don't quite understand."

Her lips quirked. "Aye, you're not a bard. We're a queer breed." She withdrew her clasp on him but not her gaze, sat back and said: "Think on this. It didn't shatter you when Sergei went, though you'd been his shipmate over and over and though you shared being human, with the insight and fellow feeling that means. Honor and affection to Fidelio's memory; but we were not close to him, it was never possible, nor he to us. Well may we mourn him, as you said, Phil. However, you meant 'grieve,' which is not so."

He winced and tightened his mouth.

"Easy, dear, easy," she said. "What's to fear? What's to be humble about? Something else broke you this day, and I'm thinking I know what it was."

A thin cloud of anger gathered on him. "See here, you mean well, but I've no patience with parlor analysis. If you'll excuse me, I'd like to turn in."

She raised a palm and chuckled. "I'll thank you to use the language of *my* profession correctly, Philip Weisenberg. I've no intention of analyzing you, in the parlor or out of it. What I said was, it's plain to see where your trouble lies, in a place that does you credit."

He gaped, caught himself, attempted to make a retort. She went on before he could, seriously, while again she took his hands.

"When Pandora failed us too, and in such a grisly fashion, when we must carry on this wild hunt, and on and on—suddenly you could take no more. You have been the tower of strength, ever calm, ever steady, more even than Dan. You may not have had your shoulder cried on, though it will be no surprise to me if you have, but yours was the presence of courage and sanity, which simply by being there helped us beyond our telling. You never took from us; in your quiet way, you always gave.

"Well, who gave to you?"

"Now, when anew you've had dashed from you the hope of coming back to the family that is so dear—"

Caitlín rose to bend over him and hug him. He stiffened and tried to pull free. She would not let him. Her tresses tumbled over his white crew cut. All at once he caught at her, lost his face in the softness of her bosom, and began to weep. *"Sarah, Sarah!"* She flowed onto his lap and embraced him more closely, not flinching when his grip grew too tight.

He was only on the rack for a couple of minutes before he fought for control. "I'm sorry, Caitlín—I never meant—"

"Hush." She kept him against her. "It is not unmanly to cry. Achilles did. Cuchulain did."

"I ... know ... but—present cir-cir-circumstances ... bad for morale—"

"Why, there's none but the two of us here, Philip, and I'll not be telling. We share, tonight, we share."

She heard him out about his wife and children and grandchildren. When during this his legs grew numb, she lowered the bed that they might sit side by side. Later, when his head drooped, she suggested he undress and lie down. He made an embarrassed noise. She laughed and buried her eyes in the crook of an elbow.

"No peeking," she vowed. "Tell me when you're acceptable. I aim to see you well asleep."

Weisenberg heeded her wish. She tucked the blanket around him, perched on the bedside, and led him to talk further. In the course of that, she related what she deemed was the truth about the Pandorans. He said it was a comforting idea.

Yet he couldn't drowse off. He kept beginning to, and awakening with a gasp. "I'd give you a bottle or a joint or a pill," she told him at last, "but for you in this hour they are wrong. They don't care."

She swung herself across him and slipped beneath the covers. "Hey!" he exclaimed as her arm went over his breast. "Wait! What're you doing?"

"You need to be held, Phil, and kissed some. Would your Sarah really mind?"

"Uh, uh ... no, but—" He grimaced. "I'm old. I'm awfully tired."

"Did I ask you for anything save that you learn you are not alone?" She reached for the nearby light switch and darkened the room. Then she caressed him and murmured to him, as a mother might do to a child, for a long while.

Finally he lay easily breathing. She began a careful

disengagement. His clasp remained, and she slipped back down beside him. "Caitlín," he whispered, half in and half out of dream.

She made slow and gentle love to him. After that, and a few endearments, he fell altogether asleep.

Caitlín shut the door behind her and turned toward the captain's cabin. Leino came around the curve of the hall. In its chilled silence, his footfalls thudded audibly and unevenly. He stopped when he saw her, put left fist on hip, brought right hand to his mouth for a drag on his latest reefer.

"Well," he said. "Good evening twice. You have been having a good evening, Miz Mulryan, I trust?"

"Yes and no," she replied levelly. "Phil and I had an important matter to discuss."

He lifted his brows. His eyes raked her tousled slenderness. Where her thighs met, the pajamas were moist. "Discuss," he said. "Yes, indeed. And what was the subject?"

"Martti, dear, you know better than to be asking that. We've little enough privacy as is. Or was it the pot that asked? How many of those have you had? Were you pacing this circle throughout the hours?"

He bridled. "Don't call me 'dear'!"

"Am I to call you enemy instead?" She stepped nigh. He made as if to retreat and preserve his personal space intact, but congealed. She laid a hand on the back of his neck. Her green gaze captured his. "You too are hard hit, you too have been flailing about trying to regain your balance, is that not so? Your way is wrong, though; it can but worsen things for you."

He showed teeth. "What's *your* way?" he snapped.

She considered him for a moment, before a smile grew upon her. "Well," she answered, far down in her throat, "it works."

He stared. Her hips undulated as she brought her free hand to his waist. "We've unfinished business, you and I, Martti," she told him.

He sought to back off. She held him. "You were overwrought last time," she said. "Maybe you've no idea how often that is the case. You gave me no chance to help, not really, much though I wanted to. Ever since, I've been wanting more and more to."

"Do you—mean—" He couldn't go on.

She plucked the cigarette from his fingers and dropped it to the deck. The carpet would take no harm and the regular cleanup would collect stub and ash. "I told you, that's the wrong way, Martti, darling."

He seized her to him.

—Not long afterward in his cabin, he lay back on his pillow, looking pleased and dazed. She snuggled. "There, now, you see, wasn't I right?" she inquired.

"You were," he muttered. "Sure. Thanks, Caitlín." With a slight effort, while he stared through half-shut eyes at the overhead: "Thank you. Uh, I'm afraid I was too quick. Would you like to spend the rest of the nightwatch here?"

"That I would. It's a shameless, greedy hussy I am." She kissed him. He responded vigorously.

—They had slept a short span, and coupled a third time, and were resting against the bulkhead, as she and Brodersen had done hours ago. The cabin felt warm and full of animal odors. Mornwatch was near.

"Can you join me tonight?" he asked. "Uh, not to intrude on Dan or anything, but if you can, it would be wonderful."

"How badly do you want me to?" she replied. "I'm sure Frieda could—" she grinned—"squeeze you in."

He hugged her. His voice dropped into Upland dialect. "Nil have I for to downsay Frieda, Caitlín, but you're longways prettier and, yea, livelier still."

"Ah, good, pretty, lively; if that's all, I'm glad."

"What?" He swung his head about to look at her.

She looked back. "Why, I feared you were in love with me. That could tear you apart."

Shocked, he protested, "I am, Caitlín!"

"You said no word about that this evening.... Wait, please. Let me finish. I'm not the least hurt or offended. Think how inconvenient it would be if every man alive desired me. I do believe you've become my good friend, Martti, and treasure that." She embraced and kissed him.

He scarcely reacted. When she let him go, he regarded her in a kind of horror. "Caitlín, heartling, I do love you," he said raggedly. "By me you're the most fair that ever did walk."

She sat erect. Her tone lashed: "Then why could you not have me until you saw me as a slut?"

He choked. She pursued, jabbing a finger at his breast: "Listen to me, Martti Leino. Bear in mind I'd not be taking this trouble did I not care for you. Easier to give you your pleasure and let you wallow in your smugness. Easier for both of us, no doubt, while this voyage lasts. But it may not last till our small doomsday. We may find our way home. In that case, in due course you'll want to marry—wait. You're about to say you'll marry me. I warn you that's impossible, but whether or not makes no difference. Surely you'll want a wife you respect, a wife you take pride in.

"Martti, *how are you going to be a husband to a woman you respect?*"

—Afterward, when the shouting was done and the pain had subsided, they lay quiet. She whispered into the hollow between his neck and shoulder: "Och, forgive me. I judged this must be done to you—for you—sometime, and how better than by a near shipmate? The more so when I know well old habits of thinking cannot be changed in a day, and here we have weeks, months, maybe years.... Never fear, I'll not be prying into how you've felt about your mother or your sister, especially Lis." He flinched. "No, dear Martti, I won't. It's not needful, nor decent, I believe. You already have the knowledge in your brain; you've only to get it into your bones. The knowledge that we women are not vessels of holiness, forever defiled if we let in the same kind of honest lust that you know. We are hardly different from you there, nor you from us in your fragility."

"Caitlín."

"The wife you get may well choose to be none but yours, as Lis has chosen thus far with Dan. There's nothing amiss with that, if it's what the two of you really wish. But she has the same right to freedom, every kind of freedom, as you do, and if she claims it she becomes not the less, she becomes the more. Aye, freedom can be lonely, can be frightening, wherefore many persons forswear it, on their own behalf or—what's truly evil—on everyone's. Yet I often think that it's what being human is about. Anything else, a beast or a machine can match. Freedom is ours."

"We ... we abuse it—"

"Indeed. We're but apes who've grown brains over-large for our bodies. If ever we meet the Others, we may begin to learn what freedom really is. Meanwhile, let's be as worthy of it as we're able."

Caitlín laughed softly. "Och, hear me preach! Martti, I must soon be about making breakfast. But first, if you're not over-wearied—which well you might be; sure, and many a lad would—if you're not, I'd like to begin proving to you what I mean."

Presently, amidst more laughter from them both, she said: "Ah, well, it will do no harm if just this once breakfast is an hour or two late, will it, now?"

Elsewhere aboard, folk slept, Frieda and Dozsa together, the rest by themselves: Brodersen and Weisenberg peacefully; Joelle heavily, under sedation; Rueda rolling about; Susanne with a smile that came and went and came again. Under robot control, *Chinook* drove on toward the transport engine.

XXXVI

I WAS A CHILD of the People, my father a man of the Corn Society, a respectable man who would never in any way seek to thrust himself above others. Yet in the tenth month before I was born, on a night when he and his fellows were in the kiva blessing their dead, my mother dreamed a strange dream. It seemed as if the kachinas came and gently bore her down to their beautiful world below the world. Therefore, as she knelt on a mat, upheld by her sisters, and brought me forth, the men of my father's Society—having been duly purified—danced certain measures, blew sacred smoke from their pipes, and prayed.

They got no sign, good or ill, and so took me for what I was, another boy baby, and presented me to the sun. Later I wailed and crowed and kicked and slumbered, was rocked in the arms of my parents and kin, drank life from my mother's breasts. She bore me on her back strapped to a cradle board while she worked in the patches of beans, squash, and cotton. At those times my head was tightly bound against the wood, to flatten my skull and make me handsome. Soon, though, I was toddling about in care of older children. We infants played many happy games, seldom broken by a tear-squall. However, my earliest memory is of a raven winging by. I stood near the cliff edge; across from me, the far wall of the canyon climbed from depths of willow, through juniper and cactus, to rise at last naked; amidst those greens deep or dusty, the tawny blue-shadowed rock, the heat and light and stillness and resiny smells, all under a sky where sight could lose itself forever: oh, there went that proud bright blackness, flying!

Our pueblo was built halfway up the canyonside, on a ledge. The heights above gave shade when summer afternoon blasted. We had neither the greatest nor the least community on that mesa where the People dwelt. Adobe walls were thick and strong, their roughness pleasant to touch; rooms within were dim but comfortable at every season; ladders went from level to level, and we were always using them, to go work or go visit. Though we set store by proper manners, I remember much merriment.

Possessing a nearby spring, we took the trail down to the river for fishing or purification or the gathering of herbs—or, in hot weather, coolness, when the young romped on sandbars while the elders sat in grave cheerfulness. Other trails led to the top, where our crops grew and we cut wood (having first explained our need to the trees), hunted, hiked to different pueblos, sought oneness with the spirits in dream or meditation. There, on a clear night, as most nights were, a man saw stars past counting, more stars than darkness, thronged around the Backbone of the World. A full moon blurred that splendor but set the land mysteriously aglow.

Yes, Creation was full of light. Even the mightiest rainstorms, cloudbursts, blazed as well as crashed. Even our dead, for whom we broke our finest pottery to bury with them, even our dead saw shiningness, in the world below the world or when they came back to us unseen.

I grew, duty by duty. For a start, I helped keep watch on weanlings. Later I helped cultivate the corn, that being a right of males. Later still I carried burdens and wielded tools too heavy for women. Led by my seniors, I went hunting, woodcutting, traveling; I partook in ceremonies suitable to my years; in this wise I learned what a man ought to know.

Apart from a few tasks that were overly hard or dull, we enjoyed whatever we did. As for those which nobody liked, besides the reward of knowing we kept the pueblo alive thereby, we made them as gladsome as might be. Thus, to name a single one, when the women ground the corn the men had brought in (after we had cleaned our buildings in order that the corn would feel happy to enter) they made a party of it, chattering away over the metates while a man stood in the door playing the flute for them.

As my limbs lengthened, everybody marked how I took after my mother in looks, nothing of my father about me. This caused some gossip among the low-minded. It died out, because the People take doings between man and woman as ordinary rather than sacred. (Yet nothing good is not sacred.) My father simply agreed this was a token I should not join his Society when I came of age, but my uncle's. It would have been the usual outcome anyhow, since we reckon descent and inheritance through the female line.

No matter what has happened since, I may not and will not tell of my initiation rites, save that they ended down in the kiva when the spirits rose from the sipapu to bless us. There I joined the Herb Society. This caused me to spend years studying which plants can heal, which hurt, which numb pain, which lend flavor, which cause weird dreams and are to be avoided, and how to talk to each kind of plant in respect and love.

Meanwhile I married, founded a household, carried on the work of a husband. My wife was an upright lass who quickly became more winsome to me than moonrise or yucca blossoms. And when she gave me my first child, to carry forth and show to the sun—!

We knew more than joy, of course. Some of us got crippled, some took sick and we could not make them well, many died young, and at best we would grow old, teeth worn to the gums, flesh wasted, blindness and deafness closing in, till we were no longer of use. However kindly children and grandchildren cared for the old, reminding them of how they had cared for the newborn, perhaps this hurt worst.

More and more, we suffered raids from the nomads below the mesa. There lopers in sagebrush, brothers of the coyote, had bows more powerful that ours, and lived for war. In my day they captured a pueblo, tortured to death what men they had not killed, outraged the women before bearing them off, and left the children to wither. This recalled to us ancient means of defense we had been neglecting; after such a punishment, we learned how to stand siege till hunger drove the wild packs off. Nevertheless I remember dreadful battles.

Their fanged souls alone did not make them assail us. Want likewise did. In my day the drought stuck. We knew of two rainless years in a row, and the legends said they had been plenty bad. Now we counted three, four, five.... Our crops shriveled, our seeds failed in the hard-baked soil, unless we endlessly lugged water.... Six, seven, eight.... Our sun smote us from a sky gone pale; and land shimmered in summer heat. Winters were dry, quiet, gnawingly cold.... Nine, ten, eleven.... We doled out what food we could scrabble together. The aged and the very young were perishing. Four of my children did, two as I watched, two while I was off helping pray....

The Summoner came to me. I was borne to the world which is not below the world, nor above, nor beyond, but which is the whole world.

For that which followed, there are no words. Far less than for a night with a dearest woman, or a night in the kiva, or a night when your mother dies in your arms, there are no words. I was every god who had ever been, and understood everything that was. It is beautiful and terrible beyond any dreaming. More I cannot in this body remember.

At the end, One said that which I can only know as: "You will return to your life. If you wish, you may forget what has been Here. Think well."

Afloat in a mighty peace, I thought, until at last I said: "No, take not from me more than must be." Do I recall a cherishing laughter, which may also have been a weeping?

I rejoined the People. They did not realize I had been gone. I had no way to tell them. I was still a man, who rejoiced in his wife and living children and friends, who grieved for his hurt and dead. They did find me strange because of the long times I now spent apart from them, under the stars.

Twelve years, thirteen.... We clung to the ancestral homes, the ancestral graves, as lichen does to a rock. But we are not lichen, it came to me. We are the People. And this is not a world forever fixed in a single harmony, which nothing but black magic can change. We do wrong to hang by the thumbs, for witchcraft, men and women who are merely ill-mannered. I have learned that the world eternally changes, and is more vast and various than we can imagine. That may be good, that may be bad, but that is true.

If we stay where we are, we die. We must move to better country.

I talked, I prophesied, I raged, I thrust myself above others, and was scorned for it. I fared off by myself and gathered knowledge of lands where we might go. With this in hand, I could reason among the People. I became a great healer too, which showed I had the favor of the kachinas.

Finally I led them away.

Now we are prospering, each year we build further on our new pueblo, in a place where summer is green and a river runs bright between the cottonwoods. I shun honors they would give me, but I do claim the right to walk solitary whenever I wish, which is often, and free my soul to the stars. Yonder lies

Oneness. Will the Summoner call me there again before I die, or shall I enter the earth? My strength is gone and my eyes grow dim. Soon I shall be no more what I am, but something else, whatever it may be. Let me thank life for all that it gave. I was Man.

XXXVII

JUMP.

There was a whirling sword of light; there was a T machine, and a wondrous pair of moons for it; there was a stellar background. There was no sun to be seen.

Slowly—it took whole seconds—Joelle drew her awareness back from the transcendence of a space-time crossing under holothesis. She need not focus vision on the spectacle in the screen; she could perceive directly through any scanner aboard. Her ears brought her Brodersen's awed, "Jesus Christ, oh, Christ, what *is* that?" from the intercom. Otherwise the computer room was silent. Weightless in her harness, she might almost have been disembodied. Yet none of the rest could conceive how fully she was in and of the universe. Data overflowed her; a gamma ray photon or a magnetic field was as real, as immediate as any sight or touch. Like a person suddenly put in an unknown setting, she turned manifold senses and magnified intellect on her surroundings and sought comprehension.

"Joelle," Brodersen begged, "have you got some idea of where we're at?"

"Yes," replied a minute fraction of her. "A pulsar. I'll need much more information, of course. Don't start linear acceleration. It may well be unsafe to leave the neighborhood of the machine. Put us in orbit around it and stand by for further orders."

"Aye. You hear, everybody? Keep your stations. Prepare to maneuver." The captain spoke shakenly.

They didn't need her for the simple task. Navigational instruments and a computer in the command center, operated by Susanne, sufficed. Joelle gave herself back to the cosmos.

Knowledge came slowly, over hours, in that unearthly

environment. She made repeated mistakes, analogous to those made by ordinary humans in a room designed to foster optical illusions. Forces, energies, free atoms and ions and subnuclear particles, were bewilderingly different in configuration and behavior from everything she was used to. The very beam of radiance, narrow, sweeping across night and stars in a blink of time, was hypnotic. The challenge made her undertaking thrice marvelous.

And: in the programs, the data banks, her own memories, was a legacy from Fidelio. Best would have been to have him in linkage with her. But as she began to learn how the information should be employed which he had left for her, she began to feel she would become the equal of the partnership they two had been. In a way, he was still aboard, a ghost within the machine and within her. That gave strength and peace such as nothing and nobody else could have done.

Concept by concept, Joelle built a recognition of what lay around the ship.

Chinook had come far through the galaxy, in the same spiral arm but thousands of light-years closer to its cloud-veiled core. She had traveled futureward also by some millions of years; where S Doradus had been, in the larger Magellanic Cloud, there was a glowing nebula. The body here had exploded, itself a supernova, but long before she left home—back when dinosaurs walked on Earth, if that statement had any physical meaning.

Rather, a giant sun had burst, strewing most of its substance into space for the nourishment of suns and worlds later to be born. The neutron star was a remnant, two-thirds the mass of Sol. Gravity had collapsed it until the diameter was a bare twenty kilometers. Few atoms existed within it. Instead was an ocean of elementary particles, as close together as quantum mechanics allowed, mercurially interchanging natures with each other, at densities which men could measure but never conceive.

A little of the star's material, caught up in the monstrous magnetic field which its spin generated, was cast outward through a pair of spirals until the speed approached that of light. Thereupon this matter gave off synchrotron radiation, in thin beams with small dispersion, whose ardor equalled that of an entire Sol. Most was at radio frequencies; the visible light was a tiny fraction of it. Astronomers with suitably tuned and sensitive receivers, on distant planets which happened to lie in the path of the ray, would mark a pulsar blinking.

The Others had built their engine to orbit in a plane normal to those energy torrents, at a distance of about seventy-five million kilometers. Closer, conditions would have been lethal, where infalling gas from space and the star's own chained violence created a maelstrom of hard radiation. Joelle wondered why the radius vector was not longer, much longer. As was, throughout its 157-day "year" the construct must repeatedly be smitten by a fury that ought to be ruinous to it, that would surely vaporize any ship which chanced to emerge just then.

No. A great round thing circled it. Joelle determined the period to be such that the object was always between T machine and star during a transit. This was not a stable situation; but no doubt the device had robotic engines which readjusted its path as necessary. It was a shield.

Another, bulkier thing likewise played satellite to the machine, in a way which, given occasional compensation, likewise put it behind the shield when protection was needed.

"And what the hell might *that* be?" Brodersen asked the heavens.

He, Dozsa, Weisenberg, and Granville took *Williwaw* forth on exploration. By telemetry and audiovisual transmission, Joelle followed along. The data flow to her would have been maddeningly slow and incomplete were a holothete not above impatience. (Between inputs she had everything else to consider, to dwell in.) Nonetheless she was with them immensely more than Rueda, Leino, von Moltke, or Mulryan, straining eyes and ears before the screens, could surmise. Understanding better what the investigators found than they did themselves, Joelle was presently telling them what to search for, and how, and what their discoveries meant.

The shield was a curved shell. Its mean density was about the same as that of the cylinder; no doubt the same kind of force bound it together. It was about five kilometers across, ample to intercept a firebeam a fifth as wide, adamant enough to reflect that energy without being damaged. The shape maximized diffusion of the image, thereby minimizing impact upon the star. Attachments around the circumference, some ponderous, some skeletal, probably generated fields to divert charged particles that might otherwise come storming past it and swing inward. A different apparatus at the center of the concave side was surely the motor that corrected the orbit. Joelle could see all those shapes in a way that nobody else was able to—for they were not readily describable in manspeech—and could appreciate their exquisiteness.

What Brodersen and company saw was impressive aplenty, the shimmering white shell athwart a black, many-glittered sky, the searing line of brilliance that whirled beyond it. Weightless though they drifted, they seemed to feel enormous powers at work; silent though the gulf about them was, hiss and crackle out of radio receivers brought them the noise of a cosmos in travail.

Joelle had but the vaguest idea of how the thing was made or how it ran. The Others knew laws of nature man or Betan had not discovered. That was no surprise. Did she ever meet them, she felt confident she, the holothete, could soon learn... converse... oh, maybe enter their fellowship!

Brodersen conned *Williwaw* toward the opposite satellite.

"Please," Caitlín said, well-nigh timidly. "Eat this sandwich, drink this milk. It's starving you are."

Beneath her helmet, Joelle blinked. She wasn't hungry. But when had she last eaten? *The circuits ought to include physiological monitors of me,* flashed through her. *Yes, that would be an interesting addition, albeit a minor one.* She decided she'd do best to heed the girl's advice, and reached for the food and squeeze bottle.

"You should sleep, too," Caitlín ventured onward. "You look like death's discarded mistress. Remember how slow and cautious they're boosting the boat. They won't reach goal for many hours." Not getting her head snapped off, she continued: "Frankly, I think it's a mistake to have a water nipple handy for you and yourself with direct connections to the plumbing. You should need to get out of that hookup several times a day at least."

In free fall, unexercised, my heart shrinks, my blood stagnates, my bones atrophy. No part of the admonition felt real. It was certainly not important, unless in symbolizing a kind of apotheosis. *The Others aren't so plagued. They don't have to cram things down a reluctant gullet and excrete the dirty residue.*

"When you're done," Caitlín pleaded, "let me take you to

your cabin, give you a little physical therapy, put you to sleep.
You're no use to anyone if you cave in. Your brain won't
function properly if your circulation doesn't."

She's right, damn her. "Very well."

—Loosely harnessed in midair, Joelle felt legs locked around
hers, hands kneading her torso or flexing her limbs for her,
through the whole of her bare skin. Caitlín was warm and
springy. She was having a period, which sharpened the odor of
her. A stray lock of hair waved past Joelle's cheek, tickled, and
carried a different scent, clean and bright.

"I must admit your treatment feels good," she said. "I hadn't
noticed how stiff I'd gotten."

"You're in better form for your age than you deserve to be,"
Caitlín replied, bolder now. "That'll not last, though, unless you
work out regularly."

"I did, you'll recall, till we arrived here. Right now I can't
spare the time." *Can't amputate myself from the glories around.
How feebly alive I am this moment!*

"You should. We've not so great a haste. I recommend men,
too."

Joelle tautened. "I'm sorry," Caitlín said. "I'd no wish to pry.
Still, you and Dan—you do truly understand, do you not, I've
no jealousy about that?"

How could you dare be jealous, the way you carry on? Joelle
considered throwing back. She decided she didn't want to. The
issue was supremely trivial. *Besides*, her nerves and glands told
her, *since I am out of circuit, I would enjoy it if he made love to
me—no, fucked me, nothing else, I passive.* The palms and
fingers along her back raised heat. *Or this creature, in this room
with me? She's not equipped, of course, and doubtless not
interested, but—no! Christine, Christine! No!*

Caitlín halted. "What's the matter?" she asked in alarm.

"Nothing," Joelle coughed.

"The hell it's nothing. You jerked and tightened as though a
thousand volts had shocked you." Caitlín brought herself
around face to face, at arm's length, lightly clinging to the older
woman. Distress took hold of her countenance. "If you care to
talk about it, I keep secrets well, and I've known a diversity of
people. This day we share dread of what may happen to Dan.
Would you like to share more?"

Joelle shook her head till she grew dizzy. "No. It's nothing, I
told you. But stop the massage. Give me a knockout pill good for

four hours. I must be alert when the boat makes rendezvous." As Caitlín hesitated, she screamed, "That's an order, you tramp!"

No Christines. No Erics. I can't afford them. They hurt too much. Why take further pain? It's the merest epiphenomenon anyway, like its sister phantom, desire, which is also its mother. In the Noumenon is peace. It never betrays. Let it be my lover, my life, while I remain sundered from the Others.

The second satellite was an argent ellipsoid, approximately nine kilometers by five, its major axis in the plane of its own orbit and the T machine's. It circled not far beyond the outermost beacon, well inside the path of the shield. The resemblance of an object at its "after" end to the object within the shell confirmed Joelle's opinion that these were motors to counteract perturbation effects. Protrusions elsewhere were less identifiable but were doubtless parts of instruments and, perhaps, communications equipment. Most of them made a lacework of metal, with here and there a phosphorescence or an aurora-like weaving of color, the whole sight very lovely against the stars.

A flange around a segment of the satellite displayed curious scallopings as well as enigmatic apparatuses. "You know," Brodersen said, "I'll bet that's the dock, made to accommodate quite a few sizes and shapes of spacecraft." He suited up and flew from his vessel on a backjet, to walk about and examine. The metal being nonferrous, magnetic soles didn't aid him, but he'd slipped on a pair of sticky-coated asteroid miner's overshoes. Through a camera in his fist Joelle saw the huge curve to his left, the unknown constellations to his right, toppling past the edge of the pier.

Excitement vibrated in his voice. "It's our bad luck nobody's around just now, but they have been and they will be. This place feels *used*."

Nothing was quite fitted to *Williwaw*. Nevertheless he found a niche into which the boat could ease. Probably one of the machines alongside would secure her, did he only know how to operate it. He settled for leaving Dozsa on unwilling watch, and led the rest off on foot and by personal rocket.

A cavernous opening in the "bow" was the entrance to a tunnel which ran three-quarters the length of the station (for station of some kind it must be). Lesser passages led off,

branching and rebranching. Every wall shone, a soft light that
spectrometers declared ranged from the near ultraviolet to the
far infrared . . . for a variety of eyes? Rails gave an opportunity to
pull oneself along. At intervals were frameworks which might be
rest stops or observation booths or—? Doors of assorted
outlines were so smoothly fitted as to be nearly invisible, and no
way appeared for opening them. "Each tenant has his key,"
Brodersen hazarded.

He said that because not every door was a silvery blankness.
For whatever reasons, a number were transparent. A few did not
even seem to be material, though if they were force-fields they
acted harder than steel. Looking, photographing, taking
spectra, the humans glimpsed half a score of separate
environments. Red murk or blue glare or mildly in between,
illuminations revealed austere cell, swirling mist, conservatory
a-riot with many-hued vegetation through which jewel-like
flyers darted, hologrammic scene of a stony land where yellow
dust scudded beneath an orange sky, moving mechanisms,
sights less nameable than these. Indications were of atmospheres
thick, medium, tenuous, which contained free oxygen or free
hydrogen or neither, at temperatures anywhere between the
boiling point of nitrogen and the melting point of lead. In every
case, what the humans saw was obviously an antechamber to a
rich complex of living quarters, laboratories, God knew what
else. (The users did, the Others did.) Brodersen said he felt sure a
centrifuge room was always included, unless something more
elegant was available, in order that visitors could enjoy home
weight when they wanted.

Visitors! speared through Joelle. *A galactic confraternity of
minds, cultures, races, whom the Others have found worthy and
have prepared this mansion for. We are not among them.*

The hurt of that exceeded the hurt of having been human
female. She cast it from her and immersed her consciousness,
baptized it, in what else she was discovering.

For actually the apartments were almost incidental to the
explorers, found piecemeal as they wandered about in the
labyrinth. What counted, what stunned was the thing at its
heart.

There the main corridor swelled to form a kilometer-wide
spherical space. A three-dimensional web of wires provided
ready access to its inner surface. Upon this were emplaced subtly
contoured devices, across which played glows and rainbows.

There were views of exterior space too, not framed in any tangible screens. And there were displays.

Displays—They were not pictures or dioramas, but moving, solid images made of light which was not confined to the human-visible octave. They portrayed no species, but were wholly abstract: shapes, hues, motions. A line, for instance, would flash into being to point at a number, which in turn was showered by an array of sparks. The nearest that any exhibit came to realism was in schematics of the pulsar.

Or thus Joelle supposed. Most of what she saw was incomprehensible, nothing but streaks, curtains, vortices, ribbands, cataracts. Probably they were intended for races whose visual conventions, maybe whose whole world-views, were totally different from hers. She concentrated on the one that made the most sense. Before long it made an enormous amount of sense. Not that it had been waiting for human beings in particular. But space-time must hold a good many creatures, besides the Betans, who perceived it and thought about it in ways not wildly unlike hers.

Have the Others prepared this for the benefit of any strangers who blunder in? Yes, I think they have.

Representations of atoms, the periodic table, quantum states and their changes—The nucleus of hydrogen-1 was a unit of mass, its neutral emission line in space a unit of length, the frequency an inverse unit of time. Between absolute zero, as indicated by the behavior of molecules, and fusion that exactly formed deuterium, the temperature scale was divided into degrees: twelve to the twelfth power. Variations and reiterations made the initial presentations clear to a holothete.

They developed. In due course came a demonstration of how to operate a specific device. You took a rod from a bracket and touched it to certain light-spots in a certain sequence. . . . "Proceed," Joelle told Brodersen. He obeyed.

Information flooded her.

It began as transmitted binary digits. They went swiftly on to form patterns she could recognize. (Enough yes-or-no points in a coordinate space will completely describe an image, tone, mathematical function—) Within minutes she learned that she ought to respond, and did through the ship's dish. Minutes afterward, the automaton had adapted its rate of sending, its whole approach, to the limitations of her equipment and the characteristics of her nervous system.

Alone in the skull, that brain might have needed years to begin fumblingly to comprehend. Holothete, it could make a hundred hypothetical interpretations in a second, test them against what it already knew: and thus, lopping off sterile branches, causing new ones to spring forth and reveal strength or weakness, work its way up a logic tree, ever closer to the bole that was truth. None in the ship but Fidelio could really have grasped what she did; and his ghost helped her onward.

Yet she needed hours to find the central fact, days to see it in anything like fullness, so incredible was it. Upon the pulsar was life, intelligent life.

Chinook swung around the T machine, its third moon. *Williwaw* had returned to her. The station being investigated as far as possible, which wasn't much, and communication started with it, which was perhaps completely open-ended, Brodersen and his group could do little else there. One time Joelle realized transitorily that while she searched and called, her shipmates must be carrying on—routines, games, intrigues, dreams, despairs—like paramecia in a drop of ditch water.

The station robot guided her to contact with the Oracle, which was a creation of the Others but no automaton.

Quasi-solid, subject to shuddering, splitting quakes, the surface of the neutron star lay beneath an atmosphere six millimeters deep. There, under a weight in the trillions of Earth gravities, at densities which were still higher multiples of Earth's, raw nuclei interacted in ways unthinkable elsewhere. Protons, neutrons, electrons, neutrinos, their antiparticles—fugitive higher elements—mesons of every kind—baryons, leptons, bosons, fermions—charm, spin, color, strangeness—fusing, sundering, turning into each other and back again, briefly orbiting, forming assemblages which might endure for whole microseconds—the matter of the star was as manifold, as changeable as the gas and water and dust that begot us.

Life is not a thing, it is a way. It is a series of happenings, it is the evolution of patterns which carry information, it is growth and decay and regrowth. Wherever the possibility of this exists, life will be.

When Caitlin heard, she said, "That's not chemistry. It's alchemy." Indeed, self-replicating structures on a subatomic rather than molecular level went beyond the physics known to human or Betan. Once she had encountered the Oracle, though, Joelle moved rather quickly toward understanding. In the mystical ecstasy of this deeper entrance into the Ultimate, she lost sorrow as she lost self.

She could have no discourse directly with the inhabitants of the pulsar. They were too short-lived. A few seconds, a few turnings of heaven, and such a less-than-microscopic being had finished its span. But so swift, so furiously energetic were the processes within it that those seconds encompassed more perception and experience, more living, than a human century. To it, she was as inert as a stone was to her.

The Oracle gave her a slowed-down playback from certain lives. She could follow mere snatches, random fragments, of the stories. The heroes were too alien to her. She did come to see that they had been heroes.

Exploring through a billion generations, they discovered the Fire Fountains, which raged in magnificence upward and upward beyond sounding. In the haze of radiation that filled the world they knew, they had had no idea of a sky. Now—

There were mountains, many of which endured for whole years by Earth reckoning, the tallest of which reared twelve and thirteen millimeters high. Seekers of knowledge set themselves to follow the course of the Fire Fountains by climbing.

Dynasties of the bold came to be, parent, child, grandchild, great-grandchild, who toiled, suffered, risked, and at last died in the great venture. Civilizations rose, flourished, and fell while the climbers fought their way on, a generation bequeathing to the next a base that was farther aloft. Many among them perished and more despaired when they reached the limits of the air. But a council of the undaunted prevailed, and work began on a tunnel up through a chosen mountain.

A million lifetimes later, through a transparent dome, a colony at the peak beheld whither the Fire Fountains went—beheld the stars.

Was that sheer indomitability? Joelle wondered. *Or did the Oracle give them . . . heart . . . to continue striving through the human equivalent of a geological era?*

She lacked language to ask that question, and doubted in any case that the Oracle would make such a claim. It was beyond pride.

It had been fashioned by the Others to dwell on the pulsar. Gigantic beside the natives, virtually immortal, it kept its place, which became a shrine unto them. Self-aware, of an intelligence to match hers when she was in holothesis, it still felt no loneliness, no dullness, ever: for it shared in the doings, the thoughts, the very souls of yonder entities. (She speculated about quasi-telepathy via modulation of the strong nuclear forces, but the vocabulary she had in common with it was too primitive—a kind of sign language—for her to inquire.) It would counsel them when they wished, though she got an impression its pronouncements were deliberately as ambiguous as those spoken at Delphi, lest it cause in them a pseudomorphosis that would stunt the maturing of their innate powers. It had recorded and gave back to them, when they desired, entire histories of theirs, vanished nations, forgotten achievements.

Mainly, it mediated between them and outsiders. Messages passed from it to the station and back over a medium which could carry them. (Quark beams?) The station relayed by various means, including radio. The Oracle slowed down or speeded up transmissions according to who was receiving.

Thus, through it, the inhabitants of the star and the visitors who fared hither to learn about the star were enabled to know something of each other. That might be the closest these people could come to sharing in the brotherhood which the Others fostered. Or it might not.

Brodersen secured himself by a handgrip on a table and confronted his folk in the common room. At his back, a viewscreen showed the revolving rays—sword blades, clock hands—nearer, brighter. Soon the shield must ward off that wrath.

"We can't stay here much longer," he told them. "You know that. Even before free fall causes irreversible changes in us, we'll have exceeded a safe radiation dosage. The background count is just too God damn high, and our protections are inadequate.

"We can retreat to a safe distance and wait, in hopes of somebody who can help us arriving before we starve. Of course, that means converting the ship to spin mode; she'd never boost again. However, it might pay off. We might get a free ride home.

"Joelle, you've said bloody little to anybody, these past weeks. We've borne with you, knowing how tough your job must be. Learning a Betan lingo from scratch was a picnic by comparison, I'm sure. But today we've got to have a report from you. I've asked you to give it to us all, because it concerns us all.

"Okay, if you please, proceed."

Floating beside him, before the rest of them, she thought wearily that she saw shock lingering on faces. *I do look awful.* The mirror had shown hair become a matted gray mane, eyes sunken and dark-rimmed and bloodshot in a visage that was hardly more than skin stretched across a skull, body turned lank and yellowish, hands which sprouted untrimmed fingernails and continually trembled. *Oh, curse this abominable flesh, that will not let me stay in communion with the Oracle!*

She mustered dryness: "I should emphasize that my exchanges have been rudimentary. In spite of computer enhancement, in spite of unstinted cooperation from my opposite number, I don't have enough years left in me to figure out the complete language. A transmission lag of minutes doesn't help, either. I may well be totally misinterpreting various things, including what's crucial to us."

"We would be nowhere without you," Susanne Granville said, arm in arm with Carlos Rueda.

Joelle drew breath. "Well, then, if you'll bear those reservations in mind— The Others built the station because they knew that spacefaring species would want to study a world so unique." *I merely guess that they trust that through this study, both the star dwellers and the outsiders will grow a little, will come a little closer to being what they are.* "I haven't been able to find out whether they manifest themselves directly to any of the races concerned, but my impression is they don't. Probably they come on their own to hear out the data, the biographies, the Oracle has been preparing for them."

"They share, then," Caitlín breathed. "Their wish is to know the lives that are on every world. The better to love?"

"They certainly knew us well before they programmed that robot at the Solar System T machine," Frieda said. "What Oracle did they plant on Earth?"

"Nothing like this'n, obviously," Brodersen said. "Go on, Joelle."

"A number of advanced societies have found their way here, presumably by trial and error," the holothete proceeded. "They send scientific expeditions from time to time. There's no set schedule, and nobody comes frequently. Remember how much else a race will have to engage its attention and effort, once it's learned the routes through several gates. Quite possibly, one or two may visit inside the next decade. But they don't know how to reach Sol or Phoebus or Centrum. How could they? The Oracle itself doesn't know."

Into a shaken hush, she said hastily: "I have made progress. If we could stay where we are, in communication range, I'd make more. The Oracle seems willing to tell me anything. But we can't. So I've concentrated on asking it about the star gates themselves. And I've gotten an inkling.

"I can't calculate where and when a particular path will fetch us out. However, given what I've learned here, I can make a probabilistic computation of the magnitude and direction of that transit. What's more important, I can make a pretty good estimate of how likely it is that another T machine will be at the end of a gate.

"The Others continue building them, you see." Laughter rattled around her larynx. "That word 'continue' is a classic example of a meaningless noise, isn't it? Excuse me. I've gotten out of the habit of being limited to my natural brain.

"The point is, the Others don't work at random. They know the plenum better than that. They're always expanding their frontiers—for knowledge only, I'm sure, not conquest—" (*For love*, Caitlín whispered; Joelle saw) "and they go to places where they're likeliest to find something besides vacuum. Remember, they have to send the materials through, maybe also the tools, for constructing a new T machine before an expedition can return. No small job, even for them.

"I think if we relay ourselves from machine to machine according to a scheme I can work out as we travel and gather more data...if we always try to jump as far as possible, in a plausible direction...I think eventually this will lead us to whatever frontier they are on. They themselves."

Joelle felt faint. Her head felt full of sand. Every cell of her seemed to ache. She free-fall slumped and longed for sleep.

Dimly she heard Brodersen: "Does everybody understand we'd be gambling? The lady does not guarantee we'll find transportation onward at any given hop. The odds may favor us; but every time we repeat, those odds go down."

"We could stay here, in spin mode and a wide orbit," Weisenberg suggested. "Apparently we've a reasonable chance that a ship will come in before we starve. I daresay her civilization can synthesize food for us and won't mind doing that. Her crew won't be able to guide us home, but doubtless we could live out quite interesting lives on her planet of origin."

"Are you serious, Phil?" Caitlín asked.

"No. I have a family. I did think one of us ought to state the case for remaining."

"And leaving humankind to the likes of Ira Quick?" Dozsa snarled.

"Whoa, there," Brodersen said. "We've time to think this over. Meanwhile—Joelle, let's get you under treatment, starting with about twenty-four hours of sleep."

She hardly noticed his embrace while he took her down the corridor to her cabin, nor did she much heed how Caitlín sponged the dried sweat from her, nor how they together harnessed her in bed and waited till she slept. As she skidded into darkness, her thoughts were entirely of the Oracle and of those who had shaped it.

XXXVIII

JUMP.

Visible stars were lessened in number, as on a hazy night of Earth. The brightest were mostly red, which suggested they were near; a few giants glared steely blue.

A sun hung large among them. Its dull blood-orange hue required no dimming by optics. The zodiacal lens was immense, though wanly lit, but the disc was featureless—no spots, flares, prominences, corona—and had no sharp photospheric edge, fading instead blurrily away into space.

Closer, broader still to the eye, was a planet which the T machine evidently orbited, in a Trojan position with respect to a big moon. Both those bodies glowed too, ember. Magnifying, Brodersen saw the primary globe molten beneath a thick, sooty-clouded atmosphere. As he stared, an asteroid drifted across the field of view, dark, pitted, tumbling end over end.

Joelle spoke: "This is a new system coalescing. The sun's energy is from contraction; it isn't yet compressed enough at the core to start thermonuclear reactions. Space remains dusty, rocks of every size plentiful. Falling in on nascent planets, they heat these to incandescence while adding to their mass. I think this one before us will come to resemble Earth rather closely."

Or could it be Earth? shivered through Brodersen. *No, that's too unlikely. Makes no practical difference anyway. I don't want to believe it. I won't.* "How long'll that take?" he asked aloud, pointlessly aside from a stunned curiosity.

"Perhaps five million years until the sun is settled into the main sequence. On the planet, formation of a solid crust may be slower. I'd need more data to give you a proper estimate."

"Sorry. We won't linger. Nothing for us here."

Except, my God, getting a fresh glimpse of the range the

333

Others move in, live in. To watch a system of worlds get born—surely then to watch them evolve and flourish and finally die—for that, they opened this gateway.

XXXIX

Jump.

"O-o-oh!" Caitlín's voice rang over the intercom. "Oh, glory, glory!" It broke in a sob.

Space blazed, stars and stars crowded together until there was hardly a glimpse of the Milky Way and hardly seemed to be any blackness left between them. The brilliance of many was like that of Venus or Jupiter seen at their brightest, ashine upon Earth. Most were of ruby color, but some ranged through rich orange to deep golden.

White-aureate was the sun to which *Chinook* had come, half a degree of arc wide, heartbreakingly like Phoebus.

"Where are we, Joelle?" Brodersen called rough-toned.

Her answer held an unevenness, a tinge of delight and ... humility? ... which had long been lacking in it. "How beautiful— We must be in a globular cluster, Dan. Old; hardly any dust or gas left free; the biggest, shortest-lived members long since burnt out, leaving mainly dwarfs, though the G types, akin to Sol, also survive— Let's stay a while, no matter what."

Everybody agreed. Besides (who could foreknow?) the Others might inhabit so regal a loveliness. The standard research programs got started. In a while the ship was accelerating. Weight felt good.

Studies terminated in a few hours. Joelle had collected most data directly and interpreted them. The yellow sun had at least seven planets. One, slightly more than an astronomical unit distance from it, appeared to be terrestroid and certainly had oxygen in its air. The T machine was in the same orbit, sixty degrees ahead. There was no detectable trace of communication going on.

Nevertheless, Brodersen decided, "We'll take a look. It's

about a three-day trip. If nothing else, we need to get out of zero gee for a spell."

"And per'aps walk on a world like 'ome?" Susanne asked wistfully.

Nightwatch.

In his bed, Leino released Caitlín and lay back beside her. "Ah-h," he said. "That was great. Afloat is fine too, but, well, we're designed for a gravity field, aren't we?"

She sat up, threw arms across lifted knees, and looked straight before her. Hair in lustrous elflocks tumbled past her cheeks and over her shoulders. Sweat sheened a little on the white skin; he caught mingled female odors, sunny and musky, and a sense of radiated warmth. It took him a few minutes to recover energy enough that he noticed the trouble on her face.

He raised himself to an elbow. "What's wrong, *querida?*" he inquired.

Still she regarded the bulkhead, not him. "Nothing," she said low. "And, in a way, everything. Not your fault, Martti. Mine."

He patted a silky thigh. "Would you tell me?"

"I'd not of my own will be hurting you."

He braced his muscles. "Go ahead. You ... always talk easily, Caitlín, usually cheerfully, and—well, the fact was slow coming to me, what a very independent and, yes, private person you are." Silence. "Please. Maybe I can help. You know I'd walk barefoot through hell for you."

He saw her gather her own resolution. "That's what's wrong, Martti."

"Hoy?" He too sat straight.

"All right, this had to come." She met his eyes. "It's truth you spoke, weight is welcome again, also for making love. This first chance should have been with Dan."

He flushed. "Uh, if I'm not much mistaken, he's got Frieda tonight. They disappeared together, at least."

Caitlín nodded. "Sure, and I'm not begrudging them that. Indeed I was glad for her sake when she succeeded, a couple of weeks ago—after I'd been spending such a deal of time with you. She's a good soul who deserves a reasonable share of the best."

He flinched. She saw, laid a hand on him, and said quietly, "I'm prejudiced, you understand. I like everyone aboard; you're each of you special; but Dan I love, and he loves me." After a moment: "I'd not have been neglecting him this often did you not need help. That well do I think of you, Martti Leino. Now the time is on us for returning to normal."

"You don't mean drop me? No! I *love* you!"

She gave him a light kiss. "Och, no. While this voyage lasts, we'll have our occasional tumble, you and I. Nor will that be a favor done you out of kindness. I've had plenty of pleasure here." Drawing slightly aside, once more grave, she went on, "But you're too emotional about me. Frankly, you've grown too possessive. This evening you well-nigh dragged me from the common room, when I had words left for Phil and an unspoken date with Dan. I thought best not to provoke a scene. . . . Don't be wounded, dear. 'Twas a fine romp. Just the same, that kind of thing has to stop, and the place where it must stop is in yourself."

He beat fist in palm. "I can't stop loving you, Caitlín."

"No, if there has not been terrible rancor, we never really fall out of love, we humans, do we? But old fires burn gentler as new fires kindle. Were we home, you'd soon be happily courting a lass quite unlike me. I dare believe I've proved to you she can be both alive and decent, and that would be what you'd most kindly remember me for.

"But, Martti," she said, a spoken caress, "a steady woman is what you want for the rest of your days, a partner, a tree for your house to stand beneath. Like Lis; like your mother, I'm sure. I must help you escape getting fixed on me. That will happen, if our search lasts for many months, unless we both take care and forethought. Then you'd be ruined for the family man your nature intends you to be. I'm never for you, unless as a friend who chances to be of the opposite sex. I'm a rover."

"Oh, I've pretty well overcome jealousy about you, I think—"

She smiled, "That's not the main thing I meant, my honey. I've restless feet. Dan himself can't hold me in Eopolis. You want a wife, not a vagrant mistress." She swung her legs over the bedside. "Martti, I know full well we can't neatly solve our problems in an hour's talk. We'll need patience and reflection and caring." She stood up. "First and foremost, we should become friends—relax—stamp on any growth of melodrama between us, but nurture any shoot of comedy that springs up—for it's comic animals we humans are, is that not so?

"We've most of a bottle of whisky left, I seem to recall."

—When they were lounging back, a trifle drunk, at enough ease that they could joke, she strummed her sonador and

remarked, "Aye, I'd not be kicking you out, not while we travel
on, have no fear. That would be a shameful waste of an excellent
talent. You must simply realize I *am* a wanderer born.... Do
you remember you teased me about my 'Outbound Song' being
in a man's mouth, the which it is not, and I said I'd fix you in my
next? Well, I've made my next, exactly for you."

The associations of the evening to which she referred no
longer pained him. "Go on," he invited.

She grinned and began.

> I'm off in space on an endless chase.
> No single world can bind me.
> As I boost along, I'll sing a song
> Of the lad I left behind me,
> > The trustiest lad, the lustiest lad,
> > The lad I left behind me.
> > Oh, he was a prize, the starry skies
> > Will forevermore remind me.
>
> Aye, he was fair to see, and it's rare
> To meet a soul so cheery,
> Though he was not tame, but kissed like flame,
> And I could not make him weary.
> > Each time I felt bad, I'd seek out my lad
> > To get him to unwind me.
> > I would purr and pounce, and soon we'd bounce,
> > All the while his arms entwined me.
>
> We said goodbye on a day when I
> Confess a little weeping,
> And although it's best to go a-quest,
> I have often trouble sleeping.
> > And so, my good sir, you may well infer
> > I cherish hopes I'll find me
> > Only one or two, including you,
> > Like the lad I left behind me.

Nightwatch.

"You are unhappy, Dan," Frieda said.

"Huh? No, no, why should I be, after the workout we've

had?" Brodersen pushed his arm against her. She arched her back and he got a clasp around her waist. "My mind just drifted. Sorry."

"It drifted far, and into no good place. The way your mouth drooped, and that tiny line between your brows—" She brushed fingertips over the creases in his countenance. Concern paled the blue of her eyes.

He attempted a smile. "Well, I am the Old Man, you know. Worry about the ship is an occupational disease. Help me slough it off."

The blond head shook. "That isn't the matter. You are tough and practical; to brood is not in your nature. Therefore when you fall into it, you are defenseless."

"Oh, never mind. How about a drink or a smoke or both?"

She pressed her solidity down to hold the arm beneath her. "Not yet, please. Dan, Caitlín could help you. May I try?"

He scowled at his feet. Frieda and he were in her cabin, which contained hardly anything else to look at, none of the small bright touches the Irishwoman had given theirs. As usual, she had music playing, a Bach fugue, tuned low but remaining ineluctably noble.

"Let me guess." She rolled onto her side and nestled against his breast, to spare him her gaze. "You feel guilt about Zarubayev and Fidelio, about the rest of us who are lost in space-time because of what you suppose is you. Dan, *Liebchen,* you know we went freely, gladly. We who you safed from the Wheel—Fidelio too, yes, Fidelio foremost, I belieff—whateffer comes on us, while we liff we will thank you. Mistakes, misfortunes, effery captain knows about those. You are too strong a captain for letting them darken you. No, you will learn from them and then go on slugging, for the good of your followers. And if in the end, what I suppose is likeliest, if in the end we do not succeed, we neffer come home . . . why, what a glorious adventure we haff had!"

"Yeah," he sighed.

"Caitlín makes you feel that in your blood. It is too bad she is not with you tonight." Frieda paused. "Or maybe it is best. Maybe she makes you too happy for looking deeper, at the roots of your sorrow. Dan, you were thinking about your family."

He drew a spastic breath.

"Your wife, your children," she said. "You suppose you haff

deserted them. When Caitlín is gone, they come back too much. From there you go on to punish yourself in effery way you can find."

His mouth writhed, his lids squinched. "Listen, let's drop the subject," he grated. "You're no...psychotech...and I'm no damn patient."

"*Ja, ja,* I know, I am simply your shipmate Frieda. Can we talk, though? Can you tell me about Lis? I would like to hear."

—Long afterward, he lay at peace of a sort, drowsy. "You're a marvelous woman," he said beneath the muted music. "I'd no notion how kind you are—helpful, understanding—"

Bitterness crossed her which he did not see. "Oh, yes, I haff my reputation, coarse old she-soldier. Well, the two grenadiers in the song, they cried, when they came back and found their Emperor was taken." She chuckled: a statement. "Now if you want to do me a fafor, Dan, you will sleep, and wake up feeling fine again before breakfast. An hour before breakfast."

His grip tightened slightly about her. "Sure. Good idea."

Impulse broke through as she said, "Dan, we had better find home soon. Else I am going to fall very hard in luff with you."

Seen from outside, the planet was a deeper blue than Earth or Demeter, marbled by clouds that bore the softest touch of amber within their whiteness. Continents made rusty blurs in that clarity, save where snow gleamed on peaks and altiplanos. Their outlines were hazy; sunrise and sunset colors, as *Chinook* orbited close, were fantastically vivid; polar caps were lacking. Three moons attended.

Massive, dense, gravity at the surface a fifth again the Terrestrial, this world held a thick atmosphere. Humans could not have breathed unaided at sea level. Their lungs would accept the oxynitro composition, but not the concentration; and greenhouse effect kept lowlands hot in the high latitudes, unbearable closer to the equator. Only on the uppermost plateaus might man survive.

Yet life overran the globe, not much different from the Earth kind, as differences go in the cosmos.

"Damn it, that *could* be the reflection spectrum of chlorophyl off the vegetation," Dozsa muttered. "Masked by something else, of course, but—"

"The chances against our being able to nourish ourselves

down there, with no seeds or synthesizers, are absurdly big," Weisenberg interrupted.

"We could investigate," Leino proposed.

Brodersen shook his head. "No. I'd like to, but the risk's too great, the stakes too small, when we've found no sign of civilization, of any intelligence."

"Besides," Caitlín said, "the Others are keeping this world for a race that can truly grow into it, the way they kept Demeter for us."

Nightwatch.

Chinook drove back toward the gate, Caitlín lay awake after Brodersen had fallen asleep, until she rose, slipped on her pajamas, and left their quarters. Entering the common room, she closed its door, turned off the lights and that viewscreen which showed the sun, and sat down in a soundless dark to be with the stars of the cluster.

Half an hour had passed when the door opened anew, to admit a person who shut it behind her. The sky, more radiant than a full Luna, showed Susanne Granville. Tears coursed along her face.

She halted when she saw Caitlín. "Oh," she stammered, "ex-excuse me," and turned to go.

"Wait, Su." The quartermaster sprang up and hastened toward her. "What's wrong?"

"*Rien*—it makes not'ing. I kn-kn-knew not you are 'ere. I will take me to my cabin."

"Like hell you will." Caitlín reached her and laid arms about her. "If anybody leaves, that'll be myself. You came in search of comfort, girl." She considered the desolate visage, bowed head, uneven breath, desperately intertwined fingers. "Or strength?"

Susanne yielded. Caitlín held her, stroked and murmured, until the storm of sobbing had passed. Thereupon she led her to a small gaming table, set her down, sat opposite, and reached across to clasp a hand. The heavens were a diademmed house around them.

Su shuddered. "It's cold," she said in a tiny voice.

"Aye, that time of the temperature cycle," Caitlín replied. "You're feeling it in a coverall, though, where I've naught but these flimsy things on me. The real cold is in you, dear. Can you be letting in some warmth?"

Su bent her look blindly outward.

"I'd not pry," Caitlín said. "Still, I am the doctor to this ship, who on Demeter has heard worse than I'd ever have you imagine, helped where I was able, and always kept silence. . . . It's to do with Carlos, is that not so?"

Su nodded violently.

"Aye, everybody's noticed you two becoming close, and been glad for you," Caitlín went on. "See here, if you tell me to mind my own business, I'll apologize and leave you be. However, you've a high heart beneath your mildness. A fight with him could make you miserable, but would not crush you like this. What happened, Su?"

The linker lifted a fist and got out, nearly too headlong to be followed: "'E 'as asked me for to marry 'im!"

"What? Why, that's wonderful. Two fine people— But you refused?"

"Yes. I must. It is impossible."

"Why?" Su giving no immediate response other than a dry gulp or two, Caitlín reconstructed in her most soothing tone: "No doubt he first propositioned and you declined. Tonight he proposed marriage. That shows he loves you, darling. He could have ample sex elsewhere, Frieda; and I confess I'd have satisfied my curiosity by now, had he not begun making you glow. True, a service Dan performed would have no legal or canonical standing, but it'd be a wedding in every honest intent, and sure I am he'd take care of the formalities if we should find our way home. Dan, who knows him of old, has told me that when Carlos gives his loyalty, that loyalty stays given."

Su bobbed her head.

"Why'd you not simply move in with him?" Caitlín asked. "Your parents are religious, you said, but to me you've called yourself a devout atheist."

"For their sakes," Su replied in a raw whisper. "I 'ave 'urt them enough already, not to come back a, a kept woman." A ghost of vitality entered. "And I would not be, regardless."

"But you'd accept a shipboard ceremony? You do love him? Then in Maeve's raunchy name, why have you told him no?"

"I am—*une vierge*."

"A virgin?" Caitlín smiled. "Well, that's unusual at your age, but no disgrace. No more than a misfortune, I'd say." Seeing the woe before her unchanged, she went on soberly, "Is it afraid of conjugal relations you are? Not pain, maybe, but inadequacy? I can give you a bit of help overcoming that, and Carlos far more. Frie—I've reason to know he's considerate.... Or do you fear being subordinated, smothered? He does have his touch of *machismo*. Yet I'll wager you've spirit to match, and to steer by your own compass. Remember Lis Leino."

"You are not compre'ending. I am never inoculated."

"What?" Caitlín was downright shocked.

"My parents—I am not angry wiz them. They are adorable. But living at 'ome, if I took my shot before marrying, they would 'ave t'ought it like a declaration I mean to ... to make me cheap like most girls."

Caitlín scowled. "That's *their* attitude."

"I do not condemn you," Susanne said hurriedly. "It is just I 'ave been raised to the making of a different choice. On Eart' too, going to a doctor for this, it would 'ave felt—sneaky?" A rueful chuckle. "No need any'ow. The problem did not come."

"And you returned, and hung around patiently in love with Dan—oh, I saw, I saw—till Carlos and you—What you fear is pregnancy."

"Yes. Abortion is 'omicide. When it is not necessary for the saving of the mother's life or 'ealt', it is murder."

"Agreed. Furthermore, we're not equipped to perform it safely. Infanticide, no! Sooner would I throw myself out an airlock."

"And we c-cannot bring children ... into this lost ship ... to need rations and shorten the few years our mates probably 'ave left to them—" Su straightened in her chair. The hand Caitlín was not holding smote the tabletop, a lonely noise. "I told 'im no. 'E wanted to talk more, but I ran away. Per'aps now I can meet 'im again. T'ank you. Do you know Dan was kind to me in this same room?"

"Hold on." Caitlín tugged her chin and frowned at the universe. "Let me think. Faith, many an agonizing human dilemma has turned out to have what our skipper calls an engineering solution.... I've not the kit or the competence to sterilize either of you. But there were once mechanical contraceptives. Maybe Phil and I between us can reinvent a thing that won't be too unpleasant." She felt resistance. "Don't get bashful. Would you not sacrifice a grain of what you consider your dignity, for your happiness and your man's?"

Susanne must struggle before she could say, "Yes. Yes."

"And it may not be needed." As ideas came to Caitlín,

enthusiasm arose and bloomed into joy. "I'll ask the data bank. It may well know of procedures—aye, vasectomy ought to be simple enough surgery if I can find out how to do it, and reversible by a bit of cloning if ever we get home—or I seem to remember reading once about intrauterine devices—or something in the chemistry— Och, we can consider details later. The point is, you poor innocent, you are not helpless. Go on! Wed him and be blessed!"

The linker seemed stunned. "No, what if we do fail and 'ave a conception?"

"Why, then," Caitlín replied, and a trumpet might have spoken, "it's no failure at all, at all. It's a triumph. It says we do not surrender to death, no, not though he offer to let us march forth with full military honors. We fight on, live on, search on—your child beside us!"

Slowly began to grow in Susanne a brightness to equal the stars.

XL

JUMP.

The stellar host was less myriad and brilliant than before, though more than around Sol or Phoebus—save that in one direction towered vast thunderheads of night, relieved only by a few gleams in their foreground. No sun was in view. The T machine had for satellite a great ellipsoid much like that at the pulsar. It orbited something which the eye perceived as a quivering blue-white spark, Joelle and the instruments as a hellish fountainhead of hard radiation.

Her judgment came to them like God's: "We've approached the core of the galaxy. Those are the dust clouds that have always hidden it from us. Here is a black hole."

The ultimate collapsar, a supernova remnant so massive that its gravitational force upon itself compressed it to a smallness, a field strength, such that light could no longer escape. . . . The known laws of physics were superseded, and matter shrank down and down toward a geometrical point, a singularity, at which no laws whatsoever would prevail. But none of this might the seekers observe. Nothing but an infinitesimal wave-mechanical leakage could return from that all-devouring potential well. Interstellar material, sucked in, gave up energy as a last despairing cry before it vanished—for eternity?

I suspect eternity is a human superstition and the Others know better, Brodersen thought. Aloud: "Yonder must be an observatory, similar to what we found earlier, except I'll bet with a lot of damned enlightening differences. We'll investigate. The background count isn't too high for us to stay a while."

"No." Joelle's voice grew urgent. "Don't. Go on. Right away."

"—Why?"

"I can't tell you. A hunch. . . . We holothetes work on

hunches, Dan, often as not, and here— Forces, energies, the very shape of space, everything feels too strange. I'm afraid we can't cope."

Without more knowledge, her self-respect said. *The Others can teach me how to come back and learn, when I find them, if I find them.*

XLI

Jump.

Again the sky was thronged with stars, almost as thickly as two leaps ago, nearly all of them a red hue, from that of blood to that of roses, but crystalline sharp. Most showed less bright than those of the cluster, more bright than those of the inner spiral arm, which fact bespoke their distances and spacings. No trace of nebulae, exterior galaxies, or Milky Way appeared. In one direction the stellar density grew greater and greater, until vision saw it melt into a ruby globe like some huge talismanic sun.

The T machine was alone, light-months from the closest astronomical body and that a dimness which merely happened to be passing by. Whatever path it followed was made for it by the entire multitude. The cylinder was twice the size of any that the voyagers had seen before. Twenty-three beacons attended it, spread across a hundred thousand kilometers.

"We are near the center of the galaxy, inside the clouds." Joelle's tone had regained steadiness, a dreamlike tranquility. "Here are many more stars than it holds elsewhere, and the survivors we see are its oldest, formed close to its beginning. There may be a black hole of monster size which has swallowed up millions of them and is still doing so. If that is true, then the rate of it has become very low—for the radiation background is only moderate—and we must have come far into our own future, when none but the longest-lived dwarfs remain shining."

Weightless in his command seat, in silence and wonderment, Brodersen heard himself ask, "Why didn't the gate we took lead to any of them?" *Pegeen might find words for what I feel right now, but my dumb brain can only bring up flat quackings—could only do that even if I weren't stunned.*

"The T machines cannot have infinte range. Relays must be necessary, placed at the optimum space-time locations for their

347

purpose. This one could serve more places, by orders of magnitude, than the galaxy has members. That, and its dimensions, and what I have already observed and calculated while we traveled, make me believe that the longer paths it generates go extremely far."

"A junction—Wait!" Brodersen roared. Revelation exploded in him. His pulse became a war-drum. "Listen, listen! A civilization, a whole set of civilizations, or, or likelier something we've no word for, no idea of—and the Others themselves—their people must pass through here. If we stay, we'll meet them!"

A shout and a babble rang through the intercom from every station in the ship. Weisenberg let it subside before he uttered his caution: "Hold on. How often does anybody come by? Probably most transits get made directly, just because the average machine can take you to more worlds than you could exhaust the possibilities of in a million-year lifetime. Maybe this is used once a century or thereabouts. On the time scale the Others know, that'd make constructing it worthwhile."

"We can't tell before we've tried," Brodersen said, calmer.

"We can't lie in free fall the whole while," Caitlín warned. "Indeed, our latest boost was much too short for keeping us healthy."

Brodersen considered. "Right." In sheer exuberance: "You've got to kick that foul habit of yours, Pegeen, of being always right.

"Okay, we need weight, and we don't want to go into spin mode before we must, but keep our options open as long as possible. So we'll boost back and forth in the neighborhood. Say—um—four hours outward, turnover, and four hours back, decelerating. That way we'd never be more than a million kilometers off, nor have too high a relative velocity. Shouldn't be any problem to detect a spacecraft appearing and punch a signal at her."

"Why should they use electromagnetic waves for communications?" Dozsa objected. "I'm told the Betans don't."

"The Betans do keep the capability of receiving it, in case of need," Rueda said. "Moreover, our jet radiation ought to register on instruments."

"And we could rig a big, fat, blinking light on our hull," Leino added excitedly.

"Well," Brodersen called, "how about it?"

Chinook flew. She went at three-fourths of a gee, less than her captain had assumed. Caitlín had pointed out that that was sufficient and would make reaction mass last longer. Folk walked lightly, on their feet and in their hearts.

Entering Joelle's cabin, the paramedic found the holothete standing amidst its bleakness. Everybody else usually kept something on the data retrieval, be it simply music or a static work of art. Here the screen was blank and mute. Unless you counted the neatly made bed, the room held no trace of personality.

In a loose blue kaftan Caitlín had made for her, Joelle seemed like a sculptured Boddhisatva. Her untidiness was gone, she was washed and groomed and reasonably well rested; but gone, too, was the last real earthliness. Huge-eyed within a coif of gray hair, her face was ivory pale, nearly fleshless, sexless, inhumanly serene. The hand she lifted and the smile she gave in greeting traced abstract curves. Her voice was melodious once more, but the melody was for no mortal ear.

"You are most obliging to come," she said: a formula.

"No trouble to me," Caitlín replied. "We do need you built up physically, and if you'd liefer begin in privacy, why, the first exercises I suppose I'll be prescribing for you require no gym equipment." She set down her medikit and opened the case. "We start with a checkup."

Joelle pulled her garment over her head and dropped it on a chair. Caitlín studied the scarecrow form, circled about, ran searching fingers across the skin. Joelle stayed quiescent save to move her arms out of the way on request.

"No harm in reasonable underweight," Caitlín remarked. "I could wish my arse were a tad less veritable. Yours, though, is positively ethereal." Her conversational gambit failing, she turned brisk. "We do have to restore the wasted muscle tissue, the which means you will eat more proteins; and a slight layer of fat is normal in a woman. Tell me, what are some of your favorite dishes? I can try to make meals you find appetizing."

"It makes no difference," Joelle said. "Inform me of how much to consume of what and I will."

A frown flickered over Caitlín's forehead, but she had no immediate answer. Proceeding with the examination, she found basic good health. That included neurological signs. The tensions, tics, and twitches were gone, reflexes were excellent, a slow and even cardiac rhythm maintained blood pressure that a person two decades younger might covet.

"End of the routine," she said at last. "You can dress. I'll be doing the standard tests on cell and fluid samples, but I make no doubt they'll prove fine."

Joelle slipped the kaftan back on. "Then I may as well commence your program, if you'll spell it out."

"M-m-m, I'm not through yet. Have a chair. I want to talk with you."

When they were seated, and Joelle had passively waited for Caitlín to speak, the latter did. "I can prescribe for your body, but that may be slim use when I know nothing of your mind. For instance, how faithful will you be about instructions?"

"Very." The promise was neither fervent nor reluctant. "I assume they won't interfere unduly with my work, and appreciate that their purpose is to keep a breakdown from interfering."

Caitlín's mouth tightened. "There's what frets me the most. How much holothesis can you take before something happens to you? What might that be? Would it be irreversible? Has it already begun? Joelle, none of your *Emissary* mates claim they ever knew you intimately, but they agree you've turned into a complete stranger. I've never heard tell of anyone spending well-nigh every waking hour in linkage. No, at home the time is limited by rules, and I wonder mightily whether Dan should enforce them on you."

"Do you fear damage?" the other woman asked, unruffled.

"Aye. Induced schizophrenia, maybe, or a condition that mocks it, or— Who can say? I'm hardly more than a nurse who's had some extra training. The medical references aboard swamp me in technicalities on this subject, then give no diagnostic symptoms nor prognoses, for the situation is unprecedented. Nevertheless, you are behaving more and more... autistic." Caitlín leaned forward. "Be honest. Are we, the rest of us, anything else to you than part of the machinery?"

"Of course," Joelle responded, still placid. The smile crossed her like a moonbeam briefly through clouds. "I like all of you, wish you well, aim to do everything in my power to get you safely home. To that end, I had better develop the power. I assure you, far from going crazy, each day I become more sane than any of our species has been before in its whole existence."

"Och, a whale of a claim to be making."

"Yes, it does sound grandiose when put in that ape-chatter man calls language. I wish you could have the experience. You're a poetess, who might be able to convey a hint of the feeling, if not of the reality. I have no eloquence, and have had less practice than average throughout my life at expressing myself to ordinary people. Furthermore, unlinked, I am, well, less than half alive." Joelle paused to search for phrases. "I suppose Susanne Granville has tried to explain how linkage is for her. That's the palest shadow of what it is for me. You don't think she's mentally ill, do you? Or—when you're composing— when you're making love, you surely more fully than most—those are transcendental experiences, aren't they? You seek them over and over, every chance you get. They don't unhinge your reason, do they? On the contrary, aren't you the stronger and stabler for them?"

"They're natural," Caitlin argued. "They evolved in us from the earliest life ever to stir on Earth. And you've renounced them altogether. That can't be wholesome. Oh, yes, priests and nuns and saintly mystics, utterly dedicated scientists and artists, they've sometimes kept a balance. Maybe asceticism suited their temperaments better than common pleasures. Yet they did keep within the human world, seeking human goals, surrounded by things human senses can respond to—not wired in a machine. I'd never be forbidding you your holothesis, Joelle. I'm but thinking you should use the rest of yourself, too."

For the first time, pain touched the countenance before her and the voice that answered, though barely. "I tried. Harder than you know. Year by year, the rewards of that shriveled and the hurts grew, till I was a silly, scrabbling crone when I was out of my linkage." Calm returned. "Meanwhile, on this flight, I began really using, really mastering what I'd learned on Beta. And Fidelio taught me more. And the incredible inputs, the whole cosmos opening to me, facets of the Noumenon that neither Betan nor human had dreamed of. Trying for insight, I've been discovering new techniques—ways to discern, think, understand—philosophies—and they give me deeper insights, which lead me onward—"

The peace in Joelle rose to a quiet ardor. "Caitlin, believe me, I've never been so happy, and the farther beyond what you call humanness, the happier and saner I become. No, I'm not better than you, but I am different, and how would you feel if a command robbed you of your gift for making songs and making love? I...I will soon be able to overcome a thing in me that I know is wrong: that I pity you. Poor sweet beautiful animal, I pity you. But I don't think the Others would, so I should not either.

"The Others— We may not find them. We may die in space, or on the world of some species that merely has superior technology to us. I can endure those things if either happens. But I'm convinced that every race, when it becomes able to, goes in search of the Others, as we've blundered into doing. What higher purpose can it have?

"And...if we should find them, if we should...I will be ready to speak with them."

—Only later, having left a pledge behind her not to limit Joelle as long as no danger signals appeared, did Caitlín think of the last sentence, the unspoken one. *I will be ready to join them.*

Chinook flew.

The common room was asparkle with newly made decorations. Organ tones pealed from a data retrieval, through whose hologrammic screen glimpses of Earth and Demeter slowly paraded, a flower garden, an ocean sunset, a mountain peak, a tree in a meadow. Elsewhere, the stars and the galactic heart shone. Clad in their best, Dozsa, Weisenberg, Leino, Frieda, and Caitlín flanked a table behind which Brodersen stood. In front of him, Rueda and Susanne were hand in hand. At the rear of the chamber waited a feast which had been days in the preparing.

Joelle alone was absent, but aware in her ascendancy of what went on. She had given the party her awkward benediction. A permanent watch must be maintained against the chance of an alien vessel emerging, to set instantly in action everything programmed, and she could replace the two who ordinarily were posted.

Brodersen lifted the papers he needed. He being neither priest nor magistrate and the couple not sharing the same faith, it wouldn't have felt right to look up and use a traditional service. Caitlín had written this, and inscribed it with calligraphic flourishes as an extra gift for her friends.

She should've presided, too, he thought. *She'd put on a better show. I'm a slouch of a parson. I...damnation, my eyes are stinging and blurring, I'm not about to cry, am I? Lis, Lis, the sunbeams through the chapel window when we—*

"Dearly beloved," he began, "upon this day of our exile we are gathered to create a home. Lost, but lost among splendors; imperilled, but charged with hope: we ask the blessing of God, or we ask the blessing of life, on these two of us, Carlos and Susanne. We thank them for the courage they have renewed, the spirit they have brightened. Shipmates, may joy be always yours! Now let us witness your vows, the while that we pledge anew to each other—"

A siren screamed.

Chinook was not far from the T machine, moving outward, to make a whole four hours available for ceremony and festivities before turnover interrupted. At electronic speed, Joelle switched the proper viewscreen to full magnification. The querning cylinder and a pair of its beacons seemed to leap into the room. But nobody glimpsed more than a blur, that whipped past sight and was gone.

After a moment wherein music was obscene against the silence, Joelle's voice came, flat: "A ship. She completed transit in thirty-seven seconds."

"Nombre de Díos," Rueda whispered, and caught his bride to him.

Before she could lose a tear, Caitlín was holding them both. Across their shaken shoulders, she called to Brodersen, "Dan, we've a larger matter to finish, aye, and celebrate, before we think about that unlucky business. Will you begin over?"

The captain sat alone in his office. Its private line was connected to the holothete. His jaws clamped hard on a pipe, which had turned the air around him acrid and was scorching his tongue. A bottle of whisky stood on his desk beside the printouts of high-speed photographs.

Those pictured a three-dimensional latticework, its widest dimension perhaps a kilometer, of no simple configuration, though graceful and fragile-seeming as a spiderweb at dawn, it also aglitter with dewdrop light. A pearly luminance cloaked the whole. That, and distance, left barest hints of any further details. The precise track it had taken had likewise escaped identification.

Joelle said: "I suspect the vessel is almost massless, almost entirely a construct of force-fields. Those could cushion passengers and cargo against the fantastic accelerations that

took her through her guidepath. If there is a cargo; if there are
passengers. She may well be robotic—no, doubtless too crude a
concept—and she may carry nothing but patterns, imposed on a
few molecules, which are information. Why send your body
anywhere? Why not a recording of your personality, that can be
activated when it arrives—in an identical, manufactured body,
or in one made for the particular purpose? It can do and
experience whatever you want. Then it can return as a pattern
and be...transcribed...into you....Why, you could live a
thousand separate lives, on as many separate worlds, and
afterward gather them all together."

"Do you know this is true?" Brodersen asked dully.

"Of course not. But I do know it's possible. I even perceive
certain details of how it can be done. If you had such a
capability, wouldn't you take advantage?"

"Yeah, I s'pose. Then they'll never detect us?"

"I didn't say that. Perhaps more primitive, material craft go
through this point too. Every race in the fellowship may not be
on the same technological level, for a number of reasons. Or
perhaps the Others come by once in a while. I don't think those
were Others, Dan. *They* would not have missed our presence."

Brodersen took a drink. "What do you guesstimate the
chances are of any of your cases being true? Somebody
happening past who's not too advanced to pay attention, the
way we're not too advanced to notice a fellow man in the woods.
Or else somebody who's so very far along that his eye is on the
sparrow."

"I'd call the chances poor."

"Yeah, me too. We may both be dead wrong, Joelle, deadly
wrong, but what've we got to go on except our best guesses, you
from your brain, me from blind instinct? If we stay here a few
more months, pacing back and forth for the sake of weight,
we'll've expended our reaction mass and have no choice but to
go into spin mode and stay on. I call it better to keep what
freedom of action we're able. I'll push for weighing anchor,
when we discuss and vote on the question."

Brodersen's pipe had gone out. He made fire to rekindle it.
"We won't debate for a couple of weeks, though," he decreed.
"Something could turn up meanwhile, just barely could. And Su
and Carlos rate a proper honeymoon."

Nothing did appear again.

XLII

JUMP.

In utter blackness, a colossal Catherine's wheel burned across a quarter of the sky. From where *Chinook* was it appeared tilted; vision crossed an arm, then the nucleus from which it curved, then an arm beyond that. It shone, it shone: the heart red-gold, the spirals blue-white, clusters scattered throughout like sparks. Elsewhere gleamed a few cloudy forms, attendants upon its majesty, and remotely the light from its kindred.

"Intergalactic space," Brodersen whispered.

"Some fifty thousand light-years out. More than that from where we were," Joelle said. Her tone held exaltation. "Judging by the colors, the relative brightnesses of inner and outer portions, there are fewer giant stars than our astronomers estimated, and less dust and gas for new ones to form out of. We must still be in our future, perhaps farther on. A billion years? Let's stay a while so I can learn!"

Brodersen regarded the cylinder and its glowing markers. "Another T machine all by itself, and big like the last. A stepping stone to whole other galaxies . . . and ages— When you reckoned what guidepath would take us the longest ways, you reckoned well."

"But still no sign of help for us," came Leino's weary voice. "How long can we keep hunting? Into what weird places?"

Brodersen grimaced. "Yeah," he said. "I begin to wonder myself. Maybe we're not wise to plow ahead. Maybe Joelle should lead us in backtracking, if you can figure out how."

"I believe I can, in a general way," the holothete told them. "But that requires more information. Which I ought to gather in any event, to improve my computations, no matter what we decide."

355

"Okay," Brodersen said, "we'll hang around a bit. Might as well." He knuckled his eyes. "A chance to think. Maybe even to get some rest, after this latest blow."

Caitlín asked gently, "Are none of you seeing how beautiful this is?"

She floated alone in the common room and adored. Clocks read twenty-two thirty hours of the day that the crew bore around with them, and what gathering there had been here had broken up early.

Dozsa came in, pushed toward her, checked himself by grasping a chair beside the one she held. The sole illumination was from outside, argent and rose, moonlight-soft. It tinged her against dappled shadows and darknesses more deep that filled the chamber.

"I thought I'd find you here," he said. "Uh, how are you?"

"Beyond joy," she answered, not looking away from heaven.

"Yes, it is a splendid sight. A shame that nobody else seems able to appreciate it. Except Joelle, I suppose, in her cold fashion.... It's for lovers."

"Indeed it is that, Stefan."

The mate smiled and laid an arm around her waist. She didn't noticeably react, for or against. He nuzzled her cheek and inhaled the aromas of flesh and loosely braided hair. "You're a more gorgeous sight, Caitlín," he murmured.

She chuckled. "Thank you, kind sir, for your mendacity." The humor faded. "If you please, though, no offense intended, but I want to lose me in what we have before us, while we do."

"Aw-w-w." He pulled close. "Caitlín, sweetheart."

She tensed and turned to face him squarely. "Stefan, we've been good comrades. You'd not be spoiling of that, would you?"

He kissed her on the mouth. She thrust back from him, not breaking his grip but gaining half a meter between all else of them. "Let me go," she demanded.

He tugged at her. "Let me go," she said, word by word, "or so help me the Mórrigan, I'll put you in sickbay."

Dozsa did. His indignation met her fury. She breathed hard. "If you doubt me," she warned, "if you rely on your karate, you'll be minus an eye at least, and quite likely the family jewels. I know how to take people apart as well as sew them together."

Wrath came under mastery. "Ah, I got my temper up," she

said with an effort. "You meant no harm, I'm sure. We'll forget the matter."

His anger waxed. "You're not Dan Brodersen's woman, pure and simple," he spat. "You're Martti Leino's too. And who else's?"

She bridled afresh. "My own and *nobody* else's."

"You throw your tail around where you feel like it, eh? And I'm not good enough."

She attempted mildness. "Stef, dear, Martti needed help. I'm not free to tell why, but he did. He does no more, most of the time. Now Dan's the one who bleeds. Decision after terrible decision must he make, never knowing if the next will doom us. I ease the bleakness for him a little. And he is my chief person, the man I love and who loves me."

"Yah! Tonight he's off with Frieda. Don't think I didn't see the three of you whispering and the two of them leaving."

Caitlín nodded. "Aye. She too has a need, I've learned. Did you ever try to know more than that big strong body? She felt so low I decided— Well, never mind."

"How about me? Has it occurred to you I might be, be capable of suffering?"

"Oh, Stefan, ring down the curtain in that theater," she sighed. "You've enjoyed Frieda many a time, and you will again. Here you just thought you saw an opportunity." She made a fending gesture. "Aye, well I know you miss your darlings at home and dread you'll nevermore see them. But you're tough-souled, like me; you don't bear the final responsibility, like Dan; nor do you— Och, the upshot is, beyond the survival help of a shipmate, we've naught to give each other but fun."

"And you wouldn't find me fun," he said bitterly.

She laughed. "Why, fellow, I've looked forward to you with much interest for weeks. It's only that conditions were never suitable."

He brightened. "Well?"

She shook her head. "Later, maybe. I told you, Dan needs me. He's being very kind this night, and nonetheless I had to urge him. There's no harm in a frolic elsewhere, but I can't risk another affair as intense as with Martti."

Dozsa looked cheerier yet. "I promise you, Caitlín, a frolic is all I have in mind."

"But you took for granted you had a right to it." Her tone was compassionate. "I'm sorry, Stef. I cannot allow that."

The mate swallowed, stared at his hands where they clutched the chair, and at last said, "I apologize."

"I felt sure you would be big enough to." She stroked his cheek. "Now let us truly forget. Let us be a pair of friends, met for the admiring of an enormous beauty."

XLIII

JUMP.

Blackness, nothing, blind and absolute. Folk moaned in a kind of terror.

The beacons around the T machine were not candles, red, violet, emerald, amber, lit against the accursed dark; they shone lost and tiny, as if at any moment they might gutter out. Then afar, the least of glimmers on the edge of being seeable, vision found a single point of light.

"Be calm," ordered a part of Joelle that she detached from herself for this. "We're in no immediate danger. I will investigate." She reunited her mind. With the ship's organs and senses, she reached forth.

Radar drew the spinning cylinder for her. It was the largest they had yet encountered. Free falling, she nonetheless felt its mass and the power locked within. Optics and radio, vastly amplified, showed her stars scattered thinly and widely, feeble coals smoldering toward oblivion. About the hull was almost a total vacuum. What radiation and material particles she erstwhile knew were almost altogether gone, leaving a hollow that it was meaningless to call empty and cold. She searched and found neighbor galaxies as cindered as this. Their forms were chaotic. She tried to find other whole clusters of them, and should have been able to spy a few of the nearest, such as the Virgo group, by the last photons they would ever breathe out; but she failed. They had receded too far.

Her awareness came back to immediate surroundings. Instruments had accumulated sufficient data for her to realize that the machine was in orbit around a wholly dead sun. Akin to Sol, it had never exploded, being too small, but passed through its red giant and variable phases, shrank to a planet-sized globe of the maximum density whereunder atoms could still be atoms,

359

and slowly cooled from white heat to a clinker. Some true planets remained, bare rocks or sheathed in their own frozen atmospheres. Save for one—

Joelle remembered she ought to descend from the heights and tell her people what had been revealed unto her.

"We're in the remote future—spatially, back inside the galaxy, but temporally, sometime between seventy and a hundred billion years after we were born. No stars are left alive except the dimmest [*the meek shall inherit*], and they are now dying, while the galaxy itself is disintegrating. The universe has expanded to four or five times the size it had in our day. If we go much onward, I think we'll learn whether it really will widen forever, or if the old idea is right after all, that it will collapse inward to a new fireball and a new cosmos."

"Us go onward?" a crewman cried. She didn't identify his distorted voice, nor wanted to. "Oh, no, oh, no."

Brodersen's came in, carefully pragmatic. "What's that mite of yellow shine we see? Must be nearby."

"It is. The black dwarf we're circling has attendants, and the light source is a satellite of one of those. I have no clear notion of its nature. We ought to take a look. The T machine is in a Trojan position with respect to its primary, and the distance is about one-point-five a.u: not quite four standard days at a full gee."

"Yes, I suppose we ought," Brodersen said.

Joelle reminded him levelly—the wonder of it stayed singing and thundering within her holothetic self—"It's doubtless a work of the Others, you know."

Chinook flew.

The viewscreens in the common room were blanked, and nobody was sure who had first proposed that; there had been no slightest argument. Instead, the data retrievals bore images, forlornly brilliant, of manwork—Pericles, Shah Jehan, Hokusai, Monet, Phidias, Rodin, on and on in multiple sequences—while music reveled. Few paid much attention.

Since the vessel was undermanned, a custom had developed that after meals, everyone not on duty helped the quartermaster and her assistant clear things away. Thus Philip Weisenberg found himself walking from the washer beside Caitlín.

"You're pretty downcast this evening, aren't you?" he asked. "What's wrong? Anything I can help with?"

"I thank you, but it's nothing," she said, sketching a smile. "A mood, a whimsy."

"Don't underrate that, my dear. As isolated as we are—no matter what grandeur is around us, we become more and more defenseless against ourselves." He brought his lips close to her ear. "You saw me through a bad night. I've not forgotten. Call on me whenever you wish."

"Well—" Abruptly she seized his arm. "Could we go somewhere and talk?"

They sought his cabin. He tuned in *Swan Lake*, a performance recorded on Luna perhaps a hundred million millennia ago, but simply to bring the room alive. No alcohol or marijuana were on hand, and she declined his offer to use the hotplate for making tea. Quietly settling into a chair, he let her pace.

"Aye, you spoke truth," she said. "About our being so cut off that our own pettinesses take us over till we become monkeys in a cage. I wasn't quite realizing of that before, for the splendors we found were always too great. But in this tomb of Creation it comes to me at last—things that have happened—and we, are we really to blame if we go mad? At home, when trouble struck, we had sunsets and sunrises, forests, heaths, loughs, larks, or simply a city, a world of fellow humans, where we could go out and *do*. Here, in a metal shell, what is left but staring, the while we follow a marshlight to nowhere?... No, worse than that, for a marshlight would at least beguile us through an honest bog, water chill and a-splash, reeds to rustle, frogs to croak, and in the end, when we drowned, peat to receive us and preserve us for our descendants to find and marvel at, in mere thousands of years!"

"You too, then?" he replied. "You also want to turn back? Nobody imagines any more that we'd find home, but—New Earth? Caitlín, there isn't a chance."

"Och, well I know. Yet we'd have stars to see. Or—Earth and Demeter are not the only living worlds. I could die gladly on Danu, among the singers and dancers."

"We can't return there either. Inbound is not a straightforward reversal of outbound, and Joelle hasn't the information, let alone the basic knowledge, to compute a path exactly."

"That I know too. But we could seek to when the galaxy was alive, could we not?"

Caitlín prowled back and forth for a time. Bright phantoms

leaped where music flowed. At last she halted, stood before
Weisenberg, and demanded, "What do you want for us, Phil?"

"To go on," he said. "As long as necessary, or as long as we
can."

"In the faint hope we may somehow pick up a pilot for Sol?"

"Yes." From his self-contained leanness, he beheld her
desperate fullness, and said, "Caitlín, I think that underneath
your longings, you agree. True, it's easier for me in a lot of ways.
I'm no child of open land and skies, I'm an engineer. A machine
is as natural to me as a tree or a rainfall. Space was always my
love, the stars, the idea of the Others . . . next to Sarah and the
kids, of course, but damn it, exploring further is the sole way to
maybe regain them, and meanwhile, whether we win or
lose— Oh, hell, I'm getting maudlin."

She stood and looked at him.

He stirred, shifted his eyes about, and said uncomfortably,
"Caitlín, you wouldn't be this troubled if you weren't trying to
shoulder Dan's load for him. Would you?"

"He shoulders the crew's," she replied.

"And still he has no notion how heavily he's drawing on
you?"

"You exaggerate, Phil. But insofar as I can cheer him who is
my life, aye, that's what I'm for."

Nearly appalled: "As independent a person as you would say
that?"

"Why not? Would he not be doing the same for me, did I have
need?"

Weisenberg sat silent, his gaze upon the deck, before he
glanced back at her and said, "All right. It's not so different from
what's—what was—what is between Sarah and me. But Caitlín,
if you'd like to let go for a while, just let the control go,
remember Ireland aloud or anything else you want, well, here I
am too."

—Long afterward, she bade him goodnight. They had
snuggled somewhat but otherwise talked, only talked, he as
much as she, though now and then her words came through
tears. "Sleep well, Phil," she said, "and thank you, thank you."

"If any thanks are due," he answered, "I owe them."

Garbed in air whose clouds gleamed white, laved by oceans in
hues of sapphire and lapis lazuli, continents green with growth,

the planet shone. Its nearby moon burned, sun-brilliant.

Chinook swung around the world and around while instruments yearned. "Earthlike," Susanne whispered.

"I fear not quite," Rueda told her. "We've obtained spectra. That isn't chlorophyl you see, and indications are that the biochemistry differs from ours in more fundamental ways still. There isn't anything that might nourish us. But it lives."

Joelle reported on the intercom: "The satellite is a gigantic nuclear reactor, consuming its own mass, apparently with an almost total conversion to energy. That violates the laws of physics we have formulated, but clearly those laws express a special case. I suspect that here we see a forced interaction directly between quarks. Probably the apparatus that brings it about is in a hollow space at the center, protected by the very fields that drive the process. Doubtless this artifical sun was originally a natural moon with the right properties—it should be good for five or six billion years—and that is why the Others chose this planet to resurrect."

"The Others?" Frieda asked shakenly.

"Who else?" Brodersen said. "I wonder, did they seed it with life, or let chemical evolution work?"

"Either way," Caitlín said in a radiant tone, "here *is* life again. Maybe—we've seen no signs, but they might be woodsrunners yet—maybe beings that think. Even though they'll never see stars, what might they become and do and love?" After a moment, softer: "Could the Others have done this because they hoped to see that question answered once more?"

The ship drove back toward the transport engine.

Gathered in the common room, her crew heard Brodersen declare: "We've got to decide. Joelle can't navigate us to any predictable exact point in space-time, though she can give us a general direction. Sooner or later, if we keep traveling, we'll pass through a gate with no T machine at the far end. That'll be where we end up, for good. It could at least be in our proper time, give or take some megayears, when the universe is bright and sort of familiar. Of course, that means dropping any hopes of finding the Others, and likely of surviving longer than our rations last. However, the plan we've been operating under has taken us to places more and more strange. The next might kill us—" he snapped his fingers—"like that. Or slowly."

He tamped the tobacco in his pipe, struck fire, drank smoke. "Okay," he said, "let's hear what each of you wants."

Seated near him, pallid and expressionless, Joelle said, "I prefer to continue. But, to be honest, that is because we may indeed encounter the Others. The idea of homecoming in itself leaves me indifferent. Whichever way we bear, once we come to rest I can search into Reality."

Leino: "Turn back. What's in the future except a universe completely burnt out? If it's cyclical, its collapse will destroy everything. If it isn't, it'll hold nothing but darkness, for eternity. Why should the Others *want* to be there?"

Weisenberg: "No, we can't quit."

Rueda: "Is it necessarily quitting? We do have a chance, microscopic, yes, but finite, a chance of getting help in the young galaxy."

Susanne: "If we tried two or t'ree more forward leaps before we reverse—"

Dozsa: "No. The likelihood of being trapped in this flying coffin is too great. I want to die in action, exploring a planet, anything, but in action!"

Frieda: "I was about to vote we continue, but what you say, Stef, makes me think twice."

Caitlín trod forth. "Do none of you understand?" rang from her. "Oh, for a while I lost heart myself, but Phil upbore me in a long talk we had, and then when I saw yonder world— Do you not understand? The Others live for life. They are death's great adversaries. Where else are we quite sure to find an outpost of theirs but at his very gates, on the very day of doom? And how else dare we ask for their aid but in the same high spirit that is theirs?"

Nightwatch.

Through her electronic senses, integrated by her electronic extra brain and its memories (Fidelio, Fidelio) into an ever more meaningful and magnificent whole, the Noumenon entered Joelle and made her one with itself. Space-time curved, strongly, subtly, mysteriously, through dimension upon dimension; energies flowed, matter like a wave that came and went across their tides; the Law, immanent and omnipotent, was no changeless equation but a music which she had begun faintly to hear.

Thank you, Caitlín, poor animal, flickered in a tiny portion of her. *I could never have raised raw emotion in your fellow animals and turned it into will as you did in a single wild hour. Now ahead of me is a dissolution I cannot fear, I who know in my inmost cell that the Ultimate is what is; or ahead of me* [existence thrilled] *are the Others.*

Nightwatch.

Light in the cabin was low and golden. The data retrieval formed an illusion of roses. Caitlín had set the thermostat for warmth and daubed around extracts of almond and cloves from her galley to scent the air. The audio played "Sheep May Safely Graze," that dearest of all melodies.

She stepped from her clothes and stood before Brodersen, hands held out to him. "God damn," he said, from down in his breast, wishing he had a gift of words, "Pegeen, you're so beautiful it hurts."

She smiled. "You are that for me, Dan, darling."

"No, wait—"

Her laughter blessed him. "Aye, it's homely you are beside the Apollo Belvedere, and I'm no flashbomb either. But you are beautiful because you are you. You look like yourself, the man I'm in love with. And likewise for you beholding me, is that not true, my own?"

In a heartbeat she turned serious—woundable—and cast herself against him. "Oh, Dan, Dan, we're bound into unknownness, we can foresee neither what will become of us nor what we will become; but we have this night. Hold me, Dan, make love to me, love me."

XLIV

JUMP.

Light, everywhere light. It was as if space had become a dewdrop in dawnlight, and they at its heart. Soft iridescences, every color that was which every seeing creature had ever known, swirled, mingled, shivered, flowed, flooded, with here and there a brief rush of starlike sparks in fountains, clusters, dancing pairs and triplets, solitaries arching through graceful great curves before they died out to be rekindled elsewhere. The sight took awareness by storm and bore the beholder off into its mighty harmonies.

They in *Chinook* had no way to tell what size was the globe of luminance that enclosed them. Surely it was vast. The T machine was dwarfed by the distance at which the ship had emerged. As remote, and of comparable hugeness, were two other things. The first was perhaps a white-hot sphere, though forces and torrents made perception waver; lesser shapes, likewise veiled, moved around it on intricate paths. The second was a sweetly curved ellipsoid which seemed to be more immaterial, quasi-solid and of ultimate strength, than the vessel which had passed through galactic center ages ago. A webwork extended from it, not identical with what the observatories bore at the neutron star and the black hole, but possessing the same intricate delicacy.

Here are the Others! blazed in Joelle. *No beings but the Others could have wrought this.*

She sent forth her probes, opened her multitudinous senses, summoned her entire comprehension of the Noumenon. *I'll not realize everything that's happening here, but I'll grasp enough that I can ask the right questions when the Others arrive, questions to prove me worthy of entering their fellowship.*

Then: she was blind, she was deaf, she was numb, she was lame. Instruments could register nothing except what they were designed to. Theory could account for nothing in an environment whose nature sprang from principles wholly beyond it. An earthworm could more readily imagine and explain birdflight than she could make this place a part of her Reality.

Stunned, she barely noticed the sudden appearance of an asteroid not far from *Chinook*. The dark, jagged mass had for companion a small golden-shining prismatic form that moved at once toward the incandescent globe. The asteroid followed. Rapidly gaining speed, the two were soon lost to vision.

Brodersen's hail reached her as if through a stone wall: "Joelle, how're you doing? What can you tell us?"

"I can't," she heard herself whimper.

"Yeah, no surprise." Through his dry words, the captain's tone resonated. "Listen, friends. Whatever we've found, and I do believe it is what we've hunted for, we can only wait till these . . . builders . . . get in touch. I imagine they will, they're bound to've noticed us. Leave your stations. We'll meet in the common room. Best to be together."

Joelle rallied. "I'll stay in holothesis," she said.

"Good. Thanks. I was hoping you would."

"You'll be with us just the same," Caitlín called.

No, not really, I'm certain. Pride and faith rose anew in Joelle. *I should not have been dismayed to discover a whole new kingdom of the Law. Rather let me be eager to learn of it and take it into myself. Let me trust the Others will teach me.*

Against the auroral skies a point of light sprang into view. Swiftly it grew until it was a nacreous arrow shape, bound straight for *Chinook* from the direction of the ellipsoid, which must be where the creators dwelt. *They are coming, they are coming. And I am she who will converse with them, who is able to, I, alone among humans, I, who have gone beyond the human.*

The crew floated waiting. Screens gave on immense and gentle brilliance; rainbow tints flew across them to make changeable the chamber they were in. They clasped each other around the waist, Rueda and Susanne, Frieda between Leino and Dozsa, Caitlín between Brodersen and Weisenberg. They shared each other's breath, sweat, animal odors, warmth— sometimes taste, in a kiss.

The stranger ship, if ship it was, drew nigh, no larger than *Williwaw*, flowingly formed but featureless behind its iridescence. By invisible means it halted alongside, a hundred meters off. And there was silence in heaven about the space of half an hour.

"Can you raise them, Joelle?" the captain asked hoarsely.

"No," he heard. "Neither laser nor radio. Nor do I detect anything from them."

"But I'll bet they're looking us over," he said, "in some way we're ignorant of, that we can't even feel."

Caitlín tensed in her man's embrace. "Can't you?" she whispered.

"What?" He snapped his head rightward to see her. Luminance played over red-brown hair; the green gaze was lost in outwardness; breasts strained at coverall as the air went in and out of her. "You can?"

"I don't know," she answered in a sleepwalker's voice. "How could I know? But I sense—no words can tell—a stirring that is bright—lost memories rise before me like merrows from the sea— Do none of you?"

Fright seized him. A scan of the whole body, nerves, brain...had she been singled out, or was she more sensitive?...Suddenly he remembered the Elf Hill story she had from her mother. "Oh, Pegeen!" He gripped her hard, and felt Weisenberg's arm tighten likewise.

"Be not afraid for me, darlings," she said, while she never turned her face from the universe. "It's a happy state. How could the Others be other than good?"

A minute or two later—many heartstrokes in Brodersen's aching chest—she trembled, looked bewildered around, and said thinly, "It's gone. It's left me."

"Gone to anyone else?" Weisenberg barked. He got mumbled negatives. "I suppose they're through, then," he ventured. "What next?"

Still the arrow lay moveless.

"A message must be going back through the T machines," Joelle said. "Our coming must be unusual even for them, quite possibly unprecedented. They'll want to consult records, perhaps call in a specialist. But I don't expect we'll have long to wait."

"No, they'd not torment us," Caitlín said. Brodersen could virtually share how she eased, moment by moment, returning from a wakeful dream to herself.

"But what will they do?" Susanne's tone stumbled. Her look at Rueda gave away that it was him for whom she feared. "We 'ave entered a, a 'ome of the gods."

"Aye, and myths tell how mortals who did that were never the same again," Caitlín replied. "Yet I think we'll be more than we were, not less." To Brodersen she breathed, "As long as I may keep on loving you—"

The half hour drew to a slow close. A second lean hull came in sight, hurtling from the direction of the T machine toward *Chinook*.

It lay to on the opposite side of the human craft from its twin. Resplendence encompassed all three and the tremendous works beyond.

On every waveband she had, Joelle radiated her salutation. *Here I am,* she proclaimed in the human languages she knew, and the Betan, and what she had mastered of the Oracular. *Here I am, she with whom you can speak, she who has awaited you as a bride awaits.*

A response welled forth in her that was a benediction:— Greeting, Joelle Ky. Be glad; be at rest. [Perception of her grew.] O poor grieved spirit, be now at last at peace!

Who are you? What are you?

—Be not afraid.

Of you?

—Yes, you fear no harm, Joelle Ky, and in this you are right. Here at the end of your quest is shelter. But a dread more deep is in you, that we will not or cannot grant you your holiest wish. A promise will not annul that, for it may well prove to be true. Can you heal the terror, and wait calmly for whatever must happen?

It ripped through her. *When will you decide?*

—After some time, we fear. We are not supernatural beings, instantly omniscient and infallible. We have come here to know you, whence you have fared and why, what you are striving for, how a victory of yours might change the course of time, perhaps for many different worlds—to know such things fully enough that we can dare to judge.

Had her arms not been bound in linkage, had she not been afloat in the firmament, she would have raised them in prayer. *I see. Here I am, then. Take me, examine me, ask me out, use me however you will.*

The kindly thought (she could feel the kindness, like sunshine

inside her) said:—You are not needed. That is well, since you are
not representative of your race; you see the cosmos askew from
your shipmates, as badly as you have been hurt. We would have
looked into them as best we could. But by the greatest good
fortune, we do not need them either, imperfect as our knowledge
would have been. An avatar of ours is aboard.

What? I don't understand—

—We must leave you now and seek her. It would be cruel to
keep your people waiting longer than the least time we can take
to learn. Let courage bring calm, Joelle Ky. Do not abide in your
holothesis. [No command; a plea:] Go to your fellow humans
and be one among them. Farewell.

The presence vanished. Joelle sat in her harness, marginally
aware of what the intercom brought her. Once she tried to weep,
and failed. After that, grimly, she stayed where she was.

A woman's rich contralto said from the intercom speaker, in
English whose lilt brought a gasp from Caitlín: "May the best
that there is be always yours. We would like to enter. Please let
us in, if you will, by your Number Three personnel lock. It's
happy we'll be to meet you."

"If we will—!" ripped from Brodersen. Nonetheless, soldier's
habit made him tell his comrades: "You stay put. I'll go, and
bring them back."

*Besides, that's sort of a cramped area for receiving the lords
of the universe*, passed within him, as ludicrously as did
consciousness of dry mouth and clamorous pulse. With shoving
legs and snatching hands he propelled himself through corridors
and companionway to the control board he wanted. Then he
must wait a minute for his shakes to subside before he could
operate the motor.

The inner valve retracted. Two came in. Silvery auras
enrobed them, which must protect against space—Brodersen
decided in his rocking mind—for they blinked immediately out
of existence. Before him poised a man and a woman.

Should I kneel? No, you can't kneel in free fall! "W-w-
welcome. We're, uh, at your service."

Both were tall, well-formed, supple, fair and blue-eyed. Long
yellow hair framed faces strong and comely, youthful and
immemorially mature. The man, bearded, wore a tunic that
might be linen, a kilt that might be wool, shoes that might be
leather, a broad cloak. The woman, whose tresses fell nearly to

her more lightly shod feet, wore a flowing gown and a mantle. The garments were embroidered and many-hued. Both persons were bejeweled in gold and silver and crystal: fillets, torques, bracelets, brooches, rings of intertwining patterns. The knives at their colorful belts gave an impression of being tools, not weapons. He carried a staff, bronze-banded, whose finial was a spray of twigs whereon grew leaves. Perched there and on his shoulders or flying about, singing, were birds, lark, thrush, linnet, robin redbreast. In her arm she bore a small harp.

Both smiled. "No, it's we who should bid you welcome, brave wanderer," said the man. His baritone rang. "Would you lead us to your fellows?"

"Aye, sir, aye." Brodersen did, in too much tumult for thinking. The pair did not require rails, handgrips, or kickspots to move. They ghosted along upright.

Through the companionway, down the hall, to the door of the common room....

Brodersen hung back to let the visitors precede him. Thus he did not see Caitlín when he heard her cry out. *"O-o-o-oh!"*—no sight in the whole journey had brought such a sound from her. Alarmed, he swung himself around the jamb. She floated in Weisenberg's clasp, arms lifted, lips parted, tears breaking loose to dance and glitter. He forgot caution and respect, launched his body at her, reached her with a force that nearly tore the engineer loose.

"Pegeen, what's wrong?"

"Nothing," she choked. "They—Aengus mac Óg, the god of love. Brigit his sister, the goddess of bards—You cannot be, can you, can you?"

The man shook his head. "No," he said quietly. "The one thing which they are not whom you call the Others, is gods. For you, though, for your solace and in homage, we have striven to be a shadow of these."

The woman moved toward Caitlín. The two men beside the girl let her go, that she might unhindered receive that touch. "Dear you are," she who was Brigit murmured, "and much do we long to know you in fullness, and give you our thanks for what you will have given us."

"What? I," Caitlín stammered, "tramp, she-fool, doggerel maker, what could I ever in the world be offering you?"

"The living you have done." Brigit set the harp adrift and took her to her bosom.

With a handhold for pivot, Brodersen twisted about to glare

at Aengus. From among his songbirds, the son of the Dagda said: "Fear not for her. Never willingly will we cause her sorrow, nor wittingly more than we must. All life is for cherishing. Oh, we too kill, we too let die, for we are *not* gods and most absolutely not God; we too are often bound to a fate. Yet as far as we may, we foster life; and we guard and revere freedom as far as we may, for that is the highest epiphany of life which we know. Should we not then honor the rights of our avatars?"

"Avatar—incarnation—" Suddenly Weisenberg looked old. "Do you mean she's a thing you made—"

"No," Aengus told them, while Brigit held Caitlín close and murmured to her. "How could a work of our own live in wholeness a life that is not our own? She is as human as you are. The differences in her are less than the differences—in the build of the cells, in the burden of the blood—between any twain of you. Had she never been Summoned, she would have ended her days unknowing what power slept in her."

"What power is that?" Leino croaked.

Brigit lifted her countenance from Caitlín. "To become one with us," she said.

Aengus: "Were we in truth gods, we could look straight into your souls. But we are only the Others, who by ourselves can only touch the thinnest uppermost part of a mind, and cannot feel at all the inwardness of an entity that has none."

Brodersen, violently: "Well, what the hell are you? Pure intellects, loose in space and time, or what?"

Brigit, smiling a little, speaking more to Caitlín than to him: "Indeed no. What but a body can bring forth and carry a mind? And were it possible, would not a spirit alone, bereft of senses and sinews and every joy that is in the cosmos, be a pitiful thing? We, your Others, are corporeal as you, the matter in us born from the stars like yours, old animal needs in us also. We are your kindred."

Brodersen: "Huh? What are you really like under those masks?"

Aengus: "Are they masks?"

Brigit: "Och, a few small, easily made changes, just for the sake of our avatar. Were she a different kind of human, as most have been, we might have thought best to appear black-skinned or slant-eyed or crag-browed or whatever seemed right. But underneath— We did not come the whole way from Earth in answer to a call, Daniel, merely because we chanced to be there."

Aengus: "We should not carry this on farther. Not until we know from Caitlín your whole story, beyond any telling that mere words or mere thoughts can give." He had become entirely grave. His regard crucified Brodersen. "You must understand, Captain, that we do not yet understand *you*. We believe you are folk of good will. Nonetheless, returning, you might bring ruin, maybe in part from knowledge of what should not be uncaged among your people in a day of peril. If we cannot give you the way back, you will have your full spans in a pleasant place we shall prepare. But I think you would rather go home."

Brodersen and the most of his crew: "Yes, oh, yes."

Aengus: "Let us defer saying more until we feel certain of what we may say. Caitlín is for us the chalice of that discovery."

Brigit: "If she wishes." To the girl she still embraced: "Darling, you will endure no harm, no pain, except what you yourself may choose afterward. Remembering has its price; but if you want, you shall be freed of every memory." She kissed her on the brow. "I do warn you, I believe you will not so desire.

"Think well, child. Take time. Never would we force you or hasten you. We cannot be wholly sure what oneness with us will do to you. Think; ask of us; ask among your comrades; be as long about this as you like, and not afraid to say no."

Caitlín raised her face to that which was a goddess' and answered through tears: "Unless I go, we won't come home, is that not right?" She laughed; the mirth sounded real. "Besides, here is the very lord of love."

The Other changed his look of concern to a smile and replied low, "We all of us love you."

"There has been enough talk," Brigit said. "Let there be song." She took her harp from the air beside her.

Afterward nobody could ever quite tell what had happened, save that in the end they followed Aengus, Brigit, and Caitlín to the airlock, and amidst music bade farewell. By then the girl was wholly enraptured. She kissed her men goodbye as she might have kissed in a dream.

Both shining ships withdrew from *Chinook*.

XLV

I WAS AN AVATAR whose lot was more strange than even they had foreseen who brought me into being. Had I remained home, likely at some time during my life those of them whose care was for man would have Summoned me. They would then have shared much joy, a measure of sorrow, many longings and wonderings, angers, calls, doings, triumphs, disasters, fears, marvels, wishes, bindings, loosings, maybe a slow slight growth of wisdom: the years of an ordinary human. But chance and desire brought me to them, at the uttermost ends of this our universe.

What happened thereafter, I cannot now know. My body recalls too little of it, and that little a phantom of the truth, though nonetheless nothing for which I can make words. The beauties and glories—can you sing a painting or sculpture a melody? And they were the least of the reality.

You see, the Others and I were not merely united, we were a whole. Their awareness, intellect, senses, recollections, outlook, feelings, souls were mine, as my soul was theirs. They were me, I was them, I was an Other.

What that was like, I am unable to think, let alone tell. The age I was born into has bequeathed to me the ideas I will use in trying, and failing, to speak of that which I have kept in me out of that which I learned. I know not whether they are more fit for this or less than the ideas of someone thirty thousand years past who was the first avatar of my race, or the instincts of an animal or the burgeoning of a plant.

The earliest Others arose on a world that took form before the coalescence of the galaxy. Perhaps a dearth of heavy metals caused them to develop technics and a high science very slowly, so that they evolved into harmony with every stage thereof before they went onward. Or perhaps they adapted themselves, psyche and soma both, to a swifter pace. Whichever, at last they were faring to stars which had by then also come to birth, in ships that went close to the speed of light. Meeting foreign sentiences and exchanging with these gave such a mighty impetus that they gained the power to build the great transport engines. At that time they were no longer a single race; and as their explorers ranged outward through spacetime, they found more beings who could be aided to join them, if those wanted that.

Most species were not ready. Few would ever be. The Others do not urge or try secretly to guide. Only in rare cases do they reveal that they exist. They do not believe anyone's proper destiny is to become like them; they do not believe in destiny. Every kind of life is equally precious, with an equal right to go its unique way. Moreover, in such diversity is the nourishment whereby their own spirit may grow.

This is not to call them indifferent. No, with knowledge, intelligence, and sensitivity such as are theirs, sharing distinct lives on many planets through the entire history of the universe, from its fiery birth to its ashen death, the Others know tragedy to depths and heights that it is well I cannot remember; this mind, alone, would not survive. Where they are able, deeming the action harmless to the integrity of a people, they help. But oftenest they must watch and mourn.

Yet they are not overly solemn. Their merriment, humor, playfulness, enjoyment, exultation go beyond my comprehending. Likewise does their creativity. They think of their very lives as ongoing works of art, to be shaped for the delight of artist and audience.

This attitude may have come about because in them the mind, the consciousness, is protean. The merging, partial or total, of personalities at will, I might call telepathy, except that that is a meager word for it. What happens is not magic. It requires a carrier wave, which obeys the laws of physics. A rudiment may sometimes occur among us. The Others have brought it to completion.

This includes the ability to map a pattern corresponding to a personality onto a different body, be that body natural or artificial, organic or mechanical or—well, there was the Oracle, for example. The map is incomplete and distorted, of course. A mind is not an isolable object. Whatever generates and maintains it must govern it as well as being governed by it.

Still, an Other can lead separate existences, eventually to bring them together in the original being. An Other can in a sense be immortal, passing an entire past from a dying body to a new one which may have been grown for the purpose, or to more than one body. Mind-merging will already have made part of this personality integral with many different entities. Recordings, too, played back into a later awareness as needed, give a kind of resurrection.

Thus the Others are not monads in any degree. Neither are they fused in an enormous overmind; that would be stultifying, if it were possible. Individuality, fluid in form, is by that same receptivity more real than it can be among us. From this root may spring their passionate devotion to freedom.

They are not gods. In our single galaxy, at any single instant, is more than they can know or foresee. However widely they range and hugely they build, they discern far better than we can how grander than themselves is the whole of reality, how eternally mysterious. Though the symbols be not things like the waxing and waning of a moon, but the birth and death of stars, they too must needs create myths, they too must dwell in awe.

Indeed, to them their technology, cyclopean or subatomic, has become incidental, a set of means to a set of ends. Much they have abandoned as no longer necessary. The achievements they seek are more subtle—too subtle for our perceiving. (If you chisel out a statue, your dog sees that a lump of stone is changed a bit in shape.) But I have to try to convey a hint, a shard.

Let me therefore say that the Others are concerned with exploring, understanding, and celebrating existence.

A way for them, among many, is through their avatars.

While they are careful and sparing about it, they do not regard as a violation the bringing forth of an avatar. Such an organism is in no way abnormal. At most, it has come into being instead of a similar bion that would else have done so. It does contain certain structures deep inside, incredibly fine, on the border between molecular and atomic. These do not affect its functioning and are not heritable. All that they do is make Oneness possible.

Slightly more may be involved. For instance, in the case of most Terrestrial vertebrates, it is simplest to fertilize an ovum parthenogenetically, while adding that micro-organ for the cell to replicate. If a male is wanted, a few minor changes in the chromosomes are required as well. Whatever the treatment for whatever kind of organism, it is very mild, it conserves rather than destroys.

An avatar, then, lives out its time as a perfectly ordinary member of its species. It may well never be Summoned. The Others do not hover constantly over any planet; the cosmos is too big. When one of its kind is brought into communion, that is an act of love. No damage occurs, no disruption; save for those that are dying, for which oblivion may be mercy, it is returned to the place whence it came, to go on as it was. There has simply been the sharing. In this wise do the Others seek to partake in all life everywhere.

True, if the avatar is sentient, shades of memory may afterward flit about in its being....

—Can I not stay? I pleaded.

—No, darling, sang that part of me which was at the heart of Brigit.—It would be a doom upon you.

From elsewhere in me spoke Aengus:—Nor would you wish to be passive, a parasite. Thankful are we for what you gave—

—But now when you have lived my life, I have no more to offer.

—If only you did!... No, that is wrong. What's right is that you be what *you* are. We Summon no avatar twice.

—Because you have awareness and thus free will, we can make you the gift of Lethe. If you accept, you will forget everything that was Here. It will be to you like a dreamless night.

—Think well, dearest. You know that if you remember, you will always be haunted.

—But by how wonderful a ghost! I answered.

—It will have many faces, and some of them terrible.

Long I mused in Oneness. Call to mind your highest moments, of love, insight, creation, beauty, victory, when for a short while you went beyond yourself. It is more than that, being an Other; and still this is the lowland beneath their peaks.

—No, I decided.—What I may keep of you, I would not give up for any reward. Aye, hard will be to know that once my soul did span so much of reality that I could even sense a little of how immensely much more remains to search for and grow by and rejoice in. But I will not altogether lose the knowledge of what your love is.

We drew closer in our farewell. For this they bore again the appearances they had first shown me, because I liked those. Not that there was anything very strange about their true aspect, or anything strange at all about what passed between Aengus mac Óg and myself. The time is not many centuries distant from my own when humans will begin one by one to become Others. They will not cease thereby to be human.

XLVI

LESS THAN AN HOUR had gone when the voice of Brigit wakened *Chinook*'s intercom. "Caitlin is returning to you. She will enter by the same lock."

Alone in his office, Brodersen bit across the stem of the pipe he had had clamped between his jaws. The bowl bobbed off through harsh blue clouds it had made. Unaided by his breath, the fire died down in free fall. He fumbled at his seat belt, got the damned thing unsnapped, surged from his chair. Behind him, a squeezer of whisky drifted forgotten.

"The word that she bears will cheer you," the voice followed him. "Through her we have found that yours is a rightful purpose. It is not absolutely right; never believe that of any purpose which may be yours; but your success would be better than your defeat. Though we do not aid you in your striving, we will send you on your way. Though we do not say that you will prevail, we wish you most sincerely well.

"But prepare to leave soon. The forces that made this place and keep it, here at the end and the beginning of a universe, are balanced as on a whirling spearhead. However tiny, the mass of your ship draws hard enough on them that while you stay, the work is at a halt. Nor have you anything left to do among us. You won this far, and thereby won your homecoming—or the right to go back and do battle for your homecoming. More we cannot bid you. At the start of your next watch, we will call upon you to depart.

"In the meantime, make Caitlín welcome. Be good to her."

"Christ," Brodersen shouted as he flew, "how could I try to be anything else?"

A few crewmen had gotten to the airlock before him. He elbowed them aside and himself admitted her. An argence entered, flicked off, and there she was. He caught her in his arms and they floated, ridiculously a-spin. The scent and warmth and lithe feel of her overwhelmed him. *God damn*, he thought, *I'm actually crying*.

"Are you okay? Pegeen, sweetheart, macushla, what happened? So soon—"

"It was long, I think," she said as if talking in her sleep. Her smile was from Nirvana. "They sent me back through time. Look." Out of a coverall pocket she pulled the notebook that spacefolk usually carried. "Written down, the patterns we'll follow, retracing the whole way we came till we get to Danu, where we jump to Beta's system. We'll arrive within a month of when *Emissary* left."

"But you, Pegeen, you!"

"Och, I'm fine. You must give me a while to...climb down—" Abruptly she clawed herself to him. He felt her shudder. "Dan, hold me, please. I should not be weeping after what I've had, I should not!"

Out of the pit where her being lay, Joelle radiated: *Won't you at least say goodbye?*

—Yes, and more, was the response.—We have learned from the avatar how stark is your need.

Then take me to you!

—It cannot be. O Joelle, can a tree fly or a bird catch sunlight? You are what you are, and you are what you may become if you will. Be glad in that.

In a few miserable years left me, knowing I will never know what you do, knowing my Noumenon is a shadow?

—If you wish, we can make you forget.

No!

—What else?

If I am not worthy of your company [—There is no special worthiness in this.] *then open Reality for me. Whether it will kill me or drive me mad, show me the Ultimate.*

—We have no Ultimate.

But what do you have—

—What fragments we possess will not harm you in themselves. [*Would a lecture on relativity harm an ape?*] The avatar could tell you....But you do have more gift and background than she does. Therefore hearken, if you will.

—[Mathematics and snatches of what might be direct perception or might not be, and:] Our space-time continuum is not the total Creation. It is a bubble in a hyperdimensional ocean which brings forth more of its kind endlessly, almost as the ancient oceans on Earth and Demeter and Beta begot life over and over, because that was in their nature. Universes die, like stars and flowers; but their stuff goes on too, worked Into something that never was before.

—Here and now, our burnt-out cosmos, expanding, fleeing from itself, has intersected another. From this union, when it is complete, will arise an entire new world of worlds. (Praised be the chance that the other plenum is old itself, that no life—we pray—will perish in the genesis!) What the next cycle will be like, we cannot foretell.

—Already the very laws and constants of physics are changing. Not you nor we could exist for an instant outside this fortress of forces. What is to come will be wholly strange. Yet we will seek to become a part of it, to understand and cherish it. We are building a machine—

—which is only a means to an end, Joelle, the end which has no ending.

After a silence:—Do you still desire a glimpse?

Yes!

—Perceive—

She screamed. That was not from hurt or fear, it was from hopelessness.

—Farewell. Fare ever well.

Caitlín stirred. "I should go to her," she said.

"Huh? What d'you mean?" Brodersen asked.

"This was laid on me, to help Joelle," she told him. "They knew what she'd suffer. They can't heal her. Maybe there is no remedy. But I must try, Dan."

"What about me?...Oh, I don't want to pester you, I don't have to have consolation right this minute, but...you've changed, Pegeen."

"Yes." She gripped him hard. "Away from you. I'll be fighting my way back, I will. Now, though—you are more strong than she is."

•   •   •

"The hour has come for you to leave," said the voices of the Others. "Bear with you our blessing."

XLVII

HUGE AND RED-GOLDEN in purple-blue heaven, the sun of Beta stood at late morning. One of the rainstorms which ruled over that part of the long day had just ended. Scattered clouds lingered, softly aglow, and a rainbow bridged the western horizon. The land gleamed wet, as if the deep hues of turf, shrubs, fronds on trees had been bestrewn with diamonds. A breeze blew cool, bearing odors as of spices. Eastward shone an estuary and rose the silhouettes of buildings, but closer at hand there was little to show that here was a chief seat of a starfaring civilization. An ancient tower did rear its bulk of gray, vine-wrapped stone aboveground.

It was the time of growth, between icy night and parched afternoon. Everywhere fresh plant life was springing up and swelling, almost visibly fast. The sky was full of wings, and song resounded from shaw and meadow.

Joelle and Caitlín approached the tower on foot. A gravity less than Earth's put spring in their stride. Yet they walked through the season unsmiling, the younger woman sober, the older woman somber.

"And why can you not be laying down your woe?" Caitlín demanded. "Aye, a shock did you have, to find what you know is but a drop of spindrift that in a moment will fall back into the sea and be lost. Yet is that any real surprise? Will it be less thrill tomorrow when you make a discovery?"

Joelle shook her head. "Worse," she said in her bleakness. "I found I am not only ignorant, I'm *stupid*. No, not even that. It would imply something in common with the Others. In spite of our holothetic tricks, we remain lower animals. We're like monkeys trying to write Shakespeare by random hits on a scriber console and unable to keep at it five minutes in a stretch. Or we're like blindworms trying to see."

For a second Caitlín doubled her fists and stared into the wind. When she had her face under control, she replied, "They don't look down on us. How often must I tell you? To them, every kind of life is noble. It's our business to be what we are, proudly."

"Easy enough for you to say."

Caitlín held back an answer.

"You're outgoing, physical, sanguine, everything I'm not," Joelle went on. "And what I believed I was turns out to be an illusion. So what I am is nothing."

Caitlín flushed, scowled, and snapped, "Are you not overdue for climbing out of that wallow of self-pity?"

"Oh, I'll perform my duties competently, never fear."

Softened, Caitlín touched Joelle's cheek. "Learn to be human again. Brain's a single facet of existence, neither the largest nor the brightest. I'll help where I can. All your shipmates will."

Scorn lifted, an acid taste. "Yes, beginning with plenty of sex. Your pet panacea, isn't it? Doubtless you can persuade your studs to do the old lady the favor of screwing her on a regular basis. No, thanks!"

"Did I make that suggestion?" Caitlín said quietly. "I'd not be doing so. It's as ugly to me as to you. Or uglier, maybe. I don't suppose you will be wanting a man as a man any more, ever. The which is no shame on you, is only your taste and choice. But dreadful it is to see you frozen in that aloneness. Let us warm you free. We can, if you will be warm toward us: if you will *care*."

"I'm still a holothete. The rest of you are still animals to me. Well-meaning, but animals; and I never did care much for pets. As for my colleagues on Earth, how can I like them when I no longer respect them? Or respect myself? Sticky sentimentalism isn't going to change any of this. . . . Here we are."

A flyer was parked outside the building, whose door had been drawn back. The women entered chill, echoey dimness and took a spiral ramp to the second story. There were those linkage units the Betans and the *Emissary* scientists had devised for their joint use. Memories of Fidelio rushed over Joelle. *We would have shared the same loss, aided each other in our pain. But he is dead.*

Three natives waited, a female looming between the lesser forms of two males. Sunbeams struck through a window to sheen off their mahogany fur. The iodine tang of them filled nostrils like the air on a beach. With upper paws and lower hands, they made gestures of greeting. The humans returned the courtesy as best they were able.

Joelle took her place. Caitlín helped connect her, then stood by. Holothesis awoke. Joelle dismissed any idea of examining the Noumenon, that shabby fiction. She simply wanted full command of the local language. Nonetheless she found the state possessing her, felt its power throughout her being, yes, this was where she belonged.

Through the vocalizing attachment she produced the full-toned, overtoned, sometimes fluting land speech. "Fair weather be yours, matriarch and her steadfast males."

"May the tide upbear you, female of intellect," the Betans responded as ritually.

"We regret we are late," Joelle explained. "The rain delayed us in camp. Our flockmates were using the vehicles lent us, on various errands connected with getting us established, and I wondered about the possibility of a dangerously strong storm."

"We did not parch," the female said.

"We spent the time calming the billows within, against what we are going to hear," added the larger of her husbands.

"You are kind to meet us, as hard at work as you must be," said his partner.

"It is the least I can bring to the wife and the brothers in household of him who was my friend," Joelle told them.

Suddenly, blindingly, she realized she meant that. She had granted the request for an interview as a calculated gesture. *Chinook*'s crew needed plenty of goodwill if they were to persuade a whole world to become their ally. But now that she was here, with those whom Fidelio had loved— Her eyes stung and blurred. She wiped knuckles across them, irritatedly, and went on, glad that her artificial voice could be kept level:

"Beside me is a female of our band hight Caitlín. He died in her arms. Before then, he had come to like her company next to mine, for he enjoyed the music she made and giving her his songs in exchange. I will interpret between you and her. Together we will seek to net for you the tale of how he fared. Ask whatever you wish."

Caitlín stepped forward till the widow bulked over her and she could proffer a box she had been carrying. "Take this, my lady," she said low. "While still in our ship, I made printouts of what recordings we have of him and enlarged the best views to pictures, for you."

While Joelle translated, the Betans saw what it was. For a while they looked at the likenesses, silent. Then the female laid claws most gently on Caitlín's head, stroked her with big unsteady hands, and rumbled and whistled—sea noises—"May you never lack for clean saltwater. May every gale blow you happiness. This in the name and presence of God."

"Och, it was a sorely little thing to do. One feels so helpless."

"Perhaps you do not catch what help you lavish if you share your memories of him. You raise those days of his that for us lay drowned."

—The meeting lasted long, hours, because the Betans wished everything, each glimpse the humans could call back. Their questions flew like raindrops on a strandwind. A camera taped the scene, but Joelle suspected they had no real need of that; what they were doing was evoking Fidelio in themselves. Caitlín unslung the sonador from her shoulder and gave them the songs and tunes she had given him. In the end she laid the instrument aside and sang for them his lullabye.

When she was done, silence dwelt for a while in the tower. Then the widow stirred, lifted an upper arm as in benediction, and said, "Mercy be upon you always, you who are merciful. I will plead your cause before the Sovereign Council, and do believe it will be moved to aid you."

"What?" exclaimed Joelle, startled. "You?"

"Had you not caught the fullness of truth about me? That bodes well, that you twain would come here only out of kindness. Know, to honor the once-being of him who traveled with you, the League of Spacefarers has lately named me its delegate. Since its members will belike heed my leadership, whatever I say in the Council should carry a full cargo."

*A lucky break. I won't disillusion her about my motives . . . or, rather, the motives I served, not expecting that anything could really matter to me any more. Besides, the implication here is alarming. If Caitlín understood—*Joelle cast a glance at the younger woman and saw her gazing out the window, face as remote from ordinary emotion as a death mask. Briefly, compassion had brought Caitlín back from those realms wherein her soul had wandered since she left the Others; but now she had returned thither.

Joelle swung attention toward the Betans. "Is there that much doubt your people will help us?" she asked.

"There has been," the female answered frankly. "The tale you brought is a terrible one. We were hoping to learn from you how we may become what we must become. Today many wonder if, instead, we—our descendants, our whole race—may not learn treachery, oppressiveness, violence, such as you report without seeming to feel they are anything very unusual. Some among us would quarantine you."

"Is your species perfect?" Joelle retorted, more in the interests of accuracy than in any defensive spirit.

"Of course not. You know what sickness is in us and what kind of parchedness has brought it about. The riddle is, would the waters you offer be healing or be poison?"

"We have more to offer than just ourselves."

"Yes, the chart of the ways you have come. Those do buoy your cause. Nevertheless—" The widow held out both hands in an embracing gesture. "Well, this day you showed us three how much decency is in your kind. Should we of this world not help it to flourish as best we can? So I will ask the Council."

Joelle was astounded at her own relief.

A few minutes later, the family said a quiet adieu and departed. They would have given the Terrestrials a ride, but the latter preferred walking.

When she left holothesis, Joelle felt none of the depression that usually followed. She couldn't think a fraction as well, but she was not driven to. Amplified reason had been holding down what began to flow up within her.

—The sun had scarcely stirred. Thunderheads were blue-black and lightning-runed in the west, clouds blew off them and across heaven before a shrill, swift air, a new storm was bound here. It wouldn't arrive before the women reached camp, though, and meanwhile it was a breath of freshness. The living landscape moved in waves before it.

Caitlín took Joelle's arm. Again the girl's countenance, her entire manner, held a quite mortal concern, with only a hint that most of her was elsewhere. "Go on and cry," she said.

"What?" Joelle blinked.

"I saw you struggle not to, often and often. Your machine lent you the strength. But why not yield? You know I dropped a few tears."

"You are different."

"How much, at heart?"

I wonder, thought Joelle.

"I'd not see you grieving for grief's own sake," Caitlín went on. "Yet a dear sign it is to me this day, that shows you can still love."

"Well—I—" Joelle swallowed. "Those were Fidelio's kin. Not human."

"What matter that? They are beings with awareness. They wish for your friendship. Grant it, receive it back, and come alive again."

No, damnation, I don't want to bawl! I—

"Our races will be in closer and closer contact," Caitlín said thoughtfully. "Earth will need a sort of ambassador on this planet, who would best be the chief of a permanent scientific mission. Sure, and nobody has qualifications to match yours."

"If the Betans will accept us."

"They will; be certain of that," Caitlín said. What wordless knowledge lay beneath her confidence? "Not only because they feel a need to study us in our lives. Indeed, while that ought to prove valuable, it will hardly be the single simple medicine they expected in their first joy. Such medicines don't exist, do they, now?

"But between us *and* the new races we can lead them to . . . why, worlds stand open! The Others would not have shown us how to go back through every gate we took on our search, did they not feel we are trustworthy enough—the whole of humanity and Beta. We must leave them in their outpost, aye, but elsewhere—"

Caitlín's voice trailed off. Her stride broke. She stood for a moment rigid, eyes turned skyward, mouth stretched out of shape, fingers hooked as if to grasp the wind. Joelle could well-nigh read her mind: *We must leave them be. Never again can we know them.*

With a rough gesture, as if calling pain to heel, Caitlín resumed walking and talking. Her tone even held some enthusiasm:

"The dancers of Danu. The Teachers of Pandora. The Oracle of the pulsar, and those from outside who come there. The navigators of that ship we saw go by at the hub of the galaxy. And more and more! Joelle, I could envy you, such adventures of mind and spirit can be yours . . . will be yours. I swear to you, the Others also live at their highest when they are questing. What else can you ask for? And—those two of them we met—children of humankind—in a way more deep than blood, they descend from you."

It may be thus. She may be right. Here on Beta, challenge, affection, inner peace.

"And from Fidelio," Caitlín finished.

Then Joelle wept.

XLVIII

THE EYE SAW NO CHANGE. Sol stood radiant against a
darkness where stars never winked in their countless brilliances,
the Milky Way rivered silver, the nebulae and the sister galaxies
glimmered remote, and the gigantic cylinder of the T machine
whirled among its beacons, a-circle in the path of Earth but
forever hidden therefrom. Any sense that anything irretrievable
had taken place could only be a foolishness begotten of
uncertainty and emotional exhaustion. Several hours ago, a ship
manned by fugitive criminals had tried to escape, blundered
through a random gate, and lost herself till the end of time. That
was all. Nothing that mattered had happened. Nothing.

*Except lives put at hazard. Except mutterings in the
crew—something is being kept secret from us, but what, and
why? Except a conscience too uneasy to let me sleep.*

Afloat alone in the control center, in silence, Aram Janigian,
commanding watchship *Copernicus*, stared out through the
viewscreen. *Is Lawes awake aboard* Alhazen? *Does he wonder if
we did right, and find what we've been told is not easy to believe,
and curse himself for lacking the guts to put his career on the
line, make the incident public, try to get an inquiry started? Or
does he know the truth and rest soundly, in the expectation that
by mornwatch he'll get his orders to come home?*

Did this truth occur to him, that important things *had*
happened, were happening, would go on happening for as long
as there was a future? It was merely that their time scale was
cosmic. The stars evolved without cease; after millions of years,
most of those that showed brightest would have flared and died.
Meanwhile the Orion Nebula and its kin would have engendered
new suns, new planets. In five billion years or thereabouts, the
slow death throes of Sol would commence. By then it would long
since have lost yonder constellations, having swung—how

often? about twenty-five times?—around in a galaxy that was itself unrestingly changeable. Afterward—

Before Janigian, a ship appeared.

Automatic alarms whooped. Men on duty yelled over the intercom. No pilot fish had warned. Nor should any have. That great blunt cylinder with the cryptic protrusions and the blue haze around it was never built by humans. But pictures of its kind lay manyfold in libraries and data banks on Earth and Demeter. A vessel much like that had passed through the Phoebean System.

"All hands to stations!" Janigian shouted. "Stand by! Not a move by us till directed, but stand by! Outercom, get me *Alhazen*."

The stranger accelerated smoothly off. A sister craft emerged and moved out of the way. A third arrived.

"Lawes, is that you? Lawes, hold your fire, do you hear?"

"D'you think I'm insane? Certainly I will. I'll beam my superiors. You try if you can raise those, those creatures. Notify me instantly and cut me in if you do."

A fourth, a fifth, a sixth— A pause, and the aliens maneuvering into a formation that might be defensive but—

The seventh vessel was different, smaller, spherical, awkward by comparison as she boosted at a standard gee...a *Reina*. "Lawes, *Emissary*'s come back. Holy Mother Mary, she's led them to us!"

"Against every order—"

"No, wait, wait. That isn't *Emissary*. Magnify your image; look close. That's *Chinook*. *Chinook*, returned from the dead."

Is this a dream? No, too much solidity, harness that holds me, meters whose dials do not melt, familiar inertia of my body, though the universe explode outside.

The aliens had englobed her, a shield-burg.

"Standard call," Janigian directed. "Switch any response straight to me."

In less than a minute, the comscreen bore Daniel Brodersen's visage. The days since last he came through to Sol had deepened the furrows therein, spread more gray across the coarse black hair, and given something else, indefinable, a look of farawayness... How was that possible?

He smiled and drawled his Spanish the same as before: "Good day, Captain, or night if that's what the clocks say. Listen, please. We are not unsuspecting innocents that you can blow out of space before they know it. But we come in absolute peace. If you shoot, we won't shoot back. No need to. I hope you won't squander the taxpayer's ammunition on us. We're proceeding to Earth. However, since we have a story to tell the entire human race, we'd like to begin with *Copernicus* and *Alhazen*. We hope you'll hear us out and send a message—to official headquarters—bearing witness. Will you?"

It trumpeted in Janigian. "Yes," he said.

Lawes took over the auxiliary set. "No," he groaned. "They're insurrectionists, I tell you, who must have recruited a fleet of monsters."

"Who told *you?*" Brodersen snorted.

"Lawes," Janigian said, "shut up. And let your men watch."

Brodersen began. He had recordings to project, and live scenes from inside the Betan ships. As he went on, Janigian's shock became anger and mounted toward berserk rage. Lawes, incredulous at first, started after a time to show wrath of his own: until he must leave his post to forestall a mutiny.

The bedside phone hauled Ira Quick out of nightmare. A crumbled house, a small dead girl accusing the sky, still holding her teddy bear, blood impossibly scarlet...Sweat was chill upon him. As he raised himself on an elbow and switched on a light, he saw how snow hissed by a nighted window. Beside him, a warm bundle, his wife moved, swimming toward wakefulness.

He accepted. A face entered the panel, a voice began to rattle forth news received. Within seconds, Quick said: "Hold. Stop. I want to take this on another line. Record whatever else comes in till I recontact, and make sure your circuit is secured."

He swung feet to floor. Alice sat up. "What is it?" she asked.

"Confidential," he replied. "Wait here." He rose.

Odd, thought a section of him, *how one doesn't feel the catastrophes immediately. Like the leg I broke skiing, or the blackmail attempt, or Bergdahl's demand for a vote recount and investigation. I met those quite well. A person becomes temporarily an efficient automaton. The anguish comes later.* He regarded Alice, judged her beautiful, regretted he would probably lose her, wished vaguely he had paid her more heed.

"Darling, it must be awful," she whispered. "Let me be with

you. Please."

"No. Wait here, I told you."

In his study, he heard the report at length. It was confused and incomplete but quite unambiguous. He made the obvious rejoinders, left the instrument on special call, and went back upstairs to knock on the door of his incognito house guest.

Simeon Ilyitch Makarov let him in. The short stout figure was attired in outrageously gaudy pajamas. "Well, what is it?" snapped the premier of Great Russia.

Quick urged him back and closed the door behind them. "Bad news," he said. "The worst, in fact."

Makarov gnawed his mustache and stood his ground.

"Seems Brodersen's returned. Leading a Betan fleet," Quick jerked forth. "*Alhazen* tried to reach me, but they entered too fast. The word is from *Copernicus* to the Astronautical Control Board. Palamas notified me. She's rattled, doesn't know what to think, but guessed I deserve a chance. What could I tell her? Essentially, 'Lies. Fraud. Preserve secrecy till we know more.'"

"But it is not a fraud," Makarov said slowly.

"I hardly think so. Somehow that devil—" Quick gulped, headed off an attack of the shakes, and went into detail.

"Well," Makarov said. "Well."

The shakes resumed, worse. "What are we going to *do*?"

"I go home, of course." Makarov wheeled, stumped to the clothes keeper, opened it, and picked up his suitcase. "You will lend me a car to the airport."

"But—sir—" Quick fought himself. "We have to plan, coordinate, alert the organization."

"Yes. Meanwhile, deny. Keep tough, is that what you North Americans say? We have a few days until the enemy arrives at Earth."

"When he does—"

"We must be ready." Makarov sagged. For a moment he looked gray all over. "Politically I am terminated, like you. And my hopes." He squared off, laid the suitcase on the bed, and commenced his packing. "I will try to get in position where I can bargain for my personal survival. Or else I arrange to disappear. I advise you do same."

No, I'm not prepared, I'm not the type, this isn't that kind of country and I don't have the right connections abroad, my time is up. Quick stared at the snowstorm. *The public will turn on me. My choices are prison or a pistol.*

"God damn them!" he screamed. "The ingrates! God damn them to hell!"

XLIX

THERE WERE FEW street lamps in Église de St. Michel, none in sight of the Brodersen house. As Elisabet Leino opened the door, she saw her lawn, flowerbeds, treetops frosty with moonlight. Both Persephone and Erion were aloft; double shadows reached across early dew. The air which entered was cool and quiet.

She checked a sound of surprise and waited for the person to speak who had chimed for admittance. Light from within was less kind to Aurelia Hancock than the glow from heaven must have been. The Governor General of Demeter stood a while, staring downward, twisting fingers together. At last she raised her eyes and begged, "May I come in?"

"Yes," replied Lis, and stood aside.

Hancock passed through. "Please, would you close the door? I'm here secretly."

Lis obliged, turned about, and confronted her visitor. The living room, carpet and hardwood floor, wainscot, picture window, fireplace that Dan had built, no longer felt serene. It felt alert. Even the cat on the sofa awoke and sent forth a yellow stare.

"Won't you sit down?" Lis invited automatically.

"I don't know if I can," the other woman said in her wretchedness. She groped in her pouch for a cigarette.

"A drink, then?"

Hancock gave Lis a startled glance. "You'd drink with me?"

"I offered *you* a drink."

"I see.... No, thank you."

Lis crossed to the hearth and leaned an elbow against the mantel above. Thereon rested a few souvenirs—heirloom candlestick from her parents, a rack of his pipes, a trophy from a figure skating contest which they had won together, the kind of

things that belong in a home. Secure beside them, Lis
demanded, "Why have you come?"

Hancock started trembling. "To, to ask for your help, your
forgiveness, and—"

Lis raised her brows. "What do you suppose I can do? The
news is out. The provisional governor ought to come through
the gate in another day or so, and the investigating committee
won't be far behind. I've no official standing."

"But you're Dan Brodersen's wife!"

"The man you did your best to get killed." Lis struck fist on
stone. "No. I shouldn't have said that, maybe. I'll believe what
you told me before, over the phone, that you'd no such
intention, that events got out of hand. Just the same, Aurie, you
assumed a responsibility and you'll have to bear the consequences."

Head bowed, Hancock drew forth the cigarette she had been
after, but instead of kindling it, she shredded it with shivery
fingers. "You don't understand," she mumbled. "I'm not asking
anything for myself. I'm asking you take pity on Ira Quick."

Lis grew stiff in surprise. "What?"

Again Hancock made herself look up. "You see him as a
monster, the one who did in fact try to do away with your
husband and, and choke off everything you and Dan hoped for."
Her voice gathered force. "But he isn't. He's made some terrible
mistakes, no doubt—though we'll never know what might have
happened if he'd won, will we? He'd've gone down in history as a
statesman, a hero. . . . Never mind. He lost, that's all. But can
you possibly realize, he didn't do what he did because of being
evil? Ambitious, vainglorious, yes; he's human. But he honestly
thought he was doing what must be done."

"I'm not too sure of that," said Lis.

"Never mind," Hancock repeated. She was crying now.
"Only ask yourself, what purpose would revenge serve?
Wouldn't it be better for everybody—wouldn't it start this new
age of yours off right—if you forgave?"

Lis was silent a few seconds before she said, "I asked you
what you expect I could do, supposing I wanted to."

"Everything!" the visitor cried. Lower: "Grant me that I, I do
know politics. Dan himself, he's the man of the hour, the man of
the century, but he does need to have charges against him
dismissed, illegal actions that led to homicide and—If he made a
public request for a general amnesty, who could refuse?" She

knuckled her eyes. "You can get him to do it. He's not a vindictive man, and...I told you, wouldn't it be a hopeful gesture? No matter me. I'll take whatever's coming to me. I was a pawn anyway, it turns out. And no matter the rest of the conspirators, either. But Ira—" She sank to the floor, half curled up, weight rested on arms. "Ira, please, Ira!"

Lis stood for a time in her own long-legged strength. Darknesses and brightnesses crossed her face. At last she murmured, mostly to herself: "They're finished in public life, the lot of them. Dare they walk abroad any more on Earth? But Demeter still has whole continents for people to make a fresh beginning."

She would not touch the huddled form before her, but she said, "Yes, Aurie, I'll put in the word you want. On your behalf also."

When she was alone except for the sleeping children, Lis returned to her study. That was a fair-sized chamber, efficiently laid out, full of up-to-date office equipment; but above the desk stood a hologram of Mt. Lorn and the undying snows. She paused, frowning at a comset, until she flipped its playback switch. Once more she reviewed the latest message from Brodersen in Lima. Image and voice alike registered weariness: "—just such a hellish lot of utter nonsense to wade through. No end in sight, either. You'd cope better than I'm doing, honey. And wouldn't it be grand to have you here! I keep telling myself that isn't really practical, then looking for ways to prove myself wrong—"

Soon, however, he mentioned Caitlín. At first Lis skipped that part, then she bit her lip and played it over, twice. Thereafter she sat down and pondered. Finally she ran through the reply that she had been composing when Aurelia Hancock interrupted. She now had considerable to say that was new and important. Before she did, something remained which might matter a great deal more.

Her electronic *Doppelgänger* looked out of the screen and declared: "—Your news is almost scary. Let me talk to her. The next few minutes of this are for her."

An awkward clearing of throat and shifting of position, followed by: "Caitlín, dear, hello. *Salud.* What Dan tells me about you does not sound good. Not that he says much, I think in part because he hasn't much to say. Apparently you go about your life in a more or less normal fashion. But, well, for instance, he hasn't mentioned any jokes between you and him, and he usually shares those with me. Or—" The tape recorded a doorchime and stopped.

Lis considered, started the machine again, and spoke into the light-years behind it.

"Dan, this is for Caitlín. Her alone. Switch off and let her have the rest. I've more to give you, but I'll put that on the next track." She knew he would honor the request.

"Caitlín, I don't think you'd better show this to Dan. Tell him it's girl talk. God knows he has worries enough. You, your grief, that's the heaviest of them.

"Please," Lis said, suddenly fighting for breath, "can you see I don't want to make you feel guilty or anything? What you've been through, I'll never be able to imagine. Or what you're longing for—that's more nearly the trouble, isn't it? You're lost in a dream of what was, and he senses you are, and—"

She marshalled her thoughts. "You have to come back. For your own sake, and his, and, yes, mine. Mine, not only through him. I could book passage to Earth, Caitlín, since he's going to be there for months yet. I would, except that you need all he can give. He mustn't lose you to the half-life you're in. I mustn't either. I've discovered how much you are to me."

She sighed. "Oh, yes, I've been envious of you, and no doubt I will be once in a while in future. But not jealous. Not any longer. We both love him, and he loves both of us. Well, shouldn't we care for each other?" A chuckle. "Could be the day will come when he envies me a little ... or feels a little jealous. Which wouldn't hurt him!

"Caitlín, come home.

"I've not been where you've been, but I am older than you and I have seen parts of life that you maybe haven't. Let me suggest, let me call to you—"

—When she was done, Lis rose and stretched, muscle by muscle. She'd scan her speech tomorrow, perhaps edit it, though merely for clarity; she knew what the counsel was, and hoped it might help. Meanwhile, how about a nightcap, some Sibelius, and bed? She'd want her full energy in the morning.

To hell with being Griselda or even Penelope. She had work to do.

L

SPRING CAME EARLY that year to Ireland. On a morning
thereof, Brodersen and Caitlín set out on a day-long ramble.

This was in County Clare. Five centuries old, long
abandoned, lately restored for renting to visitors, their cottage
nonetheless held remembrances of generations who had been
born within its walls, grown up, fallen in love, begotten and
raised children, toiled, suffered, sorrowed, laughed, sung,
dreamed, grown aged, died and been keened over. Low and
whitewashed beneath a mossy thatch roof, it stood alone on a
height overlooking the sea; they who dwelt here had mostly kept
sheep. Several kilometers off, a village in a cove still housed
fisher folk. Their manners being of an ancient kind, they did not
rush to inform the world who was staying close by, but honored
a wish for privacy that their priest had told them of. Meeting the
famous pair in street or store, taking them out in a boat,
drinking with them in the pub, the villagers were content to be
friendly.

"A fine day for sure," Brodersen said. He put the knapsack
that held lunch on his back while he looked around.

Westward, gorse and bracken came to an abrupt end at a cliff
edge. Afar, the waters shone tawny, emerald, quicksilver, in a
shiver of small waves. Closer in, they burst in surf, white
fountains, on rocks and skerries and steeps. This high up, he
heard the roaring. Southward the land was likewise rugged,
northward more so. Eastward it rolled in verdancy toward the
blue bulk of a mountain whose top was the goal of his and
Caitlín's hike. Hawthorn hedges bloomed snowy along winding
lanes. Scattered farmhouses sent chimney smoke into a sky
where a few clouds wandered. Closer stood the grassy slopes of a
rath, a circular earthwork which had guarded a homestead
before St. Patrick walked through Erin; deserted at last, it

became known as a haunt of the Sídhe, of whom the first tales were told before Christ walked through Galilee.

A cool breeze bore odors of sea and soil and growth. High overhead, a lark sang.

"Aye," Caitlín said. "As if the country would bid us goodbye with a blessing."

He turned his gaze on her. Heavy shirt, slacks, and brogans could not hide erect slenderness or take away free-striding gracefulness. Bronze hair fell below a headband; a stray lock above fluttered. In the sun-touched, lightly freckled face, her eyes were more green than the quickening fields, and her smile held a merriment he had not seen from the time she left his ship for the Others to the time when they had for a while been by themselves in this place.

"She, uh, she gave me the best blessing she can, way off on Demeter," he said. "You."

Caitlín laughed. "Why, Dan, is it a bard you'd be?"

"No. Hardly my line of work. But—oh, rats—I'm forever wanting to say how I feel about you, and never able."

"You've a better way than words for that, and you might consider a demonstration when we've rested on yonder peak. But first we must get there. Come." She led him by the hand down a path to a narrow dirt road that rambled between its flowering hedges, now right, now left, more or less in the direction they wanted to go.

When they had fallen into a steady pace—flex of muscles, swing and soft thud of shoes, lungs full, blood coursing—he ventured, "Another thing I can't figure out how to tell, Pegeen, is how glad I am to see you back to your real self. Glad? Huh! I'd have died to bring it about."

Gravity descended upon her. "Was I that mournful?"

"Oh, no. Somebody who hadn't met you before would never guess anything strange had ever happened to you."

"I should hope not." Her tone held a touch of grimness. The one secret that they of *Chinook* preserved was the fact of the avatars.

"I lay on you a geas that you keep silent about this," she had told her shipmates, "for my sake, and the sake of the Others, and likely the sake of many more." Brodersen had added weight to that last by pointing out what lunacies, deceptions, and empty hankerings the knowledge would inspire, with no benefit to anybody. Doubtless a judgment that his crew would give and abide by the promise had been a factor in the decision to let them go home. Elsewhere it sufficed to say that the Others had, after study, made that decision.

Walking beside Caitlín, Brodersen went on: "You didn't go around openly brooding or acting important or any such childishness. In fact, the child in you seemed to have died. You didn't joke or tease or skip down a corridor or, oh, the million things you used to. You never sang unless we asked, and they were never happy songs, and you didn't make new ones. In bed with me—well, sure, you took pleasure, in a way, but there was no *fun* about it. And sometimes I'd catch you crying, like at night when you thought I was asleep, or I'd see the signs on you afterward. But you shied off from telling me why, till I figured I'd better pretend not to notice."

She caught his arm, hard. "Dan, my darling, why didn't you tell me how much I was hurting you?"

"That might've made matters worse."

"Ochone! The dream of the Others had me, and naught could I do but try to live, day by day, while finding my way back from it. Yet if I'd had the wit to look from what was gone to what was around me, and who—"

"Shucks, honey, everything worked out okay. Didn't it? Meanwhile we were both lucky to be kept as busy as were, on Beta and Earth."

Well, Earth I'm not certain about. Brodersen scowled and spat. *The executive pardon for our actions, a formality, but long-drawn and embarrassing. Crowds, speeches, ceremonies, conferences, banquets, receptions, Worthy Causes, mail by the ton, calls by the thousands, and always the bloody newspeople, never a minute of ours unwatched till at last Pegeen and I managed to sneak off to here. That hullabaloo may have delayed her recovery. . . . Is "recovery" the right word? I don't dare ask.*

Change the subject. "And shortly, ho for Demeter," he said.

Their task was done. Amidst all the dismal nonsense had been these past months' jobs, duties that one could not decently shirk: helping and counselling the Betans, taking part while plans and procedures were hammered out for establishing regular relations between the two races, conveying to scientists the trove of information aboard *Chinook* and in the heads of her crew—and he had to admit that some causes were genuinely worthy. The hero of billions could raise money for ocean conservation, give politics a shove in the direction of common sense and liberty, brighten an hour for a lot of hospitalized children.

But finally, except for Joelle, *Chinook* was about to bear her wanderers home. (Carlos and Susanne wanted to greet her parents. Frieda and the husband she'd found on Earth wanted to emigrate.) The Betans had not gotten enough data for calculating how to play chronokinetic tricks in that gate. Probably no humans should anyway, at least until humans were wiser. The span of Brodersen's absence from Phoebus would therefore be approximately equal to the span of his presence at Sol.

Would Barbara and Mike have changed much? According to letters and tapes from Lis—who had agreed with him she should stay put, take care of them and the business, not let herself in for the harassment he was under—they'd mainly just gained a few skills, which they were anxious to show Daddy. However, at their ages, the time between late winter and early spring could be as long as the time to go to the end of the universe and back.

Brodersen noticed Caitlín had not responded. Perturbed, he glanced at her and saw she remained serious, her eyes on the horizon and the blue depths beyond. *No! Please!* "I'm sorry," his voice groped. "Did I say something wrong? I wouldn't make you sad again for every planet in the plenum. But I seem to have."

"Not really, dear." She patted his back. "You only reminded me."

"Blast me for an idiot! I, well, I was describing how you were before, to try and explain how you are—were—your old self. I shouldn't have raised ghosts for you. I didn't know. Can you forgive me?"

"There's nothing to forgive. I *have* won beyond the longing, the hopeless trying to regain; in truth I have." Her fingers closed around his. They halted in the middle of the road and turned to each other. A cloud shadow swept over them, then sunlight spilled anew.

"Honestly, Dan, my love. What memories are left lie deep and quiet, beyond either grief or joy. It is I must beg your pardon, for blindness to how you needed to speak of this."

"Well, I'm not awfully good at giving signals, Pegeen, macushla."

—After the kiss, walking once more, she told him, "You did say a thing that frets me, that you would have died to bring me back to what I was."

"I meant it."

"Did you indeed? You should not have. What about Lis and the children?"

He winced. "Yes, them. Right. I wasn't thinking. When a person loves another the way I love you—" He couldn't go on.

"Dan," she said, "I've told you before, I know a single reason why I would ever leave you: if I came between you and Lis. That would turn what was good and happy into a thing evil and sorrowful; and how could I abide myself?"

"No fears," he promised. "You may need to warn me occasionally, but... well, I honor my contracts; and besides, I love her too."

She smiled with her entire face. "Ah, that's my skipper speaking."

Presently: "But, my life, you're troubled in your turn. Why?"

As she had earlier, he looked into the distances. "I got to feeling—not the first time—feeling how unfair this is to you."

"How?"

"I do have a home and family and they do mean the world to me. You rate the same. Am I keeping you from them? I'm afraid I am."

She laughed aloud, which startled him enough that he caught his toe in a rut and almost fell. When he had recovered, she said, "Dan, Dan, can you really imagine me languishing in a situation I have not freely chosen, aye, purposely brought about? It took the Others to cause that, and then it wasn't permanent."

"But, uh, a free choice can be unwise."

"I always know what I want, however that may change. It may in time be a husband, if he's the right kind of man, the which includes understanding why I'll not give you up. Or it may never be, and is that tragic? I do think at last I'll want a child or two, who could well be yours. Let us see what happens. We've a whole cosmos before us."

After a minute in which the lark sang, Caitlín went on: "Already I've changes in mind—going to medical school, so I can ship out on some of the expeditions that will be off to the stars."

"What?" He stopped in his tracks.

"Don't worry, my heart." She got them started onward. "I'll return to you, as I promised in that song of mine. Or could be we'll fare together. Not on each trip. You've no right and I hope no wish to be overmuch gone from Demeter. But you do have the right and I believe the wish to stay entirely alive till you die."

He considered her. "Is this just go-fever in you, after the experience we've had?"

She answered frankly: "No. That might have been true were I what I was. You bespoke a child in me you dreaded was dead. Well, she was only sleeping, but the sleep was long and she's awakened older. I've need in me to discover and learn, to use myself to the utmost. And, yes, serve; for what our explorers do will change lives beyond reckoning. Should we not seek to make those changes harmless, or even benign? Before all else, is there not the freedom of every sentient being to uphold? I want to be where I can help, however little and mistakenly, toward those ends."

"I see." Brodersen paused. "And I've got a notion your help won't be little nor very much mistaken."

"Thank you, dear love," she murmured.

They walked. The day strengthened, brighter, warmer, greener, more full of scents. From behind a ridge, a hawk swung to hover where the sun turned its wings golden. They could feel how the land rose toward the heights.

Suddenly Caitlín cried, "Och, what are we doing instead of being happy?" She unslung the sonador from her shoulder. It was programmed for guitar. She strummed a few chords. In a short while she was singing, while her feet went blithe in the measure.

> *Go gladly up and gladly down.*
> *The dancing flies outward like laughter*
> *From blossomfields to mountain crown.*
> *Rejoice in the joy that comes after!*

16